D0887412

Smoke and Mirrors

A Mystery Novel

Ronald Lamont

KITSAP
PUBLISHING

KITSAP
PUBLISHING

Smoke and Mirrors
First edition, published 2017

By Ronald Lamont

Copyright © 2017, Ronald Lamont

Cover photo by Tara Templeton
Author photo by Stephanie Stewart, taken at the Boat Shed Restaurant
(aka "The Boat House Grill")

ISBN-13: 978-1-942661-69-6

This is a work of fiction. Names, characters, businesses, places, events and incidents
are either the products of the author's imagination or used in a fictitious manner. Any
resemblance to actual persons, living or dead, or actual events is purely coincidental.

All rights reserved. No part of this book may be reproduced or transmitted in any form
or by any means, electronic or mechanical, including photocopying, recording or by any
information storage and retrieval system, without written permission from the author,
except for the inclusion of brief quotations in a review.

Published by Kitsap Publishing
P.O. Box 572
Poulsbo, WA 98370
www.KitsapPublishing.com

Printed in the United States of America

TD 2017

50-10 9 8 7 6 5 4 3 2 1

Acknowledgments

To my brother, screenwriter James Wolf, and my former boss Mike Lawson (author of the "Joe DeMarco" series of thrillers) for inspiring me to become a writer. To my amazing friends and family whose support throughout this journey has been more than I could have possibly imagined. To my dear friend Amber Gravett whose invaluable feedback on the draft-versions of my novels helped keep me in line with my characters, along with some great suggestions to enhance the overall experience. To Kitsap Publishing who has made all of this possible. And to the Kitsap (Slaughter) County community, whose support has been nothing short of overwhelming: My book signings (local businesses offering to host and/or promote the event; and the exceptional attendance by the men and women of the community), interviewing me for the local paper, providing air-time on the local access television station, and inspiring the locations detailed within the pages of this mystery. I am truly humbled.

1

The anticipation was palpable - the rapid heartbeat, the cold sweat, the shortness of breath a gasp away from hyperventilating, the overwhelming feeling of... excitement. *"Revenge is a dish best served cold"* so the saying goes; how ironic that it was about to be served at a couple-thousand degrees. A flickering flame atop a matchstick buffeted by an early autumn breeze at one moment... a raging conflagration the next.

The *point of no return* passed hours ago; there was no turning back now. Various scenarios had been accounted for, anomalies assessed, course corrections made, and everything had fallen into place. Months of painstaking research, meticulous planning, setting the traps, covering your tracks - all converging at this particular place and time.

The midnight sky was pitch-black, save for a sliver of a crescent moon overhead. Off in the distance emanated the lights of the city, oblivious to the darkness of this deed.

Dead silence was interrupted by the sounds of nature - the rustling of leaves in the breeze... the trickle of a nearby stream.

A face suddenly appeared upon the reflection of the glass as the flame was lit – it was the face of vengeance... the face of evil.

A phone call was made just as the match ignited its *means to an end*.

A groggy, barely audible "Hello?" reverberated through the phone.

'Click' and the phone met its fate in the fledgling fire.

As the inferno began to spread a single act remained... *get the hell out of there.*

2

"Hey Nash, you've got a live one" said Sheriff Steven Clarke as Mackenzie Nash walked past his office on her way toward the aroma wafting through the space that was drawing her in – a freshly-brewed pot of coffee.

"A *live* one??" she replied as she grabbed the coffee pot and began to pour, stopping at half a cup – anticipating but a brief moment to enjoy her morning java.

"A figure of speech – SCFD responded to an early morning fire out near Blue Heron Cove."

"An apparent homicide?"

"That's their take; a body, along with indications of an accelerant. The Arson Team is on the way."

"If *I'm* getting the call I assume the Coroner or his Deputy is on the way as well" said Nash; stopping to take a sip of her coffee, "You got an address?"

"3756 Salmon Beach Road."

Nash took another sip, exhaled, and looked at her watch. She pondered the time of morning and grabbed her cell phone, "Hey Dirk, when you're done with your *morning ritual* meet me out near Blue Heron Cove – 3756 Salmon Beach Road to be specific."

Nash poked her head into Sheriff Clarke's office, "I left a message for Brogan; if he happens to show up *here* can you send him out to the scene?"

"Got ya covered."

Nash gulped down the last of her coffee, grabbed her gear, and headed out the door.

Mackenzie Nash is the Lead Detective in the Homicide Unit of the Slaughter County Sheriff's Department. She's as hard-nosed as they get – molded for this line of work at an early age. She grew up fast – not necessarily her choice; and never had a father-figure in her life as her parents divorced when she was six and 'Dear old Dad' was never to be seen again.

Being the eldest child she was always in something of a position of authority in the household; especially since her mother had to work two jobs just to make ends meet, thanks to the fact that when the XY chromosome disappeared anything resembling child support disappeared with him.

It didn't help that her mother apparently had no qualms about putting the burden of caring for the two youngest girls on Mackenzie's shoulders – routinely staying after her shift at the lounge to have a drink or two with the customers; and even worse, showing up at midnight with some *less than honorable gentleman* in tow.

When Mom remarried several years after her divorce Mackenzie thought things might change for the better, but it turned out that stepdad had no desire to be involved in the girls' lives – not in a good way at least.

One morning the two young girls confided in Big Sister that stepdad would sneak into their room late at night and *"just be creepy."* It started with him standing near the end of the bed, watching them, for what seemed like an eternity to the poor girls even though it was only a few minutes. It wasn't long before he started sitting on the edge of the bed. They'd pretend they were asleep and pray he would go away. "Why isn't Mom stopping him from doing this??" they would whisper to each other.

One night, *"Mister Creepy"* started to slip his hand under the covers of the youngest child; she let out an "Aaah!" as if she had been asleep and was suddenly awakened by the touch of *The Boogie Man*. The Boogie

Man bolted out of the room and the late night visits stopped for a while.

After that experience the girls tucked their blankets tightly under the mattress like a bunk in a military barracks. Better yet, Mackenzie set a trap – sprinkling little confetti-sized stars from the youngest girl's Glitter and Sparkle kit on the end of the bed.

When stepdad was caught strolling down the hallway in the middle of the night with the backside of his PJs covered in little stars the shit hit the fan – Mackenzie confronted him like a seasoned interrogator... a portent of her future career. Mom got a dressing-down as well for risking her kids at the hands of this scumbag. Stepdad was subsequently tossed out on his star-sprinkled ass, and the Nash family returned to normal, as it were.

3

Detective Mackenzie Nash traversed Salmon Beach Road and was struck by the surrounding solitude: The dawn sunlight reflecting off of the water, a half-dozen Cormorants perched atop old pilings rising above the bay, remnants of a long-abandoned pier that served local fishermen in a bygone era. It was a sharp contrast to the images her mind had conjured of the impending crime scene.

Her momentary daydream was broken by a row of mailboxes within her periphery on the inland side of the road. She slowed down in an attempt to read the numbers, but it was too late, they had become simply a reflection in the rear view mirror. She noticed another row of them up ahead – *2132* read the first box. She picked up the pace. Periodic rows of mailboxes came and went, along with an occasional stake, bearing a house number, at the head of a gravel driveway. She repetitively spoke the numbers of interest aloud as she gazed toward the passing properties… "Thirty-seven-fifty-six… thirty-seven-fifty-six…"

A relatively long stretch of nothingness had her wondering if she had somehow missed it. She spied a numbered stake ahead. "Thirty-four-seventy-four… almost there" she said as she reduced her speed. Another row of mailboxes quickly came into view. She slowed to a snail's pace, hugging the shoulder of the road as she anticipated the appropriate driveway to be imminent. Struggling to read the approaching mailbox numbers her focal point was suddenly shifted – she spied a Slaughter County Fire Department vehicle about a quarter-mile ahead and a hundred yards up a gravel drive – *Bingo*.

Her car tires crunching along the gravel, Nash's vista expanded to reveal a small gathering at the scene. Fire Department Lieutenant Matthew Graves – the Arson Investigator, Forensic Scientist Evan Lowell, and Deputy Coroner Valerie LaGrange all glanced over at Nash as she slowed to a stop and exited her vehicle; they were huddled near the back-end of a burned-up sedan that was facing away from the main road. The sedan rested in a field – fifteen feet from the gravel drive. The ground was relatively flat, covered with indigenous grasses and weeds, damp with the morning dew.

Nash donned her latex gloves and ducked under the yellow *Crime Scene* tape that cordoned-off a fairly large area. Arson Investigator Graves was the first to offer an opinion, "Our initial impression was that some hooligans decided to have a little *late night fun* by torching an abandoned car – until we noticed the contents of the trunk."

Nash was taken aback as she approached – a body lying in a fetal position, completely incinerated. "I guess the location... the trunk... pretty much rules out an accident or suicide" she commented.

"Oh yeah; and here's the clincher" replied Deputy Coroner LaGrange as she pointed to the corpse's jaw, "All of the teeth have been removed."

"Likely with this pair of pliers" added Forensic Scientist Lowell as he touched the plastic yellow triangle emblazoned with the number "1", identifying it as the first item of possible evidence, adjacent to the tool.

"Son of a..." commented Nash.

"You ever see anything like that around these parts?" said Lowell to Nash.

"Can't say that I have" Nash replied.

The sound of gravel beneath the tires of an approaching vehicle briefly interrupted the conversation – it was Detective Dirk Brogan.

"We're pretty much in agreement that the killer tried to destroy all evidence leading to the identity of the victim" LaGrange continued while Brogan was parking and exiting his vehicle, "...the body burned beyond recognition, all of the teeth extracted, no watch or jewelry, the skin burned off of the hands in order to remove fingerprints..."

"But there should be some residual flesh, or at least the ability to get DNA from the bones, correct?" asked Nash.

"It's possible."

"But if the vic's DNA isn't in CODIS we're going to be relying on any evidence we can dig up here, or a Missing Persons Report to point us in the right direction" added Lowell.

"Any chance a driver's license, a vehicle registration, or some other form of identification survived the fire?" said Nash.

"Hard to believe anything flammable could've survived this carnage."

"Yeah" replied Nash in a resigned tone, noticing that the sedan had been reduced to nothing more than a carcass... a mere skeleton of a car, resembling something right out of an apocalyptic movie.

"But we just started processing the scene so you never know; anything with layers like wallets, diaries, journals... we've found portions intact in the past."

"And of course a wallet could have been discarded somewhere around here near the scene, along the road, in a trash can, in the bay... you name it."

"Plus, we've got the license plate on the car. My gut tells me it's likely stolen; but you never know, even the most devious perps make at least one mistake in the commission of a crime, especially when it comes to murder."

"You know what else is missing..." said Nash.

"What's that?"

"The owners of the property; how come they're not out here hovering over us?" Nash glanced around the area and then thumb-pointed toward the gravel, "The driveway that leads back into the woods must go somewhere, right?"

"Just to an old shack; we went to check it out after we extinguished the fire, but it was locked. Judging by the dirt, dust, and grime on the windows it looks like it's been empty for months, if not years."

"What say we take a fresh look once we're done here at the immediate scene?"

"You got it."

Nash turned to Brogan who had sleepy-eye stumbled his way to the scene, "Nice of you to join us."

"I got here as fast as I could."

"I can tell" replied Nash as she pointed to her chin – mirroring that location on Brogan's face, "You missed a spot."

Brogan ran his fingers across his chin – discovering an eighth-inch rectangle of scruff, "I wasn't expecting a Sunday morning crime scene."

"What fantasy-land are you living in; you know all the cockroaches come out of the woodwork on Friday and Saturday nights?"

Brogan shrugged, yawned, and adjusted the camera strap hanging around his neck.

"So, did you happen to pick-up on our conversation?" asked Nash.

"Canvass the area for evidence, and check with all of the counties in Western Washington for 'Missing Persons'" replied Brogan.

"We may have to expand the 'Missing Persons' boundary, but that's a start."

Nash took a quick glance at the victim, paused, and then looked out toward the horizon – a full 360-degree scan of the area from the focal point of the scene, "Damn, out of the line of sight from virtually every angle." She pondered for a moment, "Who called it in?"

"A passerby" responded Graves. "A couple of nearby property owners called as well not long thereafter."

Nash turned to Brogan, "We'll start with the neighbors since we're here, but whatever the passerby saw could be crucial."

"Roger that" replied Brogan as he finally worked his way to the trunk of the burned-up sedan and caught a glimpse of the victim, "Whoa… I'm glad I skipped breakfast."

"Lieutenant" said Nash as she turned to Graves, "What's your take?"

"Obviously an accelerant was used… gasoline as a minimum based on the smell and the exploded gas can in the trunk."

"Any theories as to the sequence of events?"

"We'll be able to nail everything down once we get it back to the garage, but it appears that the first act was completely dousing the body since that was the primary objective. The accelerant was then splashed throughout the trunk and interior in an attempt to destroy all *other* potential evidence."

Nash nodded; Graves continued… "The trunk lid was left open; likely for two reasons: *One,* to be able to visibly ensure that the body was fully engulfed in flames; and *Two…* to make sure it had an adequate supply of oxygen, whereas closing the trunk might snuff-out the fire."

"You're thinking this was *not* the perp's first rodeo?"

"I'd certainly have those with *arson priors* in my pool of suspects. Plus, note how the back seat has been folded down, I'm guessing that was to help ensure the fire spread throughout the vehicle… you know, one nice big inferno and not two smaller fires contained in their respective area."

"Damn Lieutenant, are you *sure* you need to get this thing back to the garage?"

"If you're implying that I have this thing dialed-in I appreciate the vote of confidence, but my speculation is meaningless without the forensics to back it up."

Something caught Nash's attention adjacent to a yellow 'evidence identifier' near the body. "That's not a cell phone is it?"

"Yes it is" replied Lowell. "Looks like a burner… no pun intended."

Nash's eyes lit up. She went to reach for the phone but stopped herself, "You get all of the 'as found' pics of the trunk here?"

"Yep… Go for it."

Nash picked up and surveyed the phone - it was burnt to a crisp.

Lowell held up an evidence bag; Nash dropped the phone in the bag.

"The lab may *yet* get something out of this" said Lowell as he zipped-up the bag.

"We could also be in business if we get a ping off a nearby cell tower around the time of the murder" added Nash.

LaGrange opened up her gym bag-sized Coroner duffel and retrieved a large plastic sheet and a body bag. She laid out the sheet, "What say we get the body out of the trunk?"

LaGrange, Lowell, and Graves collectively removed the body from the trunk and placed it on the sheet.

Nash surveyed the area of the trunk where the body had been; hoping that a wallet had been protected from the fire via the victim's body and the trunk floor. A tire iron, a melted mini-spare tire, and a large wingnut that presumably was supposed to be holding-down the spare were the only items she noticed.

Lowell took pictures of the trunk sans the body.

Brogan peered into the trunk, "You think the tire iron might have been the murder weapon?"

LaGrange scanned the victim's head at Brogan's prompt, "No signs of blunt force trauma to the skull."

"You wouldn't think the tire iron would be *under* the victim if he'd been beaten to death with it" said Nash, "But let's mark it as potential evidence just in case."

"It looks like the cause of death is asphyxia... strangulation" noted LaGrange, looking closely at the victim's neck. "The hyoid bone is fractured."

"Any other evidence on the vic; you know, something that might have been in a pocket like a wallet or a set of keys?"

"No" said LaGrange while scanning the victim, "Nothing."

"Speaking of keys..." said Lowell while scrolling through the pictures he had just taken of the trunk.

"You found something?" said Nash.

Lowell returned to the section of the trunk that caught his eye in the photo. He placed an evidence tag near the item of note and took a close-up shot. He grabbed a pair of large tweezers, slipped it between the spare-tire well and the remains of the spare, and extracted a key that had been partially visible beneath the rim. He held it up for Nash and Brogan to see.

"What do you think?" asked Nash.

"See the two small holes here near the base? That tells me it had a plastic cover."

"Like a car key?" Brogan responded.

"Too small; more like a locker."

"I don't suppose the source is engraved on it?" said Nash.

Lowell turned the key from one side to the other, "Nope."

"A locker key?" said Brogan, *"That* could be a wild goose chase."

"We certainly aren't going to find the identity of the victim by going on a treasure hunt for a one-in-a-million locker" replied Nash, "But if we come up with a Missing Person and find out they had a locker at a gym, at work, at a Country Club..."

"Circumstantial perhaps, but an important piece of evidence under that scenario" said Lowell.

"And *who knows* what might lurk within the contents of the locker" added Nash.

Brogan had grown restless; too much talking and not enough investigating since he had arrived, "So, where do we stand on the rest of the scene?"

"The remainder of the vehicle beyond the trunk" replied Lowell, "and the surrounding grounds here."

"Well hell, let's get crackin'."

"Agreed" said Nash.

4

Detective Brogan began walking toward the front of the incinerated sedan, commenting along the way... "I noticed tire tracks up front here." He stopped and pointed them out, "I assume since they're inside the boundary of the tape they don't belong to any of you guys?"

"Correct" Lowell responded, "How about taking some shots of them from various angles, and I'll grab my casting solution to make some molds?"

"Got it." Brogan took several shots of the tracks, focusing on angles that highlighted the depth of the impressions.

Lowell arrived with his casting solution, "Let's see what you've got."

Brogan scrolled through the pictures on his camera while Lowell reviewed them. "Perfect" said Lowell.

Lowell set up his casts and poured the molds.

"I'm going to check the other side; at the back of the car" said Brogan with a head nod.

Nash was diligently working the interior of the car, and was finding nothing. She opened the glovebox – it was empty. "Who has *absolutely nothing* in their glove box?" she said aloud.

"Maybe the contents were incinerated in the fire" replied Graves, also working the interior.

"Take a look" said Nash as she pointed to the open glove box, "No ash residue."

"Removed them in order to hide the identity of the owner, perhaps?"

"Possibly, but that seems like a waste... I'm sure we can track them down through the VIN."

Brogan started tracing tire tracks from the rear of the car toward the main road; however, what were visible tracks at the front of the car were merely indentations at the rear – the grasses and weeds too thick to render tire impressions. He followed the indentations until they intersected with the gravel drive and disappeared.

Brogan paused, turned, and stood still while his head and eyes retraced the path up to the car. "Hey Nash... Lowell... when you've got a minute" he yelled up toward them.

Nash backed out of the passenger-side door and stood in Brogan's direction; Lowell walked from the front of the car and stood beside Nash.

"What have you got?" said Nash.

Brogan started walking toward them, following the path of the indentations while providing his assessment... "There are two sets of tracks" he stated. "The first car drove up the gravel drive, veered off of the gravel and onto the field, coming to a stop where the deepest impressions were made, up where Lowell made the molds. The second car, the burned-out cinder, followed behind."

"That makes sense" said Lowell as he started following the tracks in *front* of the car. "If I'm the driver of the *other* vehicle I go forward, turning back toward the gravel drive." He walked along the path in a slight arc until he reached the gravel. "But it's too tight to make a U-turn, so I stop at the drive, back-up and turn the wheel to make a Y-turn, and then head forward to the drive... down the gravel, and onto the main road and vanish into the night."

"So, the tracks you've gotten pictures of, and made the molds of, are the *killer's* vehicle?" said Nash.

"That's how it looks" replied Lowell.

"That means the victim followed the killer to this spot for some unknown reason, they got into an argument, the vic gets strangled; and *then* the killer has the foresight to remove all the teeth, lift and place the body in the trunk, douse it *and* the scene with gasoline, and turn it all into a raging inferno?"

13

"That's a lot of shit that went down" noted Brogan.

"Yeah" said Lowell, "Too well planned to be a *spur of the moment* act of rage."

"Maybe it was a drug deal gone bad?" said Brogan.

"And the killer had prepared for the possibility of things getting out of control?" responded Nash.

"Some people *do* happen to carry a can of gasoline in the trunk" replied Brogan, "And it's definitely not unusual to have tools in the trunk."

"But *no other tools… just a pair of pliers?*"

"Maybe the killer purposely left them there as a means to send a message – to screw with us?"

"A killer *that* bold?" replied Nash. "Sending messages to authorities is usually reserved for egotistical serial killers; in particular, those back in the days before extensive forensics and DNA. I'm thinking it was simply an oversight." She thought for a moment… *"Or* they figured we couldn't obtain any evidence from them."

"Hey LaGrange" said Lowell, "What do you think about our possible scenario?"

"It's possible" replied LaGrange, "But my preliminary measurements of the vic has him at close to six feet tall and more than likely at least of average build; so when you consider that there are no signs of blunt force trauma to the skull as a means to incapacitate him, I am left to wonder: *How* did the killer overpower him?"

"Drugged him maybe?" said Brogan.

"Yeah, but then how did he drive here?" responded Lowell, "Essentially he'd have to have been drugged once they were here at the scene."

"Which would imply they had planned to hangout here and do drugs" said Nash, "And that gets us to the question: *Why did they pick this spot?*"

"Like you pointed out earlier, it *is* out of the line of sight" said Brogan.

"They drove around and just happened to *find* this place?" postulated Lowell, "Or a familiarity with the property?"

"One of the many questions to solve" replied Nash.

Brogan's mind drifted back to the previous conversation. "What about a surprise punch to the head... you know, the vic got cold-cocked?"

"Knock him out and then strangle him?" replied LaGrange, "That could do it; bruises and impact marks would have been left on the flesh, but nothing on the skull."

"Then we should have evidence of a struggle" said Nash. She turned to Lowell, "You see anything along those lines?"

"No" he replied as he scanned the scene surrounding the car. "In fact, the vegetation here is only minimally disturbed. If there was a struggle, or even a single punch that knocked the vic down, there'd be at least a body-sized patch of flattened vegetation."

"Maybe the vic got sucker-punched and strangled in the car?" said Brogan.

"That would fit with the evidence" replied Lowell.

"Here's another option we haven't discussed" added Nash, "What if there was more than one perpetrator?"

"You may be onto something there" nodded Lowell.

"But what about the lack of activity in the area outside of the car?" asked Brogan.

"Well, here's a possible scenario" responded Lowell. "The two perps are in the first vehicle. The vic comes and joins them to do the drug deal or party or whatever..."

"In order for the perps to get the drop on the vic" Nash interceded, "I'm thinking one of them is in the back seat and the vic gets in the front on the passenger-side."

"I concur" continued Lowell, "They all do their thing... a drug deal, smoke some dope, do some coke... whatever..."

"And at some point the perp in the driver's seat cold-cocks the vic, and the perp in the back seat strangles him" said Nash – finishing the thought.

"That hypothesis is certainly within the realm of possibilities" remarked LaGrange.

"If there *are* two perps then a few other things fall into place" said Lowell. "The two of them carry the vic to the trunk of *this* car, which means they'd be walking along the same path... essentially single file."

"Which would explain the minimal amount of apparent activity here at the scene" Nash said as she could see where Lowell was going with his scenario.

"It also makes removing the teeth a hell of a lot easier... one guy holds the jaw down and the other yanks out the teeth" added Lowell.

"Have you found any shoe prints?" asked Brogan.

"No" replied Lowell. "Which is a bit frustrating after getting these great tire tracks; but the perp, or perps, never stepped in the softer soil in that area."

"But we haven't combed the entire area yet either, correct?" said Nash.

"Correct" responded Lowell. "What say we set up an evidence-gathering line and *have at it?*"

"Sounds like a plan; with all of the evidence here presumably destroyed by the fire let's hope we find something *somewhere.*"

"Or there's someone out there who knows something – a *witness*" added Brogan.

5

The reflection... at first glance the image was foreign, almost unrecognizable. At second glance the face was familiar, outside of the bruises; but the eyes told a different story... the knowledge of *what hath occurred* lurked within. The gravity of the moment was daunting, even overwhelming; *what thine eyes have seen* was almost too much to comprehend, but the last thing one needs is to get dragged into a murder investigation. A deep breath was taken... calm, cool, and collected was the only viable answer. Reality set in... *the time had come... the time was now.*

His thoughts were interrupted by a slight rustling sound near the door; a sheet of paper had appeared on the carpet. He grabbed and scanned the paper; as expected it was the synopsis of his stay: Five nights plus valet parking, one meal at the restaurant, two drinks at the lounge, one unidentified movie, and a myriad of taxes and fees. He folded it in half and slid it into a pocket of his suitcase.

He took one last look in the mirror – a final check that he was ready.

Another deep breath was followed by an exaggerated exhale. *"You've got this"* he told himself.

He scanned the room, donned his suit jacket, grabbed his suitcase, opened the door, and entered the hallway... almost tripping over a newspaper in front of the threshold. He bent down and picked it up. *"Hmmm... the Seattle Times... a bit of reading material during the flight"* he said to himself. He paused in thought, *"I wonder if..."*

He folded the newspaper in half, tucked it under his armpit, and trekked to the elevator.

Entering the lobby he wheeled his luggage past the Concierge desk –

no surprise that it was empty at this time of morning.

Two clerks manned the reception counter – a couple of twenty-somethings… one guy and one gal. The early-twenties guy seemed a little timid and unsure of himself, he was surely a trainee. Standing-tall and clearly in charge was a mid-twenties gal. Both were clad in black slacks, a white shirt, and a necktie; but her shirt was tailored so as to maintain a hint of femininity within the professional appearance required at such an establishment.

The woman was surprised by the man's bruised face, but a smile and cheery greeting met him as he approached, "Good morning, Sir. Checking out?" she asked.

"Yes" he said as he handed her his room key-card.

She brought up his information on the computer, "Shall the charges remain with your card on-file, Mr. Garrison?"

"Yes, thank you."

"Great – you're good to go. The valet will be out front with your vehicle in just a couple of minutes."

"Nothing for me to sign?"

Her eyes focused on his hand and wrist; wrapped in an ace bandage, "No Sir. And thank you for staying with us."

"You're welcome."

A vehicle appeared at the entryway. The valet popped the trunk, exited the vehicle, and stood-fast at the trunk to assist Garrison with his luggage.

"I'll take care of that for you, Sir" said the valet, reaching out to grasp his luggage.

The valet placed the luggage in the trunk and closed the lid. Garrison handed him a five.

"Thank you Sir; have a nice trip" said the valet.

Garrison nodded, jumped in the car, and sped away.

Turning onto I-5 South he thought to himself, *"Should have stayed at a hotel near the airport, that way you simply take the hotel shuttle in lieu of dealing with a rental car return the morning of your flight."* He considered the alternatives, *"Then again, you'd be dealing with the potential parking nightmares of downtown Seattle. And at least I'm in the reverse-commute direction, just look at those poor bastards trying to get to downtown… a sea of headlights even at this ungodly hour… I guess this was the better of two evils after all."*

He exited the freeway, drove several blocks on an arterial, and turned onto Pacific Highway South.

He spied the rental car sign up ahead. He glanced at the clock on the dashboard – he was both relieved and annoyed: Relieved that he had plenty of time before his flight's departure… annoyed that the majority of that time would be spent sitting idly-by in the airport awaiting the announcement to board the plane.

"Shall the charges remain with the card presented earlier?" said the clerk as Garrison handed him the keys.

"Yes."

"We noticed that the gas tank is not full."

"Well I…"

"Oh I'm sorry, I see that you prepaid for the gas."

"That's what I was about to say."

"Yes Sir" said the clerk as he handed Garrison his paperwork. "The shuttle is picking up passengers in the parking area and will be here momentarily."

Garrison turned around and proceeded to the waiting area.

The shuttle pulled up, the driver opened the retractable doors, and reached out to grab Garrison's luggage – a single carry-on. He placed it on the rack and moved aside for Garrison to enter. Garrison sat down, grabbed his wallet, pulled out a couple of ones, and placed them in his front pants pocket.

A couple arrived with so much luggage you'd think they were taking a vacation for the rest of their lives: Two suitcases the size of steamer trunks, an average-sized suitcase, two carry-on bags, her purse, and his satchel. The shuttle driver almost tripped over Garrison's feet as he tried to drag the first of the oversized behemoths to the luggage rack. Garrison got up and moved to the back of the shuttle.

After a lot of grunting and rearranging of the luggage, both on and under the racks, the shuttle finally got underway.

"Airlines?" said the driver as they approached the airport.

Responses rang out like roll-call on the first day of school… "United… Hawaiian… Delta." When the roll-call ceased Garrison added his two-cents worth… "Alaskan."

Barely a minute had passed when the driver announced, "First stop – Alaskan" as he pulled up to the curb. He opened the retractable door, got up and grabbed Garrison's carry-on, and carried it out to the sidewalk.

Garrison reached into his pocket and handed the driver the ones.

"Thanks" responded the driver, "Have a nice trip."

Garrison wheeled his luggage to the escalator, up a floor, across the causeway, and over to the Alaskan Airlines self-check-in kiosk terminals.

He pulled out his paperwork from a pocket on his carry-on. He entered his name and confirmation number, followed by the 'prohibited items' questionnaire, and retrieved his boarding pass.

He made his way to the security screening. It was a relatively short line, thanks to the time of morning.

He took a moment to gather himself… to reassure his need for a calm and cool demeanor. After all, you never want to look nervous in an airport; Security personnel equate nervousness to suspicious behavior.

The TSA Agent looked at Garrison's face and neck – he was curious as to the bruising, but realized it was none of his business. When Garrison handed him his Driver's License and boarding pass the ace bandage around his hand and wrist also caught the Agent's attention.

The Agent examined Garrison, his I.D. and his paperwork with the detail of a gemologist in a high-end jewelry store. Garrison thought that if he got *pulled off to the side* that perhaps it would be best to tell them what he had seen... what he knows... the *reason* behind his nervousness. But would that mean he would get stuck here in Seattle as a Material Witness? And then again, how often is it that a witness' words get turned around, taken out of context, and the next thing you know they're treating *YOU* like a suspect?

For once in his life Garrison wished the lines had been long and moving expeditiously in order to get people pushed through the process like cattle through a gate; *not* so slow that the Agent could sit and watch the beads of sweat accumulating on his forehead.

Just as Garrison thought he was about to be hauled-off to another room *to speak with someone of higher authority,* the Agent finally stamped and scribed his boarding pass and handed it back.

Garrison waited until he was well past the Agent before he finally relaxed. He took a breath, swallowed, and wiped his brow.

The screening process was uneventful – thankfully. He wheeled his luggage to the gate, stopping only to check the Arrival-Departure board – his flight was on-schedule.

Just as he sat down his cell phone buzzed – it was a text:

Hey Babe, I'll be there to pick you up... 9:30 right?

He texted back: *Yes. BTW, I didn't want to tell you earlier and worry you, but I got in a car wreck yesterday... T-boned by an inattentive driver. I'm ok but am a little beat-up. Just thought you should know before you see me.*

That's awful, but I'm glad you're ok.

Thanks. See you in a few hours.

Kk

After spending a good hour killing time: Exploring the terminal, strolling through the gift shop, grabbing a latte', and making a pit stop at the Men's Room, the announcement to commence boarding the plane finally arrived.

With no overhead ramps connecting the terminal to the small Bombardier prop planes, *through the gate and onto the tarmac* he trekked. He stopped to place his carry-on onto the luggage rack. An ironic name... *carry-on*... in this particular instance anyway... considering that the standard-sized bag was too large for the Bombardier's overhead bins there would be no *carrying on your carry-on*, hence the rack on the tarmac.

Boarding the plane he settled into his seat, placed his newspaper into the seat-pocket in front of him, and buckled-up.

Once airborne he grabbed the paper and began to read. In the *Local* section he noticed a blurb about an arson and death in Slaughter County. A spokesperson with the Sheriff's Department stated that, although unconfirmed by the Coroner's Office, they were currently treating the scene as a potential homicide. There was no word yet on the identification of the victim or any possible motive, but there was speculation that drugs may be involved. The piece ended with a request for anyone with information regarding the crime to please call a 1-800 number. Garrison pondered for a moment, and then flipped to the *Sports* section.

When finished reading the paper he flipped back to the *Entertainment* section – attempting to pass the remaining flight-time via the Sudoku and the Crossword Puzzle, but it was to no avail... his bandaged hand and wrist failed to cooperate.

The lack of shuteye due to the past twenty-four hours of tension finally caught up with him, and he fell fast asleep.

He was awakened by a prod from the Flight Attendant, "Seatback to the upright position in preparation for landing, Sir."

Walking off the plane he searched the crowd. There she was... a sight for sore eyes – literally.

Her eyes lit up when she saw him; a waving hand to flag him down, and a smile on her face.

Her beaming eyes and smile became somewhat subdued as he approached – the reality of his injuries came to the forefront.

"Wow, are you sure you're okay, hon?" she asked as she brushed her hand gently across his face and touched his bandaged hand.

She went to greet him with a kiss – he seemed a little tentative.

"Sorry" he said, "Just a bit sore."

"Not at all; I should have realized…"

"To be honest" he confessed, "everything is hazy."

"Hazy?"

"Truth be told, I actually got a concussion and the doctor told me not to fly for several days to a week. I lied and said my flight was still a week away – I just wanted to get back home."

"Sheesh hon, I don't know whether to kiss you or smack you."

"You should probably smack me because I realize now that it was a stupid move to fly home so soon. I feel much worse… headache, hazy like I was saying, even in a bit of a stupor, memory problems… you name it."

"And your voice is all raspy and your neck's all red."

"Damn air bag got me right in the throat."

"Aww Babe; we'll just have to get you home and focus on rest, relaxation, and recovery."

"I like the sound of that. And on the upside, I'm glad I purchased the additional insurance coverage through the rental car agency… at least *our* insurance company's not involved."

"That's you… always able to find the silver lining in a dark cloud."

"Not so much for the rental car company though, they had to provide me a whole new car."

6

A ghastly photograph of a charred corpse looked Nash directly in the eye. The vision etched a single thought in her mind – *justice*. Above the picture she wrote *Victim;* below she scrolled an all-too-common symbol at this stage of an investigation – a question mark.

Additional photographs and descriptors populated the white board… her *Murder Board:* The incinerated sedan, the tire tracks, the pliers, the tire iron, and the key… presumably to a locker… which would be a needle-in-a-haystack without the name of the victim; and possibly so even *with* a name.

The shack on the property was actually more like a small cabin, and peering through the windows provided nothing that would be considered *probable cause* for breaking-down the door. The cabin's owner was still potentially relevant, but was not yet known.

Information from the neighbors had been relegated to notes in the file… didn't even garner a spot on the murder board: They hadn't heard or seen a thing beyond the glow of the fire in the night sky, and they had no idea who owned the property following the death of the previous owners a few years ago. Everything was in flux at this point - more questions than answers: *Who was the victim? Why was he killed? What did the passerby see? Were there any cell tower pings; and, if so, who made or received the call?*

Nash's concentration was broken by Brogan entering the room. He walked directly to the murder board and started to scrawl under the *Passerby* item of note.

"Important info from the passerby?" said Nash.

"Not exactly; all he saw was the fire" replied Brogan, "Almost didn't call it in because he saw a cop near the scene and figured they had already reported it."

"A cop?? What the hell?! Did he describe them?"

"My bad... poor choice of words; what he saw was the *car*... a black & white."

"He didn't notice the name... the jurisdiction?"

"No; just said he saw a black & white."

"State Patrol cars are all white, so that rules them out. And we didn't have anyone in the area at that time Saturday night, did we?"

"Nope."

"So, that leaves Bennington and Scandia P.D.s."

"True. But the scene is well out of Scandia's jurisdiction so that wouldn't make sense. What about the Tribal Police?"

"They have black & whites, but they're all SUVs."

"Yeah, but some people utilize the term 'car' as a general description of a vehicle."

"Good point. Let's play it safe and check with all three" responded Nash, "See if they had an Officer in the area at the time."

"Got it." Brogan added *Bennington? Scandia? Tribal?* next to the words *Cop Car* on the murder board. He positioned himself at the item: *Cell Tower Pings*.

"Got some pings off of the nearest cell tower?" commented Nash.

"Five calls between midnight and one A.M." said Brogan as he began writing down the information.

"What's the breakdown?"

"Two of them were to taxi services: Twelve-oh-three to Dewey's Taxi, and twelve-forty-four to Crosstown Cab."

"Is there a nearby bar or restaurant?"

"Hilltop Tavern."

"I forgot about them. That's probably where the calls originated, but contact the cab companies and verify their pickup spot, rider info, and drop-off."

"Will do."

"What else?"

"Two calls from the same phone just a few minutes apart: One at twelve-thirty-three to 4-1-1, and again at twelve-thirty-six to the Washington State Ferry information number."

"Crap, maybe it was the killer checking on his preferred getaway route? If he misses the ferry he's driving south and east across the Tacoma Narrows Bridge."

"Could be, but it's not my *number one.*"

"No? What is?"

"The one at twelve-twenty-seven… it came from a burner."

"Our burner?"

"Don't know yet, Lowell's running that down: Where and when it was sold, whether they used a credit card… which is unlikely; and if the transaction was caught on video" Brogan replied. "Oh; and the number of the phone that made the call to activate it."

"Who'd the call go to?"

"A landline – 1565 Cedar Street in Bennington. The homeowner's are Daryl and Madison Wagner."

"How long did the call last?"

"All of two seconds."

"So, it could have been a misdial… a wrong number."

"Or the victim trying to make a call for help and got cut off."

"The killer grabbing the phone out of the vic's hand, shutting him up permanently by choking him, and then tossing the phone on the body in a *Take that… NOW try to make your effing phone call* kind of statement?"

"Exactly. Or maybe it was a signal?"

"A signal?"

"Yeah – *The deed is done.*"

"Maybe; but let's hold off on the conspiracy theories for the time being. And we still need to follow-up on the other numbers… you know, the cab companies and such" Nash replied. "Also, find out the subsequent pings on the number that called the ferries; I want to know if they made it onto the ferry or not, and their ultimate destination."

"What about following-up on the burner call?" said Brogan; chomping at the bit.

"Well, if we can get Donnelly working on the other stuff then you and I can go pay a visit to the Wagner residence."

"Cool… I'm all over it."

"And have her check with Lowell over at the lab to see if he has anything yet on the tire tracks… or anything else for that matter."

"Got it."

7

Nash and Brogan turned onto Cedar Street in the heart of the *old town* section of Bennington. The homes in old town were an eclectic bunch, built primarily between the early 1900's and the 1940's. Most of them were modest dwellings... bungalows of both the single-level variety or with a daylight basement, and two-story homes where the upper story had angled ceilings and dormers since the second story was essentially nothing more than a finished attic-space. An interesting thing about these old two-story homes – the stairs to the top floor seemed like an afterthought... narrow, odd turns, and very steep. One upside to the *narrow stairwells with odd turns* from Nash's perspective: The ability to kill someone by pushing them down the stairs was slim to none... the body would get stuck against the walls of the stairwell or would be stopped by a landing. After so many years in her line of work she tended to assess almost everything within her purview as a possible crime scene. Plus she'd had a case that involved that exact scenario...

"See the two-story homes around here with the dormers?" Nash pointed out to Brogan.

"Yeah?" replied Brogan. The tone of Nash's voice and accompanying glint her eye told Brogan that Nash was about to recount an old case. She always had a story to tell.

"Are you familiar with the narrow and steep stairwells that lead to the upstairs in many of them?"

"Sure, my grandparents' place was like that. When my brother and I were kids we'd take a chunk of cardboard and slide down the stairs like a sled."

"Well, several years ago, just a few blocks from here, a husband claimed his wife fell down a set of stairs such as those. She purportedly hit her head multiple times on the steps, all the way to the bottom, and died from the fall."

"How is that possible? My brother and I slipped off of the cardboard tons of times and every time it happened we'd turn sideways and get stuck against the walls of the stairwell?"

"Exactly! As you learned by your experience as a kid, forensics told a different story. The lab guys took a dummy of the same size and weight, and nudged it several times to approximate an accidental fall. Each and every time it fell and rolled only a few feet before getting stuck, *not once* duplicating the husband's description of the event."

"So you nailed the guy, right?"

"Oh yeah; blood splatter, blood trails, clothing fibers, carpet fibers... they all told a completely different story: In an upstairs bedroom he hit her over the head multiple times with a baseball bat, dragged her body down the stairs, and then positioned her *head-first* at the bottom of the stairs. He cleaned up the scene... or so he thought: Luminol indicated blood spatter in the room and a blood trail all the way down the stairs. He tried to hide the bat by burying it in the back yard, but didn't consider that the family dog would pick up on the wife's scent and dig it up... literally while he was being questioned by O'Rourke and me. It was a thing of beauty... *Forensics don't lie, so take THAT dirtbag.*"

"The dog dug-up the bat?!"

"I never would've believed it if I didn't see it with my own two eyes."

"That's awesome; I can only imagine the look on his face."

"Priceless."

A cross-street suddenly caught Nash's eye; the sign read *15th Ave.*

"Crap, we're almost there" she said, "1565, right?"

Brogan looked at his memo pad. "Yep; should be up ahead on the left."

Nash pulled into the driveway, backed up into the street, and then pulled up next to the curb right in front of the Wagner home.

Brogan noticed a curtain move slightly to the side in the home's large front window, "Somebody knows we're here."

Nash and Brogan approached the home via the walkway – Nash in the lead. She stepped onto the landing and reached for the doorbell when suddenly the door opened, very slowly, and revealed a disturbing sight. There in the doorway stood a woman in her late twenties to early thirties with a black eye and swollen lip… the rest of her face awash with bruises, abrasions, scratches, and lacerations. Nash figured she either got knocked-around as part of the *B-Town Rollers* – the local Roller Derby team, was in a car accident, or more likely, was the victim of domestic violence within the past few days.

Nash scanned the woman from head to toe – looking for indications of a struggle… of defensive wounds. There were bruises and scratches on her hands. Nash was pretty sure her arms were covered in bruises as well, but the woman was wearing a sweatshirt.

Nash regained her composure, looked back up toward the woman, and held up her badge, "We're detectives Nash and Brogan with the Slaughter County Sheriff's Department; are you Madison Wagner?"

"Sinclair" replied the woman.

"Sinclair?" asked Nash; wondering if they had the wrong address or had received misinformation from their telephone search.

"My maiden name; but Wagner is fine – what can I do for you?"

Brogan couldn't take his eyes off of Madison's face… the beating she had apparently received. He tried to peer behind her, concerned that the person responsible for her injuries might be lurking within, "Is everything all right, ma'am?"

"Yes… I'm okay."

"Are you sure?" Nash chimed in.

"Everything should be fine now" replied Madison.

Nash and Brogan subtly glanced at each other. *A curious choice of words* Nash thought to herself; she was sure that Brogan had the same thought. There was an uncomfortable moment of silence, and then Nash's focus turned back toward Madison.

"The reason we're here is in regard to a phone call" said Nash. "Did you receive a call around twelve-thirty Saturday night – Sunday morning?"

Madison had a look of confusion on her face, "It wasn't really a phone call, they hung up as soon as I answered – had to be a wrong number."

"You didn't recognize the number?"

"No; which kind of freaked me out considering the time of night… kept me awake for about an hour."

"What about your husband?"

"What about him?"

"Did he have any ideas about the call?"

"He wasn't here."

"Is he here now?"

"No."

"If he wasn't here when you received the call, do you think perhaps the call was meant for your husband and you surprised them by answering the phone?"

Madison's brow furrowed; a look of frustration on her face. The inflection in her voice confirmed the expression, "I have no idea, but I don't understand all of these questions about a *two-second wrong number phone call?*"

"I apologize. We're running-down all of the calls that were made in the vicinity, and approximate time, of a crime that occurred in the early morning hours yesterday."

"A crime?"

"A fire… looks like it might have been arson" Nash replied, "That's as much as we can share at this point."

"The one on the news this morning? Over near Blue Heron Cove?"

"Yes."

"I'm sorry, I can't help you."

Nash and Brogan looked at each other – an unspoken *Do you have anything else to ask her?*

Madison had grown weary of the questioning, "Is that all?"

Nash's cell phone rang. "Excuse me for a moment" she said to Madison.

"What have you got?" said Nash into the phone as she stepped off of the landing.

Madison stared off in the distance while she waited for Nash to finish her call. Brogan remained silent – he was fixated on Madison's bruised and battered face. Madison could sense Brogan's gaze and glanced over his way. Momentary eye contact was made and Brogan quickly, and embarrassingly, looked away.

"Yeah? Okay. Got it. Thanks" said Nash into her phone and then hung up.

Nash stepped back onto the landing. "Do you happen to know a George or Mary Montgomery?" she said to Madison.

"No" responded Madison.

"Okay... thanks for your time."

Nash started to turn around to leave. She stopped and turned back to Madison. She reached into her jacket pocket, pulled out a card, and handed it to her. "If you think of anything" she said, and then looked Madison directly in the eye, *"Or if there's anything I can do for you...* please call."

Madison glanced at the card and then back at Nash, but remained silent.

Nash and Brogan stepped off of the landing and walked to the cruiser. Nash pulled away from the curb; Brogan made one last look back toward Madison as she closed her front door.

"She looked like someone... probably her husband... beat the crap out of her recently" said Nash.

"Yeah, no shit. Let's hope that the asshole that did it wasn't still there in the house waiting to rough her up some more once we were out of the picture."

"Actually, if he *was* there then the fact that *we* were there could provide her a respite from any harm; knowing that the cops were just there, had seen her condition, and might return."

"I hope you're right."

"Now that I think about it, I doubt he was there" commented Nash.

"No?"

"She would have been acting nervously once we started questioning her about her appearance… likely even glancing back to see if he was within earshot."

"Yeah, I guess so."

"In any case, check with Bennington P.D. to see if a domestic violence report was filed."

"You got it" Brogan replied. He paused… something else was gnawing at him, "What do you think; her husband could be either the killer or the vic?"

"Anything's possible at this point" Nash responded, "But what would you make of the phone call from a burner, if, in fact, it originated from the scene?"

"If her husband's the *vic* then it could be like we discussed earlier… he was trying to call for help."

"What about your *'the deed is done'* theory?"

"Oh yeah, there's that too… *especially* since it looks like her husband has been assaulting her" Brogan replied. "But then again, she doesn't seem like the *murder-for-hire* type."

"They almost never do" said Nash.

Brogan silently pondered Nash's statement; he didn't really want to consider such a scenario.

"And if the husband is *the killer?*" Nash noted.

"A taunt from him… *her abuser*… perhaps?" replied Brogan.

"How do you mean?"

"Maybe she was having an affair, the husband found out, killed the guy, and the *'hello – click'*" Brogan gestured, "was his way of letting her know that she's been caught and he did something about it?"

"Yeah, but it was a burner phone… a number she didn't recognize?" Nash countered.

"Maybe that's all part of his game? Remember… she said she was freaked-out about the call, *specifically* because of the time of night, that it was a number she didn't recognize, *and* that they hung up immediately."

"Hmm… interesting notion; but if that's the case she does *not yet know* that her boyfriend is the vic."

"Why do you say that?"

"She was timid; not distraught. If she had an idea that her husband killed her boyfriend she would have been a total wreck."

"Good point."

"Your *'killing the boyfriend'* option could also mean that the call was meant for the husband; a murder-for-hire that *he* had orchestrated."

"And he wouldn't need to receive the call to know that the deed was done, just have his wife mention it" Brogan concluded.

"Exactly" responded Nash. "In any event, all possibilities are in-play until the evidence tells us otherwise."

Brogan nodded; and then queried… "By the way, what was the phone call that had you asking if she knew some couple?"

"It was Donnelly with the names of the property owners – *the crime scene*" Nash replied, "It was a longshot but I had to ask."

8

Deputy Laura Donnelly, dry-erase marker in hand, was adding copious notes to the murder board when Nash and Brogan entered the office.

"Somebody's been busy" said Brogan as Nash and he approached Donnelly.

"Oh hey Brogan – Nash" said Donnelly as she turned around to greet them. "Yeah, I got all the info on the cell tower pings; and Lowell I.D.'d the type and size of tires that made the tracks."

"Great; let's start with the cell tower" replied Nash.

"Sure. The call to Crosstown Cab was from Logan Dean, a sailor stationed on the Stennis. The cab picked him up in front of *Hilltop Tavern* at twelve-fifty-six and drove him to the base in Bennington – dropping him off at one-thirteen. Witnesses placed him at the tavern from nine-thirty until the cab picked him up."

"How about Dewey's Taxi?"

"Similar story. The cell phone belongs to Jennifer Atwood. The cab picked up her and a girlfriend at the tavern at twelve-fifteen; dropped them off at twelve-thirty-four at 273 Poplar Street, also in Bennington."

"And our potential ferry rider?"

"Jeff Conger – lives in Bellevue. If he was planning on catching a ferry he didn't make it."

"Cell tower pings down through Tacoma and then up to Bellevue?"

"No. Apparently he decided to spend the night here at his son's house on the outskirts of town – he was there all day and through the night."

"Well, those all went nowhere; what about the tire tracks?"

"When I told Lowell about the sighting of a cop car in the area around the time of the fire... well, *that* sure got his attention."

"Yeah?"

"He said it wasn't necessarily an *Ah-ha* moment, but was definitely curious."

"How's that?"

"The tires are Goodyear Eagle, size 235/55-17. Ironically, that's the standard tire for the Police Interceptor version of the Crown Vic."

"What the hell??" Brogan blurted out.

Nash was similarly dumbfounded. "I was hoping there may have been someone who could provide us information related to the scene" she said, "but possibly the killer?? I can't even *begin* to wrap my head around *that* notion."

"And I talked to Bennington, Scandia, and Tribal police" Donnelly added, "All of them said they had no activity in the area at that time."

"Considering the pains the killer went through to avoid leaving any evidence, if he really *was* a cop it would have been a major screw-up to have his cruiser knowingly at the scene."

"Yeah" added Brogan, "In that case the smart move would have been to be the person who *discovered* the scene; that way there's a reason for your tracks being there."

"And they surely would've been off-the-clock" said Nash.

"Just finished-up their shift?" asked Brogan.

"That would make the most sense for them to still be driving their cruiser."

"So, what do we do with this information? A tire-tread check of every department's Crown Vic?"

"That would be interdepartmental political suicide at this point; we have no direct evidence that a police cruiser was involved."

"But you just said..."

"It was an exaggerated knee-jerk reaction" Nash interrupted.

"What about the passerby saying he saw a cop car?"

"Did he actually see it *entering or exiting* the gravel drive?"

"No; just in the vicinity."

"There you go. Nothing at this point actually puts a cop car *at the scene*. Besides, the tire size might jive with a Crown Vic, but I'm sure it matches dozens of other vehicles as well" said Nash. "Get the specific details on Lowell's search; I'm guessing he has it narrowed down to a number of vehicle types using that tire since a '55' sidewall aspect ratio is not very common."

"And you know this... *how?*" said Brogan.

"Personal experience; my '94 Legend Coupe LS factory tires are 215/55-15. When I went to buy a new set there was only one manufacturer of that size and they were pricey as hell; that's when the Tire Guy informed me about the rare '55' aspect ratio. He said I could go with a more common size, with a wider tread and lower aspect ratio, and I'd be in business; so now I run 235/50-15... it's as simple as that."

"I learn something new every day. Okay, I'll get on the horn with Lowell."

"And I'll talk to the other departments about Officers that might have just gotten off-shift around the time of the crime. I won't let them know that a cop could be a person of interest; instead I'll put a positive spin on my question, telling them we are merely looking for someone who might have seen something."

Brogan was impressed, "Nash the spin-doctor... Nice."

"I'm not convinced that a cop is involved, in fact I'd be shocked if that's the case, but I've got to follow wherever the evidence leads me."

9

A mixture of black raspberry and smoke – the aroma of a recently blown-out candle, wafted through the room. Near the candle sat two wine glasses, each with a smidgen of wine at the bottom. A dessert plate sat between the glasses; remnants of strawberries adorned the plate – tiny islands in a shallow sea of melted chocolate. The room was now empty, the prelude was over, the confectionary foreplay had moved to the bedroom.

He slowly unbuttoned her blouse. "You've got chocolate on your chest" he said.

"Gee, surprise-surprise" she responded, "Since when did my cleavage become a reservoir for chocolate-covered strawberries?"

"Since you dropped it there while we were trying to share the strawberry."

"Since *I* dropped it there? So it's *my* fault?"

"Of course; it was *your* half of the strawberry."

"That's because you jerked your head when you bit into it and yanked it out of my mouth."

"Well, in the interest of fairness, I suppose I can take the blame."

"Oh, you *suppose?*"

"It's the gentlemanly thing to do."

"So you're a gentleman, eh? And that's why you are unbuttoning my blouse?"

"Of course… to make amends for my transgression" he said as he started to lick the chocolate off of her.

Still standing she closed her eyes… enjoying the attention… awaiting his next move. She soon realized he was going to need a little help to achieve his endeavor. With that in mind she reached behind her back and, with one quick flick, released her bra clasp. He grabbed the lapels of her blouse and pulled them over her shoulders and onto her arms – the blouse fell to the floor. She grabbed her bra straps and pulled them down, then unbuttoned and unzipped her skirt. Her bra landed in the vicinity of the blouse; her skirt fell to her ankles.

She pulled him back up to her face and gave him a kiss. "What's good for the goose…" she said as she unbuttoned his shirt. He went to assist, but she slapped his hand away. "I've got this one, you take care of those" she said – touching his belt buckle. He eagerly complied. She pulled-off his shirt and dropped it to the floor. He awkwardly removed his pants – there's just no graceful way to remove a pair. She stepped out of her skirt and fell onto the bed. He fell on top of her.

His mouth returned to its previous location… her breasts. He slowly worked his way down her stomach, to the lower abdomen, across to one inner thigh, back across to the other, and finally to the sweet spot. She let out a breathy whisper of a moan. He worked his magic through the increasing intensity of her moans, rising to a crescendo at the point of ecstasy… her body trembling, her skin flushed. "I need you up here" she said. He climbed on top of her and the two of them became one. The passion was intense… was heart-pounding… was relentless – until they both fell onto their backs on the bed, exhausted…

Nash was lying motionless in his arms, her mind wandering. She appeared to be staring at a painting on the wall, but that wasn't the case… the room was too dark, lit only by the lights of the city emanating through the window.

"You seem like something's on your mind" he said, "It's not about *us* is it?"

"No; it's an aspect of my current case that is rather troubling; I can't seem to get it out of my head."

"Troubling? Isn't that the M.O. for your job – working homicide and all?"

"Yeah, but this one's different. A woman I was interviewing today…"

"A suspect?" he interrupted.

"I wouldn't call her a suspect at this point, not necessarily even a person of interest, just someone that might have a tie to the case. In fact, she may have a tie to the case and be completely unaware of it, *or* she may be hiding something."

"So is that it, the fact that she may be hiding something?"

"Somewhat. But it wasn't the interview as much as it was her demeanor and appearance… sullen, almost fearful." She took a breath, "And battered and bruised… black eye, busted-open lip."

"Like some asshole beat the crap out of her?"

"Yes."

"I'm assuming you're going to do something about it?"

"As much as I'm able; but it's out of my jurisdiction unless her beatings have some connection to my case."

"Knowing you, I'm sure you'll find a way to do *something* about it."

"Dirk is checking with Bennington P.D. to see if a Domestic Violence Report has been filed. If not, I'm going to do my best to make *that* happen at the very least."

"I don't even *know* the woman and my blood is boiling. There's nothing worse than violence against women or children. Men who perform such acts are fucking cowards… fucking pussy-ass cowards who should have their asses beaten ten-times worse than the pain they inflicted."

"I can't argue with you on that." Nash paused and reflected, "Do you *personally* know anyone who has been a victim of domestic violence?"

He thought for a moment, "Not that I'm aware of, thankfully."

"Actually you do."

"I do?? Who?"

Nash turned her head and looked into his eyes. A look of surprise appeared on his face. "You??" he said.

"Back in my early twenties."

"But *you?* ...someone who won't take shit from anyone??"

"Well, it's not that simple. You grow up without any positive male role model, we're talking not a single one... none... nada... zero: Your father walked out on you, on *all of us* actually, when you were six, never to be seen again. Your mother entertained a bunch of low-lifes looking for nothing more than a roll in the sack. Mom gets remarried and stepdad turns out to be a pathetic loser scumbag that almost molests your little sisters. So your life is filled with rejection from men, and you long to find some kind of acceptance – to find love. And then you finally meet Mister Dreamboat – handsome, successful, popular... and he wants YOU."

"Things are great in the beginning" Nash continued... "He can't show his true colors because he doesn't want to lose you before he's had a chance to mold you, to condition you, to *own* you. One night you're out with friends and he's had too much to drink. When you get home he starts screaming at you because some guy was checking you out. He blames YOU... says it was *your* fault the guy was trying to come onto you when he left to go to the Men's Room."

Nash took a deep breath... "The *next time* he not only yells but he slams his hand against the wall, or he throws something at you. Then one day he slaps you. You know you should leave right then and there, but he does his *I'm so sorry I'll never do it again* routine. Eventually the slaps turn into beatings. Once again *it's all your fault,* so he says, and for some crazy-ass reason you start to believe him. And wow, does he ever put on the act... he's *Mister Wonderful* to everyone else when they are in his presence. He's the guy every woman wants, and the guy every man wants to be - they have no idea there's a monster behind the façade."

"Damn" he replied, "How long did this go on?"

"Two years."

"How did you get out of it... get away?"

"One night I got up to go to the bathroom; it was about, I don't know, two o'clock in the morning – after one of his episodes. For some reason I turned on the bathroom light... I guess to see if I had blood on my T-shirt and panties. I looked in the mirror and saw someone that resembled the woman I told you about earlier. I didn't recognize the person... the one in the mirror... not visually or emotionally. That's when it hit me... that *I* had the power... that *I* refused to be the victim any longer. The next day while he was at work I packed up all my shit and caught a bus to San Francisco; some friends that he didn't know of, so there was no way he could track me down."

"Wow, I had no idea."

"Yeah" she said in a breathy exhale.

"I can't believe you let him do that to you for *two years??*"

"You didn't hear a damn word I said, did you?"

"Whaaat??"

"Never mind" she said as she rolled over; turning her back on him. She tried to fall asleep and forget the entire conversation, but it was a lost cause... on both accounts.

10

A bedraggled figure slogged into the office. The somewhat haggard appearance was fairly rare in and of itself; even rarer was the timing of her arrival... not officially late, but a good thirty minutes beyond the norm.

Brogan looked up from behind his desk, "Geez Nash, you like hell."

"Long night" responded Nash. "And no, I don't want to talk about it."

"Forgot your umbrella?"

"It's not *technically* raining, just a thick mist masquerading as low clouds."

"It'll be burned-off by mid-morning."

"Small consolation at this point, don't you think?" said Nash as she grabbed a napkin and blotted the moisture off of her face. "Any coffee made?"

"Just finished brewing."

Nash started to head in the direction of the Break Room... "Extra strong I hope."

Staring at the coffee pot, Nash reached into her jacket pocket and extracted three small creamers... similar to those you get at a restaurant. She dumped one into her cup, grabbed the coffee pot, and topped-off her cup with the fresh brew... mixing the two elixirs perfectly. She smiled at her simple ingenuity as she took a sip... *add the cream first, then pour the coffee, and you never have to stir.* It was her first smile in about nine hours; sometimes all you've got are the silly random musings going on in one's head. She grabbed the remaining two creamers and placed them in the refrigerator.

Nash took a sip of her coffee. *The first cup of the day is always the best* she thought. She peered over toward Sheriff Clarke's office; he was sitting at his desk, seemingly fixated on his computer screen, oblivious to the rest of the world.

Nash started to head back to her desk, but decided to poke her head into Clarke's office. He looked up from his screen as she stepped into the doorway.

"Forensics is trying to hunt down the buyer of the burner phone" said Nash. "Brogan and I talked to the woman who received the call – she claimed to have no idea who called, said it had to be a wrong number."

"What do *you* think?"

"She seemed truthful, but you never know. She also looked like someone beat the crap out of her recently, so we're checking to see if any kind of report has been filed."

"Maybe she's covering for the perp out of fear of what he'll do to her if she talks?"

"I was thinking the same thing. To be honest, I'm hoping she has nothing to do with the crime and the fact that we showed up will be the impetus to get her the help she needs in getting away from the bastard that's been pummeling her."

"That'd be a nice unintentional consequence of your investigation."

"Yeah; taking down a wife-beater always makes my day."

"I agree."

"Forensics also matched the tire treads – the same type and size found on a police cruiser Crown Vic."

"But not *solely* unique to such a vehicle, correct?"

"True. Forensics is going to give us a list of all possibilities; but of course I cannot yet discount any of the local departments."

"Well it goes without saying…"

"I know… tread lightly."

"No pun intended?"

Nash half-smiled… it took her a moment to recognize the unintended pun. "Right. Oh, and we're still waiting to hear if the lab was able to extract DNA, where that might lead us, and also the Deputy Coroner's official autopsy report."

"Sounds like progress."

Nash turned to walk away.

"Hey Nash" said Clarke.

Nash turned back around, "Yeah?"

"You look like hell."

"That seems to be the consensus." She took a sip of her coffee, turned, and started to walk away... "And no, I don't want to talk about it."

Brogan made eye contact with Nash as she was returning to her desk. "Hey, I was driving by the Community Center on my way home yesterday and saw a black & white I'd never seen before" he said.

"I don't get what you mean by *'a black & white you'd never seen before'*."

"It said *Citizens Auxiliary Patrol* on the side."

"It's a new program in Bennington... volunteers that provide another set of eyes and ears to the local P.D."

"Like a Neighborhood Watch Program?"

"Yeah; but I had no idea they had their own patrol car."

"Well, it was a Crown Vic, so out of curiosity I stopped and checked the tire size... 235/55-17."

"Muddy or dirty tires?"

"No; looked like it had just been washed."

"Let's find out the activity on that car; and see if there are any others."

"Already working on it; Bennington P.D. is supposed to get back to me sometime today."

"Good." Nash took a sip, "At least someone's on top of things today."

Nash, coffee cup in hand, crossed her arms and stared at the murder board. She squinted – like someone trying to read the fine print; or in her case, seeing something she hadn't seen before. "You've been holding out on me" she said.

"What's that?" replied Brogan.

"The vic's DNA."

"Oh yeah; the lab was able to get a profile, but there's no match in CODIS."

"So the killer, or killers, went to a great deal of trouble for nothing."

"How do you mean?"

"Pulling out all of the teeth and then setting the body on fire to try to destroy evidence and hide the identity."

"Yeah, I guess so" Brogan replied. "Anyway, since they were able to get DNA they're working on getting as many samples as possible from open Missing Persons cases in Western Washington; you know, to try to match up with ours."

"Well, that's something."

Nash's eyes shifted to another section of the board. "And who's *Mike Roberson?*"

"He's the only Officer that got off shift close to the time of the crime."

"Off at eleven-thirty according to your note?"

"Yep; Bennington P.D."

"Do we know his whereabouts immediately thereafter?"

"No; I don't have your expertise at asking potentially sensitive questions without drawing suspicion."

"No problem, I'll take that one."

Brogan's cell phone rang. He grabbed his phone and looked at the incoming number – it was a call he was expecting.

"Detective Brogan" he said into the phone. "Oh yeah? Hmmm, okay... thanks." He hung up and looked over at Nash, "That was Bennington P.D. – the *Block Watch car* is only in use during daylight hours; basically just to *show the flag*. If someone used it after-hours they did *not* have permission to do so, and they would've had to get the keys from the Bennington Police Station."

"Unless someone that was using the car had a duplicate set made" replied Nash.

"That's true. Should I get hold of Lowell about doing a tire tread check?"

"Let's hold off on that for now; let me see what I get from Officer Roberson."

Nash's cell phone rang. "Nash" she said, "Really? Yeah, we'll head out right now."

Nash hung up and head-nodded at Brogan, "That was Donnelly; she's on patrol and got a call about a car that apparently went off the road and ended up in a ditch out at Eagle Point."

"A body in the car?" responded Brogan.

"Not currently, but she wonders if there may have been, and thought we should check it out."

"Cool. Should I get hold of Forensics?"

"Good idea; give Lowell a call and see if he wants to meet us there."

11

"Did Donnelly give you any details about this *car in a ditch* we're going to check out?" said Brogan to Nash as they made their way along Breezeway Drive toward Eagle Point.

"Not really; just that it piqued her interest and thought we should take a look."

Turning off of Eagle Point Road and onto a seldom-used County Maintenance road Nash noticed Donnelly's patrol car up ahead. She was standing near another vehicle, a *Slaughter Towing* tow-truck. Beyond the two vehicles was the car in a ditch, or more accurately, a deep culvert.

"Interesting" said Nash as she pulled-up near the wreck, "Not quite what I was expecting."

"What do you think, could this be our infamous *'black & white'?*" replied Brogan with air-quotes.

"Hard to say without the forensics, but I'm guessing Lowell's eyes might light-up when he sees it."

"Speak of the devil" replied Brogan as the *Slaughter County Forensics* van approached.

"Why would they be off the beaten-path like this, there's nothing out here?"

"Must have taken a wrong turn, lost control, and crashed."

Donnelly, clad in her Sheriff's Department green fatigues, stepped forward to meet Nash, Brogan, and Lowell as they exited their vehicles.

"I don't know if this could be the mystery vehicle involved in the arson homicide" said Donnelly, "But it's a black & white former Police Interceptor that was obviously removed from service and sold at auction; and it has the same type and size of tires, so I thought you all might want a look-see."

"Good call. Maybe that's why the passerby couldn't recall a jurisdiction – it's always removed before the car goes up for bidding" replied Nash as she donned a pair of latex gloves, "Let's check it out, shall we?"

Lowell started photographing the exterior scene. Something caught his eye almost immediately – near the car's rear tires. He pulled his camera away from his face to expand his vista through the naked eye, "This is odd."

"What's that?" said Nash.

"The driver made no attempt whatsoever to get out of the ditch."

"No divots due to spinning tires?"

"No; it's as if they crashed into the ditch, said *Screw it*, and just walked away."

"Maybe they got concussed from the crash and just up and left in a daze?"

"That's entirely possible considering the many signs" said Lowell as he walked around the vehicle, crouching periodically as he investigated. "They hit the ditch pretty hard based on the crumpled fender, the dug-up side of the ditch, and the bumper covered in dirt and weeds like a trowel." He stood up and peered inside the car, "And the driver's-side airbag has been deployed."

"But not the passenger-side I noticed" commented Nash. "I'm guessing either no one was on that side, or the air bag has been removed or inactivated."

"I'll look for signs of impact to the dashboard, windshield, and side window when I process the interior."

"Speaking of the interior…" said Brogan to Lowell, "Is it okay for us to take a look?"

"Not yet" replied Lowell. "With a deployed airbag there's certain to be forensic evidence in there, so we'll need to be extra careful when we go in. And before anyone enters the vehicle I'm going to dust portions of the exterior for fingerprints."

"Door handles, trunk lid, and hood-latch?" responded Nash.

"You know it."

"In that case we'll see what we can find out here… indications of tire tracks, footprints, blood. After all, the driver surely didn't just *up and vanish* into thin air."

Brogan scanned the area. "Hey Laura" he said, "How about you and I see if we can figure out the path the driver might have taken when they left the scene?"

Donnelly looked at her watch, "Sure, I can do that."

Nash noticed Donnelly's gesture. "Aren't you supposed to be getting off shift soon?" she said to Donnelly.

"Yes, but I don't mind staying and helping out here if you need me."

"I appreciate that, but go ahead and call it a day; we've got things covered."

"Yes, ma'am" replied Donnelly as she started back toward her patrol car.

"And thanks for giving us the call."

"Of course."

As Donnelly drove away Brogan turned to Nash, "It's pretty clear to me she'd much rather be a Detective than a Patrol Deputy."

"And she has the makings of being a damn good one; why do you think I asked Clarke to let her help us out earlier?"

"An audition of sorts? Grooming her for bigger and better things?"

"Something like that."

"Or maybe she just likes the idea of wearing civvies instead of fatigues" said Brogan with a wry smile.

"Yeah I'm sure that's it" replied Nash with a roll of the eyes.

Nash pointed in the direction of the woods surrounding the scene, "Why don't you see if there's any indication that the driver exited the area up that way; I'm going to backtrack down to the main road?"

"Got it."

Nash trekked down one half of the maintenance road, stopped at the main road, and then back up the other half of the road – nothing. When she returned to the scene Lowell had added the windows and fenders to his dusting for prints.

"Find anything?" said Nash to Lowell.

"Not a thing" he replied.

"I guess that means…"

"He or she wiped it clean before they left" Lowell interrupted.

"That rouses suspicion."

"True, but the explanation could be that the car is *stolen,* and not because it's the mystery vehicle from the arson murder."

"Ah, but the tires would be the clincher."

"If, in fact, they match the impressions; and I'll have that answer once I get it back to the garage."

The conversation jogged Lowell's memory, "Oh, and speaking of tire treads, a search for this particular tire size has not been as simple as you thought."

"No?"

"The stock tire for your Legend Coupe may be rare, but these rascals are a dime-a-dozen considering the thousands of police cars out there, especially old ones that are now personal vehicles and taxi cabs."

"I hadn't considered that."

Nash noticed Lowell reach out to grab the driver's-side door. "Ready to tackle the interior?" she said.

"Almost" replied Lowell as he opened the door. "But first I'd like to check the trunk." He reached in and engaged the trunk release.

Nash lifted the trunk lid to the fully-open position.

"See anything?" yelled Lowell, still with his head near the dashboard.

"Nothing obvious."

Lowell joined Nash at the trunk, scanned the area, and took a few photographs. "I agree" he said, "I'll process it in greater detail at the garage."

"Any blood or hair follicles on the steering wheel, air bag, or window?" asked Nash.

"Surprisingly… No. The force of an airbag exploding is so intense that there should be all sorts of indicators. As you know it is not uncommon to sustain some level of injuries from the explosion such as abrasions, contusions, and burns… even fractures in extreme cases; but I'm not seeing anything there."

"Any signs that they did the old *brick on the accelerator* trick to cause the crash?"

"Nope; nothing on the floorboard or gas pedal that would indicate such an act."

"So, what do you make of it all?"

"There are some fibers… probably clothing… that we'll analyze back at the lab, but for the most part it looks like the interior may have been wiped clean just like the exterior."

"That just adds to the likelihood that this is either a stolen car, or the one involved in the murder."

"Or both" countered Lowell.

"True."

"But before we haul this thing out of here I want to do a cursory look at the passenger-side of the interior, and the back seat."

"Are we done with the trunk?" asked Nash.

"For now" replied Lowell. "Hey that reminds me, the trunk on the arson car…"

"Yeah?"

"When I processed it back at the garage I found remnants of clothing beyond those found on the vic."

"Are you thinking that maybe the killer or killers got blood on their shirt or sweatshirt and threw it in the fire?"

"Or the vic had a sweatshirt or jacket with him that the perp added to the inferno."

Lowell closed the trunk lid and made his way to the front passenger-side door. Nash went to the driver's side.

Looking around the inner door skin, the dashboard, the steering wheel, the floor, and the seat, Nash offered an opinion, "I see what you mean. With exception of the blown airbag it's almost as if it came out of a detail shop; not buffed and polished, but way too clean for normal use."

"That's a fact; including the carpet... like it had been covered with paper to keep grease and dirt from one's shoes off of the floor-mat."

"Or to prevent shoeprints from being left inside" said Nash. "Speaking of evidence... or the lack thereof... any news on the license plate on the incinerated car?"

"It was bogus" Lowell replied.

"Bogus?"

"It was a real plate but it was an old one, like it came from a junkyard or a swap meet or something."

"I assume that means it didn't match the car."

"Correct. The VIN led us to a stolen car; reported ten days ago."

"So the perp swapped plates to avoid the car being detected as stolen" Nash nodded.

"Yep, but damn risky to be driving around in a car with old out-of-date plates" said Lowell, "You get pulled over and your cover is blown."

"*In a big way* if it happened while you had the body in the trunk."

"Well, that tells us one thing..."

"What's that?"

"The perp is not infallible."

"It also tells us the perp's location ten days ago" said Nash.

"Maybe – maybe not" Lowell replied.

"What do you mean?"

"We're actually looking at about a three-day period as to when the perp stole the car."

"Are you implying that the owner didn't report it right away?"

"Yep. According to him the car had broken down. He didn't go back to get it for a couple of days and it was gone, so he assumed it had been towed. After all, *who's going to steal a broken-down car that's not worth anything? ...*as he put it."

"None of the local tow companies had it?"

"Not according to them."

"Maybe one of the tow company employees took it for themselves... maybe they're the killer?"

"Something to look into."

Brogan suddenly appeared from his brief sojourn. "No indication that anyone left the area by heading up the maintenance road or through the woods" he said to Nash, "How about you; anything of note back down to the main road?"

"No. My guess is that they hitch-hiked out of here, or there was a second vehicle – a get-away car" said Nash.

"You guys find anything on, or in, the car?"

"Nope; it's been pretty much wiped clean from what we've found thus far" Nash replied.

"Well-well-well..." said Lowell as he peered under the front passenger seat, "Hold that thought, Kenz."

Nash and Brogan both perked up and looked over toward Lowell. "What did you find?" remarked Nash.

Lowell took a pen out of his pocket, stuck it under the seat, and scooped out a ring through its center. It was a man's ring – a wedding band.

"Holy shit" said Brogan.

"Please tell me it's engraved" added Nash.

Lowell grabbed it and scanned the inner surface, "It reads *Daryl and Madison 14 Feb 2010.*"

Nash looked momentarily perplexed... *there was something about those names.*

"Hey isn't that..." Brogan uttered.

"The woman who received the late night phone call – the one who was battered and bruised" Nash interrupted as her memory kicked-in.

"Yeah" said Brogan, "Daryl and Madison Wagner. You don't think…"

"I don't know, but we definitely need to check it out; it would be one hell of a coincidence if it's *not* them."

"You've got a lead on the names already?" asked Lowell.

"A phone call from a burner was received at their address around twelve-thirty the night of the arson" Nash replied, "It pinged off a cell tower in the vicinity of the crime scene."

"Damn."

"Yeah. Any chance you've been able to find the buyer of the burner that was found near the body?"

"It was sold at *Super Mart* a week ago, but they paid cash. I'm still trying to obtain camera footage to see if we have any chance of identifying the buyer."

"Do you think the ring was left by the vic as a clue?" asked Brogan.

"That's got to be it" said Lowell. "Hid it under the seat in the hopes the perpetrator wouldn't find it when he wiped-down the scene."

"I'm with you" said Nash. "I'm sure the killer only considered areas the vic would have touched and didn't take into account the space under the seat."

Nash's cell phone rang – it was Donnelly. "Hey Donnelly, I thought you were supposed to be off-shift?" said Nash.

"I am, but a new 'Missing Persons' report just came in: *Daryl Wagner*" Donnelly replied. "The guy that called it in… a coworker… said he hadn't seen him since Friday afternoon."

"Holy frickin' crap!" responded Nash, "We just found a man's wedding ring that has the inscription *Daryl and Madison.*"

"As in *Wagner?*"

"Don't know yet, but I can tell you this… their residence is going to be my next stop."

"Hey, shall I have someone check traffic cam footage for the black & white to see where it's been?"

"That would be a great idea if we were in Seattle, but we have no traffic cams here in Slaughter County, all we have are the red light cameras in select intersections in Bennington."

"Well, that's something... right?"

"Sure – let's see if we can find something... anything" said Nash, "And thanks."

Nash hung up the phone and looked into the gazing eyes of both Brogan and Lowell. "You guys aren't going to believe it" she said, "Daryl Wagner was just reported missing."

"Is that freaky timing or what?" said Brogan. "When was the last time he was seen?"

"Friday afternoon according to the guy that called it in."

"Things just got interesting" noted Brogan.

"Hey Evan" said Nash, "If you don't need us here, Dirk and I are going to go visit the Wagner residence."

"I'm essentially done; I've got a few more pics to take and then I'll get the car back to the garage."

"Great. Oh, and I'm going to need the ring for possible identification."

Lowell placed the ring in an evidence bag and handed it to Nash.

Nash turned to Brogan, "Let's roll."

12

An emphatic trio of knocks on the door invoked a sudden pang of fear. Harsh memories flooded in.

She gathered herself and walked toward the door. She stopped and looked through the peep-hole; spying a familiar, yet curious, sight.

The deadbolt unlatched, the knob turned, and the door gradually opened.

"Detectives" said Madison, "What can I do for you?"

"Good afternoon" said Nash, "We have some important questions for you."

"About the phone call the other night?"

"Well, yes and no. First of all, this may sound like an odd question, but can you tell me your wedding day?"

Madison was caught off-guard, "My wedding day??"

"If you would, please."

"February fourteenth."

"The year?"

"Two-thousand-ten."

"Did your husband's wedding ring have an inscription?"

"Yes, we have matching inscriptions" said Madison as she glanced down at her left hand; her wedding ring noticeably absent. Madison returned her gaze to Nash, "They both say *Daryl and Madison,* and then the date, *February 14th 2010.*"

Nash held up a small plastic bag, "Would this be his ring?"

Madison examined the ring; paying particular attention to the inscription, "Yes." She handed the bag back to Nash, "Where did you get it?"

"Hidden underneath the passenger seat of an abandoned car."

Madison was bewildered, "Hidden under the seat of an abandoned car??"

"Ironically, he was just reported missing this morning" said Nash. "Apparently he has been missing for at least a few days; why didn't you tell us he was missing the last time we were here?"

"I didn't *know* he was missing."

"How could you *not know* that your husband has been missing for the past several days?"

"I don't keep in touch with him; and he's not supposed to contact me, I have a restraining order against him."

Nash and Brogan had a look of surprise; not in regard to the fact that there was a restraining order against the apparent wife-beater, but they weren't expecting such a perfectly sound explanation to the question.

"When was the last time you saw him, or talked to him?" said Nash.

"Friday night."

Brogan turned to Nash, "The night before the…"

"Yeah" said Nash, abruptly cutting Brogan off before he finished, and gave him a look to let him know he needed to *zip it.*

Nash turned her focus back to Madison, "What happened that evening?"

"He came home and I told him he wasn't allowed to be here. His face turned boiling-lava-red and he said *What the hell are you talking about… it's my house?* That's when I told him about the restraining order."

"He wasn't aware of it until then?"

"No. He knocked me around and then pushed me aside, and said *No effing piece of paper can keep me away from my home.* He rummaged through the place for about fifteen or twenty minutes; filling up a suitcase. When he was ready to leave he got in my face and yelled *You're gonna regret this you effing Bitch!*" Madison's lower lip and chin started to quiver; her eyes welled-up with tears. "Then he punched me in the face; giving me a black eye and busting open my lip."

Nash was visibly moved, although she tried not to show it. She took a deep breath. She knew better than to get emotionally involved in a case, but considering the circumstances it was a difficult task.

"I'm sorry to hear that" Nash commented. "Has his aggressive behavior toward you been going on for some time, or has it been a more recent thing?"

"Why do you ask?" said Madison as she wiped the moisture from her eyes.

Nash could hear the hesitancy in Madison's voice; she realized her best recourse was to open up and reveal some of her own personal struggles, "I understand why you may not want to talk about it; I've been there myself."

"You have?"

"Back in my twenties" Nash explained. "Here I was a strong and independent woman, and yet I fell prey to a man who on the outside seemed like Prince Charming, but behind closed doors he slowly and methodically morphed into a monster. And to make matters worse, he managed to make me feel like it was *my* fault... that I *deserved* the abuse."

"What did you do?"

"After seeing myself in the mirror one night after a beating, I finally realized that I was *not* the bad person, and that I did *not* deserve to be treated that way. The next day, while he was at work, I packed-up and disappeared forever."

Madison started to tear up; she was reliving her nightmares through Nash's words. "That's how I feel right now" she said.

"Well, just know that there are people you can turn to for help in your time of need."

"Thank you."

"Did he ever offer an explanation behind his actions?"

"He always blamed it on his childhood" Madison replied. "He had great anger at his parents, which I guess he hid from them when they were alive. Now that they're dead all of his pent up anger has been released."

"Did he ever share whatever the issues were from his childhood?"

"This is the story he told me: It all started not long after his little sister was born... when the world suddenly revolved around the little princess."

"The little princess?"

"Sorry" Madison sighed, "Those were his words."

An interesting description Nash thought. "How old was Daryl when his sister was born?"

"Umm... three I think; and according to him he went from being the center of attention, to an afterthought, to *the bad kid.*"

"It's not uncommon for a child to be envious of the attention given to a new baby" Nash replied, "But being suddenly deemed *the bad kid?*"

"Apparently whenever the kids got into trouble it was *always* Daryl's fault. That's when the yelling and spankings began. But it was *the accident* that turned his life into a *living hell.*"

"The accident?"

"Daryl and his sister were playing in a little wading pool in their backyard with their dog. Suddenly the dog took off after a cat, and then Daryl took off after the dog. When Daryl returned his little sister was floating face-down in the pool."

Nash was almost speechless as the distressing vision overcame her... a breathy "Geez" was all that she could muster.

"Yeah..." Madison concurred.

"How old was she... the little girl?" Nash asked.

"Two."

Nash shook her head in disbelief.

"And *Daryl* was blamed for her drowning" added Madison.

"Daryl? Where were the parents?"

"Next door... at the neighbors."

"They left a *five year-old* in charge of a *two year-old?!*" Nash rolled her eyes. "I'm surprised Child Protective Services didn't take Daryl away from them and place him in Foster Care."

"Anyway" Madison continued, "That's when his parents started drinking heavily… and the spankings became *beatings*. His father would scream and yell and slap his mother; and his mother would take it out on Daryl… with a belt. One day she couldn't find a belt… which merely added to her anger. *Daryl had hidden them.* She looked around the room for something else to use and noticed the plastic race track to his Hot Wheels cars at one end of his room. She grabbed a section of track and wailed away… leaving cuts and welts so bad that he wished he'd never hidden the belts. The Hot Wheels track soon vanished… never to be seen again, but the emotional scars live on to this day… so he always said."

"What about the father, did *he* ever beat Daryl?"

"I guess his *dad* would only smack-around his *mom*."

"Small consolation; the sight and sound of his mother getting smacked-around could cause more damage to a kid than taking the beatings himself, and the next thing you know they end up…"

Nash stopped herself – silenced by a momentary glance at Madison's bruised and battered face.

"Daryl also said that his dad would stick up for him when it came to other kids in the neighborhood or school bullies" Madison continued… "But he'd *look the other way* when his mom was beating him. Talk about mixed-signals."

"*Mixed-signals* would be an understatement."

Nash took a moment to process the entire scenario. She had to admit that she felt sorry for the poor lad that had endured such emotional and physical abuse, but not for the monster he had apparently become. In reality, all too many kids had endured such hardships in life, and yet the majority of them went on to become good husbands, wives, fathers, and mothers. Many of them even took the next step and became great role models, pillars of society, champions of the downtrodden, and a voice of hope for the abused and neglected.

"It's a shame that such abuse occurred to a child, but there is never a valid excuse for what you've been going through" responded Nash. "And I appreciate you sharing that with me."

"You're welcome."

"Well, if you see him or hear from him I need you to call me right away, any time of day or night."

"I will."

"You still have my card with my number, don't you?"

"Yes."

"We'd like to get some of your husband's belongings, hopefully a comb or perhaps a toothbrush... something that would have his DNA."

"Why would you need his DNA?"

"Standard Procedure when someone has been reported missing."

"It is?"

"I didn't really want to go there, but Heaven forbid a body turns up, or washes up along the shoreline, DNA may be necessary to determine the identity."

"I understand. Let me see what I can find." Madison turned away and shut the door.

Nash and Brogan stood silent at the doorway. Nash glanced at her watch, then out toward the street, and back at the door.

Brogan broke the silence, "Do you think she'll find anything?"

"She said he only packed a suitcase, there's got to be all kinds of his stuff still in the house."

Brogan reached down and opened the small metal case that was sitting next to him – the Evidence Kit.

Madison returned with a T-shirt and a shoebox, "No comb or toothbrush, but this T-shirt was in the hamper; I figured since he had worn it recently and had not yet been washed, that it should have DNA on it – at least that's what they show on the TV all the time."

"That should do just fine" responded Nash.

Brogan bent down and reached into the Evidence Kit and extracted a plastic bag. He handed it to Nash, who opened the bag and held it out for Madison to drop the shirt inside. Nash zipped-up the bag and gave it to Brogan.

Madison presented the shoebox to Nash, "These should have traces of his saliva."

Nash lifted the lid, took a peek inside, reclosed the lid, and looked back at Madison. "Thanks" she said.

Nash gestured to Brogan. He got the hint… *time to go.*

Madison watched Nash and Brogan walk to their car, and then she shut and latched the door.

Pulling away from the curb Brogan relayed a question to Nash, "Were those *envelopes* in the shoebox?"

"Yes" she said. "Here the bastard pummels her on a regular basis, and yet she's kept letters from him… presumably *love letters.*"

"A sad state of affairs."

"Yep." Nash pondered the situation… "Hey, what say we pay a visit to B.P.D to see what they have on this guy – *the husband?*"

"I'm game."

13

"If it isn't *Sheriff's Department Lead Detective Mackenzie Nash*" said the Police Captain as he reached out to shake hands.

"Hey Sean" replied Nash, "Or should I say... *Captain O'Rourke.*"

"It's been a while hasn't it? ...since you and I were cracking cases here at B.P.D."

"I'll say. And speaking of... I was just telling Brogan the other day about the *Forrester* case."

"The baseball bat?"

"That's the one."

"Unbelievable" added Brogan.

"My favorite *Gotcha* moment" said Nash.

"That makes two of us" remarked O'Rourke.

"So how are Patty and the kids?" asked Nash.

"She's finally getting used to the phone calls at all hours of the night; one of the *'perks'*" he said with air-quotes, "that came with my promotion to Captain. And how about you, are you going to run for Sheriff once Clarke finally hangs up his holster?"

"I've thought about it, but that's a *long* way off."

"You and Ian still..."

"Yeah" Nash interrupted. She hadn't completely put the incident from the night before behind her, and was intent on putting a damper on the potential conversation before it started.

"When are you going to make an *honest man* out of the guy?"

"You know me... *married to the job* right now."

O'Rourke figured it was time to dispense with the pleasantries and find out why Nash had stopped by... "So, what brings you to my neck of the woods?"

"Are you familiar with a *Daryl and Madison Wagner?*"

"The Wagner residence on Cedar Street?"

"That's the couple."

"We're *very* familiar with the Wagner residence; Officers have responded to disturbances at that location a number of times over the years. Each time the wife looked like she'd been beaten-up, and every time she refused to file charges or even a restraining order – until a week ago."

"Did she call to report that he had violated the restraining order this past Friday?"

"She did; and we would've loved to lock him up, but we had not yet found him to serve the order, so we could not technically say that he violated it."

"Frickin' technicalities."

"Tell me about it" he said and then queried, "But why are you asking about them? Not that I'm throwing the *jurisdiction card* at you, *but…*"

"They may have ties to the arson murder that occurred Saturday night out near Blue Heron Cove."

"Both of them?"

"Hard to say at this point; it could be one of them, both, or it could be nothing."

"What has you looking in their direction?"

"For starters, she received a phone call from a burner around the time of the arson; and based on the cell tower ping the call originated somewhere near the scene."

"That raises one's curiosity."

"And it just so happens that we *found* a burner *at* the scene."

"The one that made the call?"

"Forensics is still working on that; although I'm not holding out much hope… the phone was mostly a melted lump of plastic so that avenue could be a lost cause."

Nash took a breath; her expression caught O'Rourke's attention... "Something tells me there's more" he said.

"When I interviewed her yesterday and asked if I had the correct address and person... *Madison Wagner*... she responded that her last name was *Sinclair.*

"Sinclair?"

"I had the same response. Then she clarified that Sinclair was her maiden name but '*Wagner was fine*'" said Nash. "Also, she looked like someone had beaten the crap out of her, and when I asked her if she was okay, she responded '*Everything should be fine now*'."

"As if her problem had been resolved?"

"That's how it came across to me."

"Interesting."

"And we *just* found out that her husband *Daryl* was reported missing this morning."

"When was his last sighting?"

"Friday night; at least according to her."

"And the arson was *Saturday* night, correct?"

"Yep."

Brogan entered the conversation, "The first thing that jumped out at me is that her husband just disappeared and she's going by her maiden name already... very curious."

"Very *suspicious* you mean" replied O'Rourke, "According to her she didn't even know her husband was missing when she reverted back to her maiden name."

"I don't know about that being suspicious" responded Nash, "The bastard has been beating her for who-knows-how-many years; I'd remove everything to do with him from my life too, *especially* his name. And remember, she had gotten the restraining order, so perhaps that was her first step at starting a new life."

"And then there's the ring" prodded Brogan.

"The ring?" replied O'Rourke.

"Yeah" said Nash. "We investigated a car in a ditch out at Eagle Point this morning and found a man's wedding ring with the inscription *Daryl and Madison 14 Feb 2010.*"

"The missing husband's?"

"According to her, yes… she *just* I.D.'d it."

"Hmmm… making your husband disappear would be another first step in starting a new life."

"I think we're getting a little ahead of ourselves on *that* conjecture."

"True. But nonetheless, it sounds like you're onto something."

"And of course if we find out that the vic *is* Daryl Wagner then we'll be having a much more pointed and candid conversation with his wife."

Brogan looked befuddled, "But she has an alibi – she was home receiving the phone call when it happened."

"A pointed conversation does not necessarily mean she's in the crosshairs; but who's the person most likely to have knowledge about his potential enemies? *She* is." Nash thought for a moment, "And you can't let the fact that she's been a victim of domestic violence to skew your investigation."

Brogan nodded agreement; but it seemed disingenuous, as if he merely felt obligated to do so.

"Well, thanks for the info, Sean" said Nash as she reached out to shake hands, "We have some of Daryl Wagner's personal effects to take over to the lab in the hopes they can extract some DNA."

"My pleasure, Kenz… if you need anything from me in regard to your case, don't hesitate to call."

O'Rourke's offer got Nash to thinking. *"You know…"* she said, "What can you tell me about Daryl Wagner's parents… and his little sister?"

"The parents died a few years back in a car wreck… drunk driving if I remember correctly. I'm not sure about the sister, but I can have someone get you the reports on both accounts."

"That would be great, thanks."

14

Her eyes bouncing between her notepad and the murder board, Nash realized that a timeline of events was starting to come together.

Brogan walked in the office to the sight of Nash at the board and Deputy Laura Donnelly at a nearby desk. Donnelly looked up to see who had entered; Nash didn't flinch – she was in deep contemplation as she gazed upon the board… paying equal attention to what lie before her, and what was still missing.

Brogan looked at his watch, "Sheesh, you two up with the chickens this morning or what?"

"Chickens?" replied Donnelly, "There are no chickens around these parts."

"Wasn't Silver City a chicken-haven back in the day; putting Slaughter County on the map before the shipyard took over that mantle during World War Two?"

"That was a hundred years ago" replied Nash – still focused on the murder board, "Are you some kind of history buff, or what?"

"Nah, I just read about it in the 'Look Back in History' section of *The Journal* last Sunday."

It dawned on Brogan that Donnelly was wearing civvies, "Hey, I see that Laura gets to play Detective today" he commented.

Nash finally turned around to physically acknowledge Brogan's presence, "Clarke assigned her to us for the foreseeable future now that things are starting to pick up on this case."

"Congrats, Laura" said Brogan.

"Thanks" Donnelly replied, "I'm looking forward to the challenge."

"Updating the board I see" Brogan directed at Nash.

"Yeah, a few things are starting to fall into place… time-wise anyway" responded Nash. "One thing that always helps is the ability to visualize the chronology; then we can start filling-in the blanks, identifying what's still missing, adding new items of interest and concern, and discarding superfluous crap and dead-ends."

"So, what's the latest and greatest?" said Brogan.

"I've been looking into persons with *arson priors*" replied Donnelly, "but nothing I've found thus far is tying any of them to the vicinity at the time of the arson. I also decided to see if any of them have ties to Daryl Wagner… the missing person that may turn out to be our vic."

"Good thinking. Any luck?"

"No ties that I've been able to find."

"Speaking of Daryl Wagner" said Brogan, "Any updates on his *Missing Persons* status?"

"Captain O'Rourke said he'd keep us in the loop" replied Nash, "No news thus far."

"Can't we do some digging on our own?"

"We *could*… but it's out of our jurisdiction."

"That hasn't stopped us before."

"Perhaps, but O'Rourke is a former colleague; I don't want to go stepping on toes unless the situation absolutely warrants it. Besides, if it turns out that Daryl *is* our vic then jurisdiction becomes ours, which is the only reason we should be interested in him anyway."

"I guess" responded Brogan in a resigned tone.

"I know you want to be the *Night in Shining Armor* for Madison Wagner, but you're going to have to sheath your sword for the time being."

"Understood."

"On a separate subject, I talked to Mike Roberson – the Officer who had gotten off-shift a little before the arson" stated Nash. "He said he drove by the area, but there was nothing out of the ordinary at the time."

"No fire?" replied Brogan.

"Not according to him. And that's in-sync with the timeline as we know it."

"What was he doing out there?"

"He said he'd been at *Hilltop Tavern* as part of the city's increased presence to discourage DUIs."

"Hmm… I guess Hilltop *is* just inside the city limits, isn't it?"

"Yep."

"Did you verify his story?"

Donnelly looked surprised at Brogan's question. Nash looked perturbed.

"I'm not going to treat a fellow cop as a suspect without a single shred of evidence pointing in his direction" Nash tersely stated.

"I guess I got a little ahead of myself there" responded Brogan.

"Ya think?!"

"Plus, I guess the discovery of the black & white kind of eliminates the whole *cop-involved* theory" Brogan nodded.

Nash's glare was interrupted by her cell phone ringing – it was Captain O'Rourke. "Hey Sean, what's up? Really? Nothing else and nothing *since?* Interesting… thanks for the update."

Nash hung up and turned her attention back to Brogan and Donnelly, "That was O'Rourke; he said that Daryl Wagner made an ATM withdrawal of four hundred dollars at eight-thirty-three Saturday night; that amount is the max that his bank allows from ATMs within a twenty-four hour period."

"What do you think?" said Brogan, "A sign that he was making a max withdrawal and taking off somewhere?"

"Seems unlikely" said Nash, "Four hundred bucks wouldn't last very long. He's been gone for four days; you'd think there would have been another withdrawal since then."

"That's true" nodded Brogan.

"And one more thing that makes this rather interesting… there's been *zero* credit and debit card activity since then; in fact, nothing since the nineteenth" said Nash. "That combination is the reason O'Rourke called with the update... possible indications that something happened to the guy."

"That doesn't seem to bode too well for him, does it?" responded Brogan.

"No, it doesn't" said Nash. "Anyway, that gives us a couple more updates for the board, along with additional questions." She turned to Donnelly, "And you've got more for us, correct?"

"Sort of" replied Donnelly, "Reviewing red-light camera photos and videos in search of both the black & white and the stolen car... *the burned-out cinder*... was a dead end."

"Did you check for both the fake plates found at the scene, and the car's *real* plates?" said Nash.

"Yep."

"Well, we gave it a shot" said Nash, "Let's switch our focus to finding the owner of the black & white."

"Got it" replied Donnelly.

"By the way" said Nash, "I got permission from George and Mary Montgomery to search the cabin that's located at the scene; so Dirk, see if you can arrange to have Lowell meet us there sometime this afternoon."

"Will do" replied Brogan. "With all this new info, how's the timeline looking?"

Nash approached the board, dry-erase marker in hand, her back to Brogan and Donnelly... "Okay, here's how it lays-out so far" she said, starting at the far left of the timeline and working her way across the board...

"The arson car... a.k.a. the incinerated sedan... was stolen between ten and thirteen days ago, which would be Thursday the 17th to Sunday the 20th.

"The most recent use of Daryl Wagner's credit or debit card was Saturday the 19th... for *what* we do not yet know.

"The burner phone was sold Tuesday the 22nd; however, the buyer is still a question-mark.

"Daryl was last seen Friday night the 25th; the last person to see him, as of right now, is his wife Madison. *But* with the news we just got about the ATM withdrawal that could change."

Brogan jumped in, "Doesn't that change his last known sighting to Saturday night when the withdrawal was made?"

"Yeah" added Donnelly, "What did the ATM camera show?"

"Good questions" replied Nash, "But O'Rourke hasn't received ATM camera footage as of yet; so we don't *know* that the withdrawal was actually made by Daryl."

"Oh… so someone could have gotten his card and PIN and used it" replied Donnelly.

"Or someone could have *forced* Wagner to make the withdrawal" said Brogan.

"Precisely" replied Nash, "So it's an *open item* until we have news on the ATM camera, or an updated sighting of him."

Nash got back to the chronology on the board…

"We don't really know when the vic was killed since the body was too badly burned to pinpoint a specific time of death. However, we can go under the assumption that he was dead at the time the fire was reported; which I think we all agree is a very reasonable assumption, but that's about it."

Brogan and Donnelly both nodded. Nash continued…

"Officer Roberson was near the scene… specifically, driving along Salmon Beach Road… around 11:40 Saturday night; he stated that there was no visible fire at the time. Considering the perp, or perps, had to kill the vic, pull his teeth out, and douse the car with gasoline before setting the fire; I'm thinking the vic was either *already dead* when Roberson drove by, or the act was *in progress*."

"It sucks that Roberson was *this close*" Brogan gestured with his thumb and pointer finger, "to catching the perps in the act."

"No shit" Nash replied, and then continued… "Madison Wagner received the mysterious call from the burner phone at 12:27 Sunday morning the 27th… about forty-five minutes after Roberson had driven by the scene.

"The passerby saw the fire and called it in at 12:35 Sunday morning. And he reported seeing a black & white near the scene.

"The car with Daryl Wagner's ring inside, which happened to be a black & white… was found yesterday morning… the 29th."

Nash put down her marker and turned to face Brogan and Donnelly, "And that brings us up-to-date."

"You're right" said Brogan, "Once you see it all laid out on the board everything really starts to gel; just think how it will be once we find out the identity of the vic."

"True, but it will also open up a whole new batch of unanswered questions" replied Nash.

"That reminds me" added Donnelly, "I haven't found anything suspicious with any of the local tow-truck drivers… you know, if one of them might have picked up the stolen vehicle, which would make them a person of interest."

"Well, better to look and find nothing than to never look at all" replied Nash, "Anything else?"

"That's all I've got for now" replied Donnelly.

"Alright; let's get the Montgomery's to meet us out at the cabin."

15

An old rustic cabin, with a porch extending the length of the front, graced the eyes of the beholder. The unpainted wood slats of both the cabin and porch had deteriorated and turned grey with age; if not for the various shades of green, orange, and yellow via the surrounding woods the vista would appear to be a black and white photograph from the 1920s.

Nash and Lowell stood on the porch outside the cabin door, awaiting the arrival of the owners – George and Mary Montgomery.

Brogan and Donnelly were too anxious to just wait around; they were peering inside the cabin windows hoping to get a glimpse of who-knows-what.

While curiosity was getting the best of Brogan and Donnelly, Nash was getting Lowell up-to-speed on the investigation.

"The owners told me they hadn't been out here in months" said Nash. "I asked them to *not* enter the cabin without us being on-scene."

"Do they know about the arson and murder here on the property?" Lowell replied.

"Not the sordid details; but yes, they know."

"Speaking of details…" said Lowell, "the tires on the black & white matched the molds I made here on the property."

"Another tie between Daryl Wagner and the crime scene; things are adding up, and they're not looking good for him."

"If the items Madison Wagner provided for DNA analysis *don't* match the vic, then that puts her husband Daryl at the top of the *suspect* list."

"Hey, I'm more than okay with nabbing the killer before we identify the vic."

"Yeah, but it makes determination of a motive rather difficult."

"All in due time Evan... all in due time" said Nash. "Although it also means we'd need to *find* the missing S-O-B."

Nash and Lowell turned their heads toward the sound of tires rumbling atop loose gravel. They stepped off of the porch expecting a vehicle to come into sight, but the gravelly sound suddenly ceased.

Nash took a few steps, stopped for a moment, and then started walking down the drive to investigate the sudden silence. Lowell followed suit.

A vehicle came into view; it had stopped at the location of the crime scene... which was nothing more than a large patch of flattened and scorched vegetation at this point.

A man and a woman, an older couple, were surveying the area. Although not elderly from Nash's perspective, which in her mind was an octogenarian or beyond, they were certainly on the cusp of being able to qualify for the *Senior Discount* at the local establishments.

The couple was circling the area of the scene on-foot... walking, talking, and pointing. Nash was sure they were assessing the scene, and likely speculating as to what might have occurred.

A combination of sight and sound interrupted the couple's conversation; it was Nash and Lowell approaching.

The gentleman reached out his hand to Nash. "You must be Detective Nash" he said, "George Montgomery."

George was an affable fellow, late-fifties to early-sixties, silver(ish) beard, wearing a fisherman's cap that had seen better days. He had the look and demeanor of someone who might play Santa Claus out at the mall during the holidays.

"Mister Montgomery" acknowledged Nash as they shook hands.

"My wife Mary" said George as he introduced his better half.

Mary was the perfect complement to George... a sweet and mostly-reserved gal who came across as George's faithful sidekick, yet likely ruled the roost at home. Her beautiful white hair was capped by a knit beret, and she was dressed as though it was the dead of winter in lieu of early fall: Wool coat, wool scarf, and even leg warmers, which surprised Nash... she was sure leg warmers had evaporated from store shelves back in the 1980s.

"Ma'am" responded Nash; who then introduced Lowell to the couple... "This is Forensic Scientist Evan Lowell."

"A pleasure" responded Lowell as he greeted them.

"I was wondering what you can tell us about your place here" said Nash to the couple.

"It all started back in my youth" replied George, "I went to school with the previous owner's kids."

Nash looked at Lowell... realizing they could be there a while, getting a first-hand retrospective of George's *life and times in regard to this property*, if not more.

"Us kids used to fish off the dock on the other side of the roadway" George continued, "The family used the old cabin as their fishing shack and gathering spot; where they stored their gear, cleaned and gutted the fish, and had family cookouts. A lot of great childhood memories."

"I can see how that would be the case" responded Nash.

"That was well before my time" remarked Mary, "Before I met George that is. But he often talked of the old dock and cabin over the years, as if it was a family heirloom or something."

"Even though the cabin had fallen into disrepair and the dock was now old and decrepit, when the opportunity came up to buy the property a few years ago I couldn't pass it up" added George.

"We have no *immediate* plans for the property" said Mary, "But once we retire we plan to build a small home here and rebuild the old dock."

"That way we can have family picnics like the old days" added George.

"And a great piece of land to pass down to the grandkids one day" added Mary.

"That sounds like a grand idea" remarked Nash, who then quickly tried to steer the conversation back to their reason for being there, "Do you suppose we could go up to the cabin and take a look?"

"Of course" said George.

"How about you two drive on up, and Mister Lowell and I will meet you up there?"

"Yes ma'am."

Nash and Lowell started walking back up the drive as George and Mary climbed into their car. "Wow, those two sure like to tell a story" Nash quietly said to Lowell as they walked, "I was afraid we were going to be here until dusk."

"Pretty entertaining though, I must admit" responded Lowell.

Nash and Lowell reached the cabin just as George and Mary were parking their car. There to greet them were Brogan and Donnelly; they had meandered back to the cabin's porch from their brief sojourn around the surrounding grounds, having long since given up on their attempt to obtain a visual of the cabin's interior through the dark and dingy windows.

George and Mary walked up to the porch; Nash introduced them to Brogan and Donnelly.

George stepped forward with his key and unlocked the cabin via the doorknob lock.

"If you don't mind Sir, we'd like to go inside and survey the area" said Nash. "Once we're done I'll ask you to come in, take a look around, and let us know if anything looks unusual or out of place."

"Yes ma'am" George replied.

Nash donned latex gloves. Lowell, already gloved, readied his camera.

Nash turned to Brogan and Donnelly, "Evan is going in first in search of shoeprints or any other items of interest on the floor so that the rest of us don't inadvertently trample over potential evidence. I'm going to follow behind. I'll give you two a yell once we're ready to process the rest of the scene."

"Roger that" replied Brogan.

Lowell started taking pictures immediately upon entering, "It may be musty and dusty in here, but there has obviously been recent activity;

the floor has been swept." He stopped and quickly shifted his focus around the room, "And a number of the surface areas have been wiped down."

Still standing in the doorway, Nash turned and motioned to George to come hither. As George approached, Nash initiated a pointed question, "I thought you said you hadn't been here in months?"

"We haven't" replied George.

"Well, there are indications of recent activity inside."

"What are you talking about?" said George as he started to make his way to the doorway.

Nash extended her arm to stop him, "I'm sorry Sir, but we aren't ready for you to enter just yet."

"What are the indications of activity?" George insisted.

"I'm not going to go into detail right now, but things have been cleaned up."

"That makes no sense."

"It does if someone else in your family, or perhaps a friend of yours, has a key."

George nodded in his wife's direction... "We're the only ones with a key."

"Did you possibly leave it unlocked the last time you were here?" asked Nash, "And whoever has been in there locked it back up when they left?"

"I'm sure I locked it" George replied.

"Maybe you locked the doorknob before shutting the door, but when you pulled it shut it didn't fully latch?"

"I always make sure it's fully closed."

"I'm sorry Sir, but there are no signs of forced entry. That leaves us three options... either it was left unlocked, someone else has a key, or you were here recently."

Mary looked concerned; the trip to the cabin at the request of the detective was starting to feel like an interrogation. "You must have left it unlocked, Dear" she said to George.

There was a moment of silence as George contemplated the conundrum that Nash had provided.

"Hey Kenz" Lowell yelled from inside the cabin, "You can come in; but stay behind me since I have not yet inspected the entirety of the floor."

Nash poked her head through the doorway, "Incoming." The floor creaked upon her first step inside; it was an uneven surface, with varying degrees of gaps between the slats.

Nash scanned the room; which encompassed the entire cabin with exception of whatever was behind two separate doors at the backend of the cabin.

There was a small kitchen at the far end: A refrigerator dating back to the 1950s, a similarly-aged two-burner stove, some old hand-built cabinets, and a counter centered by a sink.

In front of the kitchen was a table, likely hand-built a good fifty to sixty years ago, with four chairs of the same era. Between the kitchen and dining area, near the wall to the far right, stood a wood stove; presumably the only source of heat in the cabin.

To Nash's immediate left was a sofa fronted by a small coffee table; a floor lamp standing at the far end of the sofa. To her immediate right were two chairs; a magazine rack with a small table-top sat between them, a lamp atop the table.

On the floor between the sofa and the chairs was Lowell, in a crouched-position. He had a tweezer in hand; dropping a seemingly invisible particle into a small evidence bag.

"Got something?" said Nash.

"Clothing fibers and hair follicles" replied Lowell.

"Clothing fibers and hair follicles *on the floor?*"

"Someone tried to sweep it up, but the fibers and hair were wedged between the slats."

"Due to the sweeping action? Or are you telling me that someone was lying on the floor?"

"The latter is almost certainly the case; a number of the hairs still have the roots intact; as if they got stuck between the crevices in the floor and were subsequently ripped out."

"*Roots* means possible DNA, right?"

"Yes it does. If it matches our vic that tells us he was here."

"And if it *doesn't* then we have *no idea* what it means."

"An unfortunate truth. In that case we'd have to hope their DNA is on-file, track them down, and find out what the heck they were doing here."

"Which could have absolutely nothing to do with this case... could be partying, doing drugs, a little '*horizontal mambo*', squatters... you name it."

"Yep" replied Lowell as he stood up. "I'm done with the floor if you want to give Brogan and Donnelly the go-ahead."

Nash walked over to the doorway, "Hey Dirk, Laura... come on in."

When Nash turned back around Lowell had moved to the sink; he was inspecting a drinking glass. He rotated in one direction then the other, eyeballing for fingerprints. He brought it up near his nose and took a sniff.

"What do you think?" asked Nash.

"It's been wiped clean, but there's a trace amount of fluid." Lowell took another sniff, "Best guess – either Scotch or Bourbon."

"Fluid? That means someone has been here *very* recently."

"Yep" said Lowell as he placed the glass into an evidence bag.

"And only *one* glass?" queried Nash.

"So far."

"That would tend to imply only one person was here – seems odd."

"I agree."

Such a concept didn't sit well with Nash; she looked around the room, pondered for a moment, and then made a beeline to the magazine-rack table between the chairs.

"Interesting" said Nash as she focused intently on the table. "There are two circular water spots here; as if a couple of people were kicked-back in the chairs having a drink."

"The water spots are separate?"

"Yep; one close to one chair, and one close to the other; precisely where you'd set a glass down if you were sitting in each chair."

"Get a picture, would you?"

Nash motioned to Donnelly; who walked over and took some photos.

Lowell had turned his focus to the hot and cold faucets. He noticed they appeared to have the original cross-style handles; and although their threads were engaged on the valve stem they were missing their associated hold-down screw. He removed the handles and placed them in an evidence bag.

Brogan took notice of the two doors at the back of the cabin near the kitchen. "Did you guys check out what's behind the doors?" he said.

"Nope" replied Lowell, "Go for it."

Brogan and Donnelly looked at each other. They each proceeded to the door nearest them.

Donnelly opened her door first, peeked around, and dropped out of sight.

Brogan opened his door, stepped inside, and reemerged almost immediately. "Bathroom" he said, "Consisting solely of a toilet, sink, and medicine cabinet."

"No tub or shower?" replied Lowell.

"There's a shower out back" replied Donnelly as she reentered the space, "If you want to call it that. This here's a mud room of sorts" she said as she head-nodded behind her, "Full of fishing gear; with an exit to the yard."

"Anything in the medicine cabinet?" said Lowell to Brogan.

"A time warp" replied Brogan.

"A *time warp?*"

"A box of bandages from *Pinkerton Pharmacy;* a small bottle of mercurochrome; and one of those old razors like my grandfather used… you know, the ones where you drop-in a single double-edged blade."

Lowell perked up, "Is there a blade in that razor?"

"Nope" replied Brogan, "Just the razor itself."

"Damn" responded Lowell.

"*Pinkerton Pharmacy?* They went out of business over twenty years ago" stated Nash. "And who uses *mercurochrome* these days?"

"Like I said; it's a time warp in there" replied Brogan.

"Leave everything as-is" said Lowell, "I'll bag it up to take back to the lab."

"You got it."

Nash, Lowell, Brogan, and Donnelly scoured the rest of the cabin: Kitchen cabinets and cupboards, the refrigerator… which was empty and had been unplugged, shelves, and a small trunk filled with blankets and pillows.

The contents of the trunk got Brogan thinking. He looked around the room.

"What's on your mind, Dirk?" said Nash.

"The blankets and pillows" he said as he walked over to the sofa.

Brogan removed the cushions and then ran his hand along the front edge of the sofa. "Aha!" he said as he lifted.

"A sleeper sofa!" responded Donnelly as Brogan partially extracted the mattress-portion.

Brogan dropped to one knee and pointed to the floor in front of the sofa, "I was wondering what these marks were on the floor here; they're where the sleeper rests when it's fully extended."

"Good eye; and good thinking, Dirk" responded Lowell. "Go ahead and lay it out."

Brogan extended the sleeper; Lowell looked over the mattress. "Whoever was here may have been unaware of the sleeper; I'm not seeing anything within that appears to be recent."

"Maybe the sheets were removed and tossed into the inferno, or were discarded elsewhere?" said Brogan.

"Could be; but there was nothing in the sedan that appeared to be remnants of a sheet or blanket, and that would've been the most logical method of disposal."

"Or maybe they decided to forego sheets and merely used the blankets that are in the trunk?"

"That's possible; I'll get them back to the lab and examine them for evidence."

"What do you think, Evan? Ready for George and Mary to come in?" asked Nash.

"Just a sec; I want to check out the wood stove."

Lowell opened the door of the wood stove, peered inside, and then reached-in with his hand.

"Something in there?" said Nash.

A wide-eyed Lowell responded, "A skull."

Nash's eyes lit up, "What?!"

Lowell extracted his hand and held the contents for Nash to see, "I'm guessing either a rat or a squirrel."

"You're an ass" responded Nash.

Lowell grinned and then said, "You can have the couple come in now."

Nash stepped outside and approached George and Mary, "Sorry it took so long. Can you come in and let us know if anything appears to be missing or looks out of place?"

George and Mary entered – immediately noticing the sleeper sofa. "Was the bed out like that?" said George.

"No; we just extracted the bed to take a look."

George and Mary walked through the cabin. "I see what you mean about looking like someone has been here" said George, "...the lack of dirt and dust."

They opened cabinet doors and drawers, peeked out into the mud room, and strolled into the bathroom.

"Everything looks to be in order" said Mary as she turned back to

Nash.

"I agree" added George.

"Okay… thanks" replied Nash, "If you can give us a couple more minutes."

"Sure" said George, who then gestured to Mary that they should exit the cabin.

Nash watched George and Mary exit; she then turned to Lowell, "Your thoughts?"

"I think we've got all we can here."

"I agree." Nash pondered for a moment, "One thing has me curious though."

"What's that?"

"The hair with the roots intact that you found stuck to the floor crevices…"

"Yeah?"

"Well, if the hair matches the vic, why was he on the floor?"

"What are you guys talkin' about?" Brogan jumped in; unaware of the evidence discovered before he entered.

"Clothing fibers and hair follicles wedged between the floor slats; but there are no signs of a struggle" Lowell clarified to Brogan.

"That *is* weird" replied Brogan.

"Yeah" said Nash, "If they're from our vic then it begs one really big question… *what the hell went on here?!*"

The Cabin – Four Nights Ago

Slumped to one side and passed-out in a chair, mouth agape, a slight trickle of drool following *the path of least resistance* down his chin. A glass containing remnants of a celebratory single-malt Scotch rested precariously on his lap.

A terse voice rang out... "Hey! Can you hear me?!"

No response.

The glass was gently removed and placed on a small table adjacent to the chair.

A hand reached angrily toward his throat. The hand paused momentarily, and then forcefully grabbed the front of his shirt like a neighborhood bully about to make a threat.

"You thought you had it made, that you were impervious to the pain inflicted on others... but you were *wrong.*"

The grip was released. The crumpled portion of his shirt was smoothed-out by a patronizing pat on the chest. "And now *your* time has come."

Two hands grasped his shirt near the top button. "This outfit has got to go – at least for the time being."

An emphatic *ripping through the buttons* was considered, but a slow and methodical approach was deemed more appropriate.

Fingers and thumbs manipulated the release of the fabric from the first button. The sequence was repeated for the next lower button... and the next... and so on; until the flesh of his torso was completely in view. "What do you know; I guess all that crap about the gym wasn't a bunch of B.S."

The right shoe was untied and the shoe removed; the left shoe followed.

"Time to get your ass out of the chair."

A hands-on-one's-hips assessment of the next move was taken.

"Now don't go falling to one side and cracking your head open on the table; we can't have you waking up, or on the flip-side, dying from blunt force trauma right here on the floor... it's not quite your time – *not yet.*"

Both ankles were grasped. A brief tug caused him to slowly slide a few inches down the chair – just enough for his head and neck to rest on the top of the seatback cushion. Another tug and he slid the rest of the way down the chair until his buttocks rested on the floor; his back leaning against the bottom cushion.

"Alright... almost there."

The right shoulder and armpit were grabbed; the head protected by being positioned forward. A twist of the body to one side fully extricated him from the chair; followed by placing him on his back, on the floor.

A moment was taken... a brief respite... a deep breath.

"Time to get that shirt off; and it ain't gonna happen with your arms at your side."

One arm was positioned straight overhead, followed by the other.

Crouching above the head, two hands reached out and clenched the back of the shirt collar. A continuous tug and the shirt was removed and tossed to the side.

Now naked from the waist up, the pants were the next objective. The belt was unbuckled, the pants unbuttoned, the zipper lowered. Both pant-legs were gripped, and the pants slid off. The briefs were grasped and removed as well; and finally... the socks... yanked off of his feet.

Beholding the scene, breaths turned rapid and shallow; the pulse quickened, and the skin became flushed with excitement.

"Ahhh... the moment of truth."

Lying naked on the floor, the body was intimately examined from head to toe... a level of detail akin to a dermatologist looking for suspicious moles. This *up close and personal* look included the genitals.

A camera suddenly appeared.

Numerous photographs were taken – more than should have been necessary. A photographer's lament: Angst and nervousness fucking up your shots. "Come on, get it together, there are reasons we're here, and they're all about exposing what we keep hidden beneath the fabric of our façade."

The body was turned over and the examination process and accompanying photographs repeated.

Standing over the body, camera still in-hand, eyes gazing... "How's *that* for a taste of vulnerability... of being violated? All that remains now is the prelude before the final act..."

And then... the scene turned ugly.

16

"Adding the stuff from the cabin to the board?" asked Brogan as Nash scribbled.

"Yeah, but there's not much to add until we hear back from the lab: The hair follicles... the fibers... the drinking glass. And who knows, the results could provide us important clues, or could simply have us chasing our tails."

"You think ol' George and Mary were being less than truthful with us... of hiding something?"

"Nah; either George forgot to lock up the place and is too proud to admit it, or someone out there has a key."

"Detective Nash?" said Donnelly as she looked up from her desk with a file folder in hand.

Nash turned to acknowledge Donnelly.

"I don't know if this is anything you want to add to the board" said Donnelly, "but it's about Daryl Wagner's parents and his sister – the files you brought back from Bennington P.D."

"Likely a bit premature for the board, but go ahead... let's hear it."

"His parents were killed in a car wreck three years ago; attributed to drunk driving."

"They were *hit and killed* by a drunk driver? Or the father was driving drunk?"

"Actually the mother was driving... single car accident... slammed into a tree at high speed. Both of them had alcohol in their systems well above the legal limit, and several flask-sized bottles of liquor were strewn about the scene."

"His *mother* was driving, huh? I guess I fell right into the *gender stereotype* that the husband usually drives when he's with his wife."

"There may have been a specific reason the wife was driving."

"What might that be?"

"The notes suggest either a suicide-pact or a murder-suicide."

"*Suggest?* Based on what?"

"The high rate of speed... estimated to be pushing a hundred miles an hour, absolutely *no* attempt to slow down or to avoid the tree, and neither one wearing their seatbelt. Plus, it occurred on the anniversary of the little girl's death. *And* the note left on her grave."

"A note?"

"Yeah; it said *Forgive us all...* and it was signed *Mom.*"

"She left the note and then drove away and *purposely* slammed into a tree at high speed?"

"That's how it looks" Donnelly replied... "*After* they had stopped at a park where they used to take the kids – and drank themselves into a stupor."

"And the *murder* aspect if not a suicide-pact?"

"The husband's blood-alcohol content was so high he was surely passed out. And with the knowledge that he had been beating his wife for years, investigators figured that the confluence of issues... the beatings, and the little girl's death... caused the wife to hit the breaking point. Anyway, since there was no suicide note, and everything else was merely speculation, the Coroner ruled it an accident due to impaired driving."

"What do you mean there was *no* suicide note, you said she left a note on the little girl's grave?"

"The statement *Forgive us* could have been in regard to the poor girl's drowning years earlier, and not to the fact that the mother was only minutes away from wrapping herself and her husband around a tree."

"Hmm..." Nash contemplated, "Speaking of the little girl... were there any details surrounding *her* death?"

"Essentially in line with the story Madison Wagner related, but there *was* one thing that drew pause from the investigators and the Coroner."

"What's that?"

"Bruising on the little girl's chest."

"As if she might have been held under the water in lieu of just slipped and drowned?"

"That was their concern, but the father insisted they were caused by him trying to resuscitate her."

"Son of a bitch..." Nash responded in a breathy voice.

"What?"

"Madison said that Daryl's father would be protective of young Daryl from others, yet would look-away when it came to the beatings his mother would inflict upon him."

Donnelly had a disconcerting thought... "You don't think that Daryl..."

"I don't know *what* to think, except that this is *one screwed-up dysfunctional* family. If Daryl Wagner is *not* our vic then we need to make sure Madison gets protection from this guy."

"Roger that" Brogan chimed in.

Nash's cell phone rang – it was Lowell. As she went to answer the call she looked at her watch and pondered aloud, "I wonder what he's calling about; there's no way he got a match on the stuff from the cabin already."

"Hey Evan" said Nash into her phone. "No shit? Wow, we were just talking about him. Needless to say we were all wondering if that might turn out to be the case. I'm guessing that means the lab will increase the priority on the stuff you got yesterday from the cabin, right? Great; thanks."

"DNA results?" asked Brogan.

"I don't know if it's karma or irony or what, but the DNA matches Daryl Wagner" Nash replied, "The items provided by his wife Madison were the tiles that completed the mosaic."

"Ho-lee shit" responded a conflicted Brogan upon hearing the news.

He had a feeling of hesitancy in regard to investigating Daryl Wagner's death… his thoughts were that the bastard probably got what he deserved.

Brogan's deep contemplation was not lost on Nash, "I can see the cogs churning inside your head, Dirk; what's on your mind?"

"The guy's a fucking wife beater" Brogan replied. "And *who knows* what *really* happened to his little sister."

"Yeah, I get it… there's no one with a greater disdain for wife beaters than me. And perish the thought that five-year-old Daryl had something to do with his little sister's death… *and* that his father may have covered for him… we will likely never know what *truly* happened that day. Be that as it may, we have a sworn civic duty, and as much as we might like to be judge and jury on certain cases, vigilante justice or turning a blind eye is not what we're about."

"You've been practicing that speech, haven't you?"

"I had a feeling you might be a little reluctant to put a dedicated effort into solving this crime if the vic turned out to be Daryl Wagner."

"No worries, you'll get my best."

"Good; I'll get on the horn with O'Rourke and give him the good news."

"The *good* news?" asked Donnelly.

"He gets to close the book on his Missing Persons investigation and transfer everything over to us."

"For our Homicide investigation now that Daryl Wagner is no longer missing?"

"That's a fact."

"Where do we start… the *wife?* You know what they say; the spouse is always the first person on your list of suspects."

"There's no way Madison Wagner overpowered, strangled, and then yanked the teeth out of her husband's mouth; let alone the fact that she was home when he was surely murdered" responded Brogan.

"Maybe it was a murder-for-hire?" said Donnelly.

"Kenz and I talked about that possibility earlier, but you wouldn't think she'd bother with a restraining order if she already had a *hit* taken out on the guy."

Nash jumped in… "We'll take a closer look at Madison Wagner post haste, but I also want to get a bead on Daryl… his movements, his financials, his cell phone activity, you name it."

"Shall I get started on that?" said Donnelly.

Nash nodded, pulled out her cell phone and hit, 'Send'. "Hey Sean" she said into the phone, "Big news… we just got a positive I.D. on the vic in the arson murder: Daryl Wagner. Yeah… crazy huh? Anyway, I was going to have Deputy Donnelly stop by to pick up your case files on him. Oh, and I'll take care of notifying his wife."

Nash hung up her phone and turned to Donnelly, "Head over to B.P.D. and pick up their files on Daryl Wagner; O'Rourke knows you're on the way."

"What about me?" Brogan asked.

"You and I get to make yet another visit to see Madison Wagner."

"I'm kind of dreading *this* visit."

"Yeah; telling someone that their spouse has been murdered is always difficult."

"Even if their spouse has been an abuser of them?" asked Donnelly.

"Sadly, yes. They often blame themselves for the abuse… for the pain inflicted… that it was *all their fault*… just like the spouse had drilled into them time and time again. In the midst of an attack they find themselves wishing that the abuser would die a violent death; but if it actually happens they feel guilt, as if their wish of retribution had been granted, which now makes *them* the bad person."

"Wow" said Donnelly, "I had no idea."

"It's a rough world out there" responded Nash. "Be prepared for one hell of a roller coaster ride if you plan on a career working Homicide."

17

It was an unusually quiet drive to Madison Wagner's residence. No stories from Nash about *cases back in the day;* she was rehearsing her *"I'm sorry to tell you this, but…"* speech in her head. And no questions to Nash from Brogan; he was trying to determine how Madison might react to the news, and how *he* might react to *her* reaction.

Pulling up to the curb Brogan focused on the home's front window; unlike the previous visit, the curtain remained still.

Nash gathered her thoughts as she stepped onto the landing and rang the doorbell.

The door slowly opened to reveal a stone-cold-silent Madison. Her lip was no longer swollen, the bruising that had dominated her face was mostly a faded memory… physically at least. Nash calculated that Madison had a good five to six days reprieve from her last beating; possibly the longest recovery period she'd had in years.

"We have some news about your husband" said Nash.

"He wasn't really missing? He had just taken off with another woman or something?" replied Madison.

"There's more to it than that; do you mind if we come in?"

Madison gestured for Nash and Brogan to come inside. They entered the living room – hardwood floors, an area rug, and a sofa with a matching chair. Madison pointed toward the sofa, "Please… have a seat" she said.

Madison sat in the chair, on the edge, leaning forward, her arms crossed with her elbows resting on her thighs. "Now, what is it about my husband?" she asked.

"I have some unfortunate news" Nash replied, "We *did* find your husband, but I'm afraid he is no longer alive."

"What?? He's dead??"

"The car fire Saturday night…" Nash paused, looked down, took a breath, and then looked back toward Madison, "There was a body in the car – DNA confirmed it was him."

Madison stared off into space – the type of glazed-over stare that one exhibits when awakened from a deep sleep; or in her case, perhaps a nightmare.

Nash had difficulty assessing Madison's response to this news: *Was she sad? Was she relieved that her husband would no longer be able to inflict any physical or emotional pain? Did she appear unaffected by the news as if she already knew? Or was it simply the shock of it all?*

"Ma'am?" pressed Nash, "Are you okay?"

"Sorry; I guess I'm just numb" Madison replied. "What… what happened?"

"It looks like he was strangled; and then both he and the car were set on fire in an attempt to destroy the evidence."

"Strangled?? He was a pretty strong guy, how could someone have strangled him??"

"Those are the type of questions we're working on… could have been drugged, could have been overpowered by more than one person… we're not sure yet."

"But who could have done such a thing?"

"That's what we're hoping you can help us with; do you know of anyone who might have wanted to do him harm – any enemies?"

"Not that I can think of."

"No offense ma'am" Brogan jumped in, "but we know he has been physically abusive to you; it's hard to imagine that he wouldn't have some type of issues toward others as well."

"He'd get into any guy's face that he thought was paying too much attention to me – you know, when we were out at clubs or something. But those were pretty much isolated incidents."

"Isolated incidents?" said Nash.

"Well, yeah." Madison pondered for a moment, "I mean it happened a few times, but it was always different circumstances, and different guys. And I don't remember it going beyond yelling, pushing, and shoving."

"There's no particular person that he had a tiff with on more than one occasion?"

"No."

"Did any of these men seem so intense that they might have wanted to exact revenge?"

"One of them got hauled off by the cops. Usually they, *the cops*, would just break up the fight and give everyone a warning, but I guess this guy had a warrant out on him… so *off he went.*"

Nash turned to Brogan, "You got that?"

"Yeah" replied Brogan as he scribbled a note in his memo pad. "You don't happen to remember where, or when, this occurred, do you?" he said to Madison.

"About a month ago out at the *White Pig Tavern.*"

"The *Albino Swino?*" said Brogan.

Nash scowled at Brogan, "Let's dispense with the nicknames, shall we?"

Brogan looked at Nash, and then at Madison. "I apologize; it was the name everyone used when I was a kid."

Nash got back on point, "Did your husband ever strike you in public?"

Madison, shocked and offended, responded rather harshly, "Why would you ask such a question??"

"I'm sorry, but considering the circumstances there's going to be difficult questions that need answers. And I asked because perhaps someone saw you being treated poorly and felt the need to be protective of you… to *come to your rescue* so to speak."

"To kill my husband because he hit me? I can't imagine anyone going that far."

"Believe it or not, it wouldn't be the first time."

"And no, he never hit me in public other than in the car when we were in the parking lot." Her voice started to break, "That was his thing – wait until we got out to the car."

The silence was deafening... Madison momentarily caught-up in the past, Nash and Brogan quietly awaiting additional details.

Madison wiped her eyes, exhaled, and regained her composure, "Anyway, I don't think anyone ever saw that happen."

"And that was it?" said Nash.

"I mean he shook his fist at me and threatened me when we were out in public, but that was all."

"Do you recall the places where this occurred?"

"*All* of them?"

"How about in the last few months?"

"I think I might be able to write up a list."

"That would be great, thanks."

"What about neighbors, coworkers, or fathers or brothers of ex-girlfriends of your husband's that might want to do him harm?" asked Brogan.

"There was nothing out of the ordinary; at least not that I ever saw or that he told me about."

"Well, I think we've covered that subject sufficiently" said Nash, "so I'm going to go back to the night it happened."

"Umm... okay" Madison replied.

"Do you think the phone call that night could have been your husband trying to make a call for help?"

"I guess that's possible." Madison stopped and thought for a moment; something wasn't making sense, "But then I should have recognized his number. Why didn't I recognize the number?"

"Maybe he somehow got hold of the perpetrator's phone and made the call?"

"I suppose. But no one said anything; they hung up as soon as I answered, so I have no idea if it was Daryl or not."

"I understand; we're just trying to connect the dots."

Brogan looked at his memo pad and then to Madison, "You mentioned something earlier about *another woman*..."

"Well, he most certainly had a girlfriend" replied Madison.

"Why do you say that?" said Nash, "Do you know for a fact there was someone else?"

"If you mean *did I catch them together or in the act*, no; but it was clear to me."

"In what way?"

"Well, there were the long hours he'd spend on his laptop and be very secretive about it, always closing the lid when I walked into the room."

"That could be an indication that he was surfing porn sites."

"Yeah, I get that; but there was also his new grooming habits."

"How do you mean?"

"He had always bitten his fingernails and now they're suddenly well-manicured; he kept changing his look – clean shaven, then a mustache, lately a beard, grew his hair out and then a buzz-cut. And he started spending money on a new wardrobe. He'd always been a *jeans and T-shirt* guy and now he's buying clothes like he's Mister GQ."

"Those changes *would* make one wonder" said Nash. "But he never mentioned another woman, a name, maybe even someone you know but never thought of her as being anything more than a friend or acquaintance and so they never drew your suspicion?"

"No, but he'd often stay out all night; sometimes he was gone for a couple of days. In fact, that's why he didn't know about the restraining order when he showed up last Friday – he'd been away on one of his disappearing acts."

"Where did he say he'd been on those occasions... when he'd been gone?"

"At one of his buddy's. And I dare not ask for details or he'd shut me up with his fist... I learned to keep my mouth shut after the first couple of times."

"Interesting" said Nash as she scribed in her memo pad.

"Oh, and he was suddenly hitting the gym... we're talking several times a week" Madison added.

Nash and Brogan both perked up at this news.

"Do you know which gym?" asked Brogan.

"I think it was *Circuit Fitness*, why do you ask?"

"A number of reasons actually" replied Nash. "For one, we need to try to track his movements leading up to the crime, and people at the gym might be able to provide us information... not only his whereabouts, but perhaps his interactions. Also, we found what appears to be a locker key at the crime scene... could be from a gym, from work... we don't really know yet, but if it *does* open a locker at his gym there could be important clues."

"His joining a gym different from mine was another reason I figured he had a girlfriend."

"Please explain."

"I work at the largest gym in the County, so he'd get a *family discount* at my gym; it didn't make sense to join a different gym unless something was going on."

Nash jotted in her memo pad.

"You mentioned his laptop earlier" said Brogan to Madison, "I don't suppose he left it here?"

"No" replied Madison, "He never went anywhere without that thing."

"Do you happen to have a PC – a desktop computer?" asked Nash.

"Yes."

"The forensic team may need to obtain it as part of our investigation... just to let you know."

"Right now?"

"No; we'll let you know *if and when*. And I realize it may be an inconvenience, but the most important thing right now is to find evidence that might lead to your husband's killer."

"But how would my home computer play into that?"

"I'm sure he must have used it in addition to his laptop, correct?"

"On occasion I suppose."

"It will let us know who he's been communicating with, the substance of the conversations, websites he's been visiting, his search history... all kinds of potentially relevant information... maybe even the possible mystery woman."

Madison nodded comprehension.

"By the way, I know your husband's parents are no longer alive; but does he have any siblings we can contact?"

"No, his baby sister Tina was his only sibling."

"I understand... thanks." Nash thought for a moment, "Do you have any pictures of your husband that we can have? We have his picture from his Driver's License, but another picture, hopefully a more accurate rendition of his appearance, would help us out."

"You have his Driver's License?"

"No; the DMV is just the first place we checked for a photograph once he was reported missing."

"He recently renewed his license, so that picture is accurate."

"Perfect; thanks for your time" said Nash as Brogan and she got up to leave.

Madison responded with a broken half-smile.

18

Nash stepped through the doorway of the Sheriff's Office, looked around the immediate area, glanced at her watch, and then back across the room. A look of displeasure appeared on her face as she gazed upon Deputy Laura Donnelly's empty desk… the expectation of seeing Daryl Wagner's case files being sifted-through was not realized.

Brogan, right on Nash's heels, was curious as well… "What do you think?" he said to Nash, "Laura got stonewalled at B.P.D. trying to get Wagner's files?"

"That's about the only valid excuse I can think of."

"Come on Kenz, you know she's not one to be out goofing off."

"Yeah, you're right" Nash replied as she started walking toward her desk and removing her jacket. "I was just chomping at the bit to get a look at those files."

As Nash placed her jacket on the back of her chair, activity through the glass of a nearby Conference Room encroached upon her peripheral vision – it was Donnelly.

"I should have known" said Nash as she headed toward the Conference Room – feeling a bit the fool for second-guessing Donnelly's commitment.

Nash entered the Conference Room to the sight of file-upon-file spread out over the table – Donnelly compiling neat little *eight-and-a-half by eleven* stacks.

Donnelly caught a glimpse of Nash, "Too much stuff for my small desk."

"I'll say" responded Nash as she surveyed the table, "Too much for *anyone's* desk, even Clarke's monstrosity."

Brogan perked-up at the sound of Donnelly's voice. He abruptly investigated the source. "What all do we have here?" he inquired as he entered the room.

"Not only did B.P.D. give me the Missing Persons files on Daryl Wagner" replied Donnelly, "but they also provided copies of their files regarding the disturbances at the Wagner residence, *and* info about the guy that got hauled-away after getting in a tiff with Daryl at the *White Pig Tavern.*"

"What's the story on that guy… the one that got hauled-away?" asked Nash.

"His name is Trevor Cobb. The warrant was for failure to appear in court in regard to an assault & battery charge."

"Is that the guy's M.O." replied Brogan, "To go out drinking and get into fights?"

"It sure seems that way" said Donnelly. "And even though he'd had similar previous altercations, he ended up being released from jail because the complainant dropped the charges."

"When was he released?" said Nash.

"Friday the eleventh."

"That fits within the timeline of the arson car getting stolen, the purchase of the burner phone, *and* Wagner's murder" noted Brogan.

"Do they have anything on this guy between the time he was released and now?" asked Nash.

"No" replied Donnelly. "At the time that Cobb was released Wagner wasn't even a missing person let alone a murder victim, so they had no reason to track his movements."

"Obviously that reality has changed."

"I'll add Cobb's activities to my list."

"What's he do when he's not out getting hammered and trying to prove his machismo?" asked Brogan.

"Cobb?" Donnelly looked at her paperwork… "He's a machinist at *Westsound Auto.*"

"And he lives?"

"Olympic View Estates… in Bennington."

Brogan looked confused, "He makes the kind of money to live in some fancy development?"

"It's a trailer park" Nash clarified.

"Really? You'd never guess that from the name."

"I'm sure that was the point when they came up with it." Nash turned to Donnelly, "What else have you got?"

"Yeah" Brogan added, "Any news about the black & white?"

"I was thinking more along the lines of *Wagner*" said Nash, "But go ahead with the black & white, if you've got anything."

"A few notes here" said Donnelly while she reached toward a stack of papers. She flipped through the stack, "Plus I've managed an initial inquiry into the car on my own."

"And?"

"Concerning the black & white; there are no ties to this guy Cobb *or* to Daryl Wagner."

"Other than Daryl's wedding ring" Nash pointed out.

"Uh yeah… right."

"Do we know the owner?"

"Andrew Lloyd of Ruston."

"Ruston? Was it reported stolen?"

"Surprisingly… No."

"That's odd" commented Brogan, "A smart killer is going to report that their car was stolen as a means to avoid being placed at the scene… an alibi of sorts."

"Assuming he doesn't give us a viable explanation for Wagner's ring to be inside the car" noted Nash. "Hell, with the extent the killer went to destroy evidence thus far, it *would* be rather surprising to make such a gaffe if he is, in fact, our guy."

"No shit" replied Brogan. "But who knows, maybe it's our lucky break."

Nash considered the situation, and then turned back to Donnelly, "Out of curiosity, does this guy Lloyd have any other vehicles?"

"A 2009 Audi A4."

"Relatives in the area?"

"Key Peninsula is the closest… his parents."

"Well, that's not too far away."

"Yeah; only about a half-hour to forty-five minute drive."

"Maybe the car was stolen, but he doesn't know it's missing?" said Brogan.

"How could that be?" said Donnelly.

"If he only drives the Audi and the black & white was kept in a barn or detached garage or something… maybe even at his parents' property."

"If he kept it at his parents' property wouldn't they notice it was missing?"

"Not if they assumed he came and got it without telling them."

Nash was getting flustered, "Didn't B.P.D. talk to this guy?"

Donnelly scanned the files, "Crap; I didn't see this before. They talked to him and he said that he sold the car but left it up to the buyer to file the *Report of Sale*."

"A modified version of *'the car was stolen'* alibi" said Brogan with air-quotes.

"Or a calculated move by the *killer*: Obtain a vehicle to be used in the commission of a crime that has no ties to you; *and* without running the risk of being caught with a stolen car" Nash countered.

"Then you're talking about a *cash* sale unless the guy's a complete idiot."

"But doesn't it seem strange that *one* of the two cars involved in the crime was *stolen*, but the killer *purchased* the other car?" said Donnelly.

"Remember that we haven't ruled out the possibility of there being two perps, *or* that maybe *Wagner* stole the burned-out cinder" replied Nash.

"Why would Wagner steal the car?" said Brogan.

"Who the hell knows; but he *did* manage to end up in its trunk, so he may have *some* tie to the damn thing."

"Even though Lloyd said he *sold* the car we should still investigate him, right?" said Donnelly.

"Absolutely" said Nash, "We don't know if he's telling the truth; or, as Dirk pointed out, merely attempting to fabricate an alibi."

"I don't suppose you've had a chance to look into his activities... anything that puts him in the area around the time of the crime?" added Brogan.

"I haven't gotten that far yet" replied Donnelly.

"Let me know what you find" responded Nash, "It will dictate the flavor of my phone call to him." She reflected on that thought, "Or it might prompt a visit to Ruston."

"I will." Donnelly looked at her file, "And that's all I have on the black & white."

"Alright then; what do we have on Wagner?"

"B.P.D. talked to Mark Donovan, the coworker that reported him missing. He said Wagner was not the type to fail to show up for work; that he'd always call, whether it was because he was sick, missed the ferry, or whatever."

"The ferry? Are you talking Seattle? Or the foot-ferry between Port Sydney and Bennington?"

"Seattle."

"Where does he work?"

"Ancestral Heritage-dot-com... in Pioneer Square."

"What... he's some kind of researcher?"

"Tech Support."

"A computer geek?" Brogan chimed in.

"Something like that I guess" responded Donnelly.

The wheels were turning in Nash's head... "The coworker called it in on *Tuesday*, right?"

"Yes."

"But the coworker said he hadn't seen Wagner since *Friday*."

"Correct."

"So why didn't he call to report him missing on *Monday* if Wagner never misses work without calling-in?"

"He didn't want to *cry wolf* on a first time occurrence."

"Did his work try to contact him on Monday?"

"Yes, but his cell went immediately to voice mail. In fact, another portion of the file says his cell phone has been off since eight-seventeen Saturday night."

"Eight-seventeen?"

"Yep."

"What time was it that he made the ATM withdrawal?"

"Wasn't it around eight-thirty?" said Brogan.

Nash walked out of the Conference Room and over to the murder board. "Eight thirty-three" she said while returning to the room.

"An indication that he might have been abducted just before the ATM withdrawal?" said Brogan, "And the perp took his phone and either turned it off or destroyed it?"

"That would be *one* explanation regarding the timing" noted Nash. "Damn, we really need to get a copy of the ATM video."

"I'll get on that" replied Donnelly.

"Back to Wagner's work calling when he didn't show up..." said Brogan, "Did they try the home phone?"

"Don't know – there's nothing in here about that; I guess we'd need to talk to his wife Madison, or check phone records."

"If Donovan rode the ferry with Wagner every day, he must have known him better than most of his other coworkers."

"He said Wagner spent most of the ferry ride either on his laptop or catching some Z's."

"Did he have anything to share about Wagner's interaction with others, whether he talked about his home life, if he had run-ins with anyone?"

"As a coworker he seemed like a normal guy – kind of quiet, never talked about his family, and was pretty much all about work. He said that if it wasn't for the fact that Wagner wore a wedding ring he would have no clue that Wagner was even married."

"Interesting; either a classic introvert, or for some reason he didn't want anyone to know anything about his personal life."

"Maybe it was a way to make sure his wife never came up in the conversation?" said Brogan.

"Why would that be an issue?" asked Donnelly.

"If someone asks *"Hey, how's the wife?"* and the first thing that comes to Wagner's mind is the beating he inflicted on her the night before, and now he has to re-live the act *and* fumble stumble his way to an *"Oh, she's fine"* or similar response. And you also run the risk of the follow-up questions like *"What did you guys do last weekend?"* and that kind of stuff."

"I think you could be onto something there, Dirk" said Nash, "You're starting to think more and more like a devious perp... I don't know whether to be impressed, or concerned."

"I figure the more you're able to think like them, the better your odds of catching them."

"Nice" said Nash. She turned to Donnelly, "Is that the extent of it from his coworkers?"

"That's about it" replied Donnelly.

"His wife said he had a buddy or buddies that he stayed with on those nights that he didn't come home" said Nash, "Anything from them?"

"They talked to a *Gary Decker*... said he's known Daryl since high school. He's the guy Daryl would stay with when he was avoiding his home... his wife... his life outside of work."

"What does that even mean?"

"I guess sometimes he got overwhelmed with the responsibilities of being a husband."

"Overwhelmed with responsibilities??!! He's out living life like a single guy, hanging with his buds and staying out all night, yet he expected his wife to stay home and be his no-questions-asked subservient bitch?! Asshole!"

Donnelly was speechless… she hadn't seen this side of Nash before.

Silence overtook the room. Donnelly looked at Nash, and then over to Brogan.

Brogan jumped in to break the tension, "Hey Laura, do we know anything about this guy Decker?"

Donnelly was in a momentary fog. After a couple of seconds she snapped back to reality. "Yes" she said, and flipped to the next page of the file.

"He said that he and Daryl were on the football team together and started hanging out soon thereafter" Donnelly continued, "They've been best buds ever since and Decker always let him stay over when he needed a place to stay. He said that he had an idea that Daryl might have been heavy-handed with his wife, but didn't realize how bad it was until the cops showed him pictures of Madison that were taken after these alleged abuses."

Nash shook her head, "The faithful sidekick that always looks the other way… what a piece of work."

The tension was starting to build anew when it was broken by the buzz of Nash's cell phone.

"Hey Evan" said Nash as she answered her phone.

"I just sent you an email with a photo attached" replied Lowell, "It's from *Super Mart* at the moment of sale of the burner phone."

Nash walked over to her computer, "Okay, I'm opening it now."

"What do you think?"

Nash looked, paused, and leaned-in to get a closer look.

Lowell spoke up before Nash had a chance to respond… "Could that be *Madison Wagner?*"

"Damn sure looks like her" Nash replied, "but why do you only have a crappy, grainy photograph instead of the entire video?"

"That's all they would provide without a warrant."

"Those assholes; you know damn well that if they got burglarized in the wee hours of the night they'd be inundating us with every damn piece of video they could find."

"Yeah I know, but that's where we are with this, so let's get working on the affidavit and warrant."

"Will do."

"And this will really blow your mind: According to the cell phone provider there was only *one call* made from that phone... at twelve twenty-seven Sunday morning the 27th... to the *Wagner* residence."

"You're frickin' kidding me?!"

"Needless to say the combination of these two issues, along with the identity of the vic, means we should *also* be getting a warrant to seize the Wagner's home computer; there may be more going on than she's shared with us."

"I agree. What say the two of us work on that and I'll go present it to the Judge?"

"You got it."

"By the way, did you ever find out the phone that was used to *activate* the burner?"

"No big surprise that it was a pay phone."

"There can't be too many of those around these days."

"Only three in the downtown area; this one is near the ferry terminal."

"When was it activated?"

"Last Saturday... four-twenty-two P.M."

"Hmmm... presumably just hours before Wagner was killed."

"That's true."

"Can we track movements based on cell tower pings?"

"They turned the phone off right after they activated it."

"Dammit" Nash replied, "This killer is one sneaky bastard."

"They sure seem to think of everything; as if they may have traveled down this road before."

"Yeah" Nash pondered curiously, "Interesting... thanks."

Nash hung up the phone, walked over to the Conference Room, grasped each side of the door jambs, and poked her head through the doorway. "Things just took a turn that none of us saw coming" she said to Brogan and Donnelly, "Come take a look at this photo that *Super Mart* provided."

Nash turned and walked away. An intrigued Brogan and Donnelly followed.

"It's a photo of the cash register at the time the burner phone was sold… the one that was found at the scene" Nash said while walking. She stopped and gestured toward her computer screen… "Anyone look familiar?"

"That's not Madison Wagner is it?" said Brogan.

"It's not clear enough for a positive I.D., but it sure looks like her, doesn't it?"

"I'll say."

"And here's the *real* crazy part: The phone call received at the Wagner household at oh-dark-thirty the night of the murder…"

"Yeah?"

"It came from *this* phone."

"What the hell??"

"*And*… that was the *one and only* call made from that phone."

"I don't even know *what* to think right now… I'm frickin' dumbfounded."

"You and me both."

"So what do we do now?" Donnelly chimed in, "Arrest her?"

"Unless she comes out and says *"Yes, that's me"* all we have is a fuzzy, grainy photograph of a woman at a check-stand" replied Nash. "Even if she admits that she bought the phone, what are we arresting her for… suspicion of buying a phone that ended up at the scene of a murder?"

"I guess that doesn't necessarily implicate her, does it?"

"No; but it certainly makes things interesting."

"I'm starting to wonder if someone decided to take revenge on Daryl for the beatings he inflicted on his wife" responded Brogan.

"Revenge that she had a hand in?" replied Donnelly.

"I'd hate to think so, but I have to admit that damn cell phone really has me wondering right now."

"You two start looking into her friends and family" said Nash, "In fact... Laura, you might find some info right there in B.P.D.'s case files."

"Got it" said Donnelly. She stood still, anticipating additional instructions. Nash gave her a *"What are you waiting for?"* look. Donnelly jetted toward the Conference Room.

"I'll start looking as well" echoed Brogan.

Nash exhaled, "Time for me to write up an affidavit and accompanying warrant."

19

The deep, dark, orange and red clouds of sunset had faded to grey; the vision of a sky afire had given way to twilight, and the towering Olympic Mountains had become but a silhouette.

The sounds of shoes on planks announced the arrival of Nash and Donnelly into *The Boat House Grill*, a restaurant sitting atop pilings over the waters of the Port Washington Narrows.

Deputy Coroner Valerie LaGrange was seated in the bar area at a small round table... a high-topper with three stools.

"Hey ladies" said LaGrange when Nash and Donnelly walked in, "Long day, huh?"

"We just finished executing a search warrant at the Wagner home" said Nash as she perched upon one of the stools, "Talk about an uncomfortable situation..."

"I can only imagine; considering all you've told me about Madison Wagner."

"Serving the warrant, taking photographs, picking up evidence with Lowell and his Forensics team... including hauling away her computer... it was tough."

"Different from the norm, right?"

"Yeah, usually it's one of those *we're about to get you* moments; not as satisfying as the actual *Gotcha* moment, but a close second. But in this case I just don't know what to think."

"Maybe the evidence will point you in the direction of a whole new person?"

"I have to admit, I hope you're right."

Nash was lost in thought, then realized she had not yet made introductions, "Oh crap; Laura, this is Doctor Valerie LaGrange – Valerie; this is Deputy Laura Donnelly."

"Laura" said LaGrange as she extended her hand toward Donnelly, "A pleasure."

"Me too" Donnelly responded.

"One of these days I'm going to get Laura out of a patrol car and behind a Detective's desk" said Nash.

LaGrange looked to Donnelly, "You're not a Detective?"

"No; Sheriff Clarke assigned me to assist Detective Nash on this case."

"Well, with Kenz here as your mentor you are well on your way."

Donnelly smiled.

Nash grabbed the *Happy Hour* menu, "I don't know about you two, but I need some snacks."

"They've got teriyaki skewers, potstickers, artichoke dip, nachos, even a cheese and crackers plate" said LaGrange.

"The artichoke dip sounds like a good start."

"I'm game" said LaGrange, "How about you, Laura?"

"Sure."

Donnelly had her I.D. *at the ready* when the server arrived.

"Ah, the joys of being in your twenties" said LaGrange, "I don't think I've been carded since I hit the big three-oh; and we won't say how long ago *that* was."

Orders were taken and various varietals of white wine dispersed... Chardonnay, Pinot Gris, and Soave.

Nash raised her wine glass, "Another day in Paradise."

"Cheers" rang out from LaGrange and Donnelly.

"So, Val" said Nash, "Not to get into gruesome details, but I assume everything went as expected with the autopsy on our arson murder vic Daryl Wagner?"

"For the most part" replied LaGrange, "But Sandoval, the Coroner, got his nitpickers into things... taking over the autopsy in a sense, and basically rubber-stamped my *initial* assessment."

"Isn't that a good thing" Donnelly wondered, "That it shows his faith in your abilities?"

"Yes and no" replied LaGrange. "I mean sure, the cause of death was asphyxiation just as I initially reported, and there were no indications of blunt force trauma, and no lacerations that would be indicative of knife wounds."

"But isn't that the purpose of an autopsy?" Donnelly asked, "To determine the cause of death?"

"Sure, but in many instances it also includes the *manner*, which can lead us to the actual murder weapon: A specific caliber of firearm along with the proximity and angle the shot occurred, a specific type of blunt instrument, a knife, a ligature... you name it."

"But in this case you *know* it was manual strangulation, correct?" Nash interjected.

"True" said LaGrange; her focus returning to educating Donnelly, "And if there's a lack of DNA the autopsy can be vital in the identification of the victim: Dental impressions, prior surgeries, prior broken bones, birthmarks, tattoos..."

Donnelly was impressed, "I guess I hadn't considered how much an autopsy provides investigators."

"Fortunately we have DNA in this case" said Nash.

"No kidding" replied LaGrange, "Since the perpetrator obliterated all other avenues."

"I'm a little confused, Val... your mention of Sandoval... do you have concerns here?"

"I'm not implying that there are any issues, or that something might have been missed. But you know me, I'm anal retentive when it comes to my work... I want to look at every aspect of the victim's body before I put my signature on a report."

"Sounds like yet another reason for you to run for Coroner at the next election; you'd have *my* vote."

"I appreciate that, but I'm no politician. And if Sandoval decides to run again it would be a rather uncomfortable work environment to have the Deputy Coroner running against her boss."

"Yeah, but wouldn't you have a leg up on him; being a doctor while he is *not?*"

"The Coroner is *not* a doctor?" Donnelly queried.

"The County Coroner is an elected position – a medical doctor's degree is not required" said Nash, "And that's the case with Sandoval."

"That seems crazy."

"Tell me about it. Thus, he has to have a licensed forensic pathologist Medical Examiner like Val here performing the autopsies."

"It is what it is at this point" said LaGrange. "But now you know why I have issues when I feel like I can't be as thorough as I'd like."

LaGrange took a sip of her wine. Nash and Donnelly realized it was a good time to take advantage as well.

"Damn, I needed that" said Nash; setting down her wine glass. "Crap, here we are talking shop… sorry about that."

LaGrange held up her wine glass for a toast: "No more shop talk."

The three clinked their wine glasses together.

"So Kenz, how are things with you and Ian?" said LaGrange.

"Let's just say… discordant" Nash replied.

"Discordant?"

"Okay, maybe that's too harsh; *uneasy* is probably a better description."

"Wow; what's going on?"

"Issues from the other night that I'm still trying to come to grips with."

"Anything you want to talk about? You know us ladies are here for you, right Laura?"

"Of course" Donnelly replied – surprised to be emotionally accepted into the fold so quickly.

"A few days ago I had just spoken to Madison Wagner in person for the first time. Seeing her bruised and battered face really weighed heavily on me… it brought back some harsh memories. That night Ian could tell something was on my mind and so I finally let my walls down and told him about the issues that led me to the Bay Area back in my twenties."

LaGrange leaned over and quietly *filled-in the blanks* for Donnelly, "Escaped from an abusive boyfriend in the dark of night."

"Actually it was in the middle of the day while he was at work" Nash clarified, "But you get the picture."

A wide-eyed Donnelly nodded.

"Even the strongest of us get knocked down every once in a while" added LaGrange, "It's what you do when you get back up that defines you."

"I appreciate that" replied Nash, "But Ian? Not so much."

"He didn't show compassion for the ordeal you'd been through? For having the strength to escape the abuse even though it meant you essentially had to start a whole new life from scratch?"

"You know me; I wasn't looking for pity, just maybe a little understanding. But when he said that he couldn't believe that I *let* someone verbally and physically abuse me..."

"He said *that?*"

"Yep. And I've been giving him the cold shoulder ever since."

"Has he since apologized?"

"He has... said he misspoke; and that he felt such rage toward the guy for assaulting me that he let his anger toward *him* override his compassion for *me*."

"Not that I'm sticking up for Ian, but it sounds like his apology was sincere."

Nash took a moment to ponder LaGrange's statement.

"I mean, he's been pretty good to you all this time you've been together, right?" LaGrange added.

"True" Nash nodded.

"Well remember, sometimes men just don't *get* us. Do you recall that book a number of years ago *Men Are From Mars, Women Are From Venus?*"

"I never read it, but I remember the title."

"Well sometimes men aren't from Mars but rather from *Uranus*... got their head up their ass."

Nash grinned. "You've got a point there" she remarked as she raised her glass and then sipped her wine.

"So, Laura" said LaGrange, "What's your story?"

"My Dad was in the Navy so we bounced around the country a lot, ending up here when his ship came to the Shipyard for overhaul – his last duty station; in fact he works for the Shipyard now. Anyway, when you visit so many places you see a lot of diversity, a lot of people struggling... whether it was the poorer areas where we lived, or just Navy families dealing with the difficulties of their loved one being gone for months at a time. My parents always instilled on us kids the importance of giving-back... my Father by serving his country, my Mother by doing volunteer work – usually at a local foodbank. I guess the example they set held true for my brother and me; he went to college and became a school teacher, and I went to the Police Academy and became an Officer."

"Damn girl... cheers to you and your family."

The three of them clinked their wine glasses, and then ordered another round.

"What about you, Valerie?" asked Donnelly.

"The usual medical doctor path, at least initially: College and pre-med, medical school, residency, and license. I worked hospitals in the E.R., O.R., and the morgue, and found forensic pathology calling my name. A fellowship and a few years in the field and the next thing you know I'm the Deputy Coroner."

"Three totally different paths that led us together to work this case" said Nash.

"Uh-oh, we're not going to start talking shop again, are we?" asked LaGrange.

"No" Nash grinned.

"Good; although I *do* have a *semi*-work-related question for you."

"What's that?"

"What's the deal with Dirk?"

"You're not thinking of…?"

"No" LaGrange interrupted, "I'm not looking for a date with the guy."

"He's a lot smarter than he comes across" Nash replied, "At least some people get a false impression as to his intellect. He just happens to get singularly focused on an issue at times, like a laser. But I have to say, the guy is loyal like a German Shephard, and he's been vitally important in helping me solve crimes."

"Somehow I thought that might be the case."

Donnelly didn't say a word, she just smiled.

20

Nash was standing in the Break Room, sipping her coffee, looking a bit worse for wear, contemplating the events of the previous twenty-four hours.

Donnelly walked in the room – coffee mug in hand. Nash glanced over Donnelly's way.

"Good morning" said Donnelly.

"Mornin'" Nash replied, and then held up her mug, "My second cup already… one too many glasses of wine last night."

"But we only had two at the restaurant; plus we ate food as well?"

"True, but after I got home Ian stopped by."

"I see."

"I decided that we needed to 'talk'" said Nash with air-quotes.

"How did that go?"

"Surprisingly well actually; you and Val had me look at things from a new perspective. I realized I was being closed-minded, had pre-conceived expectations as to his response, and had failed to consider his point of view."

"His point of view?"

"He's only known me as a strong, independent woman who won't take shit from anyone, let alone allow them to walk all over me. So, it was only natural for him to be shocked to find that I had fallen prey to a controlling abusive asshole at a vulnerable time in my life. Once he realized that his knee-jerk reaction lacked compassion toward me he truly felt awful. And Val's words regarding how he has treated me all these years rang true." She took a sip of her coffee and smiled, "As did the whole *Uranus* thing."

Donnelly smiled and raised her coffee mug to toast the moment.

"Seriously though" Nash continued, "That event all those years ago was just one more thing that helped mold me into becoming the person I am today – striving to be a champion for the victims."

Brogan's arrival silenced the conversation. He looked around and made an ill-fated attempt at humor, "Hey, it's the ladies of the evening."

Nash glared at Brogan, "You might want to rephrase that."

"I just meant…"

"I know what you meant; I'm just flipping you crap."

"In that case I'll change the subject." Brogan looked at Donnelly and then back to Nash, "How did executing the warrant go?"

"As uncomfortable as I've ever experienced in such a situation" Nash replied.

"It was the first time I had met her" added Donnelly, "And I thought the whole process was going to bring her to tears."

Brogan was curious, "Like a guilty person who was about to be caught?"

Nash responded, "No; it was more like being inundated by a confluence of about a thousand things, essentially all of them bad. I think she's close to reaching her breaking point."

"What did she say about the photo from *Super Mart?*"

"First I asked her if she had a burner phone" Nash replied. "She said that she didn't know what a burner phone was, so I clarified that it was a pre-paid cell phone."

"And she responded…?"

"That she bought one, but didn't know where it was. Then I asked her where and when she bought it; she said she might have gotten it at *Super Mart* a week or so ago."

"It was *that recent* and she couldn't recall where she bought it?"

"No kidding. Anyway, that's when I showed her the photo and asked if that was her."

"What did she say?"

"That it *looked* like her, so she figured it must be. Then I asked her *why* she bought the phone. She said that a friend of hers recommended it when she decided to get the restraining order… figuring that her husband might start sending her threatening texts, phone calls, or even tracking her via her regular cell phone."

"She makes a good point."

"I agree. Then I reiterated about the whereabouts of the phone and she insisted that she had no idea… it was either stolen or she somehow lost it."

"I assume you told her that the phone call she received the night of the crime came from the phone that *she* bought?"

"Yes; and her response was rather dramatic… she said *'Do you mean the killer stole my phone… was in my house??!!'*"

"Whoa; I hadn't even *considered* that possibility."

"You and me both. And of course it's something we need to keep in mind as we delve more and more into this crime."

"If that's the case you've got to figure the Forensic Team will turn up something."

"I *did* ask her if she might have left a window open, a door unlocked, the garage door open or unlocked… anything along those lines. She recognized that it was a possibility, but thought it was unlikely."

"What was the Forensic Team's take on the idea?"

"They were looking for any signs of unnatural entry into the house."

"Do you mean *forced* entry?"

"That's one manner; but it also includes a slice or tear in a screen, hand or fingerprints on a window ledge, footprints outside of a window, mud or dirt *inside* the house under a window… indicators like that."

"Any luck?"

"Don't know yet."

"Any other items of note from the search?"

"The Cyber guys grabbed her computer; we'll see if that gives us anything new to work with."

Nash took a sip of her coffee; it dawned on her that they were still in the Break Room. "Top off your coffee cups and let's get back to the board" she said.

Walking toward the office area Nash relayed to Donnelly, "Hey Laura, yesterday you gave us some info about Wagner's buddy Decker; do we know the last time he saw Wagner?"

"I think that was in the file; let me grab it."

Donnelly retrieved the file and starting sifting through it, "Here it is: Tuesday the twenty-second."

"Tuesday the twenty-second?" Nash responded, "Then where the hell *was he* for three to four days?"

"What do you mean?"

"Madison said he'd been gone for several days when he showed up that Friday... the twenty-fifth; and was gone again that night" said Nash, "And, as we know, he was murdered the next day – Saturday."

"He was still making it to work those days, so he had to be staying *somewhere*" responded Brogan.

"Do B.P.D.'s files have Wagner's movements... either via cell phone or from debit or credit card usage?" Nash asked of Donnelly.

"Believe it or not he didn't have a debit card, just an ATM card; and he rarely used his credit card, primarily just for larger purchases; the most recent being an external hard-drive for his computer on the nineteenth."

"So, he was mostly a *cash* guy" said Nash.

"Or check" Donnelly replied.

"And his cell phone?" asked Nash.

"The GPS function was inactive, and he would periodically turn the phone off for some reason, so B.P.D. couldn't draw any movements of note via cell tower pings."

"Maybe he was trying to hide any movements that would place him near the girlfriend Madison thought he had" said Brogan.

"Crap, maybe *that's* where he was on those unaccounted-for days?"

noted Nash.

"I haven't been able to find anything about this alleged mystery woman" said Donnelly.

"I was just about to ask you about her... but nothing more than dead ends? Damn!"

Nash looked at the murder board, "What else are we missing?"

"Word back from Lowell regarding the cabin" said Brogan.

"The video from the ATM when Wagner made the withdrawal" added Donnelly.

"The locker key" Brogan noted, "Seeing if it matches a locker at *Circuit Fitness.*"

"And talking to Cobb – the guy Wagner got in a fight with" Donnelly finished. "Oh, and I still need to follow-up on Andrew Lloyd... the guy that allegedly sold the black & white."

"With all of that in mind, who do we get to go visit today?"

"Cobb is scheduled to work both days this weekend, so he is actually off today."

"Sounds like as good a place as any" responded Nash. "Hey Dirk, let's start with seeing if our presumed locker key works at *Circuit Fitness*; and then how about we go have a chat with Mister Cobb?"

"I'm game."

Nash turned back to Donnelly, "Laura, take a turn on Andrew Lloyd, with a priority on seeing if you can place him in the area the night of the murder."

"Will do."

Nash proceeded to her desk, opened a drawer, grabbed and donned her holster, and then holstered her weapon.

She grasped the locker key, flipped it in the air, caught it in mid-flight, and placed it in her front pocket.

Brogan readied himself as well, and the two of them trod out the office door, jumped into Nash's cruiser, and sped away.

21

A dual bi-fold electric door opened upon the presence of Nash and Brogan within its sensors. Beyond the doors stood a large U-shaped counter staffed by personnel clad in *Circuit Fitness* polo shirts. Placed strategically around the counter were two terminals, each with a computer screen and an electronic wand for checking-in members.

Nash and Brogan were greeted by a staff member with a nametag that read *Chelsie*. "Welcome to Circuit Fitness" she beamed, "How can I help you?"

Nash and Brogan held up their badges, "We're Detectives Nash and Brogan from the Sheriff's Department."

"Yes ma'am?"

Nash held up a photo of Wagner, "Do you have a member here named Daryl Wagner?"

"He looks familiar, let me check" Chelsie said – scrolling through her computer files to the *'Members'* section, and then typing his name via the keyboard.

"Yes we do" she replied, "But he's not checked-in at the moment."

"That's fine; does he happen to have a locker here?"

Chelsie scanned the screen, "Yes; locker forty-two in the Men's Locker Room."

"We're going to need to check the contents."

"Uh… sure" Chelsie replied; not used to having to grant permission for a woman to access the Men's Locker Room. "Let me get the on-duty manager to escort you."

"That would be fine, thanks."

"O-D-M, please come to the Welcome Center" Chelsie announced over the loud speakers.

Chelsie received a phone call, and explained the situation. "He's on the way" she relayed to Nash.

Within a minute a staff member approached; he was wearing a communication device... a walkie-talkie of sorts... attached to his belt loop. A second staff member was by his side.

"Good morning; I'm Kyle" he said, "I understand you need to access the Men's Locker Room and view the contents of locker forty-two?"

"That's correct" replied Nash as she held up her badge.

"Right this way" responded Kyle as he began to walk.

Past an area of cardio machines and the like: Treadmills, ellipticals, rowing machines, jacob's ladder, rope climbing machines, and stair-steppers... the group stopped in front of the Men's Locker Room door.

"Let me go in and make the men aware that a woman is going to be entering" said Kyle, "And give them time to clear out."

"No problem" said Nash, who then head-nodded toward Brogan, "Detective Brogan will accompany you."

"Yes ma'am."

Watching several men exit the locker room over the next couple of minutes, Nash donned a pair of latex gloves in preparation for examining potential evidence found within. She received several odd looks, and realized what crazy notion might be going on in the men's minds. She grinned as she pondered the possibilities.

Kyle and Brogan re-emerged from the locker room.

"Marcus" Kyle said to his assistant, "Stand guard here and keep anyone from entering while the Detectives conduct their business. If anyone needs to use the restroom, direct them to the Men's Room near the Welcome Center."

"Yes Sir."

Kyle led Nash and Brogan to locker 42. He pulled the key from his pocket. As he reached toward the locker Nash put her hand up to stop him. "We have a key we'd like to try" she said. She reached into her pocket and extracted the key.

"Of course" Kyle replied.

Nash placed the key in the slot, turned it to the right, and *voila...* the door opened.

Kyle was surprised, "Where did you get that key?"

"We're not at liberty to say."

Inside the locker was a gym bag with a *Seattle Supersonics* name and logo.

"Wow" said Brogan, "That brings back memories."

Nash extracted the bag, placed it on a nearby bench, and peered inside. She noticed that the contents were relatively minimal: Gym shorts, a sleeveless tee, fingerless gloves, a compression sleeve for the knee, and a sample-sized deodorant stick. She extracted the items one-by-one and placed them on the bench.

"What's in the bottom there?" said Brogan as he took a peek inside the bag.

"Just a couple of gum wrappers and a bandage" Nash replied.

"No" Brogan said as he pointed... "That piece of paper."

"Oh, I see" Nash replied, "I thought it was the wrapper from a bandage."

Nash pulled out a small piece of paper.

"Something's scribbled on it" said Brogan.

Nash turned it around, squinted, and read aloud... "It says *I'm watching you. Lay a hand on her again and you're fucked.*"

Both Brogan and Kyle were visibly shocked. Kyle backed away as if the author of the note was going to suddenly emerge from the gym bag.

"Whoa" said Brogan, "Can I see it?"

Nash held it in front of Brogan at eye-level.

"Son of a Bitch" said Brogan. "And go figure they got the grammar correct on *YOU'RE.*"

"That could be important if we can narrow down possible authors" stated Nash.

"Somebody obviously wasn't too happy with Wagner."

"No shit" responded Nash. She placed the note in a small evidence bag.

"I wonder why he kept it?" said Brogan.

"Likely as potential evidence in case the person who wrote it was truly out to get him."

"Somehow I'm thinking he was planning to use it as evidence in event the person beat the shit out of him; *not* from an *'after I get murdered take a look at this guy'* perspective."

Kyle's eyes popped wide-open; Nash had not mentioned the fact that the owner of the locker had been murdered.

Nash noticed the look of despair on Kyle's face, "I guess I hadn't shared the unfortunate news about Mister Wagner with you; I apologize."

"Umm…" Kyle gulped, "Not at all, ma'am."

"Is there anything you can tell us about him?"

"He'd been coming here frequently over the past several months; a good three times a week or more."

"Did he come here with anyone; or meet someone here?"

"No; he was always alone, and he kept to himself. In fact, I don't recall ever seeing him even talk to anyone – he was *all business.*"

"Alright then" Nash replied as she grabbed the gym bag. "We're going to be taking custody of Mister Wagner's belongings. And of course we will be retaining custody of this key" she said as she held up the key that had originated from the crime scene.

"I understand, ma'am."

"Thanks for your time and assistance."

"You're welcome."

Exiting the building Brogan posed a question, "I wonder if Laura might have some handwriting samples in her files that we can compare the note with?"

"Even so, we'll be limited to nothing more than a cursory comparison; any true handwriting analysis will be left up to the experts. We'll make copies for our own use and get the original to Lowell for handwriting and other forensic analyses like DNA and dusting for prints."

"Makes sense" Brogan replied, and then asked, "Next stop... Cobb's place?"

"That's a fact."

22

"So, this is Olympic View Estates" Brogan commented when Nash and he turned onto Olympic View Circle, "Not too shabby for a trailer park."

"Not at all like the stereotypical *dilapidated trailers surrounded by junked cars*" Nash replied.

Taking in the vista Brogan noticed that the area was not so much a trailer park, but rather a community of nicely kept mobile homes – mostly double-wides; with well-maintained grounds, a children's playground, and even a clubhouse with an outdoor barbecue area.

"Cobb's place is number seventeen, right?" said Brogan.

"Yep; the turquoise single-wide up ahead."

Nash and Brogan walked up the steps to a small deck covered in indoor-outdoor carpet, with a corrugated metal roof overhead. They stood at the doorway; Nash raised her fist and *rap-rap-rap* on the thin metal door she pounded.

A late-twenties man of athletic build, three-days of growth scruffy beard, and clad in a tattered and greasy *Westsound Auto* work shirt, answered the door.

"Trevor Cobb?" said Nash.

"Who wants to know?" the man replied.

"Detectives Nash and Brogan from the Slaughter County Sheriff's Department" Nash responded; holding up her badge.

"I ain't done shit, so why do you cops keep harassing me?"

"We're not here to harass you; we have some questions about an incident at the *White Pig Tavern* a few weeks back between you and Daryl Wagner."

"The night I got hauled-off by the cops?"

"That's right; I heard it all started with issues surrounding his wife?"

"Sure, I was checking her out... who wouldn't, she's smokin' hot. *What's-his-jerk* started getting in my face and we had a few words."

"And then the fight broke out?"

"Not right then; that was later on, outside in the parking lot."

"What happened while you were still in the bar?"

"Mostly male ego crap – acting tough and cussing at each other. He attempted to start a shoving match when one of the staff told us to cool it or take it outside. He looked at me for a moment and then turned to the staff dude and said *"We're cool"* and then sat back down in his seat. Since he backed down I went back to my table. Of course I kept checking out his wife... just to piss him off."

"And later?"

"When I walked out to the parking lot I saw him sitting in his car... yelling at her and smacking her around. His window was rolled down so I reached in and grabbed his shirt... by the collar near his throat... and told him to get his fucking hands off her. He told me to mind my own fucking business and to stay away from his wife."

"And then?"

"He pushed the door open with his arm and shoulder, knocking me down. I quickly got up just as he was coming at me and I popped him one right in the jaw. He took a swing at me but I blocked it with my forearm. Next thing I know a couple of bouncers grabbed us, and two minutes later the cops showed up."

"And you got taken into custody."

"Yeah; here this asshole is beating up his wife and *I'm* the one who gets hauled-off to jail."

"You were taken in because you had an outstanding warrant, not because of the fight."

"The cops still should have done something about the other guy; and they agreed with me too, but said there was nothing they could do."

"Unless they catch the guy in the act, or the wife files charges, their hands are tied."

"And then what, they sit around and do nothing until she ends up in the hospital or turns up dead?"

"I appreciate your concerns, and they are duly noted."

"Sounds like the same line of bullshit the other cops gave me."

Brogan interceded, "I understand you got out of jail a few weeks ago?"

"On the eleventh" Cobb replied. "That stint cost me a couple weeks of work; I've been workin' overtime tryin' to catch up."

"Have you seen Wagner since then?"

"The husband? Or the wife?"

"Either one" said Nash.

"I saw *him* at *The Swino* the weekend after I got out."

"Friday? Saturday? Sunday?"

"That same night... Friday... after I got released. I really needed a couple of brewskis after being locked up for two weeks."

"Did you two have words again?" said Brogan.

"He gave me a shit-eating grin when he saw me... clearly gloating about the fact that I got hauled-off by the cops the last time he saw me. And I gave him a *Fuck you too* glare, but that was it."

"Was he with anybody?" said Nash.

"He was talkin' with some chick; I think she might've been one of the bar-staff that had gotten off shift. And then one of his buddies came and joined them."

"The woman wasn't his wife?"

"No."

"Do *you* know his wife?"

"Nope."

"Are you sure?"

"Yes, I'm sure. I only know her from seeing her with him."

"Just that night?" asked Brogan.

"I'd seen them there before, and he was always acting like an ass...

and treating her like shit."

"How do you mean?"

"Yelling at her, grabbing her wrists, raising his hand like he's going to smack her... he's a first-class ass-wipe."

"Can you describe the woman that Wagner was with the night you got released?" said Nash.

"Maybe five-three or five-four... thin... cute."

"Hair color?"

"Dark. But if it's the chick I think it is she changes her hair color every week or two – brunette, redhead, blonde."

"What about the guy that joined them?" asked Brogan.

"Average height, a bit of a gut, usually wearing a *Seahawks* cap – receding hairline when he isn't."

Nash quietly said to Brogan, "Sounds like Wagner's pal Decker."

Nash returned her focus to Cobb, "Where were you the night of the twenty-sixth... last Saturday?"

"I was home" Cobb replied.

"Can anyone corroborate that?"

"Do you mean *was I with a lady friend?* No; I was alone."

"What were you doing?"

"I was clipping my toenails."

"What??" responded Brogan.

"Unless you have probable cause to take me in" Cobb stated, "I'm done playing this game."

Nash reached into her jacket pocket and extracted the note found in Wagner's gym bag.

She held up the note for Cobb to see, "Does this look familiar?"

"Nope; should it?"

"It should if you wrote it."

"I like the message, but it wasn't me."

"It mimics your earlier statement."

"What're you talkin' about?"

Nash flipped back a page in her notepad. "You said… quote… *I told him to get his fucking hands off of her…* unquote."

"Nice try but that's not *word-for-word* what your note there says."

"I don't suppose you'd mind giving us a DNA sample?"

"Now why would I want to do that?"

"I don't know if you've read the paper or watched the news, but Daryl Wagner was killed last weekend."

"And you think I wrote him a threatening note and then killed him?"

"If you didn't then why not give us a DNA sample, it would eliminate you as a suspect."

"I may have wanted to knock the guy's teeth out, but I had no reason to kill him."

"So, I take it that's a *NO?*"

"Like I said, I'm done playing this game."

"Okay then; thanks for your time."

Cobb didn't respond; he merely waited for them to leave and then shut the door.

As Nash and Brogan pulled away from the curb and drove the loop back to Olympic Avenue, Brogan wondered… "Wouldn't Cobb's DNA have been collected when he was in the slammer?"

"It's only collected in felony cases."

"Oh, that's right" Brogan recalled. "Hey, what do you think of his statement about wanting to knock Wagner's teeth out? Just a figure of speech, or was he possibly referring to the fact that Wagner's teeth got yanked out?"

"The removal of Wagner's teeth is a detail that has *not* been shared with the news agencies, so his comment gets one's attention, that's for sure."

"Then we keep looking at this guy?"

"Damn straight; I'll have Laura see if we can track his movements since he got released."

Nash reflected on another aspect of the conversation with Cobb: "You know…" she mused, "Something else jumped out at me."

"What's that?"

"Cobb's details contradicted what Madison told us. She said no one ever saw her husband hit her while they were in the car."

"Maybe she didn't realize Cobb had seen her getting smacked around; maybe she just assumed he confronted her husband because of their exchange in the bar?"

"Very true" Nash conceded, "I guess we'll have to see what she says the next time we talk to her."

23

"We hit pay-dirt at *Circuit Fitness*" Nash said to Donnelly who was updating the murder board, "Not only did Wagner have a locker there, but our *mystery key* fit the lock."

"Anything in the locker?" Donnelly replied.

"Mainly some gym clothes that we'll provide to Forensics; but this item here was intriguing" said Nash as she handed Donnelly the small evidence bag containing the threatening note.

Donnelly read the note, "Whoa, I wonder who wrote that?"

"I think we can rule out *Wagner* as the author" replied Brogan.

Nash and Donnelly both looked at Brogan; they weren't sure if he was being serious or making an attempt at humor. They decided to ignore his comment.

"We showed the note to Cobb" added Nash, "But he pleaded ignorance."

"I'll add it to our evidence" Donnelly stated.

"Actually, make a *copy* for our use… we'll be turning over the original to Forensics along with the gym bag and its contents."

"Understood."

"And be sure to wear gloves; they'll need to perform multiple analyses on it… DNA, fingerprints, handwriting…"

"Of course."

"On a separate subject, did you have any luck placing Andrew Lloyd near the scene on the twenty-sixth?"

"No closer than his parent's place in Key Peninsula. Of course he could have turned off his phone, traveled here and committed the murder, and then back to his parents' place."

"But how did he ditch the black & white and then get back to his parents?" said Brogan.

"An accomplice" Nash chimed in.

"Damn; I keep forgetting about *that* possibility."

"But what would be his motive?" said Donnelly, "I have not been able to find a single tie between Lloyd and Wagner."

"Perhaps the key is not tying Lloyd to Wagner, but rather finding a third person that has ties to *each of them*" noted Nash.

"In other words, Lloyd is the *accomplice* and a third, yet to be discovered, person is actually the murderer?"

"Now you see where I'm coming from."

"Okay, I'll look at things from that angle."

"And what about the alleged *sale* of the car?"

"Department of Licensing has no such record, so I think our only recourse is to talk to Lloyd."

"Looks like I'm going to be taking a drive to Ruston… preferably sooner rather than later" Nash proclaimed.

"I'll make the search for a commonality between Wagner and Lloyd my top priority."

"Good" Nash replied, "Anything else for us?"

"A question."

"Go ahead."

"When you talked to Officer Roberson did you ask him for any info he might have on Daryl and Madison Wagner?"

"No; why?"

"He was the responding Officer, along with Officer Gina Stahl, at several of the disturbances at the Wagner household; so I was thinking perhaps we could get some info on the Wagners from both of the two Officers… get their perspective."

"Good idea."

"You know" said Donnelly as she started flipping through her files, "I think he might have been the arresting Officer with Cobb as well."

"Really?" remarked Brogan, "Is this guy a one-man Supercop or what?"

"I think it's more a matter of a limited budget for the police force in Bennington, and getting stuck with swing-shift… the shift when most of the crazy crap happens" replied Nash.

"Here it is" said Donnelly. "Yep, he was Cobb's arresting officer."

"Was Officer Stahl with him?" asked Nash.

"No; it was Officer Adam Sheldon."

"We may not get anything beyond what's in the files in regard to Daryl and Madison Wagner, but it can't hurt to ask" said Nash. "As far as Cobb goes though, it would be very interesting to compare Officer Roberson's interpretation of events from that night with what Cobb told us."

"No shit" said Brogan, "It could move him right to the top of our pool of suspects."

Nash looked at her watch and realized it was getting late in the afternoon, "Crap, I need to get the stuff from Wagner's locker to Lowell."

Nash's cell phone rang. She looked at the Caller I.D. "Speak of the devil."

"Hey Lowell, I was just about to call you" she said into her phone.

"You want to go first?" said Lowell.

"Go ahead… you made the call."

"It's about the cabin."

"Yeah?"

"I was thinking about the lack of forced entry combined with George Montgomery's insistence that he locked the place, so I called George and asked if they had changed the locks after they took ownership."

"And he said *No?*"

"That's correct."

"Which means the previous owners would still have a key, along with anyone they had given one… family members, friends, or whoever."

"And *that* opens up all kinds of possibilities."

"No kidding" Nash replied, "Do you happen to have the name of the previous owners?"

"I literally just got off the phone with George; sorry."

"No problem, we'll take that on. What else have you got?"

"That's it for now; I'm still waiting on results from the lab for the remainder of the cabin" he responded, "And what did *you* have for *me?*"

"That key you found in the trunk of the incinerated sedan… it opened a locker at Daryl Wagner's gym."

"No shit?"

"I've got his gym bag with some clothes inside that I'll be dropping off within the half-hour."

"Anything interesting?"

"Yeah, a handwritten note that says *I'm watching you - Lay a hand on her again and you're fucked.*"

"Holy shit!"

"So of course your handwriting expert will be of importance; plus any other forensic evidence you can find on it."

"I'm looking forward to taking a look at that thing."

"Sounds good; I'll see you in thirty."

Nash hung up her phone and turned to Donnelly, "Hey Laura, do you mind adding one more thing to your list?"

"Not at all, what've you got?"

"It turns out that George and Mary Montgomery did *not* change the locks after they took ownership of the cabin" Nash replied, "See what you can find on the previous owners, we might be able to determine who has been there recently."

"Got it."

"And both of you…" said Nash.

"Yeah?" Brogan and Donnelly responded in unison.

"It's about time to call it a day. I'm going to drop off the gym bag and note to Lowell; you two call it quits soon and I'll see you Monday morning."

24

Nash walked into the office and was surprised by the aroma of freshly brewed coffee. She looked at her watch; it was ten o'clock. A few steps through the doorway yielded an even greater surprise.

"Hey Laura" Nash said, "What are you doing here, it's Saturday; you're supposed to have the weekend off?"

"I know, but there were a couple of items I didn't want to wait on."

"I know the feeling."

"Weren't you were taking the weekend off as well?" said Donnelly.

"Tomorrow maybe; but I needed to take a fresh look at the murder board."

"You could've made a digital copy and analyzed it at home."

"Home is my sanctuary from this place, you start bringing your work *home* and your entire life becomes engulfed in murder: The life that was taken physically, and the lives that are lost emotionally... which could be *yours* if you're not careful."

"I get what you're saying."

The office door opened. The sounds of shoes attempting to be scuffed clean on the doormat. A familiar figure walked through the doorway.

"Look what the cat drug in" Nash directed at Brogan.

"Either we're all extremely dedicated" Brogan replied at the sight of Nash and Donnelly, "Or each of us has *absolutely no life whatsoever.*"

"I appreciate the dedication of both of you, but let's make this a short workday and get back to doing whatever it is you do when you're not here" said Nash.

"Understood" replied Donnelly, "The first item I had for you is rather brief: I looked at County records regarding the cabin; the previous owners are, or should I say *were*, Charles and Maxine Stillwater."

"Were?"

"Yes; they both passed away almost three years ago... one from ALS, the other heart disease. I'll have to track down surviving family members to see if any of them might still have keys to the cabin."

"That's a start" Nash replied. "You implied you had a second item?"

"Yes; I found a tie of sorts between Wagner and Andrew Lloyd – the listed owner of the black & white."

"Of sorts?" replied Brogan.

"Andrew Lloyd and Daryl's wife Madison... they went to High School together... South Slaughter High... she was Madison Sinclair back then."

"Yeah, that's how she introduced herself the first time we met her" Brogan replied.

"Had they possibly known each other since they were kids?" asked Nash, "Or just High School?"

"Madison grew up in Port Sydney, and Lloyd at the south end of the County, so they were in different Elementary and Junior High school districts" responded Donnelly.

"Do you know for a fact that they knew each other?"

"No. I checked their yearbook to see if they might have belonged to the same clubs and such: Drama club, chess club, glee club, band, whether he was a football player and she was a cheerleader... anything that could have put them together, but there was nothing."

"And even if they had one or more classes together that wouldn't be telltale. Hell, every class reunion I run into someone who says *Hey, we had a class together* and yet I have no recollection of them whatsoever."

"I know it's a long shot, but it's the only potential tie I've been able to find."

"Good work."

A *ding* from a computer rang out.

"Hey Laura" said Brogan with a head nod, "Was that your computer?"

"Let me check" Donnelly replied. "Hmm... it's from Bennington P.D." She looked toward Nash, "The camera footage from the ATM at the time Daryl Wagner's card was used to make a withdrawal."

"Great" replied Nash, "Let's see it."

Nash and Brogan gathered at Donnelly's computer screen; Donnelly ran the video, a grainy black and white image emerged.

"Are you sure that's Wagner?" said Brogan.

"It's not like ATM cameras are state-of-the-art; it looks like him to me" Nash responded.

"Yeah, I guess so. He looks fidgety... nervous."

"He also looks like he's trying to communicate through the camera... mouthing a word."

"What??" said Brogan.

"Laura, back it up" said Nash.

Donnelly reversed the feed a few seconds and recommenced.

"Check it out" commented Nash, "He looks to his left as if to see if someone's watching him, then looks back at the ATM and mouths a one-syllable word, and then a quick glance back to his left... presumably to make sure he wasn't caught trying to send a message."

"Holy shit!" responded Brogan.

"Laura, can you run it again?" said Nash.

"Sure." Donnelly reversed the video feed and ran it again.

"See... right there!" Nash pointed out.

"Could he be saying 'Cobb'?" said Brogan.

"Damn sure looks like it."

"I wish we had this piece of info before we talked to him."

"I didn't have him high on my suspect list, but this video has sure caught my attention" said Nash.

"Nothing says we can't pay him another visit, right?"

"True, but I'd like to have additional ammo in my hip pocket first... so to speak."

Donnelly had stopped the feed once Wagner walked out of the frame.

Nash looked at Donnelly… "Let it continue to run; we may see whoever he was looking at."

"Got it" Donnelly replied. She resumed the feed.

"Anyone walking by in the background look familiar?" said Nash.

Brogan and Donnelly responded in unison, "Nope."

"Yeah, me neither" said Nash. She suddenly blurted out, "Wait; what was that?" as a vehicle drove by.

Donnelly reversed the feed and paused at the point where the vehicle was entering the view.

"Right there" said Nash. "Now advance it frame-by-frame."

Donnelly advanced the feed.

"Our black & white?" said Brogan.

"All we get is a side view" noted Nash, "So no plates we can attempt to read; plus it's across the street."

"It's a plain black & white, no jurisdiction on the side, just like the one we found."

"True. But there are dozens of them around here."

"The timing is interesting though" remarked Donnelly, "A black & white happens to drive by *right after* Wagner makes his withdrawal."

"Exactly" said Nash, "Any chance we can zero-in on the driver?"

Donnelly stopped the feed and zoomed-in, "Nope; too dark and too far away."

"Dammit." Nash paused in thought, "Back it up to Wagner making the withdrawal; let's see if his ring finger comes into view."

Donnelly reversed the feed.

"There it is – he's still wearing it" said Brogan.

"Do you think this is the point that he was abducted?" asked Donnelly.

"It's possible" said Nash, "But if that's the case we should have found *his* car abandoned somewhere nearby."

"Where *was* his car found?" said Brogan.

Donnelly started to rummage through her files, "Now that you mention it, I don't remember seeing anything about his car in the report."

"That should've been one of the first things they looked for when trying to seek out a missing person" noted Nash.

"You would think" stated Donnelly, "But there's no mention of his car other than the make and model."

"I suppose it could mean they looked for it, but didn't find it" said Brogan.

"If that's the case they should've identified where they looked, and why" remarked Nash.

"What's the make and model?" said Brogan.

"2002 Jeep Wrangler" replied Donnelly.

"Here's a thought" said Nash, "He rode the ferry to Seattle for work, right?"

"Correct."

"Unless he took the bus to the ferry terminal, either near his home or from a park-and-ride lot, you've got to figure he has long-term parking somewhere downtown."

"I guess it would make sense to check out both options… downtown parking lots and any park-and-rides near his home" said Brogan.

"Don't forget that he often stayed at his pal Decker's" said Nash, "So we need to check Decker's place, as well as park-and-rides near there."

"If there's a possible girlfriend we should probably look at *all* of the ones in this part of the County" added Donnelly.

"Good thinking" replied Nash. "We'll start with the most likely spots. If we strike-out then I'll talk to the various jurisdictions to include associated park-and-rides as part of their normal patrols."

"Should we get on that today?"

"If you happen to cruise by one of the lots this weekend and your curiosity is piqued go ahead and take a look, but otherwise we'll tackle it on Monday."

"So back to Wagner's ring…" Brogan prompted.

"With him still wearing his ring at this point" said Nash; pointing to the screen, "And we know it ended up under the passenger seat of the black & white, I'm thinking we can assume that the perp, or perps, are driving the car."

"But what about the car that was stolen… the burned-up sedan whose trunk was Wagner's final resting place?"

"Yeah, if Wagner was abducted either right before or during his ATM withdrawal, then the theory of one car following the other to the property seems to fall apart" commented Donnelly.

"Not necessarily" said Nash. "They could have already been at the property doing *whatever*, and at some point the perp, or perps, drove Wagner to the ATM and forced him to make the withdrawal."

"True; but does that mean that *Wagner* stole the arson car?" said Brogan. "And why the hell would he do that, it just doesn't make sense?!"

"Unless he was hiding something that we have yet to uncover" said Donnelly.

"That's definitely a possibility" remarked Nash. "Then again, if Wagner is truly saying *Cobb* in the video, maybe *Cobb's* the one who stole the car?"

"Sounds like we need to turn the screws on Cobb" said Brogan.

"I'll try to track his every movement from the time he got out of jail, until the night of Wagner's murder" commented Donnelly.

"And every move *since then* as well" said Nash, "His movements and actions *post*-murder could be telling."

"Got it."

"I'm going to go talk to Andrew Lloyd" stated Nash. "Laura, see what you can find on Cobb. Dirk, help Laura out on her search, unless there was something else you came in for today."

"I didn't have anything specific in mind" replied Brogan, "I just had a feeling that you two would be in."

"Alright then" said Nash. "And both of you… no more than a couple of hours, we can pick up again on Monday."

25

The drive to Key Peninsula was usually a time to get lost in one's thoughts, to escape the doldrums of the job, to relax and enjoy the scenery: Hills and valleys aplomb with evergreen trees interspersed with deciduous trees of yellow, orange, and red leaves reflecting early fall; along with the occasional inlet, bay, and harbor. But this drive was different – a rare excursion out of the County not in search of solitude, but in search of answers... to a murder.

Oh Nash had gotten lost in her thoughts alright, but those thoughts were engulfed in an attempt to make sense of a myriad of clues and riddles surrounding this case. It seemed that every time a question had been answered a new one arose. Not quite as frustrating as *one step forward two steps back* Nash realized; more like *two steps forward one step back*. Far from the ideal situation, *but at least progress was being made* Nash noted.

The current person of interest with whom Nash was seeking... Andrew Lloyd... could yet be just another unanswered riddle. Regardless of his claim to have *sold* the black & white former Police Cruiser that evidence shows was at the scene, he *is* the legal owner of the car. He is also known to have been in Key Peninsula the weekend of the crime... easily close enough to have traveled to Slaughter County, commit the crime, and get back to Key Peninsula in a single evening. And the fact that he attended high school with the victim's wife is an additional item of note. Are these all mere coincidences? Or is there more to the story?

Nash arrived at the address of Andrew Lloyd's parents, a rural home on the shores of Carr Inlet. She rang the doorbell; a late-twenties man answered the door.

"Andrew Lloyd?" said Nash.

"Yes" Lloyd replied.

"I'm Detective Nash with the Slaughter County Sheriff's Department; I appreciate you meeting me here at your parents' place... saved me a drive to Ruston."

"No problem. I understand you have questions about the Crown Vic I used to own?"

"That's correct."

"I'm a little confused; I already talked to some Bennington cops."

"I didn't want to get into details on the phone, but the case has been transferred to me, for reasons I will address shortly. For starters though, I was wondering if you happen to know a *Daryl Wagner?*"

Lloyd shook his head, "The name doesn't ring a bell."

"You went to South Slaughter High, correct?"

"Yes. Is he a former classmate of mine?"

"No, but how about a *Madison Sinclair?*"

"I knew *of* her, but I didn't really know her."

"How was it that you knew of her?"

"Not to sound sexist or anything, but she was one of the hottest girls in school, so she caught the attention of all of us guys."

"Did you have any classes together?"

"A few of them over the years, but as near as I could tell she didn't even know I existed."

"And you haven't bumped into her since high school?"

"Actually I have, last year at the reunion, she even walked over and said hello, which surprised me... said she remembered me from Speech class, that I had the best speech."

"That must have been one memorable speech."

"We were supposed to do a three-minute speech on *how to do something.* Most of the guys talked about how to do stuff with their car... tune-up, oil change, junk like that; and a lot of the girls talked about scrapbooking, doing makeup and stuff."

"Basically gender stereotypical stuff."

"Yeah; so I decided to be different, and hopefully a little humorous… mine was *How to get out of a three-minute speech.*"

"Very clever; I can see how that would be memorable."

"Thanks. Anyway, I didn't get to talk to her very long at the reunion because of her husband."

"Her husband? Did you meet him… talk to him?"

"No, he was over at the bar area. But Madison said she couldn't chat very long because he was the *overprotective jealous type* and might make a scene like he did earlier."

"Earlier at the reunion?"

"Apparently. She said she was talking to another classmate… a guy… when her husband came by, gave the guy a look like he wanted to kick his ass, and then grabbed *her* by the upper arm and said to her… *Who the hell is this?*"

"Referring to the guy she was talking to?"

"Yeah. She told him they were just talking about a class they had together. And then he said something like *You're with ME, right? MY wife?*"

"Like he owned her… like she was a piece of his property."

"She told him *Yes;* and then he got in the guy's face and told him to scram. It sounded like they almost duked-it-out. Anyway, he must have jerked her arm pretty bad because it was all red… you could see the outline of his fingers."

"And how did Madison seem about all that?"

"I could tell she was embarrassed by his actions; but the worst part is that she seemed really scared of him. I couldn't figure out *why for the life of me* she was *with* such a guy."

"Unfortunately, it appears to have been a recurring theme – his actions toward her and anyone who tried to interact with her."

"Why are you asking me about her anyway, I thought you had questions about the car I sold?"

"I'll explain that momentarily; but yes, let's go ahead and talk about the car."

"What do you want to know?"

"You told the Bennington Officers that you couldn't recall the name of the guy you sold the car to."

"Correct."

"I don't suppose your recollection has improved since then?"

"I thought I had it written down somewhere, but I haven't been able to find it. Thinking back though it might have been something like Overton maybe."

"First name?"

"No clue."

"Do you have a phone number for him?"

"Let me check."

Lloyd broke out his phone and scrolled through the calls. "This must be it here" he said as he showed it to Nash.

Nash wrote down the number in her memo pad.

"Thanks. Can you describe him?"

Lloyd's face scrunched-up, his eyes squinted... "Let's see... between five-ten and six-feet, average-to-athletic build, mustache, dark hair."

"Eye color?"

"Couldn't tell you; he was wearing sunglasses... aviator type... reminded me of a motorcycle cop."

"Any identifying marks or tattoos?"

Lloyd shrugged, "I saw the guy one time, for about a half-hour, weeks ago... I don't remember anything like that."

"Okay, tell me about the sale: From the point he contacted you, until you handed him the keys."

"I advertised it online and that same day this guy called about it. One of the first things he asked was if the car was in Seattle, even though that's what was stated in the ad."

"Any idea why he questioned that?"

"It was because my phone number's a 253 area code."

"And not a 206."

"Yep. I told him it was at my brother's place in the U-district; he said that was good because Seattle was much more convenient for him than somewhere in the two-five-three."

Nash jotted notes... the statement having led her to ponder the buyer's locale.

Lloyd continued... "I told him I'd be at my brother's place Friday afternoon because we were going to a car show the next morning."

"Friday?"

"The eleventh. We met downtown around four o'clock that afternoon. He checked out the car, we haggled a little, but since he was a cash buyer..."

"You gave him a deal" Nash interceded.

"Sure, when cash talks I listen."

"You also told the Bennington Officers that you didn't fill out the *Report of Sale*."

"He said he'd take care of it, so he handed me the cash and I signed-off the pink slip."

"You mean the green *Certificate of Ownership* – the Title."

"Well, yeah... *pink slip* is just what everyone calls it."

"Understood. And why were you okay with *him* filling out the Report of Sale?"

"I had the cash in-hand and he said he'd take care of it."

"You realize there's a reason for that Report: It keeps *you* from getting nailed if the *buyer* has a parking violation, fails to pay a bridge toll, the car gets towed, or in *this* case... the car gets involved in the commission of a crime."

"A crime? I had no idea; I just thought the guy crashed it into a ditch and you didn't know that I sold it."

"You really think a Detective from Slaughter County is going to come all the way down here for a car that ended up in a ditch?"

"I thought that all seemed a bit weird, but how should I know?"

Something else came to Lloyd's mind… "Another reason I didn't have any concerns about the *Report of Sale* thing is because, besides him saying he'd take care of it, he also said *'You can trust law enforcement, right?'* So, of course I figured it was all good."

"He said he was in law enforcement?"

"Yeah."

"Did he say where?"

"No; but I assume Seattle or somewhere else in King County."

"Do you remember anything else about him?"

"Not really; it was a super brief exchange, like he was in a hurry… kept looking at his watch, didn't even test drive the car: We did the deal, he handed over the cash, I signed-off the pink slip, gave him the keys, and he drove away."

"Which way did he drive?"

"Down under the viaduct… heading north."

"Well, that's about all that I had" said Nash as she folded-up her memo pad.

"You said you were going to tell me why you were asking about Madison Sinclair."

"Oh, that's right" said Nash. "Madison's husband was the victim of a crime, and your old Police Interceptor was at the scene."

"Wow… is he okay?"

"I'm afraid not – he was murdered."

"Geez; sorry I asked."

Nash extended her hand, "Thanks for your time."

"You're welcome."

Nash got in her car and made a phone call – Donnelly answered.

"Hey Laura" said Nash, "Before you leave the office, which I'm expecting will be *soon*" she hinted, "I have a phone number for you to jot down. Don't take the time to look it up right now, but I'd like it to be one of the first things you tackle Monday morning…"

26

An early-autumn Sunday in Northern California wine country: A late afternoon breeze had cooled the eighty-degree day to a comfortable low seventies; perfect for lounging out on the patio of a small boutique winery in the Russian River Valley, sipping a glass of Zinfandel, and letting the doldrums of the previous week become nothing more than a faded memory.

Wine glass in hand, feet perched upon an adjacent chair, gazing out upon rows and rows of grape vines, she took a sip... *"It doesn't get much better than this"* she thought to herself.

A voice rang out from behind her, "Hey Em, I see you couldn't wait to pop the cork."

"It's been a rough week" Emily replied.

Emily set her glass down, grabbed the wine bottle, and poured a glass for Ashley.

"Ooh, the Reserve Zin with one-hundred-percent zinfandel grapes" remarked Ashley.

"Nothing but the best for Comrades in Arms."

Ashley swirled her wine glass, held it up to examine the color, and proposed a toast... "To Comrades in Arms."

Wine glasses were clinked together, a sip was taken, and an exhale from a long day... or in Emily's case, a long week.

"Thank goodness that four o'clock is the standard closing time for wineries these days, otherwise we'd never get the chance to close up shop and relax before sunset" said Ashley.

"And we're just a small boutique winery" commented Emily, "Can you imagine the craziness of the Big Houses?"

"Been there, done that."

"That makes two of us; why do think Brandon and I bought into this little gem?"

"Yeah, how did all of that happen anyway?"

"Completely different paths that somehow converged at a single point in time."

"Kismet!"

"You could say that" Emily replied. "Brandon graduated from Berkeley with a Computer Science Degree and immediately landed at a Tech firm in Silicon Valley; I went the JC route and became a wine buyer and then a sommelier for an upscale restaurant in Carmel."

"So, how did you two meet and subsequently end up as owners of a winery way up here in the Russian River Valley?"

"Being a wine buyer and sommelier I had numerous interactions with California wineries; one day I got a job offer from a winery along the foothills of the Santa Cruz Mountains… in San Martin to be specific."

"That's a logical progression for *you,* but how does Brandon go from being a computer geek… no offense… to owning a winery."

Emily smiled, "Computer geek was quite accurate, although with a sense of style, and rather laid back; which is why the whole *Corporate Gig* didn't work for him: Long hours, almost always on-call, worked a lot of weekends, and the worst part – was required to take his laptop with him on vacations… *just in case something came up.*"

"Sounds awful."

"Tell me about it. Anyway, he'd always been into wine, learned the trade, socked a bunch of money away, became a sommelier, and one day decided to say *Adios* to Corporate life."

"You two ended up working at the same winery?"

"No, but we crossed paths at various events… one thing led to another, and here we are. It took most of his savings to buy into this place, and we were living on the edge for a while, but thanks to wine's growing popularity things are quite comfortable now."

"Sounds like an ideal match."

"It was a fairy tale for sure, but we have our hills and valleys... our ups and downs... just like any married couple, especially lately."

"The *rough week* you mentioned?"

"Yeah; he got into an accident on his business trip to Seattle a week ago... really messed him up."

"That's why I haven't seen him? I just assumed he was still on the trip. He's not bedridden or on crutches or anything like that, is he?"

"No, but he still has lots of aches and pains. Physically he *looks* much better, but he got a concussion and then took the flight home against the recommendation of the doctor. So now, beyond the physical aches and pains, are almost-constant headaches. And worse, he is mentally out-of-it."

"Out-of-it? Like how?"

"A whole array of stuff... like he's off in another world at times... difficulty focusing, memory problems, fatigue, irritability, depression, sleep disturbances. It's like an entire checklist of concussion symptoms."

"At least you know the cause."

"It's still not very comforting."

"I didn't mean to pooh-pooh it; I just meant it's not something unknown... like a possible brain tumor."

"That's true; I hadn't even thought of that possibility."

"What was the accident?"

"A car wreck – got T-boned by another car; at least that's what he says."

"You have a reason to question his account?"

"If he gets together with his buddies for drinks after work he can have too much to drink without realizing it. Because of that I'm always the designated driver when I'm with him, but if the guys don't realize he's had too much to drink..."

"They don't stop him or call a cab?"

"Unfortunately, no. He could end up like one of those *Hangover* movies."

"He gets that bad?"

"Sometimes."

"And you wonder if that might have been the case in Seattle?"

"I have no idea, I just wonder about it."

"But if that was the case he'd have gotten thrown in jail and wouldn't have made the flight home."

"Yeah" Emily conceded, "I guess I've been worrying about it for no good reason."

"Does he seem to be improving at all?"

"In some ways, but the whole thing must have been pretty traumatic, he keeps waking up in the middle of the night – jerking awake like he's reliving the crash. At other times his nightmare is not of the crash but of *being chased by a bad guy*. Even when he naps during the daytime he'll suddenly awaken and has a look on his face like he just saw a ghost."

"Wow, has he been to see a doctor since he got back?"

"No; he says he'll be fine as soon as the concussion symptoms go away. And instead of seeing a doctor he uses NFL players as an example… *'most all players in the concussion protocol are out two weeks'*."

"Men sure seem to have a thing about doctors, don't they?"

Emily rolled her eyes. "No kidding" she said; followed by a sip of wine.

Ashley took a sip as well; then replied… "Hopefully that means he'll be back to normal in another week then, right?"

"Let's hope" Emily replied, "As you can imagine it has affected our love life, too."

"Sorry to hear that. And you mentioned memory loss has been an issue as well?"

"Yeah. Sometimes it's people, sometimes events; it can be simple little things or something big, even some stuff associated with work. He's been spending a lot of time on the computer trying to get back up-to-speed, re-engage his memory and such, and it seems to be working.

On the downside, it's like being married to either a workaholic or a pornaholic... he's on the computer morning, noon, and night; in fact he's probably on his computer as we speak."

"And he's been irritable?" Ashley continued, "Toward you?"

"A little bit" replied Emily, "But mostly getting frustrated and mad at himself... like a toddler who tries to do something and keeps failing. What was *really* weird... he looked through an old family photo album and something really seemed to bother him."

"From the album?"

"I don't know, he wouldn't say."

"Maybe he suffered some traumatic event as a kid?"

"And it came back to the forefront?" replied Emily, "Could be; but like I said, he won't talk about it."

"Well, let's hope he's better soon."

"Yeah" Emily concurred, "And whatever demons out there chasing him evaporate into a puff of smoke before he, *himself*, gets lost in the nightmare."

27

Nervously scanning news agency websites he stopped and reviewed the current edition of the *Slaughter County Journal* – not a single update to his story of interest. He jumped over to the *Seattle Times* – same response. He sought out other news sources in an almost frantic manner: Other counties in Western Washington, major publications like *USA Today*, even crime reporter blogs – little or no coverage in each of those circumstances.

It had become a daily ritual – seeking news, *anything*, in regard to the arson and murder in Slaughter County that was first reported the previous Monday. For the most part, any and all news had been a whole lot of nothing... *"snippets of superfluous bullshit"* from his perspective.

Oh sure, they had updated the status from *'a potential* homicide' to *'the coroner has ruled it a homicide'.* And they had finally identified the victim, his hometown, and where he worked; but *that* story sounded more like an obituary than providing any substance in regard to a murder investigation.

The frustration was building... his mind raced... *"How can there not be periodic, if not daily, updates to this story; are the cops being mum, or are the journalists a bunch of slackers? Where the hell are the investigative reporters?! Solve the damn case already; I don't want to spend the rest of my life looking over my damn shoulder!"*

The event was taking its toll on him... the bumps, bruises, and physical scars from the accident were nothing in comparison to the emotional wear and tear. It was difficult waking up each morning wondering; and going to bed each night *still* wondering.

He considered making an anonymous phone call... *"Hey, I saw someone who might be the victim with so-and-so"*, but he decided not just yet… there *had* to be a way to solve the case without his involvement; there *had* to be sufficient evidence.

28

'Beep-beep-beep-beep' *smack*... she hit the *Snooze* button even though she had no intention of snoozing for another ten minutes; her action was simply a backup... in case, for some crazy reason, she conked-out before she was ready to roll out of bed.

She looked at the clock. She wasn't sure why; she knew it would read 5:10... *5:11* if she was slow at turning over and taking a peek. Sure enough it was five-ten – another five to seven minutes to collect her thoughts before jumping in the shower.

Fresh out of the shower and clad in her robe, she made her way to the kitchen. She opened the freezer, grabbed two frozen waffles, and popped them into the toaster.

While the toaster *did its thing* she filled a cup halfway via the insta-hot dispenser... just enough fluid to wash down the toaster waffles. Within the steaming water she steeped a tea bag.

She repeatedly checked her watch as she chowed-down the waffles and gulped-down her tea.

Her metabolism sufficiently kick-started she pulled her hair back into a ponytail, brushed her teeth, threw on a pair of pants and button-down shirt, and ventured out the door. She was right on schedule... five-forty.

Walking through the door to the office she checked her watch... *5:57.* The lights came on as she entered; as usual she was the first to arrive. She didn't even stop at her desk; number one priority – get the coffee brewing.

With coffee slowly trickling into the decanter, she finally proceeded to her desk. *"Hmm… no sticky-note updates from Donnelly or Brogan"* she thought to herself.

She walked over to the murder board. She spied a note… *Wagner's Jeep.* Underneath the note was *5th & Harbor.* Another new entry caught her eye… *Call to Andrew Lloyd.* Under that item read *Pay phone near ferry terminal…* there was a red arrow pointing to this item.

She briefly pondered the new entries on the board and then strolled back to the Break Room. The coffee was still brewing but she couldn't wait – she grabbed the decanter mid-trickle, poured herself a cup, and reset the decanter on the burner.

The door to the office opened and shut. When Nash returned to the office area there stood Donnelly.

"It looks like you got answers to a couple of items of interest this weekend: Wagner's Jeep; and the phone number I gave you" said Nash.

"I also got some crazy news about the previous owners of the cabin" replied Donnelly, "I almost called you about it."

"Why didn't you?"

"You told us to keep Saturday brief, and to *not* show up on Sunday."

"True, but for future reference a phone call is fine."

The door opened and in walked Brogan.

"Is Dirk privy to these updates?" Nash said to Donnelly while thumb-pointing at Brogan.

"Am I privy to *what?*" Brogan responded before Donnelly had a chance to reply.

"Yes, he is" said Donnelly.

Brogan looked confused; Donnelly filled-in the blanks: "Wagner's Jeep; and the phone call Kenz had us look up."

"Oh *those*" responded Brogan.

"Let's hear it" said Nash.

"I found Wagner's Jeep in a long-term parking lot downtown" said Brogan.

"Fifth and Harbor according to the board" Nash noted.

"Yep. It was locked, so I haven't done anything with it yet."

"No problem; I'll get hold of Lowell and we'll do a preliminary inspection at the lot and then get it towed to the garage."

"And the phone number you had me look up..." Donnelly started.

"I thought I told you to wait on that until this morning?" Nash interrupted.

"Curiosity got the best of me; besides, it was a quick look-up... a pay phone downtown near the ferry terminal... the *exact same* phone that was used to activate the burner phone."

"The reason behind the red arrow on the board, I assume?"

"It seemed worth highlighting."

"That could be telling; don't you think, Kenz?" added Brogan.

"A nice thought, but unlikely – it's the *most used* pay phone in the city *by far*... considering its location near the ferry terminal, restaurants, parking garages, and coffee shops."

"I get where you're coming from, but I'd like to keep that possibility in-play if you don't mind."

"Sure; you never know."

"Something else I was thinking..." said Brogan, "With Wagner appearing to say *Cobb* on the video, and a black & white driving by soon thereafter, maybe Cobb's the buyer of the black & white?"

"I was wondering the same thing before I talked to Lloyd, but it couldn't be Cobb *if* Lloyd's story about the time and date of sale is accurate – Cobb was just getting released from jail here in Slaughter County at the time Lloyd was selling the car in Seattle."

"The story you got from Lloyd eliminates Cobb as a suspect?" said Donnelly.

"No, only as the buyer of the black & white; and *that's* only if Lloyd is correct on the date of the alleged sale."

"What all *did* you get from Lloyd?" asked Brogan.

"He advertised it on the web, got called about it that same day... from the pay phone near the ferry terminal according to what you two found out. He met the buyer in downtown Seattle late afternoon Friday the eleventh, the buyer paid cash, Lloyd signed over the title, and that was it."

"Did he recall the buyer's name; or at least provide you a description?"

"He said the guy was about five-ten to six-feet, average-to-athletic build, mustache, dark hair, wore sunglasses."

"Outside of the timing and the mustache it could be Cobb. And even though the *Cobb* that *we* met doesn't have a mustache, he could have had one at the time."

"The timing not withstanding; Lloyd said he thought the guy's name was Overton or something like that, although we should always take someone's recollection of a name with a grain of salt" Nash replied. "The other piece that doesn't align with Cobb is that he said the guy was a cop from Seattle or somewhere else in King County."

"He said the guy was a cop??"

Nash flipped through her memo pad, "His exact words were: *He was with Law Enforcement.*"

"Hell, that could be a security guard, works for the Department of Corrections, a Park Ranger, a bailiff, or even one of the Parking Police... the updated version of a Meter Maid."

"Good catch Dirk, I definitely made the leap to *cop* on that one... thanks for keeping me honest."

"Sure. No first name though?"

"Unfortunately... no."

"If he was in law enforcement in Seattle or King County, why would he be calling from the Bennington ferry terminal?"

"Maybe he lives in Slaughter County, but works in Seattle?" responded Donnelly.

"Or he was over this way for some other reason – family, friends, grabbing a bite at *The Harborside Fish House*, checking out the Navy Museum..." added Nash.

"The guy doesn't have a cell phone?" said Brogan.

"Some of the job possibilities you described are not exactly raking in the big bucks."

"True, but even fast food workers have cell phones, and they aren't making diddly-squat. Besides, at the very least go pick up a pre-paid. It seems odd to me; if not downright suspicious."

"I'll start running the name and see what I can find" responded Donnelly.

"Make sure your search takes into account all of the points Dirk just made, *and* includes possible ties with the vic and with any of the persons of interest" commented Nash.

"Of course."

"The timing, along with the name Overton, kind of clinches it that it wasn't Cobb, don't you think?" said Brogan.

"For the black & white, yes" responded Nash, "But for the *murder itself* he's still on the radar screen, unless he has an alibi that clears him."

"No, he doesn't" Donnelly added, "Or if he *does* he has not shared that information."

"You traced his movements?"

"As much as I was able... he doesn't leave much of a trail."

Donnelly grabbed Cobb's file and scanned the pages, "We know he was at the *White Pig* the night he was released... the eleventh. The next day, Saturday, he bought groceries at *Super Mart* at one-thirty-seven in the afternoon; and Sunday he was back at work." She put the file down and finished... "As far as the other key dates: He *was* in the vicinity the weekend that the arson car was stolen, and there's nothing to refute, or corroborate, his story about being home alone the night of the murder... the twenty-sixth."

"No cell phone activity that night?" Nash said.

"If he has one it's a pre-paid; his only *registered* phone is a landline."

"Well, a pre-paid burner would do the trick" noted Brogan.

"What about his financials?" Nash asked Donnelly.

"Not much" Donnelly replied, "He's mainly a paycheck-to-paycheck guy."

"It looks like our best bet is to link him to the buyer, *if and when* we can determine who *that* is" said Brogan.

"I agree" stated Nash. "And before I visit Cobb again or bring him in for questioning, I'd like to have a few more nuggets beyond Wagner calling out his name at the ATM." She pondered for a moment and added, "Although I must admit that one item is pretty powerful all by itself."

"Answers like *being able to tie him to the stolen car or to the guy that bought the black & white?*" replied Brogan.

"Exactly."

"Oh, and you said that before you talk to Cobb again you wanted to talk to Officer Roberson" Donnelly chimed in, "To get his perspective regarding the night he took Cobb into custody."

"That's right" said Brogan, "And to get his and Officer Stahl's input about Daryl and Madison Wagner."

"I'll see if I can get an audience with those two this afternoon" said Nash. She took a sip of her coffee and focused back on the murder board.

"Ready for my crazy news about the previous owners of the cabin?" stated Donnelly.

"Absolutely."

"Charles and Maxine Stillwater... the previous owners..."

"Yeah?" Nash interrupted.

"They are Daryl Wagner's grandparents."

"Are you shittin' me?!" responded Brogan.

"Stillwater?" replied Nash.

"On his Mother's side" Donnelly clarified, "Thus the different last name."

"That must be the reason the property was selected" said Brogan.

"It also might answer the question as to where Wagner stayed the nights he was unaccounted-for" said Nash. "Possibly had a key; which would explain why there were no signs of forced entry."

"That would mean that Wagner *willingly* went to the property with the killer" said Donnelly.

"Or the killer was familiar with the property; such as a family friend or acquaintance" Nash replied. "I've got to get on the horn with Lowell and see if they've finished processing the cabin."

Nash grabbed her desk phone, hit the *Hands-free* button, and dialed Lowell's number. A couple of rings echoed through the phone; followed by, "Lowell."

"Hey Evan, it's Kenz; Dirk and Laura are here with me, I've got you on the speaker."

"I was just about to give you a call, but *you first*" Lowell replied.

"A couple of things..." Nash started, "We found Daryl Wagner's car in a downtown parking lot – *Fifth and Harbor*; I was thinking you could meet me there and we could do a preliminary inspection and then get it towed to the garage."

"Sounds good to me; when did you want to meet?"

"Does *soon after we hang up here* work for you?"

"Sure."

"The other thing I had" said Nash, "is that we found out that the previous owners of the cabin were Daryl Wagner's grandparents on his Mother's side."

"That would presumably explain the lack of forced entry."

"That's what we were thinking."

"Along those lines, I have results from our search there... at the cabin; that's what I was calling you about."

"Go for it."

"The glass in the sink – it had traces of GHB and saliva... the saliva yielded a DNA match to Wagner."

"So, *that's* how the perp got the drop on him... drugged him."

"Also, there was a partial print on the hot water handle, but no match in AFIS."

"That figures. But at least we can try to match it up with our persons of interest."

"I swabbed the bathroom sink and the lab found the following chemicals: Stearic acid, triethanolamine, isobutane, laureth-23, lauryl sulfate, and propane."

"Ethanol, butane, and propane? Was someone cleaning a carburetor in the sink, or what?"

"It might make a little more sense when I add the following… aloe."

"Aloe??"

"And evenly cut hairs, along with traces of blood."

"You're not telling me that all of those chemicals add up to shaving cream?"

"Yep."

"And you couldn't just say that up front, you had to be semi-cryptic and provide me a list of chemicals?"

"Sorry… couldn't resist."

"Do they match Wagner?"

"The blood does, which was all we needed."

"Are you telling me that Wagner shaved before he was murdered?"

"Or someone shaved him."

"Okay, that's just too creepy to even think about; why the hell would anyone do that?"

"I have no idea, but it's got to be one or the other."

"Were there prints, blood, or traces of DNA *other than* Wagner's on any of the items?"

"George and Mary Montgomery, but obviously they're not suspects."

"Knowing that the cabin used to be in the Wagner family I was thinking we should go take a fresh look at it."

"Great minds think alike" replied Lowell.

Something suddenly clicked with Nash, "It just dawned on me that this news could actually work against us."

"A person of interest or suspect who knows Wagner could claim that they'd been at the cabin before and *that* is the reason their DNA is there?"

"Correct" said Nash, who quickly reconsidered her concern, "But I have ways to hopefully trip them up if I run into that scenario."

"Of course you do."

"If that's all you've got what say we meet up at Wagner's car downtown; and once we're done there we head out to the cabin?"

"See you there" responded Lowell.

Nash hung up the phone.

Brogan and Donnelly had the look as if they'd just been given a shot of Novocain.

"Holy Crap!" said Brogan.

"Yeah" responded Nash. She grabbed her gear and started toward the door, "I'll give you two a call when Lowell and I are ready to drive out to the cabin."

29

The stop at the downtown parking lot to investigate Daryl Wagner's Jeep was a brief sojourn for Nash and Lowell. Nothing within the vehicle indicated foul play, which was of no surprise to them; in fact their only surprise was that the Jeep sat for a week in a parking lot and had not been broken into or vandalized. In reality there was nothing worth taking... no laptop, no briefcase, no expensive sunglasses, no fancy stereo, nothing of value whatsoever... but that hadn't stopped scofflaws in the past.

The search yielded little: Four ferry schedules – only one of which was current, a pen-sized tire gauge, various receipts which may or may not turn out to be noteworthy, and the vehicle registration. Next stop for Wagner's Jeep would be a dusting for prints and a more extensive forensic search at the garage. As for Nash and Lowell; the earlier discovery that Daryl Wagner's grandparents had owned the cabin... the property whose location hosted his hideous death... prompted a revisit to the scene in search of any overlooked pieces that might solve the puzzle.

Nash and Lowell were greeted at the cabin by Brogan and Donnelly standing on the porch. The two of them had awaited Nash and Lowell's arrival for two reasons: Professional courtesy along with the fact that Nash was the boss; and the *Crime Scene – No Entry* notice sealed on the door.

Lowell stepped up to the door with his Forensics kit in hand, extricated a fresh *Crime Scene* notice from the kit, verified all of the proper documentation, and sliced through the existing notice. He then stepped aside and gestured for the team to enter.

Nash, Brogan, and Donnelly entered and then stood still just inside the entryway.

As Lowell entered Brogan inquired, "What are we looking for?"

"Anything we might have missed" responded Nash, who immediately walked over to the magazine-rack table.

She took a fresh look at the circular water spots on the table and directed a question to Lowell… "You said the glass we found had traces of saliva and DNA?"

"Correct" Lowell replied.

"But no fingerprints?"

"Nope."

"You're telling me they made a point of wiping the glass clean, yet left evidence in the glass?"

"Go figure, right?"

"Why does this case seem to be filled with contradictions?"

"Your guess is as good as mine on that one, but I have to admit it's starting to get under my skin."

"Something else just dawned on me" said Nash.

"What's that?"

"I think we were jumping to crazy conclusions regarding the indications of Wagner shaving, *or being shaved,* before he was murdered."

"How do you mean?"

"His overnight whereabouts after Tuesday the twenty-second are unaccounted-for. Logic dictates he stayed here at least one, if not all, of those nights; so he could have shaved those mornings before going to work."

"But he had a beard in the ATM video?" Donnelly chimed in.

"I'm not talking about shaving his beard off" Nash replied, "I'm talking about under his chin and the front of his neck… you know… grooming."

"I can't believe I hadn't considered that" remarked Lowell, "But you're right, it makes a lot more sense than a creep-a-zoid killer that shaves his victims."

"Yeah; I'm still trying to erase that mental picture from my brain" responded Nash.

"You implied that he could've stayed *elsewhere* on some of those nights?" Lowell said.

"His wife Madison made some great conjectures regarding him having a girlfriend. We haven't found any such person, but we can't discount the possibility." Nash then followed with… "Have the Cyber guys found anything on the home computer?"

"No report thus far, but I expect them to be done any day now."

"How about the rest of the house; especially the idea that the killer may have broken in and taken the burner phone she bought?"

"We found no indication of forced entry" Lowell replied. "That doesn't mean that the house had not been entered, but it would've been via an unlocked door or window, or someone with a key."

"Or she left the phone in her car and *that's* where it was stolen from" stated Brogan.

"Now *there's* a thought" replied Nash.

"As far as the rest of the house goes" stated Lowell, "the only thing close to eye-popping was an empty gun case. Madison confirmed that Daryl had a gun, and a search of records shows that he's the registered owner of a three-fifty-seven magnum. Have you guys turned up anything like that?"

"No; and it obviously did him no good."

"What if it did?" Donnelly countered.

"In what way?" said Brogan.

"Did anyone check hospitals for a patient with a gunshot wound that night?"

"Good question" said Nash, "Take that for action."

Donnelly wrote down the item in her memo pad.

"Hey Evan, what about the gym bag and its contents?" said Nash.

"Forensics matched everything to Daryl. There were indications of potential fingerprints on the note, but they were smudged – unusable. We were hoping for some touch-DNA but no luck. And we compared the handwriting with samples we got from the Wagner home – no match to Daryl or Madison."

"You really thought one of them might have written it?" commented Brogan.

"No, but you can never discount *possibilities* no matter how unlikely or crazy they might seem. For example, the wife could have written the note as a means to make the husband think someone is watching him and perhaps he'd stop the abuse. And although I can't think of a reason off the top of my head why Daryl would've written the note himself, we often find cases of people trying to pass off their works as being someone else's, usually in an attempt to defraud, but also in an attempt to implicate someone else, or merely to deflect or divert the investigator's attention."

"Then where do we stand on the note?" prodded Nash.

"We're basically at an impasse until we get information that leads us to other samples for comparison" replied Lowell.

Nash looked at Brogan and Donnelly, "That's where *we* all come in."

"What about Cobb?" said Brogan.

"He's at the top of the list; it's just a matter of obtaining a sample."

Brogan looked around the cabin, "What's our primary focus this go-round?"

"We got all of the big stuff last time" replied Lowell, "But since it was considered at most a tertiary scene there could be little nooks and crannies that may not have received the attention deserved with the knowledge that the victim's family had owned the property."

"Seek out nooks and crannies, aye" said Brogan as he headed toward the area he had previously investigated – the bathroom.

With only a toilet, sink, and medicine cabinet occupying the bathroom space Brogan figured the odds of finding something new were slim-to-none, but he dove-in nonetheless. He pulled the lid off of the toilet tank – other than the water there was nothing but rusted components. The sink was wall-mounted – no cabinet underneath with which to store or hide anything. He opened the medicine cabinet; it was metal… no chance of a secret compartment within or behind it. He mentally scratched the bathroom off of his list.

Donnelly followed Brogan's lead; in her case to the enclosed back porch and mud room.

Nash and Lowell were moving furniture around as if they were checking for dust bunnies. In reality they were searching for loose slats that might reveal a repository; but to no avail. They checked under the dining table for a leaf that might be hiding something. No leaf; and no secret envelope taped underneath the table like you see in the movies.

Brogan returned to his previous discovery – the sleeper sofa. He extracted the mattress-portion. He looked underneath the mattress; then lifted it up to make sure he hadn't missed anything. The last place to check was the space between the seatback cushion and the mattress. He slid his hand between the two and came up empty.

Donnelly had struck out in the mud room, Nash and Lowell were finding nothing in the living area, and Brogan had come up empty in the bathroom and the sleeper sofa; the entire operation was looking like an exercise in futility, all that was left was the kitchen.

Donnelly was the first to focus on the kitchen – opening the cabinet doors underneath the sink. Attached to the inside of one of the doors was a small towel rack; a hand towel draped over the bar. There were two small bins on the floor of the cabinet… one with cleaning supplies, the other presumably either for trash or recyclables. She removed the bins. The bottom of the cabinet was covered in contact paper of the same type as those in the kitchen drawers and cabinets. She knocked on the bottom of the cabinet; it sounded hollow underneath… not a big surprise but it begged a question…

"Hey Lowell" said Donnelly, "Did anyone check underneath the cabinet bottom here?"

"Not that I'm aware of" Lowell replied; "It seemed to be rigidly in place, not as though it was easily removable to support storage of any kind."

"Maybe that's the point" countered Nash; "A nice tight fit to make it the perfect hiding spot?"

"Well hell… let's rip it out" said Lowell.

Donnelly started pulling and tugging to no avail; with exception that the bottom moved very slightly upward… about an eighth of an inch. "It's not nailed down" she stated, "but I'll need a screwdriver or pry bar to get it any further."

"I've got both" replied Lowell. He grabbed his kit, walked over to the sink, retrieved a screwdriver, and stuck the tip under the gap that Donnelly had created. He then slid the screwdriver the length of the board, lifting slightly as he progressed in order to provide a gap along the entire front section. With the screwdriver at one corner and a pry bar at the other, he simultaneously pushed down on them to leverage the board upward – 'Pop' went the board as it released its grip. He lifted the front of the board by hand to a near vertical position, the rear edge of the board acting as a pivot point.

"Well, what do you know" Lowell stated. In plain view was a wallet. He retrieved it, opened it, and proclaimed… "Daryl Wagner's."

Lowell handed the wallet to Nash; she immediately started to flip through the contents.

"A number of credit cards, but no cash" stated Nash.

Lowell resumed rummaging through the space and extracted a key ring; one key stood out – a key to a Jeep. The keys went to Nash and subsequently an evidence bag.

The next grasp produced a wristwatch; it followed the path of the key ring.

There was nothing else within Lowell's vantage point, so he got down on his stomach and reached in *sight unseen* as much as he was able.

"Holy shit" he said – extracting a .357 magnum revolver.

"Didn't you say that Wagner was the registered owner of a three-fifty-seven?" said Nash.

"I wouldn't be surprised if this is it" replied Lowell as he handed the gun to Nash, "I'll check the serial number when I get it back to the lab."

Nash examined the weapon, "I'm not seeing any obvious prints." She sniffed the gun, and then released and spun the cylinder, "It has *not* been recently fired; and the chambers are full." She removed the bullets, placed them in an evidence bag, placed the gun in a separate bag, and turned to Donnelly, "You can cancel that search for a gunshot victim."

Donnelly lined through the associated entry in her memo pad.

"What do you think?" said Brogan.

"I'm thinking that for some reason Wagner had his gun in his possession; the killer or killers got the gun away from him and turned it on him, and that's how he, or they, were able to control Wagner before drugging him" replied Nash.

"Why not just use the gun to kill him instead of drugging and then strangling him?"

"They were worried it would be too loud, perhaps?"

"And why stash it; why not just keep it?" said Donnelly.

"Maybe they were concerned about getting pulled over near the scene and didn't want to be in possession of a gun that belonged to a murder victim" replied Nash.

"But they could have just chucked it into the bay instead" commented Brogan.

"Since Wagner had no *current* ties to this property maybe the killer figured no one would ever look here?" said Donnelly.

"The problem with *that* theory is that the murder *occurred* on this property, so the odds would've been high that this place and surrounding grounds would be searched in detail" replied Nash. "Even if we *were* a little late regarding the depth of such a search" she admitted.

Lowell looked somewhat dejected, "If it's like everything else we've found tied to the scene it will have been wiped clean."

"Sheesh Evan, you're becoming bitter and jaded" said Nash, "What happened to Mister *'The glass is always half-full'*?"

"The perp dumped out the contents of the glass and then wiped the damn thing clean."

Lowell was not alone in his frustration, "It's like he's always one step ahead of us" said Brogan.

"A binge watcher of Forensics shows perhaps?" commented Donnelly.

"Or he knows what we look for when processing a scene" countered Nash.

"Are you implying something there, Kenz?" said Lowell.

"Just keeping an open mind."

30

Nash entered the Bennington Police Station; two uniformed Officers, one male and one female sitting at adjacent desks, looked up to see who had entered.

Nash made eye contact with the man, and then glanced at the plaque on his desk… it read *Officer M. Roberson.* She refocused her attention to him as he stood up. The female Officer followed her contemporary's lead and stood up as well.

Nash extended her hand, "Officers Roberson and Stahl?"

"Detective Nash I assume?" replied Roberson.

"I appreciate you taking the time to talk to me" said Nash as she shook hands with each of them.

"Not all, we're happy to help in any way we can."

Stahl nodded agreement with Roberson's statement.

"Shall we grab a seat in the Conference Room?" uttered Roberson with a head-nod.

"Sure."

Within the Conference Room Nash took a seat at the head of the table; Roberson sat to her immediate left – Stahl to her immediate right.

"I understand you responded to some disturbances at the home of Daryl and Madison Wagner?" said Nash with alternating glances between Roberson and Stahl.

"All too often I'm afraid" replied Stahl.

"I was hoping you can provide any insights… your perspectives."

"To help with your investigation into Daryl Wagner's murder?"

"That's correct, yes."

"I don't mean to sound like a cold-hearted bastard" responded

Roberson, "But I didn't lose any sleep after hearing that the arson vic was Daryl Wagner."

Nash wasn't overly surprised at Roberson's moral confession, but she was curious about Stahl and looked over her way. Stahl remained silent on the subject, but all indications told her that Stahl's feelings were similar to Roberson's.

Nash looked back at Roberson and questioned his response, "Because of the beatings Daryl had inflicted upon Madison?"

"Yes; it was both disturbing and frustrating" Roberson replied.

"Frustrating?"

"Because it kept happening" Stahl chimed in, "And yet she repeatedly refused to press charges."

"The bastard had put so much fear into her that she was deathly afraid of the potential consequences of charging him" Roberson added.

"Under the circumstances your only option was to catch him in the act?" said Nash.

"That's the unfortunate truth. And believe me, we tried."

"How? By tailing him?"

"In a sense, yes" replied Roberson. "I mean, it wasn't a dedicated tail... the Department had neither the time nor the manpower; but we had learned his movements, and thus made sure to adjust our patrols accordingly when we were able."

"But no luck?"

"I thought I had him when I got called to *The White Pig* a month-and-a-half ago, but missed the opportunity by mere minutes."

"Is that the night you took *Trevor Cobb* into custody?"

"That's the one."

"Why do you say you missed the opportunity to take Wagner in?"

"By the time Officer Sheldon and I got to the scene the fight had broken up."

"But you had a warrant for *Cobb's* arrest, so you ended up taking *him* away."

"We didn't know that Cobb was the other guy involved when we got the call, we only knew about Wagner."

"The caller mentioned Wagner by name?"

"Yep. Anyway, the hope was to get there in time to catch Wagner in the act of *anything* that would allow us to bring him in; and once we had him in custody then *ideally* Madison would gain the courage to open up about her beatings."

"And *your* plan under that scenario?"

"Hopefully get her to press charges; and if not then maybe we'd *at least* get her to file a restraining order."

"Any idea what finally convinced her about the restraining order?"

"Not really."

"Were you told that Daryl had smacked her around in the parking lot and *that* was the reason Cobb confronted him at that time?"

"Oh yeah, Cobb was ranting and raving about that, kept saying *'Here I try to stop this guy from beating his wife and you take ME in and not HIM'*. But we didn't actually observe it, and since she wouldn't file charges our hands were tied."

Nash looked at her notes, "Well, I guess we've exhausted that event, unless you can think of anything else that's noteworthy?"

"Uhh…" Roberson pondered, "Nope."

"In that case, I have a question related to the files."

"Sure… go ahead."

"I noticed that phone records from the Wagner landline, along with Madison's cell phone, show several calls to and from the Station. Do you know what that's about?"

"Sure; after responding to several 9-1-1 calls and her subsequent refusal to press charges, Officer Stahl and I told her she could call the Station directly."

"What was the purpose of going that route?"

"That way she could tell her husband that she had the cops on the phone. The idea was that if he knew it wasn't a 9-1-1 operator but actual *law enforcement* on the line he might have second thoughts about laying a hand on her."

The verbiage used at the end of Roberson's statement momentarily caught Nash's attention... *somewhat curious* she thought, but she quickly reconsidered, and dismissed the notion.

"And it seemed to work" Stahl added.

"Hmmm... I hadn't considered such an approach" Nash stated, "But what about the calls from the Station to *her?*"

"Basically just checking-in to see if things were okay" replied Roberson.

"We call them *health and well-being* checks" said Stahl.

"And you said that calling the Station directly seemed to work?" said Nash.

"Yes."

"So the calls were working, yet a restraining order was ultimately filed?"

"Which was a huge step forward considering the circumstances" responded Roberson, "The way things were headed it was only a matter of time before Madison ended up in the hospital."

"Or worse" added Stahl.

"Hard to argue with that" replied Nash, "But he *did* apparently manage to give her one last beating before he was murdered."

"But never again" Roberson punctuated with a look of satisfaction on his face.

Nash abruptly glanced over at Roberson... yet another curious response was made by him, and this time Nash was not so quick to dismiss it. She had no plans to press him about it at this point in time; instead she jotted down his statement, fanned through her memo pad, and then looked back at Roberson and Stahl.

"That's all the questions I had, unless you have anything for me?"

"Do you have any suspects?" asked Roberson.

"We're looking at a few people, but they're all in the category of *persons of interest* at this point."

Nash looked in Stahl's direction.

"I have no questions" stated Stahl.

"Great" Nash commented. She handed each of them her card, "If you think of anything, please give me a call."

"We will."

"Oh" added Nash as she slid her memo pad over to Stahl, "Would you mind writing down your numbers in case I need to get hold of you for anything... either your cell or home phone, whichever you prefer."

Stahl started writing down *only* her number.

"And your name too please; otherwise I might not recall what number goes to whom" Nash clarified. "You can put *Officer Stahl* or just *Stahl*."

Stahl handed the memo pad back to Nash, who then slid it over to Roberson. He jotted down the info and handed it back.

Nash stood up, placed her memo pad in her pocket, and reached out to shake hands, "Thanks again."

Out in the parking lot Nash sat in her car, memo pad in-hand while simultaneously resting it on the steering wheel. She flipped through the pages: Notes, thoughts, ideas, and questions in a palm-sized adjunct to the murder board.

She got to the last written page – the names and phone numbers of Officers Stahl and Roberson.

She pulled a pen out of her jacket pocket, flipped to the next page of the memo, which was blank, and wrote *Stahl*. She looked back at the previous page, memorized Stahl's phone number, and then flipped back to the newly-started page and wrote-in Stahl's number. She repeated the act for Roberson's name and number.

She went back to the page which Stahl and Roberson had scribed their information, grabbed the upper edge of the page, and carefully ripped it out of her memo. She placed the page into a small evidence bag, and then placed the bag in her jacket pocket.

Nash retrieved her cell phone, scrolled through the contacts, and hit 'Send'. A voice echoed through the phone... "Lowell."

"Hey Evan" replied Nash, "The note found in Daryl Wagner's gym bag..."

"Yeah?" responded Lowell.

"I've got a handwriting sample for your comparison."

31

Forensic Scientist Evan Lowell was intrigued at the prospect of a handwriting sample to compare with the threatening note found in Daryl Wagner's gym bag. He was, however, stumped as to the source – Nash had not mentioned a single word in regard to a person of interest she had in mind. Lowell was also curious as to how Nash might have obtained such a sample. Needless to say he was awaiting Nash's arrival like a six-year-old waiting to discover what Santa had left under the tree.

Nash barely made it through the doorway of the Forensics Lab before being approached by an anxious Lowell.

"So, you have a handwriting sample for me?" said Lowell, reaching out to receive the evidence bag from Nash.

"Who knows if it matches the note, but I figured it was worth a shot" Nash replied.

Lowell took a quick glance; it was not quite what he was expecting, *"Two* samples?"

"Only one of the writings truly caught my attention; the other was simply part of my ruse to obtain the sample of interest."

"Your ruse?" Lowell replied as he noticed that there was a familiarity to the piece of paper, "The sample looks like it could've been ripped right out of your memo pad."

"Good eye… that's the source."

Lowell focused on the content within the sample, "And who are the names on here – Roberson and Stahl?"

"Bennington Police Officers who responded, on more than one

occasion, to disturbances at the Wagner household."

"You think one of them wrote the threatening note as a means to put some fear into Daryl... to keep him from beating his wife?"

"Or worse."

"You're not implying that one of them is Daryl Wagner's murderer, are you?"

"To tell you the truth, I don't know what to think."

"This doesn't have anything to do with the statement you made at the cabin, does it?"

"Which statement?"

"That the killer might be someone who knows what we look for when processing a scene?"

"No, that wasn't it; but it *would* explain a few things now that you mention it."

"Then what has you looking in their direction?"

"Some statements that Roberson made" Nash replied. "They weren't to the extent of making the hairs stand up on the back of my neck, but they were enough to make me do a double-take."

"Really?"

"Yes; he started by saying that *he didn't mean to sound like a cold-hearted bastard but he didn't lose any sleep after hearing that the arson vic was Daryl Wagner.* Not a big surprise there since he had seen the result of the beatings that Daryl had inflicted upon Madison. Suffice it to say I didn't give this statement much thought until later."

"I think a number of people aware of the situation might have had the same response; even though they might not admit it."

"Agreed. What initially got my attention was when he used a phrase about her husband *laying a hand on her.*"

"Similar verbiage to the note."

"*Precisely.* And then, when I mentioned that Daryl had managed to exact one last beating on Madison before he was killed, Roberson responded *'But never again'.* And his statement was very matter-of-fact."

"Hmmm… I can see why you might wonder if he's the originator of the note."

"And at the end of the interview I asked them if they had any questions for me, and *within a split-second* Roberson asked if I had any suspects."

"Do you think he was fishing? Or perhaps merely the normal curiosity of a police officer when discussing a case?"

"Hard to say; it was just one more thing that caught my attention."

There was a moment of silence as they both pondered the information.

"Oh, and there's another thought that came to me while I was driving over here" added Nash. "It's probably just my mind running amok and there's nothing to it, but I can't shake the notion."

"What's that?"

"Roberson also used the term *law enforcement.*"

"Yeah? So?"

"So that's the same term the guy who bought the black & white used… at least according to Andrew Lloyd, the owner."

"But didn't you say that it was a guy from Seattle or King County, and that the name was different?"

"I was thinking about that as well, but a few things dawned on me… *For One:* They did the deal in downtown Seattle near the viaduct; which, as you know, is near the ferry terminal."

"True."

"And he was only *guessing* on the name, which was *Overton…*"

"Essentially rhymes with *Roberson*" Lowell recognized.

"That was my thought."

"Anything else?"

"The description of the buyer – same height, same build, dark hair, mustache…"

"An interesting series of coincidences at the very least; so what's your plan?"

"For starters, I'm going to see if Donnelly has found a possible buyer named Overton. If so then we'll follow that lead; and if *not* then I'll ask

Lloyd if the buyer could have been named *Roberson* in lieu of *Overton,* and I'll also show him Roberson's picture and see what he says."

"And I'll get the handwriting sample to Riggs; I'll let you know what we find."

"Sounds good" Nash replied.

"By the way" said Lowell, "I've got some info regarding the cabin..."

32

Nash hadn't even made it to her desk when Donnelly's probing curiosity rang out… "How did your chat with Roberson and Stahl go yesterday after you left the cabin?"

Brogan piled on before Nash had a chance to respond, "Yeah; anything good?"

Nash draped her jacket over her chair and then turned to acknowledge them, "Roberson made enough interesting statements that I had both of them write-down their names and phone numbers before I left."

"I'm confused" responded Donnelly, "I'm not getting the tie between *'making statements'* and *'writing down phone numbers'*."

"Let's just say there were statements that led me to believe that Roberson might have more than a passing concern regarding Madison Wagner's safety and well-being; *and* one of those statements bore a resemblance to the note found in Daryl Wagner's gym bag."

"Whoa" replied Brogan, "Do you think he might be involved somehow?"

"And what was the purpose of their phone numbers?" added Donnelly.

"I didn't really care about their phone numbers, I could always get them from O'Rourke" Nash replied, "I just wanted a handwriting sample."

Brogan was impressed, "Obtaining a sample under the guise of needing a phone number… Nice."

"And as far as him being involved somehow, that's anybody's guess at this point; it could be simply him writing the note in an attempt to get Daryl to stop the beatings, or it could be no involvement whatsoever."

"He didn't say?" asked Donnelly.

"I didn't mention it."

Brogan turned to Donnelly to explain, "You start asking questions with nothing more than a weird feeling... no facts to back it up... and the guy gets defensive and uncooperative."

"Which means you don't get your handwriting sample; *and* you get shit raining down on you from his boss" Nash clarified.

Donnelly connected the dots: "So, your request for his phone number was merely subterfuge to get a handwriting sample?"

"That's a fact."

"Subterfuge?" said Brogan.

"A ruse... a trick."

"Oh."

"But why ask Officer *Stahl* for *her* number?" said Donnelly.

"The con doesn't work if it's obvious" replied Nash, "I needed to ask in a way such that Roberson wouldn't give it a second thought."

"How'd you manage that?"

"I asked for their numbers *while* I was handing my memo pad to *Stahl*. Putting the emphasis on Stahl *first* deflected attention from Roberson. She wrote down her info, passed it back to me, and then I slid it over to Roberson. He merely mimicked what she had done... just as I had hoped."

"Wow, I never would have thought of that."

"Tricks of the trade you learn over time."

"Where's the sample now?" asked Brogan.

"I delivered it to Lowell right after I left B.P.D."

"It will be interesting to find out the results."

"If it matches Roberson he will have some explaining to do" noted Nash. "Even if he was just trying to scare Daryl it will have been very poor judgment on his part – definitely outside the bounds of proper police protocol."

"And if it doesn't?" said Donnelly.

"We're back to square one as far as the note goes."

"Was there anything else about Roberson that piqued your interest?" asked Brogan.

Nash pondered the question as she reflected upon the many items she had relayed to Lowell.

The silence, along with Nash seemingly staring off into space, led Brogan to question as to whether Nash had heard him.

"Kenz?" he prompted.

"Mmm… not at the moment" Nash responded; preferring to keep those thoughts under wraps for the time being.

"That means we're done with him for now?"

Nash paused once again as she considered her game-plan. "Not exactly", she said and turned to Donnelly, "Laura, can you build a timeline, spreadsheet, or *whatever* regarding everything in B.P.D.'s files that relates with Officer Roberson and the Wagners?"

"Of course" Donnelly replied.

"Okay, *now* I'm done with that subject… for the time being."

"Since you talked to Lowell, did he have any info from the cabin?" said Donnelly.

"Yep; the gun we found *is* the one registered to Daryl Wagner. But, as we suspected, there were no prints on the gun itself, only the bullets… which are presumably Daryl's since they match those found at the Wagner home."

"His prints are not on file?"

"Nope."

"How about the wallet?" asked Brogan.

"They're still going through it… credit card-by-credit card, business card-by-business card… looking for possible clues."

A chime rang-out from Nash's computer.

"Hey Kenz" said Brogan.

"Yeah, I heard" responded Nash while taking a look at her computer screen.

"Well it's about frickin' time" Nash blurted out.

"What's that?" replied Brogan.

"The video from *Super Mart* finally showed up."

"No shit?" said Brogan as he crowded around Nash's desk. Donnelly joined him.

With Brogan and Donnelly gathered in front of her computer screen, Nash clicked on the associated icon.

The opening screenshot was that of Madison Wagner at the cash register; it was the same shot that Nash had received previously… the photograph of the moment-of-sale of the burner phone.

"Okay, here's Madison; just like we saw in the photo" noted Nash.

She selected 'Play'.

"That guy right behind her" Brogan immediately commented, "Is he *with* her or is he simply the next customer in line?"

"Could it be Daryl… her husband, but scruffy-faced and mustached and not his beard?" added Donnelly.

"Don't get too antsy, let's watch and see if the video answers some of those questions" Nash replied.

The video continued and the man leaned closer and began to speak. Madison turned as if to acknowledge him. Nash pondered while the footage continued: *Does Madison know the man? Were they together? Or did he simply strike up a conversation with the attractive woman in front of him?* Madison proceeded out of the frame; the man made a purchase and walked out of the frame as well. The video ended.

"What do you make of that?" said Brogan.

"Separate purchases" replied Nash, "So at first glance it just looks like some guy attempting to flirt with the woman next to him."

"Hey, it's starting again from a different camera angle" reported Donnelly.

The next feed showed Madison exiting the store through the automatic doors. A few other customers approached from different angles and passed through the exit as well, and then the man… seemingly in a bit of a hurry… passed through the doors.

"That angle didn't tell us anything except that *Mister Smooth Talker* was in a rush" said Brogan.

"Hang on, we may get the parking lot" responded Nash.

Another feed started; it was from the vantage point of the building's exit looking out to the parking lot: Madison exited the building, stopped briefly to let a car pass via the main drive area, and then she proceeded up one of the parking lanes.

A man came jogging up behind her; he appeared to be the same man that spoke to her in the store. She stopped and turned around as he approached. *Was her action due to him calling out her name? Or was it due to hearing someone running up behind her?* Nash wondered.

The man caught up with her and they chatted briefly. Madison turned and resumed her trek to a light-colored car. She got in, backed out of the spot, and drove away.

The man went off in a separate direction, got into a dark-colored vehicle, drove straight ahead since there was no vehicle in front of his, and exited the lot via the same exit as Madison.

Nash turned to Brogan, *"Now* you can ask the question."

"What the hell do you make of *that?"* Brogan reiterated.

"Unfortunately, the video is too grainy and too far away to get a bead on the guy; not to mention the high angle and that all of the shots are either from behind or a partial side-shot."

"Plus the ball cap he's wearing" said Brogan. "And if it *is* Daryl, like Laura pointed out, his beard is not grown out as much as his driver's license photo or the day he was killed... his appearance on the ATM video."

"You wouldn't think a guy's beard could go from scruffy-faced to Grizzly Adams in just a few days" said Nash.

"Even though I realize you're exaggerating, I see what you mean" said Brogan, "But hey; what about *Cobb?"*

Nash turned to Donnelly, "Any chance we know who that guy is... what he purchased?"

"No luck on his I.D.; he paid cash. But his purchase was *also* a burner phone."

"Are you shitting me?!" responded Nash, "With the phone purchases only a minute or two apart, how do we know that *his* phone is not the one that called the Wagner house at the time of the murder?!"

"I have no idea" replied Donnelly, feeling she had stumbled into the unfortunate position of 'Kill the Messenger', "I guess we'll have to ask Lowell."

"Son of a damn bitch!" Nash vented.

A hush fell over the room; with exception of the muffled breaths of Nash's frustration.

As the tension eased Brogan posed a question, "What next?"

"I'm adding this to the shit I'm going to throw at Cobb and see if any of it sticks" replied Nash.

"The other item being Daryl's ATM video?"

"You got that right."

"Today?" wondered Donnelly.

"I talked him in to stopping by for another chat."

"How'd you manage that?" said Brogan.

"I gave him a choice; *stop by here and we can talk, or I can embarrass you in front of all your coworkers...* He chose option one."

"Anything you need from us?" said Donnelly.

"Now that you mention it, have we gotten anywhere on the theft of the incinerated car?"

"No; what little we had turned into nothing but dead ends."

"Alright then; we figured he could've been the one to steal the car, so I'm thinking it's a good starting point for my conversation with him... a little something to soften him up."

"Or to break him right out of the gate" noted Brogan.

"You know me well."

The annoying pitch of a buzzer, indicating a request to enter the building, echoed through the office. Nash looked up at the security monitor – it was Cobb.

"Looks like our *Guest of Honor* has arrived."

33

Nash opened the door to allow Cobb's entry into the building. Apparently Cobb had a singular sense of style – once again he was wearing an old and tattered *Westsound Auto* denim shirt. One minor exception, this version was lacking sleeves – they had been ripped right off of the shirt; seemingly to show off what were, in his mind, *his trembling biceps.*

Cobb looked around, "I like what you've done with the place."

Nash didn't respond.

"It's smaller than B.P.D.'s digs" Cobb continued.

"A smaller budget yet larger jurisdiction than those guys" replied Nash.

"Kinda sucks for you guys."

"We make it work."

Nash led Cobb to the Interview Room. It was similar to a conference room but slightly smaller; yet larger than the Interrogation Room – an isolated box literally nicknamed 'The Box'. At one end of the room was a television screen.

Nash and Cobb sat across from each other – Nash with a file folder in front of her, along with a remote control.

"It's your dime" stated Cobb.

Nash opened the folder and then looked at Cobb, "You work at *Westsound Auto*?"

"The *shirt* give it away? Besides, you know I do, we had that conversation a couple days ago."

"Sleeves get caught in some machinery?"

"It's my summer shirt."

Nash looked at her watch as if it told the time of *year* vice the time of *day*.

Cobb responded accordingly... "Hey, it's supposed to be seventy degrees today" he reasoned. "Besides, the ladies like the look."

Nash shook her head and then got back on track, "Are you a mechanic? Or in sales?"

"A machinist; but I cover the *parts desk* on occasion... why?"

"I take it that means you know a lot about cars?"

"Sure."

"What say I throw a hypothetical at you?"

"I didn't kill the guy."

"That wasn't my hypothetical."

"Okay, I'm listening."

"Suppose a buddy goes out and has a few beers at his favorite bar, but when he goes to leave his car won't start; are you the guy he asks to help him out?"

"Nine times out of ten."

"And you can get the car running?"

"It depends... if it just needs a jump, there's a loose connection on one of the battery terminals, there's an interlock between the ignition and the gearbox and he doesn't have it fully in Park... same thing if it's a manual tranny and he didn't push the clutch in sufficiently... a lot of simple options like that on the newer cars. On older ones I'd check to see if he's getting a spark to the plugs... maybe one or more wires to the coil is disconnected; and I'd check the starter motor, the solenoid, crap like that."

"It sounds like you know your stuff."

"I know my way around an engine compartment. So, what's the deal with the *'hypothetical'?*" Cobb said with air-quotes.

"A car broke down not far from one of your favorite hangouts... the *White Pig*, back on the seventeenth. The owner didn't bother coming back to get it for a couple of days, and when he did, it was gone. First thought is that it got towed, right? But that wasn't the case. Best guess is that a Good Samaritan came by, fixed the car, took it for a test drive, and darn the luck… he forgot to give it back after the test drive."

"Now why would I fix some guy's clunker and then take it?"

"How do you know it was a clunker?"

"For starters it broke down. And then the guy didn't bother to go retrieve it for a couple of days?? It wasn't worth his trouble?? Sounds like a clunker to me."

"We know you were in the vicinity within the time-frame that the car went missing."

"Well, I can tell you with *one-hundred-percent certainty* that you didn't find my prints or DNA in the car."

"Because you torched the car?"

"Because I was never *in* the car."

"How can you possibly know that when I haven't given you any details about it?"

"What do details about the car have to do with anything?"

"Maybe the car was a friend's or family member's; in which case you may have ridden in it, driven it, done repair work on it… you get my point?"

"Fine; whose car was it then?"

"Do you know Jared Jensen?"

"Jar-Jar?"

"Excuse me?"

"If it's the Jared Jensen I know we all call him Jar-Jar."

"What kind of clunker does this Jar-Jar guy own?"

"An eighty-five Mazda six-two-six."

"Is there anything unusual, odd, or unique about his car?"

"Yeah, the driver's seat broke and he replaced it with a seat from an old Honda Civic… it looked ridiculous."

"That's the car."

"Word at the shop was that it broke down and he had it towed away."

"It was stolen... and ended up at the crime scene."

"Okay you got me; I've been in the car before so there's possibly some of my hair strands or other DNA in there; but I had nothing to do with the crime."

"So you say, but what do you make of this?"

Nash grasped the remote, hit 'Play', and nodded toward the television screen – it was Daryl Wagner's ATM video.

"The guy's making an ATM withdrawal; big deal" responded Cobb.

"He looks a little nervous, don't you think?"

"Yeah... so?"

"So what about this part here where he's saying your name?"

"*MY* name?? That's ridiculous!"

"Looks that way to me."

"Based on what?! There's no audio; all you can see is him opening his mouth like a fish; he could be yawning for all we know."

"Yawning? No, he's definitely saying something."

"You're just seeing what you *want* to see; he could be saying Bob, Rob, Mom, Pop, even *Cop*... what do you say to that?"

"I'd say I have another video for you."

"*Now* what?" Cobb responded.

"I understand you do most of your shopping at *Super Mart*?"

"Like half the people in the County; what's your point?"

Nash switched from the ATM video to that of Madison Wagner purchasing the burner phone. She pointed to Madison, "The woman here making a purchase is Madison Wagner. Now pay attention to the guy right next to her... he starts talking to her, she makes her purchase and leaves, he makes *his* purchase, and then catches up with her in the parking lot. They chat some more, and then go to separate vehicles."

"Once again... what's your point?"

"That's not *you* in the video, is it?"

"Nope."

"You're not chatting with Madison Wagner, buying a pre-paid cell phone, and then running out to chat with her some more before driving away?"

"Like I said, it's not me."

"You drive a dark colored Jeep just like the one in the video."

"So does her husband."

"How do you know?" responded Nash; hoping that Cobb had just inadvertently revealed potentially incriminating information.

"He knocked me over with his frickin' car door at the *White Pig* a month ago. Besides, my Jeep is a CJ."

Nash hadn't considered Cobb's acute recognition and recollection of Wagner's Jeep, *"although I shouldn't have been surprised, he is a car-guy after all"* she thought to herself. She quickly regrouped…

"Why would she and her husband drive separate vehicles to the store?"

"I have no idea, why don't you ask *her?!"* Cobb crossed his arms and added, "Are we done?!"

"Just one more thing; don't leave the area."

"What do you mean by *the area?"*

"The Olympic Peninsula."

"Hey, you can't keep me from going to Seattle or Tacoma or Olympia or wherever."

"Fine, then don't leave the state."

"Where am I going to go? I'm sure you checked out my financials… nothing but chump change."

34

"Get anything from Cobb?" Brogan queried Nash.

"A whole lotta not much" Nash replied. "I threw the stolen arson car, Daryl Wagner's ATM video, and Madison's burner phone video at him and he was having none of it."

"Do you mean he refused to talk?" said Donnelly.

"No; he maintained his cool and had a reasonable response to each of them."

"What about Daryl mouthing his name when making the ATM withdrawal?" Brogan replied.

"He said that we were only seeing what we *wanted* to see. And I have to admit he has a point; with no audio it's the kind of argument a Defense Attorney would use."

"Damn."

"He also said that Wagner could be mouthing the word *'Cop'*."

"As in *the alleged cop that bought the black & white?*"

"That's what popped into my head when he said it; but I hadn't shared any of that information with him, the whole *law enforcement* statement from Andrew Lloyd that is, so I'm thinking it's just his way of screwing with us."

"So, he's off the hook?"

"Let's just say that we don't have enough to reel him in at this time."

"You're not worried about him doing a disappearing act?"

"I *did* tell him not to leave the state, although technically I have no grounds to prevent him from doing so, but he doesn't know that."

"And if he bolts?"

"It's not like he's some high-roller who can sneak off to a foreign country and start a new life; in fact he doesn't even have a passport, so I'm not too worried at the moment."

"Alright" said Brogan. "Well, I have some news."

"What have you got?" Nash replied.

"I didn't get a chance to mention it earlier, but I stopped by the *White Pig Tavern* after work yesterday."

"Are you bragging… or confessing?"

"Good one" Brogan replied, "Anyway, I got the name of the woman who was with Daryl Wagner back on the eleventh… the night Cobb saw him there."

"Oh, you were doing a little recon."

"Yep; her name is Sarah McKinney – she's one of the cocktail servers."

"Were they seeing each other behind the scenes?"

"Not according to her."

"You talked to her?"

"And to some of her coworkers. They said that Daryl was a regular at the tavern, mostly coming in by himself or with his pal Gary, and only occasionally with Madison. They didn't know Gary's last name, but it's gotta be *Decker*. The staff said that Wagner was always sitting at either the bar, or at a high-topper, and that some of the staff would join them and hang out a while if Daryl and Gary were there when they got off shift."

"I assume that was the case with this gal Sarah back on the eleventh?"

"That's what she said; and her coworkers corroborated her account."

"Did they give you any other info about Daryl, his buddy, or Madison?"

"Yep; they said that Daryl was generally a decent guy when he was there, but had a completely different personality when he'd come in with his wife… quick to get jealous and tended to blame her if any guy was giving her attention. It got to the point where the staff dreaded when he showed up with his wife because they knew there was going to be some kind of drama."

Nash rolled her eyes… "That story keeps repeating itself."

"They also said that if he had a girlfriend on the side he never mentioned her or brought her to the tavern."

"And you're sure this woman Sarah wasn't hiding the fact that she had a relationship with Wagner?"

"You never know for sure in those circumstances, but she seemed upfront to me."

"I just can't believe in this day and age that we can't seem to find this mystery woman."

"Well, maybe there isn't one?" Donnelly chimed in. "Or maybe it was a one-way-street… he was obsessed with some woman but the feeling wasn't mutual?"

"Like he was doing all of that stuff to try to impress some woman that didn't want anything to do with him?" said Brogan.

"It might explain why we aren't finding any alleged girlfriend."

"Maybe so, but if he's obsessed with some woman who doesn't want to be with him, then why does he keep beating up his wife?"

"Why does *any* asshole do that shit?" responded Nash.

Brogan and Donnelly didn't respond; they realized Nash's question was rhetorical.

"You guys got anything else?" asked Nash.

"A couple of things" responded Donnelly, "I talked to Lowell about the newly-discovered burner and he said they'll get right on it."

"Great. And the *other* thing?"

"My search for anyone named Overton that might have been the buyer of the black & white."

"Why am I getting the impression that another dead-end is on the horizon?"

"Unfortunately, that seems to be the case; shall I refrain from giving you what I found?"

Nash was resigned to the inevitable, but was curious nonetheless, "Go ahead."

"There's a Jerry Overton who's a Corrections Officer at the King County jail, but outside of the mustache he doesn't match the description… he's five-nine, two-eighty."

"I'm assuming his physical stats are not that of a super buff no-necked weightlifter type?" replied Brogan.

"Nope" said Donnelly as she held up Jerry Overton's photo.

"Whoa! Don't they have fitness requirements for that job?"

"He was also working swing-shift the date of the sale… from three P.M. to midnight."

"I see why he's out of the picture; who else?" asked Nash.

"There's a Douglas Overton that works for the Vancouver Police Department."

"Vancouver *Washington,* not *Canada,* correct?"

"Correct."

"And he wasn't in the Seattle area on the eleventh?"

"Correct again."

"The last one was Burt Overton – Spokane Police."

"Same story as the Vancouver guy?"

"Yep."

"I can't say I'm surprised" Nash replied.

"What is that… *three* dead-ends so far today?" stated Brogan, "It's getting a bit frustrating."

"Hey, it means we're eliminating crap that, unbeknownst to us *initially,* was out on the periphery" responded Nash, "And *that* allows us to narrow our focus."

"But to whom?" said Donnelly, "Andrew Lloyd didn't pan out, nor did Cobb so it seems; we haven't been able to find an alleged girlfriend that might provide us with a suspect or at least a person of interest, and the name *Overton* went nowhere?"

"How about Officer Roberson?" Brogan replied.

Nash and Donnelly gave Brogan a curious look.

"If it turns out he wrote the note?" Brogan clarified.

"We're going to need a lot more than a threatening note before we put a cop in the crosshairs" stated Nash, who then gazed over at Donnelly.

"I'm working that angle" said Donnelly, "…just in case."

"Good" said Nash; suddenly interrupted by the buzzing of her cell phone.

"It's been a morning rife with dead-ends" said Nash into the phone, "I hope you've got something good."

"I've got a *maybe*… and a *holy shit*" replied Lowell.

"Now that's more like it, what've you got?"

"The *maybe* is about the handwriting sample you gave me. Riggs said that he couldn't say *definitively*, but if he were a betting man he'd say it was *Roberson's* handiwork."

"Son of a bitch. Definitive or not I'm going to broach the subject with him."

"Isn't that a bit risky?"

"Not at all, if it *is* him then his only option is to admit it."

"How can you be so confident that *he'll* see it that way?"

"Because if he *denies* it and we get additional samples that shows he's *lying*, then his career is basically over. So, his best bet is to bite the bullet and admit he wrote it; at that point he simply gets a reprimand."

"And if he *didn't* write the note?"

"Then he has no worries because additional samples would confirm he's not the author."

"I like the way you think."

"Thanks. Now how about the *holy shit* item?"

"It's about the second burner phone. We don't know the buyer, but I can tell you this little tidbit… it has been making calls to the Wagner home; they started soon after Daryl's death."

"Holy shit!"

"Told ya."

"Why weren't these calls *flagged?*"

"Probably because they occurred *after* Daryl's death; so no one considered them to be suspicious."

"Better late than never I suppose. Do you know the phone utilized to activate it?"

"The infamous pay phone near the ferry terminal."

"What the hell is it with this pay phone?!"

"No kidding" Lowell replied. "What's your next move?"

"It looks like I need to have yet *another* chat with Madison Wagner." Nash paused in thought, "Along those lines, what's the latest on her computer?"

"It has been a little more work than the Cyber guys initially expected; they're working on recovering some deleted files, but they *promise me* they're getting close."

35

Nash reflected on the latest information and pondered the logistics regarding her next move. Leads that had come up empty and those awaiting a defined conclusion notwithstanding; the matter of a threatening note and a second burner phone were at the forefront.

The next step suddenly achieved clarity... she picked up her phone, scrolled through her contacts, and hit 'Send'. "Hey Sean" she said, "I've got a little something to talk to you about."

"Go ahead" replied Captain O'Rourke.

"This needs to be in person."

"What did you have in mind?"

"I plan on having another talk with Madison Wagner and figured I'd stop by your office either before, or after, I speak with her."

"Why don't you have her come here; you can use our Interview Room?"

"Hmm... I hadn't thought of that, but... okay, I'll see if she's game."

36

As Nash walked through the doorway of the Bennington Police Station she wondered if she had inadvertently *made a deal with the devil*. Not that Captain O'Rourke had assumed the role of Lucifer, but he had convinced Nash to allow one of his young Officers to assist with the interview of Madison Wagner. In reality Nash had been caught off-guard, and her momentary silence in regard to O'Rourke's request had been mistaken as a sign of agreement.

The wondrous gaze of a late-twenties uniformed Officer almost stopped Nash in her tracks. He was a spindly lad, standing at attention, perfectly pressed pants and shirt, spit-polished shoes, hat tucked under his left arm pit, and not a hair out of place on his head. He reached out to shake hands as Nash approached. "Detective Nash" he said, "Officer Clarence Wilberforce."

Nash wasn't one to judge, but she had to wonder what Wilberforce's parents were thinking when they chose his name. *"He must be a 'Clarence Wilberforce the third' or 'fourth'… that's got to be it"* she thought to herself.

"Officer" Nash replied as she shook Wilberforce's hand.

"I have the Interview Room set up per your request" stated Wilberforce.

"I appreciate that" said Nash as she looked at her watch, "How about we check it out before Ms. Wagner arrives?"

The Interview Room had changed little since Nash's days on The Force. The notable difference was that the old-style picture-tube television on a tall rolling stand had been replaced by a wall-mounted LED screen. Wilberforce had set up the interview to occur at one end of the table… Nash and Madison across from each other since Nash was the lead interviewer, Wilberforce at the end... to Nash's right, Madison's left. He had also set up the monitor with a remote for Nash.

Nash was pleased with the arrangement, but had no idea what she was in for; not with respect to the room, but to the misguided novice with whom she would share the interview. Officer Wilberforce's personality was a diametrically-opposed combination of 'delusions of grandeur' and 'feelings of inadequacy and insecurity'. Now that Wilberforce was in a position of power, courtesy of his badge, his attitude was an overzealous attempt to be someone who was to be feared by *John and Jane Q. Citizen* while also looking to impress higher authority by his domineering approach. They were traits that he lacked in his youth... where he would cower in the presence of stronger individuals.

Nash stepped out of the room to await Madison's arrival. She looked around the office – both Roberson and Stahl's desks were empty. She casually walked through the space, attempting to be inconspicuous, but what she really wanted was to take a peek at those desks. The chance that anything noteworthy would be laying out for all to see was slim-to-none, but Nash's curiosity was getting the best of her.

Her roundabout stroll was brief; just as she had slithered near the two desks to catch a glimpse, Madison entered the building.

Nash greeted Madison and led her to the Interview Room and the somewhat uncomfortable introduction to a man she had never met.

"Ma'am, this is Officer Wilberforce with the Bennington Police Department" said Nash, "He's going to assist in the interview."

"Okay" a meek and slightly confused Madison replied.

A figure walked by the Interview Room window and suddenly stopped. Madison abruptly looked out that way as recognition caught her eye – it was Officer Roberson. The two made eye contact. Nash turned around to see what had captured Madison's attention. Roberson felt the intensity of Nash's gaze and immediately turned away; quickly resuming his trek. Nash turned back to Madison; she too looked away... as if she'd gotten caught with her hand in the cookie jar.

Nash, Madison, and Wilberforce took their preassigned seats.

Nash didn't even get a chance to open her mouth when Wilberforce glared at Madison and immediately jumped-in as if he was running the show... "Where were you around midnight Saturday the twenty-sixth, early Sunday the twenty-seventh?"

Nash was taken aback; a startled Madison responded, "I was at home, just like I said before."

"Can anyone corroborate that?" Wilberforce countered.

"No, I was alone." Madison turned to Nash; her tone was emphatic, laced with frustration and displeasure, "But you *know* I was there; I received the phone call you asked me about."

Nash attempted to respond, but Wilberforce kept the heat on... "Or the reason you knew about the phone call is because *you* are the person who *made* the call?"

Madison had the look of a deer in the headlights.

Wilberforce kept on the attack, "And I understand that the other day, when Detective Nash asked if you were okay, that you responded *'Everything should be fine now'*. Is that because your husband was *now* dead?! Murdered by you or someone you hired or were in cahoots with?!"

The *Wilberforce experiment* was over before the Bunsen burner could even heat up the beaker, Nash had had enough. She grabbed Wilberforce's arm and sternly said, "Officer – a word" while head-nodding toward the door of the Interview Room.

Nash turned to Madison. "Excuse us" she said, and then walked out of the Interview Room with Wilberforce in tow – figuratively grabbed by the earlobe and led through the doorway.

Once the door to the room was closed, in a harsh yet muffled voice, Nash laid into him... "Who the hell are you trying to impress? This *in your face Drill Sergeant bullshit* is just that... *bullshit!*"

"I'm trying to make a point here" Wilberforce reasoned.

"What point?"

"Turn up the heat and get her to confess."

"That kind of crap is nothing but theatrics… this isn't a damn TV show, it's a real-life investigation into the *truth*."

"Well I just…"

Nash cut him off and continued her tirade… *"Well you just WHAT??* You don't know *squat* about this woman. Regardless of what circumstantial evidence is out there, you don't know if she has anything to do with the murder or not. For all we know she is completely innocent but may have information that is vital to our investigation… information that will be *lost* to us if she clams up because of your *"I'm going to beat it out of you"* mentality."

"It's worked for the Captain before."

"There's a time and a place… *and this ain't it!* Did you even *read* the report on her?? Do you know anything about her?? She's been a victim of domestic violence for who-knows-how-many years by a husband who is supposed to be her protector but instead has been pummeling her on a regular basis. Right now she's at the point where her *one and only* protective response is to curl up like a cocoon and not say a word… nada, nothing, zip!"

"If she's been abused then she has a prime motive to want him dead."

"No shit; why do you think I have her here? But interrogation is an *art;* you need to understand your quarry and adjust your method accordingly; you don't try to paint a portrait with a frickin' pickaxe!"

"What if she's guilty?"

"Then we rely on the *facts*. No matter what story a guilty person tells, when the facts contradict their story they ultimately trip-up over the mountain of lies, deceit, fabrications, and falsehoods. It may not be today, or even tomorrow, but eventually they cave."

"Got it."

Nash grabbed the door handle to the Interview Room.

Wilberforce stepped forward as if to join her.

Nash stopped, put her hand up, and in a commanding voice responded,

"Nope. I'm flying solo the rest of the way on this one."

Nash walked back into the room and immediately noticed that Madison's eyes were red and puffy.

"I apologize" Nash said and then head-nodded toward the door... "A rookie trying to impress his boss – he won't be back."

"Thank you."

"I realize we've met several time now, but I hope you understand that an investigation is a dynamic process; constantly churning up something new until the case is solved."

"I understand."

"A few things have surfaced lately; and I'll start with Daryl's locker at the gym: We found a threatening note in his gym bag... were you aware of such a note?"

"He mentioned the note, but I never actually saw it."

"Do you know where he found it?"

"He said it was on the windshield of his car when he left the gym one day."

"Did either of you know who wrote it, or at least have an idea as to who might have?"

"I had no clue; and if he knew he didn't say. But he started carrying his gun with him after that."

"Interesting" Nash replied, and jotted it down in her memo pad. She then reached into her jacket pocket, withdrew the note, and held it up for Madison to see. "Do you recognize the handwriting?" she said.

Madison looked it over closely, "No... not at all."

Nash placed the note back in her pocket. "Alright then; on to the next item" she said. "The last time we talked you said that no one ever saw your husband hit you while you were out in the car, but what about the night the one guy got arrested?"

"What about it?"

"I talked to the guy and he said that he *specifically* showed up at your car because your husband was hitting you, and even told your husband to get his *effing hands* off of you."

"All I remember is him reaching in the car, grabbing Daryl, and a lot of yelling. I just assumed it was a continuation of the issue they'd had in the bar; if he said that he saw Daryl hitting me none of that registered with me at the time."

"I thought that might be the case, but I had to ask."

Nash gave Madison a moment to collect her thoughts, and then continued... "Since this guy had told your husband to get his hands off of you, and the note had similar wording, do you think he might have been the one to write it?"

"You don't know if it was him?"

"We have not yet collected a handwriting sample."

"I have no idea, you would know better than me."

Madison had made a rather relevant observation, and Nash felt somewhat foolish having put herself in a position to get called-out by Madison's astuteness.

Nash did not have the time to wallow in her minor faux pas, and quickly transitioned to the next item of interest. She picked up the remote and pointed to the screen, "We received the video from *Super Mart* when you purchased the cell phone; I'd like you to answer a few questions related to it."

"Okay" Madison replied.

Nash started the video... "The guy that starts talking to you and then follows you out to the parking lot; do you know him?"

"Oh sure, that's Mike."

"Mike?"

"Officer Roberson."

Nash was stunned; she'd had a feeling that Roberson might have had more than a passing concern regarding Madison's safety and well-being, *but to be on a first-name basis*... this was an entirely new revelation. "Why was he there with you?" she asked.

"Like I mentioned before, he told me that I should get a pre-paid cell phone in case Daryl started to send me harassing and threatening calls or texts after I got the restraining order."

"You never said that the person making the suggestion was a police officer."

"I didn't see why that would make a difference."

"Why did *he* get a pre-paid cell phone at the same time that you did?"

"I don't know... he didn't say."

"Didn't it seem odd to you that he'd get a pre-paid phone when he already had his *own* cell phone?"

"Maybe he was afraid Daryl would figure out that he was helping me and would make calls to Mike?"

"Your friend *Mike* is a *police officer;* if Daryl was going to make threats to a cop he was going to end up in jail."

"I guess you're right" Madison conceded. "Then I have no idea why he bought the cell phone... for a family member maybe?"

"That hardly seems the case; several calls from *that* phone have been made to *your* number in the past week."

"Do you mean that his new number is *that* phone?"

"You tell me."

"There's not much to tell, he just said he had a new phone."

Nash's frustration was building: *Was Madison as naïve as she seemed, or was there more to the story? And what the hell was Roberson thinking?!*

"What exactly is the nature of your relationship?" Nash probed.

"There is no *relationship;* he's just been helping me."

"Then what specifically is the *help* he has been providing you?"

"Both he and Officer Stahl said I could call them anytime if Daryl was threatening me, they checked up on me to make sure I was okay, he helped me file the restraining order..."

"Whoa, whoa, whoa" Nash interrupted, "He helped you file the restraining order??"

"Yeah."

Nash was visibly angry; but remained silent. *"That son-of-a-bitch said he had no clue who gave Madison the idea about the restraining order!"* she said to herself.

Nash awoke from her trance and continued… "What else?"

"And he told me about getting a pre-paid cell phone" replied Madison.

"But you never activated the phone?"

"He was going to show me how to do that, but it went missing before he had a chance to."

"You realize all of this does not paint your friend *Mike*… Officer Roberson… in a very good light."

"I don't understand; all he has been doing is helping me… isn't that their job, *to serve and protect?"*

"Yes, but he crossed the line when he met you while he was off-duty… when the meeting was *not* in an official capacity. And he made it worse by contacting you via a pre-paid cell phone."

"He probably saved my life; I don't want him to get in trouble because of me."

Nash grew wide-eyed, "What do you mean he *saved your life?"*

"Being there for me, the restraining order, keeping an eye on Daryl to make sure he wouldn't hurt me again…"

"But Daryl still hurt you the night before he died, correct?"

"Yeah, but it could've been worse."

"Are you telling me that Officer Roberson intervened?"

"He didn't confront him or anything, but he showed up outside in his patrol car" Madison explained. "And when Daryl saw a cop car pull up he left."

"Did he get out of his car?"

"Mike? Not while Daryl was there."

"What about after Daryl left?"

"Mike came to the door and asked if I was okay. When he saw the bruises and my busted-open lip he told me I needed to officially report it."

"He didn't take matters into his own hands?"

"No; he just made sure I called to report it."

Silence prevailed as Nash processed all that she had heard. "Okay, just one last thing to cover" she continued... "Are you familiar with the area where the crime occurred?"

"Just what I saw on the news."

"You didn't recognize it?"

"No; why should I?"

"The crime occurred on the property of your husband's grandparents."

Madison looked confused.

"Out near Blue Heron Cove" Nash elaborated, "There's a small cabin on the property and a run-down fishing pier."

"I had no idea that's where Daryl was killed."

"You know the property?"

"Yes, but we hadn't been out there in years."

Nash closed her memo pad and placed it in her jacket pocket, "Alright then, that's all I had."

Nash's cell phone rang – it was Donnelly.

"Yeah, I'm finishing up with her right now" she said into the phone. "Really? Wow. Okay... thanks."

Nash hung up and turned to Madison, "Tell me about the recent increase in Daryl's life insurance."

"A few months ago he said that the fifty-thousand dollars each of us had would not be enough if something happened; he said we should have enough to cover expenses and to pay off the house. I told him I didn't think we could afford it, but he said that since we're still young... me under thirty and him in his early thirties... that it wouldn't be that expensive."

"So, why was *his* policy the only one that was increased?"

"What're you talking about, I signed two sets of papers... one for him and one for me?"

"Your insurance company's records show a pre-existing policy for you at fifty-thousand dollars, and a newer policy for Daryl at *three-*

hundred-thousand dollars."

"That's the right amount, but they must have misfiled the policy for me because I signed papers for *both* of us... I *swear.*"

"Okay" said Nash, *"Now* that's all I had... unless you have any questions for me?"

"What's going to happen to Officer Roberson?"

"That's up to Captain O'Rourke... assuming there are no more surprises."

Madison, with a look of concern on her face, remained silent.

Nash stood up from her seat. "Thanks for coming in" she said.

"You're welcome" Madison replied.

Madison left the room and immediately looked toward Roberson's desk. He looked up from his paperwork. She gave him an apologetic smile; fearing that what she had shared in her interview was about to get him in hot water. He smiled back.

Madison turned and proceeded out of the building.

37

Nash walked out of the Interview Room – closing the door behind her. She glanced over at Roberson seated at his desk. Roberson could feel Nash's presence, but had no intention of acknowledging her.

Nash turned and started toward Captain O'Rourke's office... a planned visit, but with a new sense of urgency.

O'Rourke looked up from his desk as Nash entered, "Hey Kenz; go ahead and shut the door if you would."

Nash reached back and gently pulled the door until it latched.

O'Rourke gestured toward a chair; Nash took a seat.

"How'd it go?" O'Rourke inquired.

"I had to kick Officer Wilberforce out of the interview."

That was not the response that O'Rourke was expecting, "What happened?"

"Apparently he's been watching too many cop shows where the interrogator tries to beat a confession out of a suspect."

"He didn't...?"

"Physically – no" Nash clarified, "But verbally – yes."

"I'll have a talk with him."

"That would be a good idea."

"So, you said you had something you needed to talk to me about in person?"

"Before I get to that, there was a surprising revelation that surfaced during my interview."

"Really?"

"Yeah; and just so you know, I'm not looking to go all *Internal Affairs* on one of your Officers, but I'd be doing you a disservice if I didn't make you aware."

O'Rourke looked concerned, "What have you got?"

"Actually I'd like to show you" Nash replied. "I sent over the video from *Super Mart* at the time that the burner phone found at the crime scene was purchased. If you can access it on your computer I can show you what I'm talking about."

O'Rourke performed a few keystrokes and mouse clicks and announced, "Okay; I've got it" as he pointed to a large screen on the wall of his office.

"If you hit 'Play'..."

O'Rourke complied.

Nash pointed to the screen, "The woman there is Madison Wagner, the wife of the vic."

"Okay" O'Rourke responded.

"Now pay attention to the guy next to her: He talks to her, makes a purchase of his own, and then catches up with her again in the parking lot."

"A person of interest?"

"I asked Madison and she identified him as *Mike.*"

The name was not clicking with O'Rourke, "Mike?"

"She clarified that it was Officer *Mike* Roberson."

"You're shitting me?"

"Nope. She said he'd been helping her out; and in this particular case, according to her anyway, the burner phone that she purchased was recommended by him."

"And they were on a first-name basis?"

"So she says. What makes matters worse is that *his* purchase was *also* a burner phone, and he's been using it to communicate with her... the calls started just *after* her husband Daryl's death."

"Son of a bitch!" said O'Rourke while getting up from his chair, "Time to have a little chat with him."

"Before you do, I have the item I *originally* called you about" Nash replied while she extracted the evidence bag containing the threatening note.

O'Rourke sat back down – Nash handed him the note. He read it and responded, "Who was the recipient of this?"

"The vic… Daryl Wagner. We found it in his gym bag."

"I assume Riggs analyzed the handwriting?"

"He couldn't say *definitively*, but it *appeared* to be Officer Roberson's handiwork."

"What did the Officer say?"

"I didn't ask; I just got the results and wanted to show it to you first."

"I appreciate that. Anything else before I call him in here?"

"That was it. And hey, it's not like I'm looking to charge him with a crime, but I'm sure you can see that even if he has been genuinely trying to do nothing more than help a victim of domestic violence, the whole thing is a bit messy."

"To say the least" O'Rourke said as he walked toward his office door… clearly annoyed, "This is the type of crap that drives me nuts – goddamned self-inflicted wounds."

O'Rourke opened the door, stuck his head out, glared at Roberson, and loudly voiced, "Officer Roberson!"

A startled Roberson looked up from his desk, "Yes, Captain" he replied.

O'Rourke gave Roberson the *get your ass over here* finger wave – Roberson sheepishly made his way to O'Rourke's office. It wasn't until he walked through the doorway that he saw Nash… his heart sank at the sight of her; anticipating fallout from Nash's interview with Madison.

"Officer Roberson" said O'Rourke, "I have a few questions."

"Sir?" Roberson replied.

O'Rourke started the video and pointed to the screen, "Any idea who *that* guy is?"

"I believe that's me, Sir."

"Care to explain yourself?"

"Madison... uh... *Mrs. Wagner*... was concerned about what her husband Daryl might do after serving him the restraining order. I suggested she get a pre-paid cell so that he couldn't harass or intimidate her by phone."

"Madison?? Really??"

Roberson had the look of a student who just got caught cheating on a test.

O'Rourke continued... once again pointing at the screen... "You were in civvies there... *off-duty*. Did you *completely forget* about proper police protocol?!"

"I was just trying to help a woman get out of an abusive relationship; I guess I had a lapse in judgment."

"You think?!! And what is it that *you* are purchasing?"

"A pre-paid cell phone."

"You *have* a cell phone."

"I just thought it would be better to use a pre-paid than my personal cell to communicate and make sure she was okay through all of this."

"Have you lost your damn mind?!"

Roberson remained silent; he knew there was no correct answer to the question.

O'Rourke held out his hand toward Nash; Nash handed him the threatening note. He held the note in front of Roberson, "Do you know anything about *this?*"

"I wrote it" Roberson confessed, "And placed it on Daryl Wagner's windshield when he was parked outside of *Circuit Fitness*."

O'Rourke was speechless; his blood was about to boil.

Roberson attempted to explain his actions... "I thought that if he knew someone was watching him he'd stop the abuse."

"By threatening him?!"

"I was just trying to scare him; I had no intention of actually doing him harm."

"You realize that if Daryl Wagner found out that *you* wrote that note then *he* could have filed harassment charges against *you*... against the *entire Department* for that matter."

"I guess I hadn't thought of that."

"Right now you are potentially interfering with a criminal investigation... a *murder* investigation. Your actions are not only ill-conceived, they actually draw suspicion."

"Suspicion? Sir?"

"You wrote a threatening note to someone who turned up murdered only a few days later; you were meeting with his wife in an *unofficial* manner *before* his murder; and you've been communicating with her via a burner phone right *after* his murder."

Roberson had no response.

O'Rourke made his final declaration, "It needs to stop... *NOW!*"

"Yes Sir."

O'Rourke gave Roberson a *'Get your ass out of here'* head-nod.

Roberson turned and walked out of O'Rourke's office.

Nash and O'Rourke stood in momentary silence – Nash in a state of surprise that Roberson didn't try to bullshit his way of his predicament – O'Rourke exasperated at the entire event.

Nash broke the silence and extended her hand, "Well, thanks Sean... I'll keep you posted."

"I appreciate it."

38

Brogan and Donnelly, in tandem, walked into the office to the sight of Nash at the murder board.

Nash turned around, took notice of their arrival, and turned back to the board. "If you two are dating" said Nash while still facing the murder board, "I don't want to know about it."

Donnelly blushed; Brogan replied somewhat defensively, "Not at all; we just pulled into the parking lot at the same time."

As Brogan and Donnelly approached they were shocked by a new entry and associated photograph on the murder board – it was *Officer Mike Roberson*.

"I don't understand" remarked Donnelly, "Roberson is a *suspect?*"

"It's not that simple" responded Nash. She turned to Brogan, "Of all the names and photos that have donned the board over the course of our various cases, how many, percentage wise, were actually the guilty party?"

"I don't know" Brogan replied, "Maybe five to ten percent?"

"Which means ninety to ninety-five percent were innocent?"

"I guess so... yeah."

"And how did we come to that conclusion?"

"Once we laid everything out it became clear that they weren't the perp."

"Bingo."

"So, the ability to visualize the details on the board brings clarity to their innocence" Donnelly concluded.

"Well, there's always the five to ten percent where the details end up putting them in the crosshairs" said Nash.

"Then the purpose of putting Roberson on the board is to show without a doubt that he's not our guy, and thus we can focus on the real killer?" said Brogan.

"Let's hope that's the case; but the purpose of putting him on the board is that every time we turn around he has some sort of involvement and we need to figure out W-T-F."

"There's something new pointing at him?"

"That would be an understatement."

Nash moved to the side to reveal the additional items under Roberson's name.

Donnelly was the first to raise her eyebrows and inquire… *"Roberson* wrote the note?"

Brogan added, "And *he's* the guy who was with Madison at *Super Mart?"*

"You got it" responded Nash.

"Did he explain his actions?"

"Regarding the note; he said he wrote it to try to scare Daryl into leaving Madison alone. In the case of *her* burner; he talked her into getting it in the event that Daryl tried to make harassing phone calls after she filed the restraining order. And he bought *his own* burner so he could keep in touch with her and make sure she was okay."

"Those all sound legit."

"A police officer writing a threatening note to a member of the general public is *legit?"*

"Well, when you put it *that* way…"

"How did Captain O'Rourke react?" asked Donnelly.

"He was pissed" replied Nash, "In fact he's probably ripping Roberson *a new one* as we speak."

"So, what do we do with this new info?" said Brogan.

Nash pointed to the murder board, "We start *populating the crap* out of this thing and see where it leads us."

Nash posted another picture next to Roberson's on the board.

"Madison Wagner??" stated Brogan.

"These two seemed to be joined at the hip, so it only makes sense to place them adjacent to each other and see what ties them together, and what does not."

39

The murder board was starting to fill up like a bucket under a leaky roof. None of the team really wanted to see a fellow cop implicated in Daryl Wagner's murder, and even more so any hint of Madison Wagner's involvement; but every addition to the board tended to point a finger in their direction in lieu of exonerating them.

Item after item seemed to lend credence to Roberson and Madison's guilt, yet every so often there would be an item that made no sense; at least not *common sense*. One of the overriding nonsensical issues in Nash's mind was murdering Daryl right after Madison had *finally* taken out a restraining order against him.

This conundrum was not lost on Brogan or Donnelly either, with Donnelly commenting, "Why not see if the restraining order works and the abuse finally stops? I mean it had been what... only one day??"

"And to make the leap to murder and risk a life in prison instead of waiting-out the restraining order?" Brogan added, "It's ridiculous."

"Maybe Daryl threatened to kill Madison when he found out about the restraining order? And if so, then maybe Roberson and Madison felt that they were out of options?" stated Nash.

"You think that's a viable reason?"

"Hell no; but someone had convinced themselves that murder was the proper recourse."

Trevor Cobb was still in-play of course... he'd had a beef with Daryl Wagner, and he had no alibi for the time of Daryl's murder. But if he *was* involved it was looking more and more like it would have been as an accomplice; and even *that* would be difficult to prove barring a confession – considering the minimal amount of evidence tied to him thus far. However; it was something that Cobb had said *off the cuff* that was wearing on Nash's mind: Maybe he was right, maybe Daryl was actually saying 'cop' and not 'Cobb' when he was attempting to communicate via the ATM camera? And if that was the case, maybe the 'cop' was Officer Roberson. After all, more and more pieces of circumstantial evidence were pointing in his direction, if not *directly at him*.

Nash had sent a picture of Roberson to Andrew Lloyd, asking if he was the guy who had purchased the black & white. Lloyd responded that it looked like him, but he couldn't testify to it without seeing him person. However, when Nash mentioned the name *Mike Roberson* Lloyd had responded, "That's it! That's the name of the guy!"

Donnelly had also uncovered a two-thousand dollar withdrawal made by Roberson just two days before the purchase of the black & white. Andrew Lloyd, the owner, said he sold the car for eighteen-hundred dollars. These instances added to the *possibilities* in Nash's mind.

At every turn, so it appeared, Roberson was in the vicinity and had opportunity; or at the very least his whereabouts were in question and could not be corroborated otherwise. He had admitted to purchasing a burner phone at the same time Madison had made her purchase; and his phone had been activated at a pay phone near the ferry terminal... as had Madison's phone, which had ended up in the lap of Daryl's charred corpse. That particular pay phone was also used to inquire into the sale of the black & white – the vehicle that had been at the scene *and* had Daryl's wedding band hidden under the passenger seat.

By Roberson's own account he'd been in the vicinity of the crime the night of the murder. And his patrol area earlier that evening also took him in the vicinity of the ATM where Daryl, appearing to be under duress, made the withdrawal.

While the murder board was doing anything *but* exonerating Officer Roberson, things were not so clear when it came to Madison Wagner. She had purchased the burner phone that had ended up at the crime scene, but she had also been home to receive the call from that phone. *Motive* was the only true item pointing in her direction at this point, and it was twofold: Being a victim of abuse by her husband; and the recent increase in his life insurance. But motive alone wasn't going to convict someone of a crime... you need evidence to back that up, and in her case evidence was sorely lacking; until Nash's cell phone rang...

"Hey Lowell, what have you got?" Nash said into the phone. "What?? Wait a minute; let me write all this down."

Nash grabbed her memo pad, "Okay; go ahead." She scribbled line after line as Lowell spoke, and then stated, "Holy crap, I did *not* see that coming. Ironically, we were literally in the middle of laying out everything we had learned about Madison and Roberson, trying to make sense of it all. Oh, and by the way, Roberson *did* admit to writing the threatening note. Yeah... one more tick-mark against him. And with the information you just gave me about Madison I may have to reassess my game-plan... I'll keep you posted."

Nash hung up her phone and stared off into space... processing what she had just learned.

Nash's exclamation of surprise at the onset of her conversation had stopped Brogan and Donnelly in their tracks. Standing motionless throughout the duration of Nash's phone call they were waiting with baited breaths to discover the source of Nash's angst, but neither of them had the courage to interrupt her moment of contemplation.

Nash finally broke her silence and faced Brogan and Donnelly... she looked concerned. "That was Lowell" she said, "The Cyber guys were able to recover some deleted files on the Wagner's home computer; the contents of which do not bode well for Madison."

Donnelly had the look of someone whose interest had been piqued; Brogan had the look of anticipation... the gut-wrenching anticipation a guy feels when his girlfriend just told him *'We need to talk'.*

As she prepared to break the news Nash took a deep breath and shook her head... it was the barely visible head shake of disbelief.

"I'm not implying that everything Lowell shared with me was a gotcha moment or a smoking gun" Nash finally revealed, "But a couple of them are eye-openers, if not downright game-changers."

Brogan and Donnelly looked at each other, and then back to Nash. "There were *several* items of interest?" said Brogan.

"For starters" said Nash as she flipped open her memo pad, "Web searches on homes and shelters for victims of domestic violence."

Brogan immediately came to Madison's defense, "That just shows that she was finally looking for a way to escape Daryl's abuse."

"Then why delete the search?"

"I'm sure she figured that if Daryl found out about the search he'd beat the crap out of her."

"I concur with your assessment, but I'd like to hear it from *her*."

Nash glanced back at her memo pad, "Then there was a search on pre-paid cell phones."

"That doesn't mean anything; a lot of people check to see what pre-paid phones are all about without some evil intent behind the search."

"Agreed; but if you give me a chance you'll see where all of this is going."

"Sorry... go ahead."

"Dental records; and a follow-up of DNA within tooth pulp."

"There was a specific search on *DNA within tooth pulp?*"

"Yes. And here's the coup de grace... a search of homicide cases that had successfully used *'The Battered Wife Defense'.*"

"You're telling me that Madison was planning for Daryl's murder, how to prevent his identification, and a method of defense in event she was implicated?"

"Can you provide me any other explanation? It's not like *Daryl* would have made these searches."

"What if someone else, like Roberson, used her computer for the searches?" responded Donnelly.

"That *does* seem more plausible" Nash admitted. "Look into the timing of Madison and Roberson's communication versus the date and time of these *Battered Wife Defense* searches. If Roberson didn't specifically perform the search, perhaps he at least planted the seed."

"Will do" said Donnelly.

"That's *got* to be it" noted Brogan, "There's *no way* Madison planned some elaborate scheme to kill her husband."

"The woman we've encountered... No" Nash responded, "But you have no idea what someone is capable of when they are cornered. Or worse, when they feel their life is in danger... when they are faced with a *kill or be killed* alternative."

"So, what do we do with this information?" asked Donnelly.

"We start piecing together everything we have on Roberson and Madison."

"But haven't we pretty much done that on the board here, other than a few loose ends we need to run down?" asked Brogan.

"This would be in file form; in preparation for presenting it to Sheriff Clarke and the Deputy Prosecutor."

Things suddenly got real for Brogan; he had taken Madison's ordeal to heart from the moment he first met her... battered and bruised from the beatings her husband Daryl had inflicted upon her. The idea that Madison might have been involved in Daryl's murder was gut-punching... almost too much to comprehend.

Nash was equally troubled, but as Team Leader she had to maintain her composure... her professional approach... this was not the time to let her personal feelings become an impediment to the search for the truth.

Donnelly's mood was somber as well, and she had not even experienced the horrifying results of the beatings that Daryl had inflicted upon Madison.

Nash looked at her watch, "While you two are compiling the files on Roberson and Madison I'm going to take one last run at each of them; perhaps they'll provide me something that steers us in a totally different direction."

"Let's hope" said Brogan.

"I'm not holding my breath" replied Nash as she walked out the door.

40

Nash kept running various scenarios through her head, trying to determine if there was something she had missed, that someone *other* than Madison... a frightened and battered wife, and Roberson... a decorated police officer, were the prime suspects in a murder case. But to no avail, there was a mountain of evidence pointing toward Roberson, and although the evidence against Madison was minimal, it was damning. Nash feared this one last interview was going to be nothing more than a mere formality.

Nash rapped on the door of the Wagner home. Madison opened the door with a smile; which quickly faded at the sight of law enforcement. It was the first time Nash had seen even a hint of a smile on Madison's face, and found the situation to be rather ironic; all those years of Madison's constant beatings the arrival of police at her door had been her momentary savior, now they were potentially the source of her undoing.

"Detective?" questioned Madison, "What can I do for you?"

"It's about your computer" Nash replied.

"You have it for me?"

"Unfortunately, no; it has become an official piece of evidence."

"Evidence?"

"We've uncovered some deleted files with apparent ties to your husband's murder."

"What?! How's that possible??"

"That's why I'm here; to get answers to those questions."

"Like what?"

"Did you perform a search of shelters for victims of domestic violence?"

"I was looking for ways I could escape from my husband and his abuse."

"Why did you delete the files... the search history?"

"Are you kidding? Daryl would have killed me if he found out I was going to leave him. And if I *did* leave he could've found my search and then he would have known exactly where to look for me... all the places I had looked into."

"What about a search for pre-paid cell phones?"

"That too. When Mike... umm... Officer Roberson... suggested I get one I had no idea exactly what they were, so I did a web search to find out about them, how much they cost, and where they were sold around here."

"And you deleted that information and search history as well?"

"Yes; for the same reason... Daryl would have asked me why I was looking up pre-paid cell phones."

"What about searching information regarding dental records and DNA... specifically *DNA within tooth pulp?*"

"What?? I've never looked up any such thing; and I've never even *heard* of *DNA within tooth pulp*... what does that even mean?"

"You realize that all of Daryl's teeth had been removed, which made identification by use of dental records an impossibility, and DNA within his tooth pulp unavailable in the event all other sources were destroyed?"

"You never told me he had his teeth removed; what kind of sick person does that?"

"Someone who's trying to prevent the identification of their victim."

"This makes no sense, there has to be some kind of misunderstanding."

"And what about searches for cases utilizing a *Battered Wife Defense,* is that a misunderstanding as well?"

"What are you talking about? This is crazy!" Madison paused in thought, "Maybe Daryl did the search?"

"Why would he do that?"

"He was the one *battering his wife*, so maybe something got to him… maybe one of those *48 Hours* or *Dateline* shows?"

"I suppose that's possible" Nash replied. "So, let me ask you this: Would anyone else have had access to your computer?"

"Not routinely; but only my email is password-protected, not access to the internet, so if one of Daryl's friends were here they could've used it."

Nash jotted in her memo pad, "Was Officer Roberson ever inside your home?"

Madison didn't respond right away; her demeanor spoke volumes – she didn't want to answer the question. Nash gave her a stern glare.

Madison relented, "He had been here a few times to check up on me."

"Before your husband died?"

"Yes."

"Did he ever use your computer?"

"He helped me look up the shelters."

"Anything else?"

"Not that I can think of."

"Did he do the research *for* you, or did he merely assist you with it?"

"Actually he did the look-up and then called me in to see what he'd come up with."

"So he could have done some other searches while you were away from the computer?"

"I suppose. But he wouldn't have looked up the other stuff you mentioned."

"How do you know?"

"Because he's not that kind of person."

Nash had expected such a response from Madison; after all, she had repeatedly tried to avoid implicating Roberson in any way.

Just as silence had taken center stage Madison was struck with an idea and suddenly blurted out, "Wait; if the killer got into the house to steal my cell phone, then maybe he also did the computer searches?"

This notion seemed extremely implausible to Nash, although it triggered something she had not previously considered, and *this* idea made *perfect* sense... perhaps *Roberson* took Madison's phone without her knowledge? *"Holy crap; that would explain a lot"* she thought to herself.

"Detective?" said Madison; wondering if Nash had heard her question as she appeared to be momentarily lost in space.

Nash snapped back to reality with a response that was merely intended to placate Madison, "We will certainly take that into consideration."

Another idea popped into Nash's mind, "You said Officer Roberson checked on you periodically?"

"Yes."

"How about that weekend?"

"He stopped by Saturday night after his shift. He was concerned since Daryl had hit me and threatened me the night before... after I told him about the restraining order."

"How do you know it was right after his shift?"

"Because he was still in uniform and had blood on his shirt."

"Blood on his shirt?!"

"Yeah; I thought it was from a bloody nose cuz he looked like he got socked in the face, but he said it was from breaking up a fight."

Nash was so stunned by this news that she had trouble hiding her surprise, but she knew she had to maintain a poker face. "And what time was that?" she asked.

"I don't know... sometime between midnight and one o'clock I suppose."

Nash was tempted to dig deeper, but the wheels were now turning in her head and she didn't want to be obvious and run the risk of Madison tipping-off Roberson.

"Okay then... I guess that's all I have for now."

41

Nash had given Captain O'Rourke a heads-up of sorts regarding her need to interview Roberson one more time. She hadn't provided details, only that new information had surfaced regarding Madison Wagner and the Officer.

When Nash walked into the Bennington Police Station Roberson was already seated in the Interview Room. Roberson's body language told a story – he was clearly annoyed with the prospect of being interrogated. Nash had not used that term, preferring the word *interview,* but Roberson knew when to call a spade a spade.

Captain O'Rourke had noticed Nash's arrival, and joined her at the doorway to the Interview Room.

"Anything I need to know before we start?" asked O'Rourke.

"Don't worry, I won't blindside you."

"Okay… it's your show."

Nash and O'Rourke entered the room. Nash sat directly across from Roberson; O'Rourke moved back out of the way but remained standing. Nash wasn't sure what to make of O'Rourke's stance… was it intended to be an intimidation factor toward Roberson to ensure he kept on the straight and narrow? Or was it simply to stay in the background and allow Nash to do her thing?

Nash directed her first question to Roberson, "You were in the vicinity the night of Daryl Wagner's murder, correct?"

Roberson was immediately flippant, "I don't know… if you say so."

"You told me a week ago that you were there." Nash opened her memo pad… "Quote – *I drove by the area around eleven forty but there was nothing out of the ordinary at the time* – unquote." Nash closed her memo pad.

"Yes, I drove by what was later determined to be the scene. I was heading home from my patrol area at the end of my shift."

"But you didn't go directly home."

Roberson was hesitant; he looked over to O'Rourke. O'Rourke gave him the *"answer the question"* stink-eye.

"That's correct" said Roberson, "I made a brief stop to make a well-being check on Mrs. Wagner."

"Can you define *well-being check?*"

"She had just informed her husband the night before that she had filed a restraining order against him... his response was to punch her in the face. I stopped by to make sure he had not returned, and to make sure she was okay."

"She stated that when you stopped by you looked like you'd been punched in the face, and had blood on your shirt."

"Yeah, I had just broken up a fight at the *Hilltop.*"

O'Rourke immediately interjected, "Why is this the first time I am hearing about this?"

"There was nothing to tell, Captain" responded Roberson, "A couple of guys got into a fight and one of them got bloodied. I jumped between them to break it up, got elbowed in the chops, and also got the one guy's blood on my shirt. I made sure the situation cooled down, gave them a warning, and let them go."

O'Rourke nodded to Nash as if to say 'Go ahead'.

Nash continued with Roberson, "What time did you stop by the Wagner home?"

"Around midnight."

"Are you sure it wasn't closer to one A.M.?"

"No; it was around midnight."

"Madison said she thought it could be as late as one o'clock."

"Well, she's mistaken."

"How long were you there... at her house?"

"Ten to twenty minutes maybe."

"So, you were there when she received the phone call?"

"What phone call?"

Nash glared at Roberson. "You're kidding me, right?" she said.

"No, I wasn't there."

Nash scribbled in her memo pad, "So, back to that shirt…"

"What about it?"

"You're sure the blood was from breaking up a fight at the *Hilltop Tavern?*"

"Check with their staff, they'll corroborate everything."

"Where's the shirt now?"

"It was ruined so I tossed it."

"Interesting" replied Nash as she jotted down Roberson's response in her memo pad.

"Just what are you implying, Detective?"

"You threatened Daryl Wagner, you were in the vicinity at the time of his murder, and you showed up at his wife's house with blood on your shirt…"

"Had I known that Wagner was going to get murdered and that I would subsequently get *railroaded* I would have kept the damn thing."

"Did you ever use Mrs. Wagner's computer?"

"Yeah, I helped her look up shelters for victims of domestic violence."

"Anything else?"

"Nope."

"No searches about forensic evidence, you know… dental records, DNA, tooth pulp, Battered Wife Defense… stuff like that?"

"Hell no."

"There was a black & white former Police Interceptor Crown Vic that had been at the scene; and Daryl Wagner's ring was found inside."

"Yeah? So?"

"So, the seller of the car identified you… by name *and* your photo… as the buyer."

"That's a bunch of bull; I never bought such a car."

"Then how do you explain him identifying you?"

"We all know that names and faces attributed to so-called '*witnesses*' are ridiculously unreliable; he is obviously mistaken."

"First Madison was *mistaken* as to when you stopped by her house the night of the murder; and now the seller of the vehicle tied to the scene, who identified *you* as the buyer, is also *mistaken*" said Nash... "It seems everyone who contradicts your version of events is *mistaken*."

Roberson sat silent while attempting to maintain his cool; but his scowl directed toward Nash spoke for itself... he was clearly annoyed at the implication.

"Not only that, but the car was sold for eighteen-hundred dollars" Nash continued... "And you *just so happened* to withdraw two-thousand dollars from your savings account two days before the car was purchased."

"You've been looking into my financials?!! That's it, I'm done talking!" Roberson responded as he sat back in his chair and crossed his arms.

Nash looked over at O'Rourke. O'Rourke gave her a head nod toward the door of the Interview Room. The two of them exited and began a hushed conversation...

"Are you telling me that you think Officer Roberson is Daryl Wagner's murderer?" said O'Rourke.

"I hate to say it, but beyond this stuff today, and what we addressed *yesterday* when I was here, I've got about another dozen things that point his way."

"What was the deal with the computer searches?"

"That's what the Cyber guys found when they recovered deleted files."

"Damn, that looks bad."

"Yeah."

"Motive?"

"The only thing that makes sense is fear that Daryl was going to take revenge on Madison for filing the restraining order. After all, he had told her that if she ever left him he would kill her." Nash paused, "And the fact that there was a recent increase in his life insurance just adds salt to the wound."

"So, what're you thinking?"

"Right now we're compiling everything we have on both Madison and Roberson to see if it warrants taking to the Prosecutor."

"Can you give me a heads-up if it gets to that point?"

"Sure."

"This is one of those days when I hate my job" said O'Rourke.

"You and me both" replied Nash.

42

Nash was flipping through Roberson's file when Donnelly walked into the room. "You and Dirk did a great job compiling all this stuff yesterday" Nash commented.

"Thanks" responded Donnelly.

"Yeah... thanks" echoed Brogan as he approached.

When Brogan got up next to Donnelly he inquired of her... "You tell Kenz about Clarke?"

"What about him?" Nash intervened.

"He stopped by and did a quick review of the files and the murder board" Donnelly replied, "I think he wants you to present it to him and the Deputy Prosecutor sometime today."

"Today??"

"From *his* perspective we were building a credible case against both Madison and Roberson... *especially* Roberson" said Brogan.

"I kind of figured he might be pushing us to take the next step in this case" replied Nash.

"That's a good thing, right?" said Donnelly.

"It's an almost overwhelming amount of evidence, although solely circumstantial" replied Nash, "But to implicate a battered wife and a decorated cop... it's like getting smacked in the face."

"Tell me about it" said Brogan, "But it's not like we can drag this thing out forever... I mean, what would be our reason for delaying the inevitable?"

"The truth."

"What are you talking about, everything in the files are facts; it's not like we're making up crap just to close a case?"

"True; it's just the way this case is coming together."

"Are you kidding; it's coming together stroke-by-stroke like a painting."

"Yeah... like a Picasso."

"A *what??*"

"Never mind."

A gentleman in a suit and tie walked into the office. This was a rare sight indeed, usually reserved for a State or Local Official 'showing the flag' during some high profile incident; or a local politician trying to make points with the Law Enforcement Community.

"Who's that?" Donnelly whispered to Nash.

"Deputy Prosecutor Alan Dansby" Nash replied.

Dansby spied Nash and walked directly toward her. "Detective Nash" he said as he reached out to shake hands.

"Mister Dansby, what brings you to our little nook here?"

"I understand you have the *Daryl Wagner murder case* prepared to present to Sheriff Clarke and me?"

"It's coming together, Sir. But at its current state it is also one-hundred percent circumstantial... no eyewitnesses, and no physical evidence such as fingerprints or DNA."

"Well, it wouldn't be the first time I've prosecuted a case that was solely circumstantial."

"Of course, Sir."

"And this must be the rest of your investigative team?" said Dansby as he reached out to shake hands with Brogan and Donnelly.

"Yes, Sir" responded Nash who followed with introductions... "This is Detective Brogan... and Deputy Donnelly."

"Deputy?" said Dansby as he shook hands with Donnelly, "I'm a deputy as well... Deputy Prosecutor Dansby."

"Sir" Donnelly and Brogan acknowledged in unison.

Nash rolled her eyes at Dansby's overt attempt to be personable with Brogan and Donnelly, as if he was talking to five-year-olds. *"Ever the politician"* she thought to herself, *"What's he going to do next, look around for a baby to kiss?"*

Dansby turned back to Nash, "I assume your presentation will include a possible scenario… a sequence of events that ties all of the evidence together?"

"Yes Sir."

"Excellent; I'm sure you won't let us down."

Nash wasn't sure what to make of Dansby's statement – it sounded condescending. *"What the hell is he up to?"* she wondered.

Dansby disappeared into Sheriff Clarke's office.

"Why would he show up here asking about a case?" Brogan said to Nash.

"Beats me… he sounded like a politician trying to garner votes; it's a good thing there wasn't a toddler around for him to play patty-cakes with for a photo-op" Nash replied. "I hope there's no political B.S. behind his inquiry."

"What do you need us to do?"

"As soon as Dansby leaves I'm going to go have a chat with Clarke; but in the meantime we need to continue to prepare everything for my presentation."

Dansby's visit with Sheriff Clarke was brief; as soon as he exited the building Nash high-tailed it to Clarke's office.

"You ready to present your case?" Clarke said to Nash before she had even finished walking through the doorway.

"Not as ready as I'd like" she replied.

"Scanning your files yesterday it looked perfectly presentable to me."

"Something tells me there could be more to the story."

"More of *what?* You've got pages and pages of stuff that clearly puts the wife and her cop buddy in the crosshairs" Clarke replied. "Dansby is pushing to get this case resolved; the Prosecutor is retiring and, as Deputy Prosecutor, Dansby is the logical choice."

"The logical choice?"

"For County Prosecutor; and this would be a nice feather in his cap."

"A feather in his cap? What the hell is that?!"

"With all the bad press going on around the country regarding law enforcement these days, it's a perfect opportunity to show that *here*, in Slaughter County, justice prevails for *everyone*."

"For everyone?"

"Yes; cops will be held accountable just like every other citizen in the County… they will receive no special treatment, and there will be no sweeping their crimes under the rug."

"Sounds like a bunch of politics to me."

"Not everything in the world is black and white."

"When it comes to justice, and the law, it should be."

"I don't know what's gotten under your skin; you have scads of evidence against this guy, so let's get to presenting it."

"And the woman who's been getting the shit beat out of her for who-knows-how-many years… what about her?"

"It's unfortunate… but she made her choices."

"She made her choices?? To get the *shit* beat out of her??"

"To get involved with a cop who apparently decided to take matters into his own hands and make her problem go away – *permanently*."

Nash turned around and started to walk out of Clarke's office.

"Dansby will be here at three o'clock" remarked Clarke as Nash was leaving.

Without turning around Nash raised her hand and replied, "Got it."

Brogan and Donnelly, working feverishly on Roberson and Madison's files, ceased action as Nash approached.

"How'd it go" Brogan inquired of Nash.

"Apparently there's some political motivation behind getting this case to the Prosecutor and subsequently to trial."

"Political? How?"

"I'll fill you in on that crap later." Nash looked at her watch, "Right now we need to get this stuff ready for me to present by three o'clock."

"Three o'clock??"

"Yep."

Nash thought for a moment and then turned to Donnelly, "Hey Laura, you started compiling information about Daryl Wagner earlier in the investigation..."

"Yes I did, but it fell by the wayside as we started to close in on our suspects."

"Understood; but once we get Roberson and Madison's files ready, I want you to get back on Daryl Wagner's trail... I want to know *every damn move* he made over the past few weeks."

"Will do."

43

Nash walked into Sheriff Clarke's office carrying a stack of file folders. She had prearranged with Clarke to show the two videos that were a part of her evidence: The purchase of the burner phones by Officer Roberson and Madison Wagner; and Daryl Wagner's ATM video.

"Gentlemen" said Nash as she placed the stack of folders on the table, "If you'd like to take your seats I'll go over the case against Madison Wagner and Officer Mike Roberson as the evidence suggests."

Deputy Prosecutor Dansby and Sheriff Clarke each took a seat facing Nash. She handed them two folders apiece, and retained two for her use.

"One folder applies to Madison Wagner; the other to Officer Roberson" Nash commented.

Dansby and Clarke commenced flipping through the files.

"The bulk of the files are the compilation of facts, evidence, and other supporting documentation" Nash continued, "My goal is not to go through every piece if information contained therein, rather, I've prepared a sequence of events… a *possible scenario* if you will… supported by the evidence."

"Weaving the facts together via conjecture in order to create a realistic story?" responded Dansby.

"That's correct, Sir."

"Alright, let's hear what you've got."

Nash flipped to her synopsis… "Daryl Wagner was a wife-beater; inflicting physical and emotional abuse on Madison for years" she stated and looked up to clarify her statement, "This information was gleaned directly from Bennington Police Department files."

Nash continued… "Officer Roberson had responded to multiple domestic violence calls to the Wagner home, witnessing *first-hand* the results of Daryl's beatings; but each and every time Madison had refused to press charges. Roberson had grown fond of Madison and vice-versa."

Dansby interrupted, "What proof do you have to support that statement? Are there texts, emails, love letters? Caught them holding hands, kissing, or in a compromising position?"

"Well, no; but they *were* on a first-name basis" replied Nash, "They slipped-up in front of both Captain O'Rourke and me during our interviews."

"So, what you're saying then is that they had *'forged a friendship that grew beyond that of a police officer and a member of the general public'?*" Dansby hinted.

"That's correct; I'll revise my wording."

"Good; let's go with that."

"As *friends*" Nash continued, "Roberson could no longer sit back and witness the results of the beatings inflicted upon Madison. He tried to convince her to leave Daryl, but she was too afraid of him as he had told her on numerous occasions that if *he* couldn't have her *nobody* would, causing her to fear for her life if she took any action. That's when Roberson decided to do something about it."

"In what manner?" said Dansby.

"Roberson wrote a threatening note in the hopes that Daryl would have second thoughts about harming Madison."

"A threatening note?" Dansby asked.

"Yes; there's a copy of it in your folders" Nash replied.

"Do we *know* that Roberson wrote it?" said Dansby as both he and Clarke flipped through their associated folders to view the note for themselves.

"Yes; he admitted as much to Captain O'Rourke and me. And,

unfortunately, the threat didn't work. In fact, the beatings escalated as Daryl became angered about the note – blaming Madison."

"Son of a bitch" said Dansby as he viewed the note, "Not a smart move by a police officer."

"Correct. Thus Madison started looking for ways to escape the abuse, starting with web searches on shelters for victims of domestic violence, but she remained too frightened to act. That's when, I believe, Roberson came up with a plan they figured was the *only option* to avoid Madison eventually being killed at the hands of Daryl… to get rid of him. As a cop, Roberson knew how to avoid leaving evidence at a crime scene and had convinced Madison of this, but Madison made her first mistake… researching *DNA evidence* on her computer. She deleted her searches but the Cyber team was able to recover it."

"Was that the *only* damning evidence they discovered on her computer?" asked Dansby.

"The two big items were about *dental records;* and *DNA within tooth pulp.* Note that the victim… her husband… had all of his teeth removed."

"Whoa" Dansby replied.

"Yes Sir. Also, Daryl Wagner's life insurance was bumped-up from fifty-thousand dollars to three-hundred-thousand dollars just weeks before his murder. Madison claims she signed papers to bump-up *both* of their policies to that amount, but insurance company records indicate that *only* Daryl Wagner's coverage was increased. The bottom line is that she stands to collect three-hundred grand."

"Like a jury awarding damages for her pain and suffering" remarked Dansby.

"Whether it was her idea or Roberson's, I'm sure that's how they considered it."

Nash continued with the next item… "Madison was familiar with the property where the crime occurred, a secluded area that was not in use… the perfect spot for the murder."

"How do we know Madison knew of the property?" queried Dansby.

"She'd been there before; it used to belong to Daryl's family."

Dansby nodded; Nash continued... "Roberson agreed with the selection of the site, *especially* since it was close to the *Hilltop Tavern* where it would provide him with a reason for being in the area without drawing suspicion."

"The tavern gave him a reason to be in the area?"

"Yes Sir; an increased presence had been instituted by Captain O'Rourke as a means to reduce potential DUIs."

Nash continued... "Roberson reasoned he'd need an operable vehicle with which to abduct Daryl, figuring it would be too risky to abduct him and throw him into his cruiser – people tend to pay *way too much* attention to activities involving a police car. He didn't want to risk stealing a car, so he looked for one he could buy 'on the cheap', and just so happened to find the ideal ride... an old police cruiser Crown Vic. A vehicle that looked like a cop car would give him something of an alibi... or more accurately, a plausible alternate vehicle."

"What do you mean by *a plausible alternate vehicle?*" responded Dansby.

"If his *own* cruiser was spotted at the scene there would surely be someone who saw this *other* vehicle that could take the blame. Worst case scenario he could make an anonymous phone call to lead police to the black & white we ultimately tied to the scene."

"Interesting. And how did you tie the car to the scene?"

"Tire tracks" Nash replied. "We also found Daryl Wagner's wedding band stashed under the front passenger seat."

Dansby was impressed; Nash continued...

"He called about the car from the pay phone near the ferry terminal. The next day he jumped on the ferry and did the deal."

"Do we have *proof* that Roberson purchased this car?"

"Unfortunately, no; a Report of Sale was never filed so the car is still in the name of the previous owner."

"Then what ties the car to Officer Roberson?"

"Andrew Lloyd, the owner of the car, identified Roberson by name and by photograph."

"Is he willing to make that statement in Court?"

"Not without first seeing Roberson in person."

"Please clarify."

"Roberson matches the description he had given me, and when I showed him Roberson's picture he said *'Yeah, that looks like him, but I'd need to see him in person and hear his voice'*."

"So all of that raises doubt unless we can get him to see and hear Roberson in the flesh and *then* he makes a positive I.D.?"

"Correct. But an additional piece of circumstantial evidence is the fact that Lloyd said he sold the car for eighteen-hundred dollars, and Roberson made a two-thousand dollar withdrawal from his savings account two days before the purchase of the car."

"He's the kind of guy that would just throw away eighteen-hundred bucks for a car he's going to abandon?"

"That amount is not a concern when Madison would be getting a nice *three-hundred-thousand dollar* payday.

"Alright... we can use that."

Nash continued... "The actual crime scene was a nineteen-eighty-five Mazda six-two-six... it had broken down and was subsequently reported stolen. Roberson's patrols took him past the car. After seeing it there for a couple of days he figured it had been abandoned and saw the perfect opportunity to use it in conjunction with the crime – one that couldn't be traced back to him. He figured no one would question a car being towed by the police. Since all cruisers include a tow bar, he towed it to the property. In event the car was subsequently reported stolen he changed-out the plates with a pair that he picked up at a swap meet, or maybe even got out of the impound lot."

"That's an awful lot of conjecture" replied Dansby.

"Yes Sir, but the car had to get from the side of the road to the crime scene *somehow*."

"Very well; but let's *verify* the impound lot before we try to present such a possibility. If we can't verify it then we don't want to mention it as a *'what if'*… a good Defense Attorney would actually use that against us."

"Understood Sir" Nash replied, and then continued…

"A decision was made to file a restraining order against Daryl Wagner for one of two reasons: Either to make one last attempt to stop Daryl from beating Madison without resorting to bloodshed… which seems an unlikely reason because then it means Roberson truly *did* throw away almost two-thousand dollars for the black & white Crown Vic. Or, more likely, they filed it simply as a means to provide reasonable doubt to their guilt."

"Explain" replied Dansby.

"She could say *'why would I file a restraining order if I planned to have him killed in the first place?'*" responded Nash.

"Good point" said Dansby.

"However, before filing the order Roberson convinced Madison to get a pre-paid cell phone. This was based on the concern that Daryl would react by making harassing or threatening phone calls. Roberson bought a pre-paid cell at the same time as well. I have a video of the two making the purchases; plus they both admitted the purchase, and to the reason *behind* the purchase I just stated."

"You have the video?" said Dansby.

"Yes, Sir" replied Nash as she grabbed the remote and pointed toward the screen in Clarke's office.

Nash ran the video; pointing out Madison and Roberson.

"And they both admitted to being the pair we see in the video?" said Dansby.

"Yes. And these burner phones will come into play later."

Nash continued… "The restraining order was filed, but when Madison informed Daryl about the order he once again beat her up. Roberson decided it was time to execute the plan, and now it was merely finding the right opportunity, which occurred the very next night."

"The next night?" Dansby replied, "Was that merely a stroke of luck, or was it strategically planned?"

"Hard to say for sure, but both Officers Roberson and Stahl admitted that they had been tailing Daryl, so I'm thinking that Roberson tailed him again that Saturday, or he knew where he might likely find him."

"Do you think Officer Stahl had any role in all of this?"

"I haven't uncovered anything that would implicate her."

"Very well... continue" said Dansby.

"Just after dusk Roberson abducted Daryl; probably under the guise of placing him under arrest for smacking Madison around the night before. Roberson then forced Daryl to make an ATM withdrawal."

"Forced him to make an ATM withdrawal??" replied Dansby, "You're going to have to enlighten me as to why you think Officer Roberson went that route."

"I believe it was to make it look like Daryl's murder was tied to a robbery, *and* it was done as a means to provide Roberson with an alibi."

"An alibi?" asked Dansby.

"Yes... that he was *on-duty* at the time of the abduction" Nash replied. "But what he failed to consider is that his patrol area at that time of night... before he landed at the *Hilltop Tavern*... placed him near the location of the ATM."

"What makes you think his withdrawal had any tie to Roberson and was not simply Daryl grabbing a few bucks for himself?"

"I'm glad you asked. I have a video of the transaction."

Nash grabbed the remote and ran the video.

"He looks like he's in distress" stated Dansby as he watched Daryl's transaction. "And he's mouthing something into the camera."

"We think he is saying 'Cop' as a means to identify his abductor."

"But why not mention his abductor by name?"

"I believe that trying to mouth *'Roberson'* would've been too obvious. Notice how he does a quick look to his left, mouths the word, and looks back" Nash responded, "I think he's attempting to make a statement without getting caught. Also, notice that he is still wearing his wedding ring."

"Good call" replied Dansby. "But what's the importance of the wedding ring?"

"Roberson takes Daryl back to the cabin, but unbeknownst to *Roberson* Daryl had slid off his wedding ring and placed it under the seat of the black & white."

"Leaving a breadcrumb for investigators to find" Dansby nodded.

"Yes Sir; and once at the cabin Roberson gave Daryl a drink laced with GHB."

"Are you *speculating* that he was drugged?"

"No; we found a glass with residue that contained Scotch, GHB, and saliva that matched Daryl Wagner's DNA" replied Nash.

"Is that the sole evidence that Daryl Wagner was inside the cabin?"

"No. There were hair follicles wedged between the slats in the floor; and we found his wallet and his gun stashed under the floorboard beneath the kitchen sink."

"A gun? Obviously it didn't do him any good."

"Very true. Anyway, once Daryl was passed out Roberson strangled him. I'm guessing at this point he loaded Daryl into the trunk of the Mazda and then proceeded to his patrol duty at the nearby *Hilltop Tavern*. Once his shift was over he returned to the scene and pulled out all of Daryl's teeth in an attempt to keep him from being identified via dental records or by DNA within his tooth pulp. This could have been the source of the blood on Roberson's shirt."

"He had blood on his shirt?"

"Yes Sir; he said it was the result of breaking up a fight at the *Hilltop*."

"I'm sure you commissioned a DNA test; what were the results?"

"Unfortunately, we had no such opportunity – Officer Roberson got rid of the shirt."

"One more act that draws suspicion."

"Yes Sir."

"Alright… please continue."

"He then lit the fire, made the call to the Wagner house via Madison's burner phone, threw the phone on the body, and departed the scene."

"Why do you think his teeth were removed in the Mazda and not inside the cabin?"

"The cabin was too clean. The act of pulling out someone's teeth would have surely left blood droplets as a minimum; plus, pliers were found in the trunk next to the victim."

"You think that Roberson did all of the heavy lifting… literally… in this case?"

"It would've been a heck of a lot easier with an accomplice to overpower Daryl, haul his body to the car and place it in the trunk, and then hold his jaw still while Roberson pulled out all the teeth; but thus far we haven't been able to tie anyone else to that portion of the crime."

"But you're still looking into such a possibility?"

"Of course."

"Understood. And you mentioned that a phone call was made from *Madison's* burner phone and then tossed onto the victim?"

"Yes. I believe it was a *'the deed is done'* signal. I also believe that either Madison gave Roberson the phone for that purpose, or Roberson took it from Madison's home for that purpose… intended to be untraceable, but they messed up on that account."

"And what about the fact that Roberson had two vehicles to deal with… the black & white and his own patrol car?"

"I believe his patrol car was left at *Hilltop Tavern*, which is just a short walk through the woods to the cabin."

"He still had to dump the black & white and then get back to his patrol car though?"

"I think he departed the scene in the black & white, went to Madison Wagner's house, she followed him out to Eagle Point where he ditched it, and then she drove him to *Hilltop Tavern.*"

"A very plausible scenario… seemingly no stone left unturned… nice work, Detective."

"Thank you, Sir. A couple other items of note: The phone calls from Roberson's *burner* to Madison's phone started just *after* Daryl's death... as if they no longer had to worry about Daryl finding out but were still trying to hide their relationship from authorities who were investigating Daryl's murder. And when I interviewed Madison for the very first time, just a couple of days after the crime, I noticed she was battered and bruised. As such I asked her if everything was alright. She responded *'Everything should be fine now'.*"

"Referring to the fact that her *problem*... aka *her husband*... was no longer an issue?" said Dansby.

"That's certainly one way to read the statement. Of course a Defense Attorney could say that she was referring to the issuance of the restraining order."

"That is likely how they would present it. In fact, with all that you've presented you realize that on one hand the evidence ties both Roberson and Madison Wagner together, but on the other hand you actually have very little on her... just the life insurance, the computer searches, and the purchase of the burner phone that was found at the scene."

"Yes, and I'm guessing the biggest issue for her are those computer searches, which implies conspiracy to commit, correct?"

"Correct. If not for those searches a good Defense Attorney could say she had nothing to do with it... that Roberson took matters into his own hands without her knowledge."

"Unless he gives her up."

"True; you could end up with the proverbial *'he said she said'.*"

"What about the *Battered Wife Defense* considering that Daryl had been physically assaulting her for a number of years?"

"The Prosecutor and I fully expect her attorney to go that route if they feel a verdict of *innocent* is not achievable."

"I assume that since the strongest case is against Roberson he'd be the first to go to trial?"

"That's correct. And who knows, she might opt to testify against him in exchange for a deal."

"It's all a shame though; she seems like a naïve abused woman that got in over her head."

"That may be, but it's not our place to decide; that's up to the jury."

"Yes Sir. Oh, and one last thing…"

"What's that?"

"It's that Roberson, as a cop, would be well-versed in the things that detectives look for at a crime scene… hence how they had been wiped clean and lacked DNA other than Daryl's. In fact, if it wasn't for the foresight of Daryl to leave his ring under the seat of the one car, and the misguided *'the deed is done'* phone call via the burner, this case could have easily gone cold."

"Agreed" said Dansby as he stood up and grabbed his copies of the files. He abruptly stopped in his tracks. "Something just dawned on me" he said.

"Sir?"

"The timing of the Officer's *'the deed is done'* call and him stopping-by to see Madison…"

"I'm glad you brought that up, Sir" Nash replied. "I had the same thought when I questioned Officer Roberson in that regard; and he made a 'rookie mistake'."

"How so?"

"He said he was *not* at the Wagner home when Madison received the call."

"So he failed to seize the opportunity for an alibi: *I was with her when she received the call so I can't be the one who made the call, and thus I can't be the killer.*"

"Yes Sir. And if he changes his tune he gets caught contradicting his initial statement, along with the fact that the first time I questioned Madison she said she was alone when she received the call."

"Nice work" said Dansby, "I'll take it from here."

"Great job, Detective" added Sheriff Clarke.

"Thank you" Nash replied.

Nash picked up her copies of the files and departed Clarke's office.

44

"How'd it go in there?" Donnelly said to Nash as she approached her desk.

"After laying out all of the facts, along with the possible events that could tie them together, I almost convinced myself that we've pretty much wrapped this up."

"You *almost* convinced yourself?" said Brogan.

"Yeah" added Donnelly, "What has you on the fence?"

"It's not so much *being on the fence* actually, it's just the fact that there's not a *single* piece of *physical* evidence tying Roberson to the crime."

"But we've got more circumstantial evidence than pretty much any case *I've* worked. Plus, like you said, he's a cop so he knows what investigators look for at crime scenes, and would know how to avoid leaving evidence."

"True, but you'd need to don an anti-contamination suit to *not* leave a single trace anywhere. Think about it, there's nothing in the black & white and nothing in the cabin… how is *that* possible?"

"What about his cruiser?" said Brogan.

"Daryl's *ring* was found in *the black & white*, and his *DNA* was found in *the cabin*, so Roberson's cruiser wouldn't really tell us anything. In fact, with as many scofflaws and perps he's had in there it would be a *DNA primordial soup* at this point."

Brogan wasn't sure what Nash meant, but he nodded comprehension nonetheless.

Nash was struck by her own statement. *"All those scofflaws and perps"* she said with a furrowed brow in a quiet, contemplative tone.

"What's that?" said Brogan.

"In Roberson's cruiser."

"What about 'em?"

"One of them was *Cobb*."

Donnelly speculated on what Nash was implying, "Cobb has no alibi, we determined that the killer likely had an accomplice, both Roberson and Cobb had motive, *and* they crossed paths at least once... *including* recently."

"Remember how Roberson arrested Cobb on an outstanding warrant, but he was released when the complainant subsequently decided not to press charges?" said Nash.

"Do you think Roberson might've had something to do with that?" asked Donnelly.

"Who the hell knows" said Nash as she looked at her watch and then the wall calendar, "But we need to maximize our available time."

"Available time?" said Brogan.

"I figure we've got twenty-four to seventy-two hours before you and I get a new case, or get assigned to delve into a cold case" said Nash; who then nodded toward Donnelly, "And before Laura's back on Patrol Duty."

"I assume you're talking about twenty-four to seventy-two hours to see if we can tie *Cobb's* movements to *Roberson's;* and to track Daryl Wagner's every move leading up to his death?" said Donnelly.

"That's correct."

"But why would a cop hitch his wagon to a troublemaker like Cobb?" said Brogan.

"Your guess is as good as mine... maybe he had something on him, or is setting him up to be the patsy" replied Nash.

"And for *Daryl;* what exactly are we looking for?"

"Anyone seen with him that we *haven't* spoken with... any unusual activity by him... anything that doesn't add up. In fact I just had a thought" Nash pondered aloud... "Madison mentioned, as did Daryl's coworker, that Daryl was always on his laptop; but it wasn't inside the burned-up car, it wasn't at the cabin, and it wasn't at his home. So where is it?"

"The killer took it and tossed it?" commented Brogan.

"Or they still have it."

"Roberson?" said Donnelly.

"That would be a nail in his coffin" remarked Brogan.

"I'll talk to Lowell and see if he's been directed to do a search of Roberson's place" replied Nash. "Hmm… something else comes to mind now that I think of it…"

"What's that?"

"There's no internet access at the cabin."

"So he'd have to go elsewhere to access the web" noted Donnelly.

"Precisely. Thus, if he was staying at the cabin between the twenty-second and the twenty-sixth, he had to venture out to log on to the internet."

"That's a great point" noted Brogan.

"We need to do some good ol' fashioned boots-on-the-ground investigating" said Nash, "Checking the local libraries along with cafés and coffee shops that provide free wi-fi."

"Looking to see if Wagner had been frequenting any of them?" said Donnelly.

"Yes; specifically, looking to see if he met up with anyone and, if so, get a name if possible, or at least a description."

"The cabin is almost equal distance between Bennington and Silver City, so I'm guessing we're checking establishments in both locations?"

"Correct."

"What about *Hilltop Tavern* since it's just a walk through the woods from the cabin?" Brogan asked.

"There's no wi-fi there. Taverns are interested in patrons socializing, sharing a few laughs, and of course a few drinks… *not* someone sitting on a computer taking up space."

"So bars, clubs, and taverns are out."

"For this particular assignment... yes. The bottom line is placing someone... *anyone*... with Daryl before his murder."

"I have an idea of a starting point" said Donnelly.

"Let's hear it."

"We know Daryl wasn't a debit or credit card guy for the most part; and instead frequented ATMs. Well, the one that he frequented *the most* was the one downtown where we received his video, so coffee shops nearby seem like an obvious place to start."

"Agreed; Laura you take that area, Dirk you take Silver City, and I'll check the libraries."

"I have another item about Daryl since you told me to start taking a closer look at him before you briefed the Prosecutor."

"What's that?"

"He recently revised his will."

"In what way?"

"Just one minor item actually – he added a *Consent for Cremation*."

"Geez Laura, you had me thinking it was some bombshell" commented Brogan, "What's the big deal with wanting to be cremated?"

"I didn't say it was a big deal, but Kenz wanted me to peel the onion on him and that was something I uncovered."

"Did he specify what he wanted done with his cremains?" said Nash.

"No" replied Donnelly.

"Interesting" Nash responded as she mulled over the information. "And to answer your question Dirk, you're right, there's normally no big deal with preferring cremation; hell, some people see a horror flick where someone was assumed to be dead and wakes up inside a coffin – the next thing you know they're like '*Screw that, I'm being cremated when I die*'. The timing of it causes one to pause and wonder though, but I can't think of any reason to be suspicious; in fact I'd be more suspicious if the body had only been preliminarily identified and the *wife* insisted on immediate cremation."

Nash pondered the situation... "Still, we can't be too careful." She grabbed her phone, scrolled through the contacts, and hit 'Send'.

Brogan and Donnelly looked confused.

"Hey Val" Nash said into her phone, "I assume you still have Daryl Wagner's body on ice?"

"Yes I do" replied LaGrange; "What's up?"

"We discovered that his will has a *'Consent for Cremation'* rider and I want to make sure his body isn't released from evidence until the killer is brought to justice."

"Are you still zeroed-in on his wife and the Bennington Officer?"

"Yes; in fact I just presented my case to the Deputy Prosecutor, so I wouldn't be surprised to see charges filed sometime soon."

"You're concerned that his wife might push for cremation, which would prevent us from taking a second look at the body in event something fishy comes up?"

"I think it's unlikely, but you never know."

"No problem, I've got you covered."

"Thanks, Val."

Nash hung up the phone and turned to Donnelly, "Hey Laura, send a copy of that *'Consent for Cremation'* rider to Lowell; tell him we need to evaluate it for a forged signature."

"Whoa; I hadn't thought of that" responded Donnelly.

"Okay, let's get after our assigned tasks" said Nash.

45

This wasn't a typical ferry ride to Seattle for Nash. Normally she'd be chatting with a girlfriend or heading over with Ian to catch a Seahawks, Mariners, or Sounders game, or perhaps a night out at the theatre. No, this ride had her working a case, a case whose first act had almost come to a conclusion, at least according to Sheriff Clarke and Prosecutor Dansby. Not that Nash necessarily disagreed, but in her mind phase-one was not yet complete, more evidence was yet to be gathered; which might *strengthen the case* against Roberson and Madison, *or* could shift the attention in an entirely new direction. Considering the extent of circumstantial evidence against Officer Roberson, and to a lesser extent Madison Wagner, the former seemed likely, but Nash had long since learned to never discard the notion of *possibilities*.

She pondered the previous twenty-four hours: Her trips to local libraries that afternoon had come up empty – no one recognized Daryl Wagner, and his name was not in the system as a member. Brogan had the same result at Silver City cafés and coffee shops. Donnelly appeared to have better luck... one of the workers at a downtown Bennington coffee shop thought that the picture of Daryl Wagner looked familiar; Donnelly was going to return that morning to speak to the owners since they were away catering a luncheon yesterday afternoon. Nash was crossing her fingers.

Nash had talked to Lowell right after she jumped on the ferry; catching him just in time – he was on his way to Officer Roberson's home with his forensic team. She told him to keep an eye out for Daryl Wagner's laptop since it hadn't turned up anywhere thus far; she also thought there was a chance it could be at Wagner's place of employment... *her* next destination.

Nash spent the majority of the ride jotting down a list of questions she would have for Daryl's supervisor. The hour-long ferry ride arrived more quickly than anticipated, and before she knew it she had strolled to Pioneer Square and walked through the doorway of *Ancestral Heritage-dot-com*. She was greeted by Jenna Wu, co-founder of the company.

Nash extended her hand, "I appreciate you meeting with me; as I mentioned on the phone I have a few questions to ask you about Daryl Wagner."

"We heard what happened to him… such a sad story" Jenna replied. "How can we help?"

"Did he have any issues with his coworkers?"

"Not at all" said Jenna. She paused and added, "He might get a little frustrated if he thought someone wasn't pulling their weight, but he was never confrontational about it."

"So, there was no one here that might have wished him ill will?"

"No… not at all."

"How was he *in general?*"

"He was a bit of a loner, didn't interact with others much; he was all about doing his job and doing it well."

"What exactly did his job entail?"

"He primarily worked with clients when they were being introduced to, or had questions about, the site."

"Primarily?"

"Yes; he also had a few ancillary duties."

"You said he worked with clients; how are they assigned?"

"On a rotating basis: A person signs up and the next tech in the rotation takes the email and sends them a Welcome Kit that explains all of the aspects of the site, provides links to various search categories, identifies additional services… that sort of thing."

"What kind of links?"

"Military service records, death certificates, and census reports to name a few."

"And the *additional services?*"

"The primary one is the DNA testing; it provides you with a breakdown of your heritage based on your DNA... you know, a certain percentage of Danish, Irish, Native American, Asian, Hispanic for example."

"What role did Daryl Wagner play?"

"All of that and more."

"I got the impression from one of my Deputies that Daryl worked in Tech Support."

"That was the *'and more'*... the ancillary duties I spoke of."

"Please explain."

"Initially he helped set up the site and the logistics behind it."

"He was here from the beginning?"

"Yes. Daryl was recommended by my former business partner; they went to college together. Anyway, once the site was up and running it was like a nuclear reactor operating at power – basically self-sustaining. That's when Daryl branched out to working direct-interface with clients, mainly helping them navigate the site, but also answering questions."

"Where's your former business partner now?"

"He got an offer from another, similar, website and bolted for them around a year ago." Jenna offered a bit of unsolicited advice, "Word to the wise – never start a business venture with your fiancé."

"I'll keep that in mind." Nash smiled, and then got back on point, "And you said your site is self-sustaining?"

"Only in principle; of course there are periodic updates, adding features, troubleshooting problems; that's why Daryl was so important, he could do it all... and did."

"You also said he helped people navigate the site and answer their questions?"

"Yes, but ninety-percent of the time it was via online chat; not on the phone."

"Is there any chance he could've had some issues with one of his clients?"

"That hardly seems likely; interaction with clients is minimal, and I would have been made aware of any threatening correspondence."

"Nonetheless, I'd appreciate it if you could provide me a printout, or send me an email attachment that identifies those he had provided assistance over the past few months?"

"That might take a bit of work, but I think we can make it happen."

"That would be great; thank you very much for your time."

46

Nash reflected upon what she had just learned about Daryl Wagner as she rode the ferry *Quinault* west across the open waters of the Puget Sound; unfortunately, what she had learned was minimal, nothing that got her any closer to a new suspect or a possible accomplice. She was holding out hope that Brogan or Donnelly might have uncovered something, but she wasn't feeling all that optimistic. Not that she considered Roberson to be innocent, it was just the feeling of the Deputy Prosecutor to be in a rush to judgment; and one thing she had learned over the years... undue haste tends to lead to something being missed. The last thing she wanted was to either have an innocent person go to prison, or to have a guilty person go free due to a technicality. More than simply a mantra, Nash had a specific person in mind for each scenario.

She looked at her watch... a reflex action when time is passing too slowly... a common occurrence when biding your time on an hour-long ferry ride and you have nothing to occupy the minutes. She considered calling Brogan and Donnelly for an update, but too many times she herself had experienced a loss of momentum on a task due to interruptions such as requests for status, and she didn't want to be *that person*. Besides, the ferry had just passed Bainbridge Island, so she should be back in the office in a half-hour or less.

Just as she was about to get up and stroll around the decks to pass the time her cell phone rang – it was Brogan.

"Hey Dirk" said Nash as she answered, "What's up?"

"Are you still on the ferry?" replied Brogan.

"Not for much longer... Why?"

"I made another trip out to the *White Pig* and talked to Sarah McKinney – the gal that Daryl was seen with back on the eleventh."

"And whatever you got couldn't wait until I'm back in the office?"

"She said she had seen him at *The Harborside Fish House* on the twenty-sixth around six P.M.; since it's right next to the ferry terminal I thought you might want to check it out before heading back here."

"Good call; what all did she see?"

"Just that he was with another guy, and they were there for over an hour."

"Did she provide a description of the guy?"

"No; he had his back to her, but she did notice that he was wearing a wedding ring, for whatever that's worth."

"She specifically noticed a wedding ring?"

"I asked the same thing. She said that being a single woman pushing thirty it's one of the first things she looks for."

"Ah the single life" Nash mused, "Anything else?"

"Both Laura and I have a few things for you, but I figure we'll go over all of that once you get here."

"Sounds good; I'll be there after I visit *The Harborside*."

Nash hung up her phone. She had the look of optimism on her face.

47

Nash had barely walked through the doorway of the office before she was bombarded with questions...

"Get anything from Daryl's work?" said Donnelly.

"And what about the mystery guy that was with him at *The Harborside* the night he was murdered?" Brogan piled on.

"To answer *your* question *first* Laura; there was nothing earth-shattering from my visit to his work, but I found out that he did more than provide Tech Support, which was our initial impression" replied Nash. "He actually helped set up the website, and more recently he assisted clients navigate the site and answer questions."

"He helped set up the website?" said Brogan.

"Yep."

"So he was a *major player* in the company and not just your everyday tech support guy?"

"That's a fact."

"Did you learn the details of his working with clients?" asked Donnelly.

"I did. And they're sending over all of his client contacts over the past few months."

"What do you expect to get from that?" said Brogan.

"To be honest I have no idea; maybe someone wasn't happy with the site and made threats? It's a longshot, but perhaps we'll find something worth a closer look" Nash replied. "Anyway, that was it as far as his work goes."

"What about Daryl's visit to *The Harborside* the night he was murdered?" Brogan asked.

"Not much. Neither the manager nor the few crewmembers that work Saturdays recognized his picture. And his name didn't show up on any credit card transactions that evening."

Brogan was disappointed, "So, Sarah McKinney was mistaken as to the night she saw him."

"Not necessarily; remember, he last used his credit card on the nineteenth, so he could've paid cash; or the guy he was with might have picked up the tab."

Donnelly chimed in, "The crewmembers you talked to... did they work the restaurant area or the lounge area?"

"I didn't ask, but I think I know where you're going with that."

"When a couple of guys meet up they usually sit in the lounge or bar area unless it's full."

"That's true" nodded Brogan.

"Well, I left Wagner's picture with them, so maybe we'll get lucky" said Nash. "Beyond that, they gave me a printout of all of the credit card sales that evening."

"That's got to be about everyone in the joint that night" commented Brogan.

"A fair number of the bar patrons pay cash, but you're right. However, the list identifies the number of patrons per bill, so we can focus on those with two people."

"And what are we looking for?"

"Anything that jumps out at us for starters; and if not, then merely add the names to the murder board for a possible link later" stated Nash as she handed the list to Brogan.

"Got it" replied Brogan.

Nash turned her focus to Donnelly, "Okay Laura, you're up."

"It turns out that Daryl had been frequenting *The Java Hut* in downtown Bennington... just a few blocks from the ferry terminal, and a block away from his bank's ATM" replied Donnelly. "According to the owners he had been there a lot that week; not only on his laptop, but on the phone. With that information I checked his cell phone records... there's nothing to indicate he was there."

"So, for some reason he was using a burner" commented Nash.

"That's how it looks."

"I don't suppose they happened to overhear any of his conversations?"

"No details like a name or anything, but they had the impression that someone was coming to visit... maybe family or an old friend or something."

"Couldn't be *immediate* family since none of them are still alive... parents, grandparents, little sister..."

"Maybe *extended* family such as an uncle or cousin; or like they said – an old friend?" said Brogan, "And maybe that's who he met up with at *The Harborside?*"

"I have an even *more* intriguing thought" said Nash as she turned to Donnelly, "Maybe you've stumbled onto the alleged girlfriend?"

"How do you mean?" replied Donnelly.

"Think about it... his laptop, a burner phone, a meeting..."

"So, the burner was all about communicating with the other woman – the girlfriend?" said Donnelly.

"And her jealous boyfriend or husband found out and killed him?" added Brogan.

"Could be" replied Nash.

"But Daryl's murder invoked extreme anger based on yanking all of his teeth out" said Donnelly, "How could someone he didn't really know have that level of anger toward him?"

"I have to disagree with your assessment, Laura" countered Nash, "Yanking out the teeth was an attempt to prevent identification of the victim; extreme anger tends to show up as a continuing assault well after the victim's death... forty-seven stab wounds, emptying an entire gun clip into them, two-dozen blows to the head..."

"But if that's the case... a jealous boyfriend or husband... how come there's no evidence of anyone else at the scene?" said Brogan.

"Yeah, there's no way someone could act in a jealous fit of rage and *not* leave a single trace of evidence" added Donnelly. "Plus, what about all of the stuff we have against Officer Roberson?"

"You're right Laura; there would be a definite contradiction to unravel if we want to tie our horses to a *jealous boyfriend or husband* scenario versus everything we have against Roberson" replied Nash. "And speaking of our apparent *lone wolf* cop... did you find any ties between him and Cobb?"

"Not a thing."

"It figures" replied Nash, "The lack of physical evidence with this crime is both baffling and frustrating; you'd have better odds of winning the damn lottery."

"We're due for a break in one manner or another, that's for sure" said Brogan.

"Finding Daryl's laptop would be a huge step in that direction" said Nash.

"And you said Lowell and his forensics team are searching Roberson's home, correct?"

"Yep."

"But we can't discount the stuff we've discovered in the past twenty-four hours" noted Donnelly. "And Dirk and I have more."

"Let's hear it" replied Nash.

"I went back to the calls made to taxi cabs the night of the murder and expanded my call-zone. It turns out that Crosstown Cab got a call around one o'clock that morning from a guy that said he had crashed his car out near Eagle Point."

"Holy crap; did you get a name or description?"

"No name; and the description's minimal – average build and a mustache."

"What was their destination?"

"The ferry terminal."

Nash considered the options as to the reason the ferry terminal was chosen: *Were they catching the ferry? Was it because it was a convenient downtown location? Or was it a diversionary tactic?*

"That tells us that if *Roberson* was the guy, then Madison did *not* pick him up at the scene of the ditched black & white" said Brogan.

"It also means that *Cobb* did not pick up Roberson at the black & white" responded Nash. "But he could have picked him up near the ferry terminal."

"Understood. And speaking of the ferries, I got hold of footage of the various ferry runs the afternoon of the eleventh when the black & white had been sold, but there was no sign of Roberson on any of the runs."

"There's no way you're going to see *every single person* on the ferry, so maybe he just got lucky?" said Nash, "Plus he could have been wearing a ball cap to hide his identity... like he did when he was purchasing his burner phone."

"True; although they *do* get a shot of every person making a purchase as they *drive* on, but there's nothing there either."

"So, *if* he managed to miss getting caught on camera on the way over, *and* he bought the car..." said Donnelly, "Then obviously he drove around across the Tacoma Narrows Bridge in lieu of taking the ferry back."

"And just our luck cameras are only installed on the eastbound traffic where you pay the bridge toll, not the toll-free westbound lanes" noted Nash.

"Anyway, that's all I had" commented Brogan.

"Okay; you two add everything to the board, I've got a call to make."

Brogan and Donnelly proceeded to the murder board with all of their notes; Nash dialed a number on her phone and hit 'Send'.

"Prosecutor's Office" said the voice on the other end of the line.

"Deputy Prosecutor Dansby please, this is Detective Nash from the Slaughter County Sheriff's Department" replied Nash.

"I'll see if he's in, ma'am."

Nash knew what that statement *really* meant: *I'll see if he wants to talk to you.*

"What can I do for you, Detective?" said Dansby on the line.

"Sir, I have some new information regarding the Daryl Wagner murder case that might be relevant insofar as affecting your decision to charge a suspect with the crime in the immediate future."

"Go ahead."

"Crosstown Cab picked up a guy matching Roberson's description out near Eagle Point around one A.M. the night of the murder; that's the location of the ditched black & white where we found Daryl Wagner's ring."

"It sounds like one more piece of evidence against the Officer?"

"Potentially... yes, that's true. But it *also* would tend to indicate that Madison Wagner did *not* drive him back from ditching the car."

"So her possible involvement is even less than we had surmised?"

"Yes Sir. We also looked at footage of all the ferry runs between Bennington and Seattle the day the black & white was sold, but there was no sign of Roberson within the footage."

"I take it that was an attempt to rebut his statement that he had no knowledge of the car?"

"Correct; and a video of him making a transaction within the car at the ferry's toll booth on the return trip would have been a 'gotcha' moment, but instead we have nothing."

"But since the ferry cameras wouldn't catch *every* person on the boat he could've gone undetected on his way over and then driven the car back."

"I agree; I merely wanted to make you aware since a Defense Attorney could use that information to plant the seed of doubt."

"I appreciate that; was that all?"

"I still have a few irons in the fire Sir, so I'd like a little more time to pursue them before we issue any arrest warrants; unless we get a major breakthrough from the forensics team's search of Officer Roberson's home of course."

"I want to put this case behind me and am not interested in dragging out the inevitable…"

"But Sir…" Nash interrupted.

"If you'll let me finish…"

"Yes Sir."

"I'm not interested in dragging out the inevitable, *but* I'll give you through the weekend, along with one more crack at Officer Roberson, before I issue the warrant."

"Thank you, Sir."

Nash hung up the phone. Brogan and Donnelly were staring at her; they hadn't moved a muscle since they heard Nash utter the name *Dansby*.

"That was the Deputy Prosecutor" Nash relayed to Brogan and Donnelly, "He gave me through the weekend to come up with anything additional before he throws the book at Roberson."

"He only gave *YOU* through the weekend?" asked Brogan.

"Well, I can't ask you two to throw away your weekend to delve into what could be nothing more than an exercise in futility."

"To heck with that; I don't know about Laura, but I'm in."

"Me too" added Donnelly.

"I appreciate that" replied Nash. "You two get back at it; I'm going to call Captain O'Rourke and let him know what's up, and then I'm going to make one last run at Roberson."

48

Nash was surprised that Roberson had shown up without a lawyer; considering his final statement in the previous interview was that he was no longer going to talk. Then again, perhaps he was just going to sit there and not say a word; which wouldn't be a total loss in Nash's mind, she could say her piece and get a read on Roberson simply from his non-verbal response.

Nash sat down across the table from Roberson. He didn't budge, just sat there leaning back in his chair with his arms crossed. He had the look of a teenager who was about to get the *'you need an attitude adjustment'* speech from his stepdad – in other words, somewhat perturbed and completely disinterested.

After several seconds of silence Nash decided to test the waters, "I appreciate you taking the time to come in."

"As if I had a choice" Roberson replied.

"The last time we talked I asked you about a former Police Interceptor Crown Vic that had been at the scene of Daryl Wagner's murder, and that also contained his ring... hidden under the passenger seat..."

"And I told you I never purchased such a car; why would I?"

"An actual patrol car is going to draw attention."

"And one that *looks like* a cop car *isn't?*" Roberson replied. "Plus, you think I'm just going to throw away a couple grand? You know as well as anyone that cops aren't raking-in the cash... Give me a break."

"You can afford to throw away a few bills if Madison Wagner is going to receive a nice payout from Daryl's life insurance."

"You really think she and I had something to do with Daryl's murder?? That's such a crock; if I was the killer I would've been the cop who *'stumbled upon and discovered the scene'*" he punctuated with air-quotes... *"Especially* since I already had a reason to be in the general area with my assignment at *Hilltop.* Your so-called *conjecture* is idiotic."

Nash remained silent, but she realized Roberson had made a good argument... the same point that Brogan had made days earlier... one that would likely cast reasonable doubt in a courtroom.

Roberson leaned forward, put his elbows on the table, and continued... "Not only that, but I read the *Crash Report* on the Crown Vic and it stated that the driver's-side airbag deployed; so how is it that I left no DNA?"

"Maybe you covered your face somehow, and then wiped down the scene afterward?"

"And how do you suppose I left the scene?"

"Maybe Madison picked you up? Or maybe you called a cab? Crosstown Cab reported picking up a guy with a mustache out near Eagle Point and dropping him off near the ferry terminal."

"As if I'm the only guy in the County with a mustache" he stated, "Hell, between cops and sailors in this town it's a frickin' *Tom Selleck convention* out there."

Nash remained silent.

"Check my cell phone records and cell tower pings... you won't find me anywhere near the ditched Crown Vic" Roberson continued. "And why would I go to the ferry terminal?"

"To meet up with your accomplice so they could take you back to your cruiser" Nash replied.

"My accomplice? I wouldn't need an accomplice to get the drop on *Daryl Wagner*... I've got a *Glock*" responded Roberson as he patted his holster.

"Is that a confession?"

"Screw you."

"Nonetheless; your threatening note to Daryl, your secret meetings with Madison, lying about your relationship with her, your purchase of burner phones together – one of which was subsequently found at the scene, getting rid of the shirt you wore that night that had blood on it, and your lack of an alibi at the time of the murder has you directly in the Deputy Prosecutor's crosshairs."

"The only thing I'm guilty of is poor judgment in regard to trying to help a woman who's been repeatedly assaulted by her husband. So go ahead, arrest me for being a stupid shit, waste the taxpayer's money on my trial, and let the *actual* killer go free."

"That's up to the Prosecutor's Office" Nash responded. "As for now… you're free to go."

49

It was nine o'clock on a Saturday morning; and instead of lying in bed sipping a cup of French-pressed coffee courtesy of her beau Ian, Nash was walking through the doorway of the Slaughter County Sheriff's Office.

Not that working weekends was an unusual event... not when you're a Homicide Detective; but in this particular case Nash was feeling under the gun... figuratively speaking of course. She was getting heat from both Sheriff Clarke and Deputy Prosecutor Dansby to close the book on this case, which meant *throwing* the book at Officer Roberson if Nash didn't come up with compelling new evidence to at least buy her more time. It also meant that Madison Wagner would likely be collateral damage at the hands of a Deputy Prosecutor looking to make a name for himself.

Nash entered the office to the sight of Brogan and Donnelly huddled around the murder board.

"Solved world hunger before I got here?" said Nash as she approached the board.

Brogan responded as if the question was serious, "No, but here's a crazy thought for you; what if *Daryl* made the computer searches?"

"What??" replied Nash.

"What if he was planning to disappear and start a new life; figuring the best way to start a new life is to make it look like you're dead... like you've been murdered and your body was dumped somewhere... never to be found?"

"And the computer searches were a way to frame his wife for his disappearance and alleged murder?"

"Sure. And maybe Madison was telling the truth about the insurance policy… that she signed papers for both her *and* Daryl, but he only submitted the one on *him* to make *her* look guilty when he disappeared?"

Brogan awaited a response. Nash figured he had come up with an entire scenario along those lines, so she egged him on… "Keep going, you're on a roll" she said.

"And Roberson too perhaps; maybe that's why Daryl saved the threatening note? *And* maybe he was faking the whole ATM-thing… mouthing the word 'cop'?" Brogan continued, "Add that to the computer searches and you're looking at a missing person, with evidence of foul play, pointing toward his wife and a cop that she'd been communicating with behind the scenes."

"How do you explain the black & white; and the stolen Mazda?"

"Uhh…"

"And maybe he was the second gunman on the grassy knoll, too?" Nash said sarcastically. "Are you sure you're not just trying to come up with ways to exonerate Madison?"

"What about the secret phone calls he made at *The Java Hut*; possibly with some woman that he either already knew, or had met online and was going to meet?"

"Yeah Kenz" added Donnelly, "Like you said, maybe we had stumbled onto proof of the mystery girlfriend?"

"Not necessarily *proof*" responded Nash, "But sure, it adds to the possibilities."

"Then again" Donnelly conceded, "Even if Daryl *had* planned to disappear and make everyone think Madison and Roberson were responsible for his disappearance, someone killed him before he could fully execute his plan."

"Bingo" said Nash with a finger-point. She turned toward Brogan, "And no matter what frame-up you think Daryl might have attempted, the bottom line is that *he* is the one who was murdered, and somebody… most likely *Roberson*… did it."

"I still like the idea of a secret girlfriend with a jealous boyfriend or husband" said Brogan.

"Then *find* them" responded Nash, "And you'd best hurry... time is running out."

Although Nash felt as if Brogan might be living in a Fool's Paradise, at least when it comes to Madison Wagner and her possible involvement in her husband's murder, his off-the-wall ideas often caused her to ponder avenues not previously considered. And when it comes to investigating a crime, the ability to see beyond the obvious could be the difference between a case solved, and a case gone cold.

"I made a list of names of those who made credit card purchases at *The Harborside* the night of Daryl's murder" stated Brogan as he pointed toward the murder board, "Nothing stands out though."

"And I got cell phone usage in the vicinity of *The Java Hut*" said Donnelly, "There were more burner phones in use than I expected, so I couldn't really pinpoint which one might have belonged to Daryl."

"Not only that, but with nothing more than cell tower pings we don't even know if the calls originated from *The Java Hut*, they could be *anywhere* downtown" noted Nash; the frustration beginning to show.

"That's correct; but I've got the numbers for the parties at the other end of the line... that may turn up something."

"So, in both instances we've got nothing new to go on" replied Nash. "Another round of grasping for the carrot that is out of reach; *if* in fact there is even a carrot to be grasped."

"What about the search of Roberson's house?" Brogan said.

"Lowell called me before I left home, and there *were* a couple of things that are working against Roberson."

"Like what?"

"For one: A pad of paper that detailed Daryl's movements."

"That looks incriminating."

"To a Prosecuting Attorney you're damn right; it makes it look like he was stalking Daryl" Nash replied, "But on the other hand, he *did* admit that he and Officer Stahl had been tailing Daryl, so a Defense Attorney could argue that it was all part of his job."

"And you said there was more?" said Donnelly.

"Notes showing conversations he'd had with Madison" said Nash. "And it's a good thing that he admitted to his questionable relationship with her; otherwise the Prosecutor would've had a field day with that. Even so, I'm sure it's going to be a focal point for Dansby."

"I take it Daryl's laptop did *not* turn up?"

"Nope" Nash sighed, "I have a sinking feeling that we could be in for a *long* weekend."

50

It had been a nerve-wracking couple of days for Nash. She'd made minimal progress; due in part to the fact that she was still awaiting records from Daryl's place of work. Not that the Client Contact List from his employer would necessarily provide answers, or even new clues to follow; but she was running out of options, and more importantly, out of time. She knew that Prosecutor Dansby was ready to serve a warrant for Officer Roberson's arrest, possibly Madison Wagner's as well; and there was nothing tangible in-hand she could use to intervene with what was rapidly becoming *the inevitable*.

Nash was staring at the murder board, looking for previously-unidentified ties, or something that might have been overlooked, when Brogan and Donnelly arrived.

"Hey Kenz, anything new since we left last night?" said Brogan as he approached.

"Nope" Nash replied, "You two have any brainstorms over the past twelve to eighteen hours?"

"Yes and no" responded Donnelly, "Of all the calls from burners that might have been made from *The Java Hut*, I've compiled a list of those made to, or received from, women; and those made or received via another burner."

"And?"

"Unfortunately, none of the ones tied to women seem to be likely candidates for a secret girlfriend."

"Why not?"

"Either too young, too old, or too far away."

"You never know about a guy's taste; and the *far away* ones would actually have potential based on him describing how to get to Bennington."

"That was my thought too, but the ones that fit into that category never left their state that weekend… one in Florida, and one in Virginia Beach."

"The *too old?*"

"Gladys Belmont; age eighty-two. Since he's thirty-something I figured that would be a reach."

"And the *too young?*"

"Fifteen. I figure she's chatting with a school chum or something."

"Yeah, let's hope we aren't adding pedophile to his list of character flaws" Nash replied. Something dawned on her… "I hope you took into account the obvious?"

Donnelly looked confused.

"If *Daryl* was the common denominator of the calls" Nash said, "they should've stopped the night he was murdered."

Donnelly didn't respond; Nash then clarified: "The burner he was using would no longer be active *unless* the killer has it; *or* somebody found it and started using it."

"Crap" Donnelly replied, "I'll revise my list accordingly."

Nash turned to Brogan, "You got anything?"

"I got nothin'" Brogan replied.

"Alright then" Nash said as she started toward Clarke's office, "Wish me luck."

There was a certain sense of trepidation as Nash walked into Sheriff Clarke's office, but she felt she was out of options.

Sheriff Clarke looked up from his desk, "Detective, what can I do for you?"

"I re-interviewed Officer Roberson Friday afternoon and I'm starting to wonder if maybe there's more to the story, maybe even someone else out there we need to take a look at, or at least talk to."

"What are you talking about; *YOU* are the one who built the case against him and the vic's wife?"

"Maybe that's what they wanted to happen… leaving bread crumbs to lead us to Roberson and Madison?"

"Who's this *THEY* you're talking about?" said Clarke with air-quotes, "And since when did you become a conspiracy theorist?"

"Okay, I'll grant you that I don't have specific evidence of a third party master-manipulator, but things just don't add up."

"What do you mean they don't add up; they add up perfectly?"

"That's my point… it's *too* perfect."

"*Too* perfect? Did you forget how much work you and your team performed to put this case together?"

"Of course not, but the convenience of those computer searches… I mean really, who looks up *DNA within tooth pulp?* It's ridiculous! And specific searches on *Battered Wife Defense?* Come on… someone's setting Madison up and we walked right into their trap, took the bait, and reeled her in."

"Perps perform dumbass computer searches all the time. They think that they can simply delete their search history and it's gone forever – never to be discovered. And then the Cyber geeks find their ill-fated attempts at hiding their searches and they are busted big-time."

Nash essentially ignored Clarke's statement and forged on with her next item of note… "And Roberson made a great point: If he was the killer it would've made *much more* sense to be the person who *discovered* the scene instead of *fleeing* the scene; in fact, he would've had the perfect alibi having been on-shift nearby."

"We both know that people make stupid decisions when in the heat of the moment while committing a crime. And if you think someone set-up Madison Wagner *maybe* it was Roberson… maybe that's *his* game, setting up enough contradictions to try to make us question our evidence? Maybe *he's* your master-manipulator?"

"Okay, I concede that perhaps you're right… maybe Roberson's a sneaky some-of-a-bitch who's trying to play me… play us all. I just want more time before we put all of our eggs in one basket and ignore other possibilities."

"Do you have new evidence that points to someone else?"

"Not exactly; but we've come across new information that could yield new leads."

"You want more time for something that is nothing more than a *maybe?*"

"Well yeah… today's *maybe* could be tomorrow's *final piece of the puzzle;* and we won't know that unless we have the time to investigate and see for sure."

"That's up to the Prosecutor, so I wouldn't hold my breath."

"You won't back me up?"

"Like I said… it's up to the Prosecutor."

Nash wanted to continue to plead her case, but realized it was a lost cause, at least for now. An exhale of frustration followed. She turned and walked out of Clarke's office – not uttering a word.

51

"I take it things did not go as well as planned with Clarke?" commented Brogan as Nash walked into the area.

"Why do you say that?" Nash replied.

"The look on your face."

"It's *that* telling is it?" responded Nash, "But yeah, Clarke's basically washing his hands of anything, saying that it's the Deputy Prosecutor's call if we're going to get more time to work this case."

"Well, there's more that went on while you were in there" stated Donnelly.

Normally *"there's more"* meant something good... additional leads, new evidence, a missing link; but Donnelly had the look and sound of someone who was about to be the bearer of bad news.

"What are you talking about, I was only in there for what... ten minutes maybe?" responded Nash.

"We just got word that Deputies were dispatched to arrest both Roberson *and* Madison."

"Are you frickin' kidding me?! Clarke had already ordered their arrest before I even had a chance to plead my case for more time?!"

"Or Prosecutor Dansby made the call" said Brogan.

"Son of a bitch!" Nash responded, "Any news about a Bail Hearing?"

"Word has it they're planning for this afternoon."

"They've both been assigned Counsel already?"

"Court-appointed attorneys" said Donnelly.

Nash rolled her eyes... "Oh, that's just terrific."

"So now what?" Brogan asked.

"See what ties, if any, you can glean out of the credit card purchases from *The Harborside* along with any burner phones used downtown whose usage stopped right after Daryl Wagner's murder" Nash replied, "Oh, and if the email shows up, include the Contact Client List from Daryl's work."

"But isn't the Client List being emailed to *you?*" said Brogan.

"It should come to all three of us; I called earlier and impressed upon them the importance of getting us the information, and to include both of you on the email just in case I was otherwise engaged."

"Do you plan on being somewhere else?" said Donnelly.

"I do *now*" Nash replied, "I'm going to spend the rest of the morning prepping for the Bail Hearing; and once the Hearing is set I'm outta here."

"You're going to the Hearing to back-up the Prosecutor?"

"I wouldn't say *that* exactly; but I'm interested in the content of the Deputy Prosecutor's presentation. And if I end up putting in *my* two-cents worth then who knows, the next time you see me here may be as a *former* employee cleaning out their desk."

52

Nash sat quietly in the Courtroom as Judge Karen Langley examined the weight of evidence against Madison Wagner and Officer Mike Roberson in regard to their Bail Hearing.

Nash had made eye contact with Madison when she entered the courtroom; Madison's demeanor was that of a frightened child, but when she looked at Nash there was a sense that she'd been betrayed by someone who had supposedly stood by her. Nash wished she could explain the situation, but it was not to be.

"Shall we start with the case against Madison Wagner?" stated Judge Langley.

"Yes Your Honor" responded both Deputy Prosecutor Dansby and Court-appointed Attorney Angela Armstrong respectively.

"Attorney Armstrong" announced Judge Langley – indicating that the attorney had the floor.

"Yes ma'am" Armstrong replied and began to lay out her case, "Misses Wagner has never been cited for a crime, in fact she's been a victim of domestic violence for a number of years."

"*Alleged* victim" Prosecutor Dansby jumped in to the surprise of both the Judge and Attorney Armstrong, "Her husband was never charged with such a crime, Your Honor."

"But several calls were made to the Wagner household in regard to a domestic disturbance, correct?" stated the Judge.

"Yes."

"And responding Officers filed reports stating that there were indications that Misses Wagner had been beaten?"

"Yes."

"And she filed a restraining order against her husband?"

"Yes."

"Might I remind you that this is merely a Bail Hearing and not a *trial*, Mister Dansby?"

"Yes ma'am."

"Attorney Armstrong – continue" directed the Judge.

"Along those lines Your Honor, I submit to you that Misses Wagner is *not* a danger to others in the community."

Dansby jumped in once again, "She's being charged with solicitation to commit murder; I would call *that* a danger to others."

Judge Langley was getting perturbed... "Deputy Prosecutor, you can make your case when I call on you."

"Yes ma'am" he replied.

Judge Langley returned her gaze to Attorney Armstrong.

"Misses Wagner has very limited financial resources" Armstrong continued, "She has only a couple thousand dollars in the bank, her Mother is a Home Health Nurse, and her Father is on Disability."

"What about a life insurance payout?" asked the Judge.

Armstrong nodded toward Dansby, "The Deputy Prosecutor contacted the insurance company; and thus they are withholding payment pending the outcome of any actions against Misses Wagner."

Judge Langley directed a look of displeasure toward Dansby.

Armstrong continued... "As stated previously Your Honor, Misses Wagner has no criminal history, no history of drug or alcohol abuse, and has been a resident of the County for her entire life. I submit that she is not a flight risk, and should be released on her own recognizance."

"On her own recognizance??!!" Dansby blurted out as he jumped to his feet.

"Deputy Prosecutor" Judge Langley sternly responded, "Do I need to have the County Prosecutor *replace you* in these proceedings?"

"No ma'am" replied Dansby as he retook his seat.

Nash saw an opening; she stood and addressed Judge Langley...

"Your Honor; if I might speak?"

"And you are?" replied the Judge.

"Detective Mackenzie Nash; with the Slaughter County Sheriff's Office."

The name rang a bell with the Judge; she looked at the case file and then looked back at Nash, "You're the Lead Detective on this case?"

"Yes ma'am."

"Very well... proceed."

"Your Honor, I believe there is more to this case than currently provided you."

"You have additional evidence, Detective?"

"Yes Your Honor" Nash replied. "Well, to be accurate... some new evidence that potentially contradicts some of the case against Misses Wagner, and some possible new leads as well."

"So why are we here?"

"Not my call, ma'am."

"Do you have this additional information with you?"

"Yes ma'am" Nash replied as she held up some papers.

Judge Langley motioned for Nash to come forward with her information.

Nash approached the Judge and presented her a file folder; she then walked over and provided folders to both Dansby and Attorney Armstrong; she subsequently returned to her seat.

Judge Langley scanned the paperwork – the courtroom stood silent.

The Judge looked up from the paperwork and then directly at Dansby, "Deputy Prosecutor."

"Yes Your Honor?" Dansby replied.

"This case against Madison Wagner, as you have presented, is weak at best; nothing but computer searches and the purchase of a cell phone that the victim *himself* could have taken and later used in an attempt to call for help."

Dansby remained silent; the Judge continued... "You have zero physical evidence, zero evidence that Misses Wagner was anywhere near the scene, and no direct evidence of solicitation to commit murder: No text messages, no voice mails, no emails, no secret recordings, no witnesses to such an act... nothing. Based on that, Misses Wagner is released on her own recognizance."

Madison had a look of elation; Attorney Armstrong a look of pleasant surprise and satisfaction. Deputy Prosecutor Dansby looked stunned and forlorn.

"As such" the Judge continued, "I suggest you reexamine your case against Misses Wagner pending the discovery of additional evidence."

"Yes ma'am" Dansby replied.

Judge Langley flipped back to Roberson's file. "And your case against Officer Roberson is entirely circumstantial... not a single shred of physical evidence."

"Yes, but the amount is overwhelming" Dansby defended.

"I'll leave that to the Grand Jury" replied the Judge. "However; in light of the information provided by Detective Nash, along with Officer Roberson's impeccable service record, I'm inclined to release the Officer on his own recognizance as well."

Both Roberson and Attorney Armstrong were shocked; neither of them had expected such a positive outcome.

Dansby was in shock as well... at the opposite end of the spectrum. His demeanor quickly transitioned to frustration and anger... directed specifically toward Nash.

The Judge then looked at Roberson, "However, Officer; if you plan to venture out of the Olympic Peninsula you shall first obtain the permission of your Police Captain."

"Yes Your Honor" replied Roberson.

"Very well" stated the Judge, "This proceeding is concluded."

The Judge exited the courtroom and all in attendance began to disperse.

Madison looked over at Nash and mouthed "Thank you." Nash

smiled in return.

Nash walked out of the courtroom; Sheriff Clarke immediately accosted her – Nash had no idea that the Sheriff had been observing the proceedings from the back of the room.

Clarke motioned Nash to a secluded corner and, in a muffled yet emphatic voice, said… "What the hell was *that?!!*"

"I told you that there were unanswered questions and I needed more time on this case" said Nash in defense.

"What is this, *blackmail?!* A Lead Detective in a case does *not* speak on behalf of a *suspect* at a Bail Hearing!"

"Blackmail? That's ridiculous; the information I had was relevant to the proceedings."

"Then it should have been provided *before* the Hearing."

"I tried, but I got stonewalled. And I wasn't about to let Madison Wagner get thrown in jail based on flawed evidence."

"There you go again with this *flawed evidence* bullshit. The Deputy Prosecutor was presenting evidence that *YOU* gathered, and under a scenario that *YOU* presented!"

"My scenario was based on the evidence that I had *at the time;* and by the Deputy Prosecutor being in a rush to convict someone before we had gathered all the facts. And why? So that he can put a frickin' notch on his belt??"

"You're letting your own personal demons affect your judgment: Your father walking out on you when you were a child, your stepfather trying to molest your younger sisters and your mother not doing a damn thing to stop it, and now you're trying to protect Madison Wagner because she has been suffering the same physical abuse that *you* suffered back in your twenties!"

Nash was in stunned disbelief; she never would have imagined that the very personal information she had shared with Clarke in confidence years earlier was now being used to attack her character and motives.

"You fucking asshole!" she responded.

53

The drive from the Courthouse to the Sheriff's Office was all a blur to Nash; she had been preoccupied with a myriad of thoughts and emotions ranging from satisfaction, to being conflicted, to anger and disgust. *Satisfaction* that she was able to bring to light some of the flaws in the Prosecutor's case against Madison Wagner; *conflicted* in that speaking up for Madison also invited questions regarding the case against Officer Roberson, who was likely guilty of Daryl Wagner's murder and Nash may have inadvertently gotten him released on his own recognizance; and *anger and disgust* at Sheriff Clarke's inappropriate comments regarding Nash's past, and his apparent questioning of her character and judgment.

A level of surprise greeted Nash as she walked into the office. Considering the late hour she'd expected Brogan and Donnelly to have gone home for the day; yet there they were, like loyal canines anxiously awaiting their master's arrival.

"How'd it go?" asked Donnelly.

"Yeah, you didn't get fired did you?" Brogan jokingly added.

"That remains to be seen" Nash replied to Brogan, "It could become a reality as soon as Clarke shows up."

That wasn't the response Brogan had expected, "Why do you say that?" he queried.

"Because I told him to fuck off."

"Are you shitting me??"

"Nope. At the hearing I spoke up on Madison's behalf... telling the Judge that we were continuing to follow leads and that the information she... the Judge... had, was outdated."

"You didn't?"

"Yep. Both Clarke and Dansby were pissed. Clarke accosted me right after the hearing, made a few choice statements which crossed the line; and I told him to fuck off." Nash paused and then added... "Well, *technically* I told him he was a fucking asshole."

"Wow" responded Brogan.

"And what happened to Madison and Roberson?" said Donnelly.

"The Judge ordered them both released on their own recognizance" replied Nash.

"With all that evidence against Roberson?" said Brogan, "Holy Crap!"

"So, before I'm back on the streets... either as a Patrol Officer, or as a civilian... how about updating me on our status?"

Brogan beamed as if he'd just won the lottery, *"We've got a name."*

"Brandon Garrison" Donnelly chimed in, "He showed up on *both* of our lists: Credit card purchase at *The Harborside Fish House*; and calls to and from a burner at the approximate times that Daryl Wagner was downtown at *The Java Hut.*"

"And Daryl's workplace provided us the clinchers" added Brogan, "Daryl had set up his work phone to transfer calls to another phone."

"One of the burner phones used at *The Java Hut?*" said Nash.

"Yep. *And* guess whose name shows up on the Client Contact List?"

"Garrison?"

"You got it."

"So who is this guy?"

"Good question" Donnelly responded, "From what we can tell he has no ties to Daryl Wagner whatsoever... doesn't even live here in the state."

"You're telling me that the only connection is that this guy had a question or problem with the website and Daryl was his helpdesk support?"

"Thus far; but we *just* got the info, so we haven't had a chance to dig any deeper."

"And he lives out of state?"

"Northern California… a town called Healdsburg."

"But he was here in Slaughter County, apparently with Daryl at *The Harborside*, the night Daryl was murdered?"

"Nothing *specifically* places the two of them together at *The Harborside* that night" responded Brogan. "Everything is circumstantial and speculative."

"Educate me."

"Sarah McKinney said she saw Daryl there with some guy. Garrison's credit card puts him there within the timeframe. And earlier that day there were phone calls between the burner we tied to Daryl, and to Garrison's cell."

"They had talked earlier in the day?"

"Yes; my guess is that the calls were to finalize the logistics of their meeting up."

"What would have caused them to go from online website assistance, to communicating on a regular basis, to meeting up? Especially for *Garrison* since he lives in California?"

"The frequent communication could be as simple as finding a rep you're comfortable with and wanting to continue to work with them" replied Donnelly, "And thus they, the rep, will typically provide you with their phone extension."

"Okay, I suppose I get that; but meeting up?"

"This may be a little outside the box" said Brogan, "But maybe they found out they're old pals or something… you know, how people find old friends and classmates on social media sites?"

"Or perhaps they discovered that they have mutual friends or acquaintances?" added Donnelly.

"In today's digital age I guess anything is possible" replied Nash. "Let's find out what we can about this guy: Who he is, what he does, why he was in the area, his background, and if we can make any connection between him and Daryl Wagner beyond some ridiculous *website tech support* baloney."

"Will do; but I have more on Daryl himself if you want to hear it?"

"Absolutely."

"I discovered that Daryl had set up some secret bank accounts... one in Bennington and two in Seattle."

"How much is in there?"

"Nothing now; the Seattle accounts were closed-out Friday the twenty-fifth, and the Bennington account Saturday the twenty-sixth."

The timing was not lost on Nash... "The Seattle accounts the day *before* he was murdered... the one in Bennington the day *of* his murder."

"Yep."

"The amounts *before* he closed them?"

"Each account was just under ten thousand dollars."

"He was walking around with nearly thirty-grand in cash?" asked Brogan.

"Possibly" responded Nash, "But most people close out accounts via a cashier's check made out to themselves which they typically deposit into a new bank, credit union, brokerage firm, or whatever."

"So the guy had thirty-grand in cashier's checks or a wad of cash... either on him, or lying around somewhere, when he was murdered. Holy shit."

Nash looked to Donnelly, "Where would he have gotten the money?"

"I ran his financials and he received a bonus from work every January" Donnelly replied, "Twenty-five-hundred dollars of each bonus would go into his shared savings account with Madison, and seventy-five-hundred would go into a secret account."

"So, apparently he was minimizing the amount of his bonus when he'd mention it to Madison, and was keeping the lion's share for himself."

"That's how it looks. The remaining funds were via periodic deposits over time – small enough that Madison would be none the wiser. He'd get one account up to around nine-thousand and then he'd open up a new one."

"How long has this been going on?"

"Almost three years."

The cogs were turning inside Brogan's head; it was time to revisit a previous notion… "Maybe the idea of Daryl planning to disappear and start a new life wasn't so far-fetched after all?"

"Maybe" replied Nash, "Or perhaps he was stockpiling a hidden cache in the event that Madison filed for divorce – trying to avoid her getting what *he* perceived was *his* money."

"But if he wasn't planning to disappear, why close out all the accounts?"

"To keep her from discovering them and get half of it in a divorce settlement."

"But then he'd either have to stash the cash somewhere, or hand it over to a trusted friend for safekeeping."

"In the case of cash… yes; and nothing like that was found at the Wagner home."

"I'm thinking that *the cabin* would have made the most sense" said Donnelly. "Maybe he stashed it in that hidden compartment under the sink where we found his wallet, and then the killer took it?"

"But if Roberson's our guy you checked his financials and there weren't any large deposits, right?" said Nash.

"That's true; the only noteworthy transaction was the withdrawal of two-thousand dollars that he never explained."

"Then again, making a thirty-grand deposit would be suspicious" noted Nash, "Did he have a safe deposit box?"

"I hadn't thought of that" said Donnelly, "I'll have to check."

"If Daryl *was* hiding the money in event of a potential divorce, did we find any indications that either of them were planning to file for one?"

"There's nothing in the case files; we'd have to talk to Madison on that one."

"Of course the restraining order could have been her first step toward a divorce."

"Maybe he gave the money to his pal Decker for safekeeping?" commented Brogan.

"But Decker said he hadn't seen Daryl since Tuesday the twenty-second" replied Nash.

"How about our mystery man Garrison? Maybe *he* was going to help Daryl disappear and *that's* where the money ended up?"

"Do we have any way to verify where the money landed?"

"Not without a warrant."

"I was afraid of that. There's no way Clarke or Dansby will support me on that... not after my little stunt at the Bail Hearing."

"Do you need their okay?" asked Donnelly, "Can't you just go directly to the Judge that presided over the hearing?"

"You've got a point there, Laura; I'll have to think about that."

"Since the bank has already provided us with financial info, maybe we can just ask them for that additional piece?" said Brogan.

"That's true" said Nash, "What's the worst that can happen... they say no and then I draft a warrant and present it to Judge Langley."

Donnelly looked at her watch, and then glanced toward the windows – realizing the afternoon had given way to dusk. "I guess I'll have to hit them up first thing in the morning" Donnelly noted.

"I concur" said Nash, "But just the bank in Bennington; no need to run to Seattle just yet."

"Got it."

"And take copies of what they already gave us, that way you can say *'You provided me this information about Daryl Wagner in support of our murder investigation and I simply need the details as to whether he obtained a cashier's check when he closed the account, and if so, to whom it was made out'.*"

"Will do."

54

It had been a night of very little sleep for Nash… tossing and turning while her mind tried to grapple with continuing concerns about the case, along with the verbal punch-in-the-gut she'd received from Sheriff Clarke after the Bail Hearing.

She found it interesting that Clarke never made it back from the Courthouse the previous afternoon; *"Perhaps it was a calculated move on his part to allow a cooling-off period between us"* she thought to herself. Even so, she was anticipating a potential confrontation once they finally crossed paths. Not that she would initiate such an event, but how many people can call their boss *a fucking asshole* and not suffer consequences… some sort of repercussion… maybe even *'a stint on the beach'* as they call it?

As Nash pulled into the parking area of the Sheriff's Office the first thing that caught her eye was the sight of Sheriff Clarke's cruiser. Her gut figuratively wrenched itself into a knot. The anticipation of being confronted by Clarke overshadowed the fact that both Brogan and Donnelly had also made an early start to their workday.

Nash walked into the office and immediately made a visual sweep around the space – no sign of Clarke. Her focus turned to Brogan and Donnelly adding notes to the murder board – Brogan the reader, Donnelly the scribe.

"It's a half-hour before official start-time and you two are already hard at it" Nash said as she draped her jacket over her chair, "Are you bucking for a raise or what?"

"Like you said the other day, we figure we're on borrowed time when it comes to this case, so we're doing what we can" replied Brogan, followed by a head nod toward Sheriff Clarke's office… "Before the hammer comes down."

"With that in mind, what have we got?"

"We found a tie between Wagner and Garrison beyond the website; it's minimal but it might explain the nature of their relationship."

"Garrison's family lived here in Slaughter County back when he was a little kid... a toddler" Donnelly clarified. *His* father and *Wagner's* father served together on a ship that was in the shipyard for overhaul, *and* both families lived in Base Housing."

"It's possible that the two kids spent some time together back then" Brogan added. "But they were just kids, so once the families went their separate ways it's hard to believe they could even remember anything from back then."

"The families went their separate ways?" said Nash.

"Yes; Wagner's father got out of the Navy and stayed here in the area... going to work at the shipyard; and Garrison's family returned to the San Francisco Bay Area with the ship when the overhaul was completed."

"They didn't keep in touch?"

"Hard to say for sure; the parents might have, at least for a little while, but you wouldn't expect a couple of little kids to keep in contact."

"I take it there is no known communication between them prior to Garrison logging onto the *Ancestral Heritage* website and needing assistance?"

"Correct."

"What does Garrison do for a living?"

"He and his wife own a small winery near his home" Donnelly replied.

"There was a Winemaker's Convention in Seattle the week of the twenty-first" said Brogan, "That was his reason for being up here around the time that Daryl was killed."

"So it wasn't a special trip to get together with Daryl, it was merely one of those *'Hey I'm going to be in the area on business so maybe we can catch up'* scenarios?"

"Seems that way."

"Okay, so maybe they played in the sandbox together when they were just out of diapers; that's not a whole lot to go on" remarked Nash with a tinge of frustration building.

"I'm thinking our best bet is to call Garrison and get his side of the story" said Donnelly.

"I agree, but if at all possible I'd like to know what happened to the funds from the accounts Daryl closed-out before I do… just in case Garrison's name pops up."

"I was going to head over there in about a half-hour… figuring I can catch the manager as they're opening up the branch."

"Alright; you two keep working the board here, I need some coffee."

Nash grabbed her coffee mug and started toward the Break Room. She purposely focused straight-ahead as she passed by Clarke's office, looking to avoid the anticipatory uncomfortable eye contact that she'd been dreading. If Clarke glanced up from his desk Nash didn't see it.

She opened the fridge, reached in and grabbed one of her mini creamers, and poured the contents into her mug. She topped off her mug with coffee and took a sip. She paused and reflected on her hesitancy to talk to Clarke, realizing she needed to *suck it up and face the music*. And who knows, perhaps he'd make no mention of the prior day, chalking it up to emotions running wild in the heat of the moment.

As she stood in the Break Room and prepared herself for the inevitable, Nash noticed Clarke walk out of his office and head in the direction of her desk. This was odd; Nash was sure Clarke had seen her, so why did he head toward that location when she wasn't there?

Nash returned to her desk; Clarke was nowhere in sight.

"Did Clarke come through here?" Nash said to Brogan and Donnelly.

"Yeah" Brogan replied, "He stopped and asked us what we were up to."

"We told him we were following leads regarding the last person to see Wagner alive" Donnelly added.

"Then he said *Do you mean Officer Roberson?*'" Brogan stated, "And we said *'No... Brandon Garrison'.*"

"Then he just shook his head, turned, and walked out of the building" Donnelly finished. "He seemed a bit perturbed."

"Shit; obviously he's not happy that we're still working this case" Nash replied. "Hey Laura, get over to the bank ASAP and see if we can tie Garrison to Wagner's withdrawals. Dirk, let's you and I keep working the board until we either get some breaking news, or Clarke shuts us down."

"Roger that" both Donnelly and Brogan replied in unison.

55

Donnelly had hit pay-dirt at *Slaughter County Bank:* Daryl Wagner had, in fact, closed out his account via cashier's check… made out to Brandon Garrison. Not only that, Donnelly had also spoken to the two banks in Seattle where Wagner had closed out accounts and, with the *Slaughter County Bank* manager's assistance, they had confirmed that Brandon Garrison was the recipient on Daryl Wagner's cashier's checks there as well.

It was time to talk to the mystery man himself. Nash punched in his number on her cell phone and hit 'Send'.

"Hello?" emanated from the other end of the line.

"Brandon Garrison?" Nash replied.

"Speaking" said Garrison.

"I'm Detective Mackenzie Nash with the Slaughter County Sheriff's Department; I was wondering if you know a *Daryl Wagner?*"

"That lives up in the Seattle area?"

"That's correct."

"I knew him, but not very well… why do you ask?"

"You *knew* him?"

"Yes."

"Why did you use past tense… you *knew* him… in lieu of you *know* him?"

"I saw a tribute to him on the *Ancestral Heritage* website – so sad."

"Are you aware of his manner of death?"

"Just what I read online; that arson was involved and it was ruled a homicide."

"You said you didn't know him very well, yet you two met up that weekend... the night he was killed?"

"Our initial introduction was a fluke actually; I needed assistance with the website and he happened to be the on-duty tech support guy. He helped me navigate the site and said that if I had any further questions or issues I could contact him directly, and he gave me his extension. So whenever I needed assistance I'd just call him."

"But something took you beyond tech support... to actually meeting in person."

"That's true. One day he noticed a familiarity between my background and his... that our fathers served together in the Navy and that both our families lived in Base Housing back when we were kids. We figured we probably played together as little tykes; we got a good laugh out of that one."

"And what about the two of you meeting up on the twenty-sixth?"

"I was in Seattle for a convention and we thought it would be nice to meet in person and talk more about the old days, and where our lives had gone since then. I rode the boat over to Bennington that afternoon and we grabbed a bite and a couple of drinks at a restaurant near the ferry terminal."

"How did he seem that day; was he worried about anything... anxious... concerned?"

"He seemed fine. But why do you ask; I read that the police had the killers in custody?"

"They're not *killers* until convicted; but yes, two suspects were arrested. However, we're still trying to piece together everything that occurred the evening of the twenty-sixth... the events leading up to his death."

"I don't know what I can provide; we hung out at the restaurant for an hour or two, and then I caught the boat back to Seattle."

"Did he mention anything about his wife... how they were doing... their relationship?"

"He said things had not been going well, and that she might be having an affair… he was pretty pissed about that."

"An affair? Did he say with whom?"

"He didn't give me a name; and I hate to point a finger at one of your contemporaries, but he said it was a cop."

"A cop?"

"Yeah. He said he wanted to talk to the guy's boss or some other person in law enforcement, but he was afraid as to what the cop might do – figuring cops would cover for their own."

"I thought you said he didn't seem concerned about anything?"

"I didn't think of the whole thing about a *cop* until you brought up his wife."

"What was he going to do? Did he say?"

"He talked about packing up and leaving… getting a divorce and maybe move out of the area and start fresh."

"And that's where you came in" Nash responded rather matter-of-factly.

"How do you mean?"

"He had secret bank accounts that he closed out; and they were closed out via cashier's checks made out to *you*."

"Yes they were. He was afraid his wife would *'take him for all he's got'* as he put it; so he asked me if I would hang on to the funds until the divorce was final."

"That seems awfully trusting of someone he barely knew."

"That's what *I* told him; but he said there was no one else he could trust, that even the closest of his friends would be too tempted by that amount of cash. He figured since I'm pretty successful and financially comfortable that I'm not someone who would take the money and run."

"Where's the money now?"

"I haven't done anything with it… I still have the cashier's checks."

"Why is that?"

"I had been waiting for word from Daryl in case he changed his mind; he was supposed to contact me the following week after we met up."

"Did you try to contact *him* to find out what was wrong?"

"Yes I did, but all I got was his voice mail."

"Do you know of anyone who might want to do him harm?"

"Like I said, I barely knew him. The only person he seemed to have concerns about was that cop I mentioned." Garrison paused, "And speaking of... the news reports said that a cop was arrested... is he the one?"

"I hadn't heard about a cop that Daryl was concerned with, but it's possible we're talking about the same person."

"Daryl never told me a name, so I was wondering if it was the same guy." Garrison took a breath, *"Thank God* he was caught."

The tone of Garrison's voice caught Nash's attention... it was almost a sigh of relief.

"Are you sure there was nothing unusual about your visit with Daryl?" Nash probed, "Something he might have said that seemed innocuous at the time, but in hindsight, knowing what you know now, might be relevant?"

"Just what I already told you about the cop. I'm curious though, with the guy in custody why call me; is it because of the cashier's checks?"

"For the most part; but also because you were the last person known to see him alive."

"I was?" said Garrison; such a revelation brought a concerning thought, "It makes me wonder..."

"It makes you wonder?"

"If we'd hung out longer, would that have prevented his murder? ...merely delayed it? Or worst case scenario... would I have been collateral damage – a second victim?"

"Hard to say, but I'd be thankful that the worst case scenario did not materialize."

"Yeah" he sighed. "And the reports said that his wife was arrested as well?"

"I'm afraid so."

"Unreal."

"How's that?"

"You just never think a wife is capable of such a thing; not outside of those 'real life' mystery programs anyway." He paused in thought, "It's a shame that he didn't file for divorce and get the hell out of there sooner."

"Yes... quite a shame. Anyway, like I said earlier, we're just trying to tie up a few loose ends. If you think of anything else please give me a call."

"I will."

Nash hung up the phone... she had a perplexed look on her face.

"Hey Kenz" commented Brogan, "I can see something's on your mind... what gives?"

"I have a feeling that Garrison knows more than he's letting on" Nash replied.

"What gives you that impression?"

"He seemed genuinely relieved that Roberson had been arrested for Daryl's murder."

"He mentioned Roberson by name?" said Donnelly.

"No; just *'the cop that Daryl was concerned about'*" Nash said with air-quotes.

"Daryl talked to Garrison about a cop?" said Brogan.

"Yep... that he thought Madison was having an affair with some cop, and he was concerned what the cop might do, *especially* if Daryl notified higher authority about it."

"So this guy could testify for the prosecution."

"His statement would be nothing but hearsay... inadmissible in court; but if he actually *saw* something, well that would be a whole different story."

"He didn't say if he saw anything?" asked Donnelly.

"He said *'no... didn't see a thing'*."

"Then why do you think he was relieved by Roberson being arrested?"

"I can only speculate at this point, but I just wonder if he knows more than he's letting on, like perhaps he really *did* see something."

"Like Daryl's abduction?"

"Probably not that overt" responded Nash. "If I was going to construct a scenario it would be something like this: Garrison is walking back to the ferry terminal and happens to turn around and see some guy get in Daryl's face. He probably didn't give it a whole lot of thought initially; but when he failed to hear from Daryl, and then got news of his death, he put two-and-two together. He figured the guy was watching Daryl, and hence *him*, at *The Harborside*, and was afraid that the guy might come after him, too."

"So, he could potentially place Daryl and Roberson together the night of the murder?" said Brogan.

"Potentially… yes. But as long as he holds to his story there's nothing we can do."

"Does that mean we forget about this guy, and focus on everything else we have?"

"Let's just say that we keep him in our hip pocket."

56

The mystery of Sheriff Clarke's whereabouts suddenly became moot – he walked through the entryway of the building. As he passed Nash, Brogan, and Donnelly he looked directly at Nash and, with a head-nod, stated, "Detective... my office."

Nash gave Brogan and Donnelly a *'here it comes'* look and followed Clarke's path.

Through the entire trek to his office and across the threshold of his doorway Clarke never turned around, but he knew Nash was right on his heels. As he turned around to take a seat at his desk Clarke stated to Nash, "Shut the door."

Nash complied.

"What's this *wild goose chase* you've got Brogan and Donnelly working on?" Clarke said.

"We're following leads" replied Nash.

"What leads? Both of the prime suspects have been arrested; and thanks to YOU, they are currently out on bail... correction... *out on their own recognizance* instead of sitting in jail awaiting trial where they should be!"

"I don't grant bail... a Judge does."

"Yeah; because you went behind my back and then embarrassed the Deputy Prosecutor with some so-called 'new evidence'" said Clarke with air-quotes, "...in the middle of a damn Bail Hearing!"

"Went behind your back?? I *told you* I had uncovered information that contradicted a portion of our theory as to Madison Wagner's involvement, and I told Dansby as well. You were supposed to back *me* up, but you two chose to ignore it."

Nash took a breath and added... "And I don't remember reading anything in the *Sheriff's Department Code of Conduct* that says *'thou shalt not embarrass the Deputy Prosecutor'.*"

"Dansby wanted you suspended" said Clarke.

"For what??"

"For making a mockery of the Hearing."

"That's so ridiculous, if anyone made a mockery of it *he* did; do you know how much *in the shits* he would have been if it was discovered that he was withholding evidence? And that would've been *on top of* the dressing-down he got from the Judge before I even spoke."

"What dressing-down?"

"Did you miss the part where he kept interrupting the Defense Attorney and the Judge asked him if she needed to call the Prosecutor and have him replaced?"

Clarke remained silent.

Nash continued... "And in addition to the new information I provided the Judge *and* the Deputy Prosecutor, we've discovered someone who might have seen something."

"This guy *Garrison* that Brogan and Donnelly mentioned?"

"Yes."

"Was he at the scene?"

"Well no, but he could have seen Wagner and Roberson together and thus debunk Roberson's statement that he had no contact with Wagner that night."

"Did he *say* he saw them together?"

"No, but I'm pretty sure he's hiding something."

"So your *'witness'* didn't actually *witness* anything?"

"So he says, but if we keep digging we might be able to determine otherwise."

"For what purpose? We already have a boat-load of evidence against Roberson; we don't need to waste time *and* the taxpayer's money on some guy that was *not* at the scene *and* said he didn't see anything...

that's insane!"

Nash had no rebuttal to Clarke's statement.

"And where does this guy live?" Clarke continued.

Nash was hesitant – she responded in a muffled voice, "California."

"Where??"

"California" Nash repeated more loudly.

"Are you kidding me?! California?! This crap stops *now!* Pack up all your shit on this case and get it to the Prosecutor. And Donnelly... she's back on patrol duty in the morning."

Nash turned and walked out of Clarke's office – not uttering a word.

57

Brogan and Donnelly looked up from their desks as Nash approached; she had the demeanor of someone who had just experienced a rare defeat... whose self-confidence had been beaten-down. They decided not to broach the subject of Nash's talk with Clarke unless Nash brought it up.

"Our orders are to pack up everything by the end of shift today" said Nash.

"We're done working the case?" responded Brogan.

"*Officially*... yes."

Brogan grinned... he knew the meaning behind the inflection in Nash's voice.

"But we can continue to work it today, right?" said Donnelly.

"As long as we're packed up by the end of the day" replied Nash.

"Good; because your intuition that Brandon Garrison might not be telling us the whole story was correct... check out these surveillance photos" responded Donnelly as she nodded toward her computer screen.

"What the..." Nash started, "Are you sure that's him?"

"These were all taken at his hotel: This one he's entering the lobby area from the street; here he's entering his room; here he's *exiting* his room the next morning; and so on."

"How do we know it's Garrison?"

"The room number" said Donnelly. "Plus, I have a later shot of him checking-out early Monday morning the twenty-eighth."

"What the hell happened to him?" said Nash

"He was on foot, so it's not like he was in a car wreck or something" replied Donnelly.

"Are we sure about that?"

"He told you he *walked on* the ferry; and his hotel is only a few blocks away."

Brogan was curious as to Nash's statement, "Do you think he was lying?"

"Possibly" replied Nash. "Or he ventured out after he got back to Seattle."

Nash looked at the photos and added, "What's the time-stamp on these?"

"His arrival at the hotel the night of Daryl's murder is at three-thirty-two A.M." said Donnelly.

"Three-thirty-two in the morning? As in *Sunday* morning?"

"Yep."

"He was seen at *The Harborside* around six o'clock Saturday night; he said he was there for an hour or two and then caught the next ferry back to Seattle... that would put him on either the 8:20 or 9:30 ferry at the latest."

"I thought the same thing" said Brogan, "So I looked at surveillance footage on both of those runs, but there was nothing definitive."

"Which we all know is a hit-and-miss endeavor in the first place, so that doesn't really tell us anything" noted Nash, "Did you check any of the later runs?"

"Not yet."

"He could've hit some clubs along the Seattle waterfront or Pioneer Square" said Donnelly, "They're within walking distance of his hotel."

"Or he could've caught a cab or Uber and headed to Belltown or Pike Place, or anywhere else in the city" added Brogan.

"You know; we could be jumping to conclusions on him being all beat up following his trip to Bennington" said Nash, "Maybe he got roughed-up earlier?"

"Not unless it happened between his hotel and the ferry terminal Saturday afternoon" said Donnelly as she pointed to surveillance footage… "Here he is leaving the hotel at three-forty-five Saturday afternoon – not a scratch on him. I figure he had to catch the 4:20 ferry to be in Bennington before six o'clock since the next one would put him there at six-forty."

"So, sometime between eight o'clock Saturday night and three o'clock Sunday morning he got in a bar fight, a car wreck, or trampled by Bigfoot" said Brogan.

"Good one, Dirk" responded Nash. She shook her head and turned to Donnelly, "Laura, see if there are any police reports on him during that timeframe – Seattle P.D. Also, check for any hospital E.R. visits."

"Will do."

"Oh, and check with his rental car company; even if he *was* in a wreck and managed to avoid a Police Report there's no way his rental car company wouldn't know."

"Got it."

"Hey, I didn't get a chance to tell you yet" Brogan piped-up, "But I came across some info that might back me up in my suspicion that Daryl was trying to set-up Madison."

"Okay Sherlock, let's hear it" replied Nash.

"I talked to Daryl and Madison's life insurance agent, and he said that Daryl had discussed increasing coverage for *both* of them, but for some reason he… the agent… only received the paperwork to increase Daryl's."

"Did he have an explanation for receiving just the one?"

"He called Daryl and left a voice mail, but when he didn't hear back from him he went ahead and processed what he had, figuring that Daryl or Madison would get back to him and he'd process the revision on Madison's coverage once he received the paperwork."

"That's *one more* nugget a Defense Attorney would use to cast doubt as to Madison's guilt."

"Yeah; it would throw a monkey wrench in the *insurance payout motive* and leave only the *fear for her life due to years of abuse* motive."

"Which a good Defense Attorney would refute based on the filing of the restraining order."

Brogan was about to sit back in his chair and relish in his momentary gratification when something caught his eye on his computer screen... "Wait a minute" he said as he leaned-in toward his screen.

"What have you got?" said Nash.

"The footage for the 2:10 A.M. ferry." He pointed to the screen as Nash and Donnelly gathered around, "Could *that* be Garrison?"

"That's quite a leap you're making; the guy's covering almost his entire face with a rag or a T-shirt or something."

"Yeah; but it also looks like a *bloody* rag or T-shirt or something."

"It could be that the guy simply has a bloody nose. Do we get a clear shot of his face at any time?"

"Nope."

"Garrison wasn't covering his face with anything when he arrived at his hotel early Sunday morning" noted Donnelly.

"He could have tossed it in a trash can before he got to his hotel" replied Brogan.

"I have to admit that the timing works out perfectly... the arrival of the ferry in Seattle around three A.M, and then Garrison showing up at the hotel a short time thereafter" commented Nash.

"Well, if it *is* Garrison then *this just got interesting.*"

"Should I cancel my other searches... police reports, E.R. visits, and Garrison's rental car company?" said Donnelly.

"Let's not get ahead of ourselves; we never see the entirety of this guy's face, so we have no idea if it really *is* Garrison."

Nash paused in thought. She felt obligated to inform Clarke of the latest information regarding Madison Wagner – the life insurance contradiction. Under normal circumstances she'd provide him the latest info about Brandon Garrison, someone who looked more and more like he knows something, possibly even a witness of some sort; but for some unknown reason Clarke seemed to have Dansby's hand up his backside manipulating him like a puppet. With that in mind she decided that the curious news regarding Garrison would have to wait until she had something definitive.

"Time to jump back into the fire" stated Nash as she started toward Sheriff Clarke's office.

Brogan and Donnelly watched Nash walk out of sight, and then looked at each other with an expression akin to a grimace.

"This could get ugly" Brogan noted.

Clarke looked up from his desk as Nash entered his office – he had a *'Now what?'* look on his face.

Nash provided Clarke with the statement from the Wagner's insurance agent... that he corroborated Madison's story. Clarke was unfazed except to respond, "So now you're working for the Defense Attorney?"

"I am neither the judge, the jury, nor the executioner... I'm an investigator – I *investigate*. If I uncover evidence that contradicts our theory of events it is my duty to report that contradiction. What the hell?"

"You're getting too personally involved in this case; why don't you take a couple of days off?"

By the tone of Clarke's voice Nash knew his *question* was, in reality, an *edict*.

"Fine."

Nash turned and walked away.

As she grabbed her jacket off of the back of her chair Nash turned to Brogan and Donnelly and stated, "I've been told I need to take some time off."

"What??" Donnelly replied.

"Yep. So I'm going to get out of here since there's something I need to do. Keep me posted if you dig up anything before you wrap all of this up today."

"Will do" responded Brogan.

"I can neither confirm nor deny my continuing to follow leads during my time off."

"If you need anything, give us a call."

"I can't ask you two to keep working on this."

"Our choice; right Laura?"

"Absolutely" said Donnelly.

"I appreciate that" responded Nash, "But keep it on the down-low, lest you end up in my shoes."

"Roger that" replied Brogan.

58

This was not a trip that Nash had expected to make, but she felt it was necessary in light of recent events. It wasn't just the curious videos of Brandon Garrison, or Daryl Wagner's life insurance policy; Nash's action was prompted by the apparent two-person crusade by Sheriff Clarke and Deputy Prosecutor Dansby to cast aside virtually anything that didn't fit within their narrative regarding the murder of Daryl Wagner.

A look of concern fell across Madison's face as she opened the door to the sight of Detective Nash. She looked around the area for other patrol cars... other police officers... she was sure she was about to be arrested.

"Detective?" said Madison while she continued to scan the area.

"I'm sure you weren't expecting me" said Nash. "To be honest, I wasn't expecting to make this visit, but I have some important information for you. *However*, if you attribute any of what I'm about to say to *me*... I will vehemently deny it."

Madison was perplexed, "Umm... okay."

"This may sound confusing at first, but please hear me out: I think you've been set up to take the fall for your husband's murder."

"I have?"

"I think so, yes. But you need to know that the person setting you up could be either your husband... or possibly Officer Roberson."

"You're right, I *am* confused; how could my husband set me up for his murder?"

"All I have is my gut telling me that something is hinky, but there's a possibility that he was planning on disappearing and starting a new

313

life… and making his disappearance look suspicious, which would point directly at you."

"Starting a new life?" responded Madison, "With the girlfriend?"

"Possibly; but we haven't been able to verify that such a person exists. And sure, when someone's running away to start a new life it is often because of a secret love interest; but sometimes they are simply running *from* something."

"I don't understand how he could up and vanish and make *me* look suspicious?"

"Case in point: Did you perform the computer searches on *DNA* and *tooth pulp?*"

"Of course not; I already told you that."

"As you know, those searches, along with the recent increase in Daryl's life insurance coverage, put *you* under suspicion."

"But the life insurance was *his* doing, and it was supposed to be for both of us."

"I know."

"You *know?*"

"Your lawyer should have looked into this, but we contacted your insurance agent and he corroborated your story that *both* of you were supposed to receive increased coverage; however, he only received the paperwork for your husband."

"Daryl's the one who took care of all that."

"That's what I figured."

"But if he wanted to start a new life, why not just get a divorce?"

"Some would consider that, if you *really* want to start fresh… a clean slate… the best way to do that is to get rid of your previous life; and the best way to do *that* is to make it appear that you're no longer alive."

"To fake that he'd been murdered?"

"Sure; that you were murdered and the body disposed of. You plant some evidence that implicates someone – *like incriminating computer searches and a recent increase in life insurance"* Nash emphasized. "And then to punctuate the set-up you leave blood evidence somewhere, and then vanish... to another state, another country... with a new identity. When you add it all up who are the cops going to focus on? The person with the most to gain; and with all of the evidence pointing at them."

"But there was no blood found anywhere, was there?"

"That's because his plan never came to fruition... instead of *faking* his murder he actually *was* murdered."

"So everything he did to make me look guilty for his *fake* death ended up making me look guilty for his *real* death?"

"Assuming my suspicions are accurate... that's correct."

"But why would he pick me?"

"Someone had to take the fall, and you were the easiest target. And you only have to look back at the woman you saw in the mirror two weeks ago to get an understanding as to his treatment of you."

"Wow, it's a good thing I didn't agree to the Prosecutor's offer."

"He made you an offer?"

"He said if I pleaded guilty to a lesser charge and agreed to testify against Mike, that I would only have to serve a few years instead of twenty-five years to life."

"And you actually considered it?"

"I didn't want to because I didn't *do* anything. But my lawyer said that the Prosecutor inferred that Mike was going to implicate *me,* and if that was the case then I should consider it. He said it would be a good deal under those circumstances... better than spending the rest of my life in prison for something I didn't do."

"*He* said? I thought your lawyer was Angela Armstrong?"

"I guess she was only my lawyer for the Bail Hearing; I was assigned someone else."

"Who's that, Doofus McClueless?"

"No... Carl Jordan."

Nash had a feeling that Madison wouldn't comprehend her smart-assed nickname for Madison's new lawyer.

"Well, the Prosecutor is blowing smoke up your lawyer's ass. There would be no upside for Officer Roberson to implicate *you* because if he *does* then he's admitting to the murder. If he stays silent he has a better chance of being found *not guilty;* not a great chance mind you concerning all of the circumstantial evidence against him, but a better chance than admitting guilt."

"I see what you mean."

"Anyway, I'm not a lawyer so my opinion may mean nothing; but if it were me I would say *'no deals... I'll take my chances in court'.*"

"He... my lawyer... mentioned that if it went that route *The Battered Wife Defense* might be an option."

Nash rolled her eyes. "If you're *guilty* then yes, it basically means that you killed him in self-defense... that you felt your life was in danger. But remember, the search on your computer for *cases involving the Battered Wife Defense* makes it look premeditated, and you'll be hard-pressed to claim self-defense for a premeditated act... in the eyes of a jury anyway."

Madison nodded.

"And here's another thing that *hopefully* your lawyer is looking into" said Nash... "Your husband had three secret bank accounts where he had socked away almost thirty-thousand dollars."

"What??"

"Which is one more reason to believe he may have been planning to disappear."

Madison looked as if all of this information was confusing... possibly even overwhelming; Nash realized she needed to bring Madison back to reality...

"But remember" Nash continued, "No matter *what* your husband might have been *planning,* we can't ignore the fact that he was murdered, and right now all of the evidence points to Officer Roberson."

Nash wasn't sure if Madison had comprehended her statement, so she decided to clarify, "I don't know if you are continuing to communicate with him, but I would advise against it – the more you *do* the more it makes you look like an accomplice."

"I understand. So what should I do now?"

"You get this info to your attorney. If he doesn't jump on it then request that Attorney Armstrong be reassigned to represent you."

"Yes ma'am."

"And when he asks where you got this information, what are you going to say?"

"A source who did not identify themself?"

"Exactly" Nash responded with a thumbs-up gesture.

Nash stepped off of the landing and was heading toward her car when her cell phone rang – it was Donnelly.

"Hey Laura, you got something?" said Nash into the phone.

"The call to Crosstown Cab around one A.M. the night of the murder..." said Donnelly, "You know... to pick up who we *think* was Roberson out near Eagle Point..."

"Yeah?" Nash interrupted.

"It came from Daryl Wagner's *burner.*"

"Son of a bitch!" said Nash, "No wonder Roberson was so *matter-of-fact* about us not being able to trace that call to *him*... the bastard used *Daryl's* phone."

"So... what now?"

"I have an idea... let's hope it works."

59

Nash considered the irony of still working a case when officially off-duty... *temporarily kicked to the curb by your boss* as it were. Was it dedication... stupidity... or a complete lack of a life outside of work that had her still *hard at it?* She liked to think it was the former, although she had to admit to herself that an *'I told you so'* moment with Sheriff Clarke and Prosecutor Dansby would be quite gratifying. Then again, if her plan worked, the *'I told you so'* speech would go both ways. Yep... irony at its finest.

Nash was sure that Clarke had told Dansby that she... Nash... *was spending a few days on the beach* – implying that she had been suspended when in fact she was merely taking some long overdue vacation days. A *'working vacation'* mind you, but a vacation nonetheless. And what had her taking this unusual step? The revelation that Daryl Wagner's burner phone was used to make the call to pick up his killer after ditching the black & white. Nash figured that at this late stage of the investigation she had one last hand to play – one that, if she played her cards right, could seal Roberson's fate.

"Please return your seatbacks to their upright position and tray tables stowed" rang out over the intercom system. Next stop: *Northern California Wine country.*

Nash stepped onto the porch of a classic Victorian home. She wasn't sure what to expect when the door opened, but even a seasoned veteran like herself was caught off-guard. It was a sight to behold... and for all the wrong reasons. There before her stood a woman... beaten, battered, swollen, and bruised. Nash was in disbelief, *"What the hell??*

Why do I keep running into women who apparently have been beaten to a pulp by their husband??!!" She scanned the woman from head to toe – her hands and arms had suffered the same fate... *"Surely defensive wounds"* Nash determined. She regained her composure and held up her badge...

"Ma'am, I'm Detective Nash; is everything alright?"

The woman seemed disoriented, "Umm... I don't know... uh, yeah... fine I guess... why do you ask?"

"You look like you've had a rough go of it."

"Oh that... no, I'm okay. What can I do for you?"

"Actually, I'm looking for Brandon Garrison."

"That's my husband, but he's not here right now."

"Then you're *Emily* Garrison?"

"That's correct" Emily responded. "Why are you looking for my husband?"

"I need to follow-up on a conversation he and I had yesterday morning by phone" Nash replied, "It concerns a crime that he might have information about."

"He might have been involved in a crime?"

"Not so much *involved...* more like a possible witness."

"He never said anything like that to me. When did this happen?"

"A little over two weeks ago... Saturday the twenty-sixth."

"What? You must have the wrong person because he wasn't even *here* at that time, he was in Seattle."

"It occurred while he was in the Seattle area; I'm with the Slaughter County Sheriff's Department."

"Slaughter County? I've never even heard of it. And why would you travel all the way down here if you already talked to him?"

"We've uncovered evidence indicating that he might know more than he let on when I spoke with him, so I figured perhaps he'd be more comfortable sharing whatever he knows *in person* instead of over the phone."

"He should be back later this afternoon; I can call you when he returns."

"That would be fine. But in the meantime do you mind if I ask you a few questions?"

"Uh… okay."

"We noticed on surveillance videos at your husband's hotel in Seattle that he had received some sort of injuries."

"He said he got in a car wreck and received a concussion. It really messed him up; it has been difficult for him… for all of us, since his return."

"How do you mean."

"He hasn't been himself at all… paranoid, aggressive, even abusive… totally out of character."

"Concussions can have deleterious effects on a person… the type of symptoms you just mentioned. Do you feel your safety is at risk?"

"I don't really want to talk about it."

"Okay then; how about his car wreck, did he say much about that?"

"That he got T-boned by an inattentive driver."

"Actually ma'am, there's no record of a car accident involving your husband."

"There *has* to be… he said it was so bad that the rental car company had to replace his car" responded Emily – clearly befuddled, "Maybe it was in a town *outside* of Seattle?"

"We checked with every law enforcement agency within the entire Puget Sound area and came up empty. And according to his rental car company your husband returned the same car that he rented… not a scratch on it."

"But he was all bruised and scratched, his throat all red, his voice all raspy, had a large wrap covering his forearm and wrist…"

"We noticed that as well… from surveillance cameras at the hotel, the rental car company, and also at the airport."

"Maybe he's remembering it wrong; maybe he was a passenger in someone else's vehicle?"

"It's possible, but it seems unlikely unless he departed the scene without seeking treatment."

"But he said that a doctor told him he had a concussion and that he shouldn't consider flying for another week?"

"Perhaps he departed the scene and sought treatment without mentioning a car crash as the reason for his injuries?"

"But why would he tell me something different?"

"Well, I have a possible scenario for you: A car was crashed into a ditch in Slaughter County, and we've tied that car to a crime scene."

"Slaughter County? Not Seattle?"

"It's a ferry ride away from Seattle."

"Are you saying that *this* car crash might be the one that my husband was involved in?"

"I don't know for sure, but it's possible."

"But why would my husband have been there… in Slaughter County?"

"He told me he was meeting someone from his childhood… from back when his family lived there."

Emily was dumbstruck, "He told me before he left on his trip that he was hoping to catch up with an old friend, but when I asked him about it after he returned home he said the meeting never happened."

"Not only did the meeting happen, but the man ended up being the victim of a crime – murdered; and as near as we can tell your husband was the last person to him alive."

"Murdered? You don't think my husband had anything to with his death do you?"

"We think he was a witness; either to the abduction of the victim, or to the crime itself."

"That could explain…"

Nash inadvertently cut Emily off: "In fact it could be worse; I think it's possible that your husband was an unintended victim himself."

"How do you mean?"

"I think he was abducted along with the intended victim" Nash replied, "He may or may not have witnessed the murder, but somehow he got away."

Emily stood silent; Nash provided a possible scenario... "Your husband could have taken off in the car that was at the scene and, in his haste, accidentally crashed into a ditch; *or* he could've been a passenger in the car and when the crash occurred he managed to make a run for it. Either way, it appears he just happened to be in the wrong place at the wrong time."

"Wow. But at least he got away."

"Yes. And I'm sorry, I think I interrupted you... you were saying that his being a witness *could explain something?*"

"That's okay; I was just going to tell you that it could explain his nightmares. I can't believe it, but it fits your story perfectly."

"His nightmares?"

"Yes; of the crash and being chased by a bad guy. I thought it was all the result of his concussion, all in his head, *not* that it could actually be real... the *being chased by a bad guy* part that is."

"It sounds like he is possibly reliving the event."

Emily just had a scary thought, "If you were able to track down my husband, doesn't that mean the *killer* could track him down, too?"

"We have two suspects in custody; plus the killer would not have access to the surveillance footage and electronic evidence we gathered to track down your husband."

Nash's lies were twofold: Yes, two suspects were arrested, but they were subsequently released on their own recognizance; and, as a cop, Officer Roberson *would* potentially have access to the methods utilized to track down Brandon Garrison. However, Nash felt these false statements were necessary to alleviate any possible concerns for Brandon Garrison's safety, and hence his willingness to talk. Besides, if Roberson defied the Judge's orders and showed up in California... well, such an act would seal his guilt, and his fate.

"I guess the fact that they're in custody eight hundred miles from here makes me feel a little more at ease" Emily responded.

"That's good" Nash replied. "Needless to say I hope you can see why I really need to talk to your husband."

"I'll let you know when he returns."

"Thank you; I appreciate that... and your time."

60

Nash was flipping through the files of *'The Daryl Wagner Murder Case'*. She smiled at her sleight of hand when embarking on her unofficial *working vacation*; having absconded a copy of the case file for her own personal use prior to departing the office the previous afternoon.

Nash's temporary office – a local coffee shop – had one minor flaw, the ding of a bell every time a customer entered and exited. She had considered working out of her hotel room; but being surrounded by textured wallpaper, generic furniture, a floral bedspread, and walls covered with dollar-store reprints masquerading as paintings completely inhibited her ability to focus. It also didn't help that the intensity of this case... the long hours, the sleepless nights, the early morning flight... had taken a toll on her. She was but a quiet moment away from conking-out like a toddler whom had run herself ragged chasing fairies; or in Nash's case... a phantom. With that in mind the bustling activity of her surroundings was actually a welcome stimulant... along with a triple-shot latte'.

She had settled into a comfortable easy-chair in a little nook at the far end of the coffee shop. She soon realized it was a bit too comfy: Her eyelids growing heavy, the 'ding' of the café door becoming muted, the line between a dream and reality becoming blurred. A sudden head-jerk made her aware that she was losing the battle. She scanned her surroundings to see if anyone had noticed her nodding-off; a middle-aged woman hiding behind a romance novel gave her a sympathetic smile. She returned the gesture.

She refocused on the task at hand – updating her files. But *The Sandman* was a staunch adversary; and she found herself drifting between the physical act of updating the files, and the visions held within: Daryl Wagner's charred corpse, a bruised and battered Madison Wagner, a bloodied and bandaged Brandon Garrison, Brandon's beaten and disoriented wife Emily, and prime suspect Officer Mike Roberson... whom Nash had inadvertently gotten released from custody. *Had her actions put other lives in jeopardy? Had Madison's innocence and naiveté been simply an act?* Nash realized she was second-guessing herself.

She closed her file folder. A 'ding' from the café door rang out... simply another unremarkable sound to be ignored, yet something caused her to look toward the entryway. The sight was nothing more than a silhouette, but there was a familiarity to the specter. As the shadow receded and a face emerged, panic ensued... *it was Roberson!* Nash jumped up and grasped at her weapon...

Bzzz... bzzz... Nash jerked awake. She frantically looked around – nothing but the calm and innocuous activity of a coffee shop... no phantom bearing down upon her.

Bzzz... bzzz... Nash snapped back to reality and fumbled to grab her cell phone. She took a glance at the screen – it was an unfamiliar number.

"Detective Nash" she struggled through rapid breaths into the phone.

A frenetic voice responded, "Detective Nash, it's Emily Garrison, you need to get over here right away!"

Nash didn't ask a single question, she merely responded, "On my way", gathered up her files, and bolted out of the coffee shop.

Nash's heart was racing as she jumped into her car; stoked by the nightmarish vision of Roberson bearing down on her in the café, along with the impending scene at the Garrison home.

She reached to engage the lights and siren – quickly realizing that she was driving a rental car... "Dammit!" she said aloud.

With no flashing lights or siren to pave her way, Nash had to skirt the traffic laws in order to make haste to Emily Garrison's house; luckily for her it was a short trip.

She pulled up to the Garrison home and jumped out of the car... her weapon drawn – *just in case*.

Emily was standing on the porch anxiously awaiting Nash's arrival. Her eyes grew large at the sight of Nash's gun.

"What's the emergency?" stated Nash.

"I'm sorry to alarm you; you won't need that" replied Emily as she nodded toward Nash's gun.

Nash holstered her weapon while stating, "You mean your husband is *not* here?"

"He was, but when I mentioned that a detective was here looking for him, he replied *What the hell did you do?!* I told him that I didn't do anything, but he raced out of here anyway."

"He probably thought you called the cops because he assaulted you."

"Uh, I guess so, but there's something else... the thing that *really* freaked me out, and why I called – *THIS*" said Emily as she held up a cell phone.

"He accidentally left it on the end table when he was in such a hurry to leave" Emily continued, "I was curious, so I scrolled through it and found these pictures."

Emily handed the phone to Nash.

As Nash scrolled Emily commented, "I don't understand; why are there pictures of my husband naked and apparently passed-out on the floor?" She was becoming frantic, "What the hell is going on here?!!"

"Son of a bitch" replied Nash as she continued to scroll, "This looks like the cabin where DNA traces of the victim were found."

"DNA traces of the victim?!"

"Hair follicles wedged between the slats of the floor, and saliva in a drinking glass."

"Was there some creepy sex-thing going on? Is that why my husband is having nightmares?"

"As if the perpetrator performed some lewd sex acts on both the victim and your husband, but somehow your husband managed to escape?"

said Nash, "I don't know, but it looks possible."

"Oh my God, no wonder he's such an emotional wreck! To have this happen; and also a concussion? He needs professional help before it's too late!"

"Are you sure these pictures are your husband and not of the victim?"

"Yes. When you've been with someone for over seven years you learn every inch of their body... from moles to birthmarks to skin-tags on their privates."

Nash hadn't expected that extent of detail in Emily's response, and was not about to question it.

"Based on these pictures the killer is even more depraved than we thought. I really need to get hold of your husband; do you have any idea where I can find him?"

"Some nights he stays over at the property... the winery; there's a caretaker's cabin that's currently empty."

"Great; I'll start there" replied Nash, "Oh, and I'll need to take this" she said, referring to Brandon's phone.

61

The sun had just disappeared behind the rolling hills of the Russian River Valley. Nash turned onto a dirt road and pulled up to the gate of *Vino D'Emilia Winery* – it was closed.

Nash got out of her car and approached the gate on foot. She inspected the mechanism and noticed it was a simple manually-operated gate… no lock, no chain. She pulled the gate open, jumped back in her car, and drove through – leaving the gate open.

She drove up to the parking area – it was empty. With no car in the lot she figured Emily's guess as to her husband's whereabouts was a no-go. She decided to get out and explore the grounds anyway… *"Perhaps Brandon will yet show up"* she reasoned.

She walked along the outside of the building, periodically glancing through the windows; there was no activity within.

When she got to the far end of the building she noticed two lanes of dirt the width of the track of a car. She followed them around a corner and spied a car a few hundred yards down a ways. Beyond the car was a cabin.

Nash trekked down the path, expecting Garrison to emerge from the cabin as she approached; but the only sign of life was a hawk circling overhead.

Nash was running her eventual conversation with Garrison through her head. She wanted to *rake him over the coals* for the beatings he had been inflicting upon his wife, but she knew if she did he would be completely uncooperative in regard to her murder case. Unfortunately, solving a murder was a higher priority than throwing him in the slammer for being a wife beater. Thus she had to suck it up, bite her lip, and pretend she had no clue in regard to his domestic abuse... for now.

Just as Nash stepped onto the landing of the cabin her cell phone rang – it was Emily; but as she went to answer the call the door opened. Nash ended Emily's call without answering.

"Brandon Garrison?" said Nash to the man in the doorway.

"And you are?" he replied.

"Detective Mackenzie Nash."

"Nash? Why does that name sound familiar?"

"With the Slaughter County Sheriff's Department."

"Oh, the detective I talked to yesterday. You're a bit out of your jurisdiction, don't you think?"

"Yes, but I had some vacation time coming and figured you'd be more inclined to talk openly in person than on the phone."

"You're here on your own time and your own dime?"

"Go figure, huh? What can I say, I don't like loose ends."

"Well, I'm afraid you've wasted your time and money unless the primary purpose of your trip was to do a bit of wine tasting; as I told you over the phone, I didn't see anything."

"I may not have evidence that you *did* see something, but I know for a fact that you didn't give me the whole story."

"Based on what?"

Nash held up her phone and scrolled through the surveillance photos she had of him, "This is you at your hotel, the rental car company, and the airport."

"Your point?"

"You're all *beat to hell* right after your trip to Bennington."

"I got in a car wreck."

"So I heard; but the details you told your wife were not quite accurate, were they?"

Garrison didn't respond; he wanted to hear whatever Nash *thought* she knew.

"We checked accident reports throughout the entire Puget Sound area and *none* of them involved you."

Garrison started to open his mouth to respond but Nash cut him off... "And before you claim you got T-boned to the extent that you were injured and yet no report was filed, we also checked with your rental car company; they said the car you turned-in was as pristine as when you drove it off the lot."

She let the information percolate in Garrison's head for a moment and then added, "So, what's the *real* story?"

"You seem to be the one with all the answers, you tell me."

"Very well" she responded. "You got in a car wreck alright... in a black & white Crown Vic on a County Maintenance road in Slaughter County... and then you fled the scene because you were in fear for your life."

Garrison remained silent; Nash knew she was onto something.

Nash continued... "Your meeting with Daryl Wagner didn't go exactly as planned; or should I say, didn't *end* exactly as planned. The two of you left the restaurant via the elevator" she paused and clarified, "We have surveillance footage" and then continued, "The elevator takes you to the parking garage and also access to the boardwalk. I'm guessing you were going to split up at that time... Daryl to his car and you to the boardwalk and the ferry... but unfortunately Daryl got abducted, and you happened to be in the wrong place at the wrong time. You got abducted right along with him, didn't you?"

"I don't know what you're talking about."

"You're really going to play that game?"

Nash reached into her back pocket, pulled out *Garrison's* cell phone, and held it up.

"Where did you get that?" Garrison demanded.

"You left it at your house; and your wife discovered some disturbing photos" Nash replied as she handed the phone to Garrison.

"What the hell?! That's an invasion of privacy!"

"Those photographs were taken at a cabin tied to Daryl Wagner's murder" Nash stated, "Were the two of you sexually assaulted – raped by some sadistic psychopath who took photos of you with your own cell phone?"

Garrison realized he could no longer plead ignorance, "I have no idea what the creep did to me while I was passed-out, except that I know I wasn't raped."

"And Daryl?"

"Not a clue; as you noticed I was passed-out."

"You didn't see what happened to him?"

"Just foggy bits and pieces: The killer on top of him like he was choking him, things went blank for who-knows-how-long, and when I opened my eyes again he was gone."

"Daryl? Or the killer?"

"Both. The next thing I knew I was in a car, but it was stopped and I was alone. I remember a fire, but I couldn't see what was burning. He... *the killer*... suddenly ran and jumped into the car and we took off. I pretended I was still knocked-out. My clothes were all askew; I didn't realize until after I looked at my phone that I had been naked and he must have haphazardly put my clothes back on."

"Any idea why he would have done that?"

"Probably in case he got pulled over" replied Garrison. "He could explain a guy passed out in his car as a buddy who had too much to drink, but a *naked guy passed out in his car*..."

"Any idea why he would've stripped you naked and taken photographs?"

"Because he's some psycho, perv, sick son-of-a-bitch?? How the hell should I know?!"

Garrison's breaths had grown rapid, his body trembling; as if he was reliving the nightmare. A sudden realization overtook him. As a disturbing thought came to mind his heightened state immediately transformed to that of a lost soul. "I can only imagine what sick, twisted photos he took of Daryl... maybe even capturing the murder itself"

Garrison murmured as he shook his head.

Nash contemplated the horror that Garrison had posed. She gave him a moment to collect himself, and then gestured for Garrison to continue.

"Anyway" said Garrison, "We were driving out in the middle of nowhere. I figured he was taking me someplace remote to kill me like he did Daryl, so I jumped up and grabbed the wheel and we slammed into the ditch. His airbag deployed which I guess knocked him for a loop. It also hit my right hand and arm since I was holding the wheel, along with the side of my face. Then I jumped out of the car and ran like hell."

"How did get your cell phone?"

"It was sitting right next to me on the seat. I wasn't even sure it was mine, I just grabbed it."

"And after you discovered the pictures you decided to save them as evidence against him?"

"Just in case... yeah. But as I told you before, I'm not flying to Washington to be your witness for the prosecution; you've already got your guy... you don't need me."

"But your *eyewitness account* could seal the deal on this guy?"

"Sure; and then he gets off on some technicality and, being the one and only witness, I'm the next poor bastard to get his teeth yanked out and then get set on fire."

Garrison's response struck a nerve with Nash, "If you were passed-out, how do you know that Daryl's teeth had been yanked out?" she said.

"Say what??"

Nash emphasized her point... *"How do you know that Daryl's teeth had been yanked out?"*

"I didn't say I was passed-out at *that* time, I said that I saw foggy bits and pieces while I *pretended* to be passed-out."

Nash flipped back to a page in her memo pad and read aloud, "You said the foggy bits and pieces were when the killer was on top of Daryl choking him, and when you opened your eyes both of them were gone, and the next thing you knew you were in a car *alone*." Nash closed her memo pad and reiterated, "So... about the teeth?"

"Cuz the crazy killer dude was ranting and raving about it while we were driving, okay? Sheesh!!" Garrison retorted.

Nash wasn't buying the entirety of Garrison's response, but something else had caught her attention, "In addition to grabbing your cell phone, you also managed to grab your ring when you escaped?"

"How's that?" replied Garrison.

Nash pointed at Garrison's cell phone, "Those pictures of you passed-out... you're not wearing your ring."

Garrison looked at his ring, and then started to scroll through the pictures; but before he could respond Nash's cell phone rang – it was Donnelly.

"Excuse me" Nash said to Garrison as she held her cell phone up to her ear, turned around, stepped off of the landing, and turned her back in order to answer the call with some level of privacy.

"Hey Laura, what's up? Yeah, I'm talking to him right now" said Nash as she looked back toward Garrison. "What do you mean there's *another* reason all of Wagner's teeth were yanked out?" she said as she turned her back to Garrison and realized the eerie timing of Donnelly's statement, "And I'm not going to believe *what?*"

Donnelly explained her surprising news, and immediately followed with a photograph. Nash pulled the phone away from her ear to view the photograph that Donnelly had just sent.

"What the hell??" Nash said aloud.

Nash was in disbelief... confusion... even *shock* from the news. She slowly turned around to the sight of Garrison standing in the doorway.

Garrison could see in Nash's eyes that she had discovered something... *too much* of something.

Nash looked back at the picture on the phone, and then back to

Garrison – he was racing toward her… his eyes filled with rage.

She let out a yell of surprise, dropped her cell phone, and reached for her weapon, but it was too late – Garrison tackled her like a linebacker… slamming her to the ground. Her weapon went flying from the impact.

Donnelly's voice reverberated through Nash's cell phone… "Kenz, what's going on? Kenz?? KENZ??!!"

Garrison was now straddling her and started to pummel her with his fists; Nash covered up like a boxer to deflect his punches. She momentarily reached out with her right hand and patted the ground in search of her weapon, but it was not within her grasp.

Garrison went for Nash's throat. Nash reached around and punched him in the face, but it barely fazed him.

As Garrison leaned forward to apply more pressure to Nash's throat he made himself vulnerable – Nash kneed him in the groin and he momentarily released his grip. She immediately took another shot, using all of her strength and momentum to push him aside enough for her to attempt to get away.

Now on her stomach she spied her gun and tried a lunging bear crawl toward it, but he grabbed her legs. She spun around causing him to lose his grip. She kicked him in the chest, knocking him on his ass.

She was able to get to her feet and race toward her gun. As she reached down to grab it Garrison kicked it away while he once again tackled her; but this time his momentum carried him past Nash. As Garrison hit the ground Nash was able to immediately regain her feet; however, so was Garrison… and he grabbed her from behind via choke hold.

"STOP!" suddenly rang out.

Garrison, surprised, immediately jerked his head around to find the source of the directive. As he did so his grip relaxed. Nash elbowed him in the ribs and then dropped to her hands and knees to get out of the line of fire.

Gunshots rang out until they were replaced by the clicks of empty chambers.

Garrison fell to the ground – dead.

Nash walked over to Emily; who was shaking, in tears, and holding Nash's gun. Nash held out her hand – Emily handed her the gun.

Nash looked Emily directly in the eye and said… "You were never here."

EPILOGUE

The scenario that Nash had painted... *her case against Officer Mike Roberson*... was more accurate than she could have imagined; there was only one minor flaw in her assessment – *Roberson* wasn't the killer after all. And no, it wasn't Brandon Garrison either, because *this* wasn't Brandon.

The news that Donnelly had given Nash just before her attack had sealed it, and everything had fallen into place.

Nash was kicking herself; not so much that she hadn't considered such a possibility... after all, who would have; but she had relied on the single photograph of the bearded Daryl Wagner as she plowed through the investigation of his murder. When the surveillance photos of Brandon Garrison surfaced there was nothing obvious to connect the two. In hindsight Nash realized that *that* was Daryl's plan from the get-go, *'his ever-changing appearance'* as Madison Wagner had put it.

Daryl Wagner and Brandon Garrison were twins... identical twins and thus identical DNA... born to Wayne and Betty Garrison. Ironically, the two boys had different birthdays: Brandon was born at 11:53pm March 31st – Daryl at 12:07am April 1st.

It was a difficult decision for Wayne and Betty to give up the baby that would ultimately bear the name of *Daryl*, but they thought they were doing the right thing. They had been blessed with a healthy pregnancy while their friends John and Cindy Wagner had suffered a great loss... a miscarriage following years of attempting to conceive. This loss was magnified just a few months later when Cindy's doctor told her that, in his opinion, a viable pregnancy would never be an option.

When Betty Garrison discovered she was carrying twins, Wayne and she made a heartfelt, yet gut-wrenching and extremely difficult decision: If she delivered two healthy babies one of them would be the ultimate gift to an infertile couple... the gift of a child.

Firstborn Brandon was immediately placed in his mother's arms – an event that sealed the second twin's fate; there was no way that Betty could give up her firstborn... the child she had held against her bosom upon his arrival into this world. When the second-born arrived just minutes later Betty chose not to hold him... if she did so *it would be too difficult to then give him up* she reasoned. She wept over the decision.

John and Cindy Wagner were overjoyed, and they decided to name him *Daryl* in honor of John's uncle who had died in the Vietnam War. The adoption records were sealed, and the two couples made a pact that their secret would never be revealed to either of the boys.

Daryl was a few months shy of his third birthday when a miracle happened – against all odds his mother had become pregnant... a baby sister would be joining the family. The anticipation was exciting for all. Sadly, the excitement was short-lived for young Daryl; when baby Tina arrived Daryl became an almost-nonexistent entity. The more he tried to reclaim the adoration he had received as *the only child*, the more he was seen as a nuisance. He came to resent *"the little princess"* – the title his parents had bestowed upon his little sister. When the *unfortunate accident* befell young Tina the Wagner family began to spiral out of control; and Daryl's life would be forever changed.

At the funeral of Daryl's parents a well-intentioned friend of his mother divulged to Daryl that he had been adopted. He was blindsided. He felt betrayed by the only parents he had known for keeping such a secret, but now *it all made sense:* The favoritism his little sister received, how Daryl had become the black sheep of the family... *"The rent-a-kid... the throwaway... the kid his parents picked up at the pound"* Daryl would angrily say to himself. His hurt and anger also extended to his birth parents, knowing that they had abandoned him... rejected him. He came to hate that day... his birthday... to him he was nothing more than "The April Fool." He had grown up to be a violent and abusive man, and this revelation made matters worse... *far* worse.

When Daryl inadvertently crossed paths with Brandon Garrison he had remarked how their birthdays were only one day apart, and how they had been born in the same hospital. Further investigation led to the knowledge that their fathers served together in the Navy, and of the boys playing together at each other's Quarters on Base Housing as little tykes.

The more Daryl researched Brandon's past the more intrigued he became; and when he saw Brandon's picture on social media he realized something crazy was going on. They say that everyone has a double, but this was much more than an Old Wives Tale. He convinced Brandon to submit a DNA sample through his *Ancestral Heritage* website *"in order to determine specific details about your heritage"* Daryl told him. That was the clincher. He provided Brandon his ancestral makeup, but he kept *'the secret'* from him… he had to; he was beginning to formulate *a plan.*

The more that Daryl delved into Brandon's life and compared it to his own, the more jaded, bitter, angry, and resentful he became. While Brandon had lived a charmed life… had been provided every opportunity… Daryl's life had been exactly the opposite – *a living hell.*

Every milestone, every life event, every windfall recounted by Brandon was just one more way of reminding Daryl that he was a pathetic loser… the discarded trash. If Daryl had to listen to *one more* of Brandon's *"my life is fantastic"* stories he was going to choke someone. A figure of speech of course… *or was it?*

When Madison sought refuge from Daryl's control and beatings behind the badge of a police officer, Daryl decided that it was time to act. Taking over Brandon's life was the primary concern, but Daryl would make sure that Madison would take the fall in some capacity. And Officer Roberson sealed his fate as the patsy when he placed the threatening note on Daryl's windshield.

There was a method to the madness behind Daryl's ever-changing look: Workouts at the gym to attain Brandon's physique, the mustache to impersonate Roberson when needed, and finally the beard to ensure he looked different from Brandon *'once all the shit rained down'.*

Nash had pretty well nailed the scenario... just plug in Daryl's name for each action: The stolen Mazda, the purchase of the black & white while masquerading as Roberson, the suspicious computer searches, and the life insurance policy. And then there was Daryl's acting performance at the ATM... making it appear as if he had been abducted by some *'cop'*.

Brandon had unwittingly given Daryl access to his personal and financial information – he had used the same username and password that he had used for his login to the *Ancestral Heritage* website.

When Daryl saw Madison's newly-purchased burner phone the night before the murder he saw an opportunity. It had not been a part of the plan... placing one of her belongings at the crime scene... but what a perfect, unanticipated gift courtesy of karma.

Brandon had been an easy mark – he had a tendency to drink to excess, so getting him to the cabin after a few drinks at *The Harborside* was no problem at all; he even took his drink glass with him. Once they were at the cabin Daryl added the GHB... just to be sure.

There were a few technicalities tied to assuming Brandon's identity: Exchanging clothes, and putting on Brandon's wedding ring and watch. He also had to determine if Brandon had any scars, birthmarks, tattoos or anything that would differentiate between the two of them – hence the numerous up close and personal photographs for him to study before showing up in California to start his new life. The buildup of Daryl's anger as he took the photographs was a telltale indicator as to the person he had become... an evil, vengeful man whose rage would culminate in a cold-blooded death-grip to the throat.

He carried Brandon to the Mazda and dumped him in the trunk... right on top of the gym locker key he had planted. He couldn't let dental records foil his charade, so Brandon's teeth had to go; he yanked them out and placed them in a zip-type bag.

He was disgustingly calm, cool, and collected after the act. He pulled off his blood-covered sweatshirt and tossed it on the body. He then casually walked back to the cabin, cleaned up, and shaved off his beard... retaining only the mustache in the event that anyone saw him in the black & white they might think he was *a certain cop.* He also stashed his wallet, watch, and handgun in the secret compartment under the kitchen sink.

He returned to the car, drenched Brandon's lifeless body in gasoline, lit the fire, and placed a call to his home phone. He hung up the phone as soon as Madison answered, and then threw it into the fire. He scrambled to the black & white, planted *his* wedding band under the passenger seat, and sped away.

Careening down a County Maintenance road he purposely ran the car into a ditch – a necessary move to utilize a car crash and a purported concussion for his initial venture into his new life.

He called a cab via his burner phone and strolled out to the main road to catch a ride to the ferry terminal; making the 2:10 A.M. ferry run. He used a t-shirt to cover his face and the bloody lip and nose he had received from the crash. He continued to cover his face while riding the ferry. Once in transit he walked outside, opened the zip-type bag, and poured Brandon's teeth into the waters of Puget Sound. His burner phone also found its way to the bottom of the Sound. He then went to the Men's room and shaved off his mustache in preparation for his appearance as *Brandon* at the hotel.

He milked the part of the injured and concussed alter ego for all it was worth, but it wasn't long before his true colors shone through... first verbally abusing, and later physically assaulting, Emily Garrison.

When Nash arrived on Emily's doorstep with tales of a murder, and inconsistencies regarding her husband's sequence of events, Emily began to see things in a whole new light. The discovery of the disturbing photographs on her husband's phone got Emily to wonder what *really* had occurred that fateful weekend. When she had put the pieces of the puzzle together she literally vomited at the realization that the photos she had discovered were likely documenting the last moments of her husband's life, and that she had shared her bed with an imposter... *the monster that had murdered him*.

When Emily arrived at the winery to the sight of *the monster* attempting to choke the life out of Nash, the only answer was to intervene, even if it meant joining her husband in the afterlife. She spied Nash's gun lying on the ground, grabbed it, and took the action necessary to stop him... the only option that *the demon* had given her.

Nash sent Emily home to grieve; and, once Emily had driven out of sight, Nash called 9-1-1.

The report would state that Nash had freed herself from the perpetrator and stopped the attack via her weapon. She had expected to be asked why a seasoned Detective would have needed to empty her entire clip into her attacker; but Brandon Garrison had been a pillar of the community, so when his imposter... his killer... was *taken out in a hail of gunfire*, it was really no surprise that no one posed the question.

In the end, Daryl Wagner, *the evil that he had become*, left behind a trail of carnage... a trail of tears. A single vicious act had taken two innocent lives... Brandon Garrison physically – his wife Emily emotionally. And although irony... or more accurately... *karma*... had granted Emily her revenge, she would have traded a thousand lifetimes to have never crossed paths with such a monster. Another life had been damaged from years of Daryl's abuse. Madison was now free, but would she ever fully recover? Only time would tell. And Daryl's baby sister? Her tragedy was too much to bear for all involved. It could be said that *four* lives were lost that fateful day: A sweet, gregarious, precocious child; the hopes and dreams of her grief-stricken parents; and a young boy's innocence. Guilty or not, he had been convicted in The Court of Public Opinion, and by the worst possible judge and jury a young boy could imagine – *his parents*. It was a decree that would ultimately become a Death Sentence. *"Sticks and stones may break my bones, but words will never hurt me"* so the saying goes. Nothing could be further from the truth.

CPSIA information can be obtained
at www.ICGtesting.com
Printed in the USA
BVHW04s1708051018
R9187600001B/R91876PG529149BVX6B/6/P

9 781942 661696